FOREST AT THE EDGE
~ Book One ~

The

# FOREST

at the

# EDGE

of the

# WORLD

### TRISH MERCER

2<sup>nd</sup> Edition, revised

Cover design and photography by David Mercer's wife, who forced him to dress up and stare "meaningfully into the distance," which, for the dear sweet life of him, he just couldn't figure out how to do.

Contact author via website: forestedgebooks.com

Because my sisters Judy and Barbara
knew how to hold their tongues,
but usually wouldn't.

# MAPS

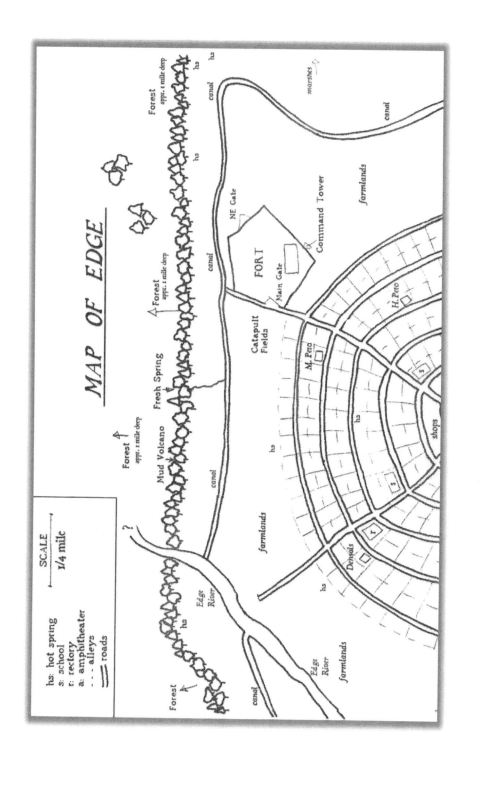

MAP OF EDGE

SCALE
1/4 mile

hs: hot spring
s: school
r: rectory
a: amphitheater
- - - alleys
—— roads

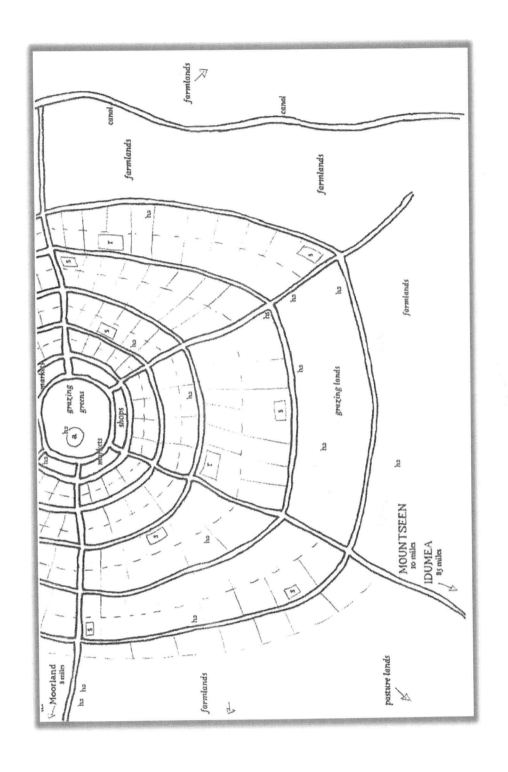

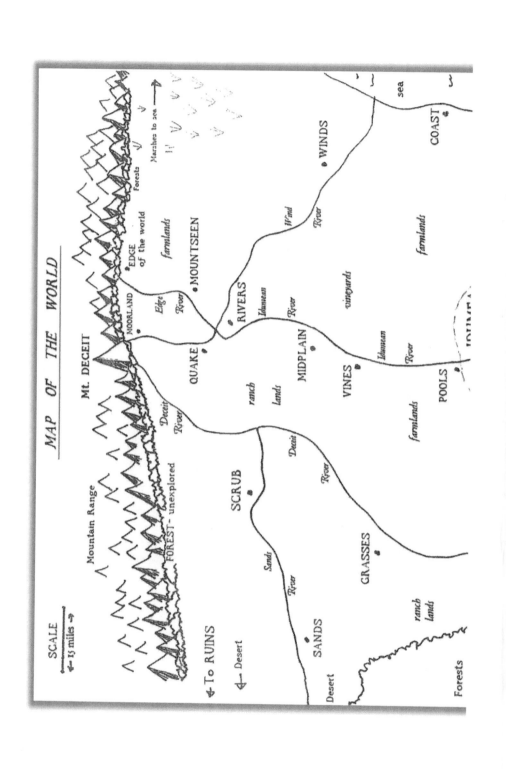

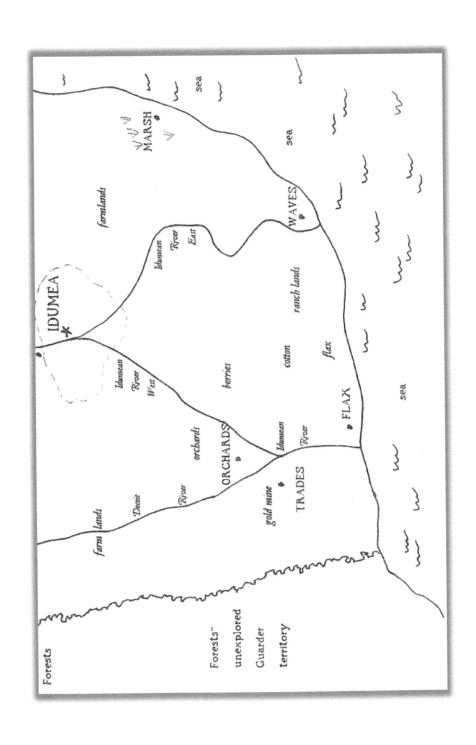

# A pronunciation guide to some of the more unusual names . . .

| Nicko Mal | NEE-koh  MAL |
|---|---|
| Querul | KWER-el |
| Idumea | i-doo-ME-uh |
| Hogal Densal | HOE-gal  DENS-al |
| Mahrree Peto | MARR-ee  PAY-toh |
| Cephas Peto | SEE-fus  PAY-toh |
| Hycymum Peto | HIE-si-mum  PAY-toh |
| Hierum | HIE-rum |
| Tuma Hifadhi | TOO-muh  hi-FOD-hee |
| Sonoforen | sun-uv-OR-en |
| Terryp | TARE-up |
| Jaytsy | JAYT-see |
| Brisack | BRIZ-ak |
| Gizzada | gi-ZAH-duh |

For background information on all character names and derivations, visit
forestedgebooks.com/characters

# Prologue ~ "Words for Weeds?"

"So . . . you really destroyed the world?"

The old woman kneeling in the pumpkin patch sat back on her heels and looked up at her accuser. The sunlight illuminated his worried look, betraying his attempt at nonchalance.

The woman smirked. Thirteen-year-olds weren't known for their subtlety. She tucked a wisp of gray hair behind her ear. "Not exactly."

But the look in the boy's eyes suggested he didn't believe her. She'd seen this happen before, with other thirteen-year-olds. He was now ready for the knowledge, and for many moons he would struggle to regard her as he used to, because the old woman he thought he knew turned today into something much *more*. There had always been the stories, but today he heard *the* story.

The old woman noticed a movement behind the boy. His cousin was picking her way through the pumpkins, wearing the same anxious-stunned look. She was thirteen too.

"Now I understand why you didn't teach the lesson," she said when she reached them. The girl warily eyed the small woman. "So, Muggah . . . is it all true?"

Muggah positioned herself more comfortably in the dirt—that was why she wore her brown cotton skirt and tunic—and put her hands on her hips. "Depends on who told the story this time."

"We were told that you are—" the girl swallowed nervously before continuing, "—the most dangerous woman in the world?"

Muggah rolled her eyes dramatically. "Let me guess: a *certain general* told you that?" Her voice dripped contempt.

The children nodded and, for the first time, began to relax.

"You know how he likes to weave a story," she reminded them.

Finally the cousins smiled. Muggah was still as they remembered her.

Sort of.

"I can give you the real story, the more *accurate* version." She winked at them.

They grinned. "That's what we were hoping," the boy said, sounding relieved.

"Ah, but I have so much weeding to do." Muggah sighed sadly. "So much work . . ."

The cousins exchanged a knowing glance, and then dropped to their knees. Their mothers had purposely sent them out in their work clothes.

"Words for weeds?" the girl asked.

Muggah nodded. "Words for weeds, Hycie. And Vid, it wasn't *exactly* destroyed. The world's still there, right?"

The boy shrugged. "I don't know, Muggah. Is it?"

She gestured to the garden. The children immediately started pulling unwanted vines and yellow flowers.

Muggah smiled and leaned back to let the sun beat down upon her. The afternoon was going to be easy, just as she expected.

"Now, we'll begin with Oren, in the year 317. I always like to start with an end, because that's the way to get a beginning . . ."

# Chapter 1 ~ "The chicken thing was just a misunderstanding."

It was his Last Day.

For any other person, that would have explained the lost-in-thought expression on his face as he sat alone in the quiet hall. But the thickest ruler of the world had only ever been "lost." He gave other people slips of gold to do the "thought" part for him.

He also didn't know it was his Last Day. But that was about to change.

---

"King Oren!" shouted the voice across the empty throne room.

The middle-aged king looked up from his gold and leather throne. He saw the old professor—white-haired and squatty—enter into the long hall filled with windows. He had a way of perpetually trembling, Oren had noticed some time ago, which made his tufty hair quiver like an agitated skunk. Oren always liked skunks.

The afternoon sun illuminated the other professors that Oren employed as his advisors, as well as the High General and about a dozen soldiers in blue woolen uniforms who followed.

Oren didn't like the High General. Everything about him was too hard and gray, like a rock come to life, and it wasn't happy about it.

Oren gulped.

"We all are here this day," the professor gestured to those behind him, "to deliver our judgment and punishment, on the 47th Day of Planting Season, the year 317—"

"I know what day it is," King Oren offered helpfully.

"—to announce to you that . . . *what?*" the old professor squinted.

"The date. You don't need to tell me anymore. I figured out how to read calendars a few years ago, remember?"

"Did you hear that?" the professor announced to the men behind him. "Forty-four years old, and Oren now knows how to tell the date!"

"Right after I hired you, we spent several days going over the dating system," Oren continued, not recognizing the sarcasm in his advisor's voice. But Oren did realize that Professor Mal was trembling even more than usual. He usually did that just before he'd start yelling. "We have four seasons, 91 days in each, and each year starts again in Planting Season, although I always thought it was in the middle of Raining, but—"

The professor, incredulous, turned to the High General. "Do you still insist he deserves my carefully prepared speech? Listen to him babbling!"

"—it does make more sense for the year to begin in Planting, since dogs—"

The High General, a hulking man in his fifties, sighed loudly. "Nicko, we went over this."

"—although I'm sure the cats disagree—" Oren scratched his chin and lost his thought. The High General's gravelly voice always made him forget what he was talking about.

It was cats, Oren suddenly remembered.

He liked cats—not skunks.

Simple mistake. Both are the same size, same shape, just different coloring. It was easy to confuse a skunk for his cat lost in the mansion's compound at night.

But do it four times, and the servants begin to complain.

"King Oren deserves to know why this judgment is being handed down to him." The High General's face tightened as the king raised his hand to say something.

"Whatever happened to my cat? Mal, I haven't seen her around for—"

"Oren!" Professor Mal bellowed, his white hair shaking. "Shut up!"

The King of the World clamped shut his mouth and cowered on his throne. Mal never did like his cat.

Or maybe it was the skunk he didn't like. *The smell, Oren—don't you notice the smell?* Mal had yelled that at him once when he wrestled the skittish, terrified cat into the mansion, only to realize he had the wrong animal. It was the smell of worry, Oren had thought. He knew that smell intimately. Surely his cat would feel worry, too—

Mal straightened his woolen jacket. "We're here to explain to you why you'll no longer be ruling our world nor occupying that chair."

"This has to do with the market last week, right?" Oren squeaked, beginning to make his own scent of worry. "The silk cloak?"

"Among other things, yes!"

"Because I have that figured out now," Oren said, trying to avoid the steady glare of the High General. Normally he enjoyed looking at all the shining medals, counting the stitched patches on his blue uniform, and admiring the silverwork on the hilt of his sword. But today the High General of Idumea's army had an even harsher expression which refused to let Oren focus on his uniform.

"You see," Oren started, "you explained to me that even though I possess the world—"

"That's only what your grandmother claimed," Mal reminded him.

Oren kept going, because Mal always said that and he didn't know why. "—I just can't take from it what I want. People get mad when I raise taxes so that I can make my mansion lovelier. But I can't get more things if I don't have more slips of gold or silver, and I have to take those from the people. So when I took that silk cloak last week, I didn't give any slips of gold because I didn't have any, and I didn't want to take any. Instead of taking gold that's mine but being held by the people, I just took the cloak!" He smiled proudly. It had taken him all night to work that out, but finally he got it. And without any of his advisors' help.

He never followed what they said anyway.

Mal closed his eyes. "High General, do we really have to continue this? He's a waste of my breath—"

"Nicko, tell the man. This will be put on the message boards, remember?" he said out of the corner of his mouth. "You know full well that how history is recorded is how it's *understood*. The world needs to understand *this* in the right way."

Oren heard his low muttering, but just didn't worry about it. Life was so much easier when you stop worrying about the bits that make no sense.

The High General glanced over at the nervous scribe in the corner who was trying to read his lips. The man immediately hunched back over the stack of parchment on his small desk and returned to his scrawling.

Mal grudgingly opened his eyes. "Your *theft* in the market place caused a riot," he resumed his explanation to Oren. "Remember us telling you about that?"

Oren nodded slowly. It had seemed to be a rather good party.

"And that riot spread to nearly each of the seventeen villages surrounding Idumea. We've been hearing reports of deaths and chaos, and the army has been dispatched to quell the riots in villages where we didn't even need forts before. The world has been devastated by your ineptitude!"

Oren silently mouthed in-ep-ti-tude. Mal liked big words. Oren didn't.

The scribe hurriedly dipped his quill in the ink and scribbled on the parchment.

Mal cleared his throat and resumed his speech. "Since your ancestor

Querul the First took control of our world in 190, he didn't stop the chaos, but added to it. Starting in 195 we suffered from the Great War for five long years. Two hundred thousand were dead at the end of it."

*Oh, another lecture,* thought Oren glumly. How many lectures had he sat through, bored to squirming because Mal said he needed an education? He'd done school. Lots of it. It was all the same. Words, writing, reading, staring out the window and waiting for something interesting to happen. As a boy he'd look at his piece of chalk and wish it could turn into a . . . into a stick, or something.

Maybe that wasn't too interesting. But maybe *two sticks*—

"Oren?"

The king blinked and sat up straighter to face the snarling voice that said his name.

Mal had his arms folded, his hair so jittery that Oren knew the explosion of temper was coming at any moment. He gritted his teeth and braced himself. "Yes?"

"*Where are you?!*"

The king blinked twice at that. He looked around and considered that maybe Mal had been wrong to yell at him for years about being stupid. Clearly Mal was the one struggling right now. "We're in the throne room," Oren said kindly. Mal was an old man, after all.

"Oren!"

"Yes?"

"Pay attention!" Mal bellowed.

Oren jumped in his throne and nodded. That was the only way to calm Mal—silent obedience.

Professor Mal cleared his throat, shot a furious look at the High General who ignored him, and continued on the same dull lecture.

"The violent faction who prolonged the war—the Guarders—were carelessly allowed by Querul the First to escape their punishments by fleeing to the dangerous forests beyond our borders. We weren't saved from them. They *still* attack us and steal our goods!"

Oren knew better than to sigh loudly. His grandmother's slap always reminded him that she never approved of that, and neither did Mal. Sighs always made the old professor shake more, and right now he was quivering as if he stood on his own land tremor. All Oren could do was focus on the brass buttons on the High General's uniform, and wonder what they'd look like hanging in the windows where they could catch the sun's light.

Maybe his cat would come back if he saw them shining . . .

"Querul didn't bring peace," Mal droned on. "Neither did his son

Querul the Second, a brutal and paranoid king who employed twenty percent of the population to spy on each other looking for evidence of Guarder collaboration and bringing the need for execution squads. Under his rule another twelve thousand perished, according to our best guesses. Many of them simply vanished."

Too many big words. But something Mal said . . .

Oren's thoughts shifted away from wondering if skunks liked shiny things, and he looked into Mal's enraged eyes.

Maybe he *should* pay attention.

"His son, Querul the Third, was no better, continuing the reign of terror of his father. And his wife—your grandmother, Oren—was the most evil woman to ever stalk this world. Since she died seven years ago we've done all we can to undo her influence upon the world and you—"

"She wasn't *that* bad," Oren feebly tried to defend her. He couldn't help it. Even though she'd been gone for years, somehow she was still in his mind, pinch-lipped and pointing. That finger was gnarled and bony, but somehow it was the scariest finger in the world. And you couldn't turn your back on it, or it'd get you.

"She *disposed* of your wife and two daughters, Oren!" Mal shouted. "Do you know what happened to them?"

That was one of those worrying things Oren found it easier to just not worry about. He timidly shook his head.

"Never bothered to ask, did you? Your wife couldn't produce a son, and you can't legally have more than two children, so your grandmother cleared the way for you to have more children by various women in the world to finally produce a male! And what about your own mother, Oren? What happened to her?"

Another worrying thing. Mal seemed to be strangely interested in those today. "Umm," Oren began, although his grandmother also smacked him whenever he began a sentence so inarticulately, "they went for a walk. She just disappeared."

"Just disappeared," Mal repeated tonelessly. "The wife of the king, out walking with her mother-in-law, in a city of tens of thousands, and she just *disappears.* I know you believed that as a boy, but still? Oren, no one would ever have accused your grandmother of kindness. She didn't want anyone else to influence her two grandsons but her."

Oren's mouth dropped open, and he absently rubbed his face where she hit him every day for the thirty-seven years she ruled his life. No—she was mean, certainly, but not . . . She'd never have—

"Then your father, Querul the Fourth, was an idiot! Not as big as you, granted," Mal conceded, "but—"

"The chicken thing was just a misunderstanding," Oren insisted. Here was something he did know about. "He didn't want the pocks to—"

"The chickens were never infested with pocks, Oren!" Mal barked. "Any other thinking man would have asked for a second opinion, instead of taking the word of *cattle ranchers* that the chickens were ill and advancing disease! Any other man would have asked a scientist before killing off ninety percent of the world's poultry. It took the world years to recover from your father's gullibility."

Oren bit his lip. Without even knowing what all those words were, he was beginning to suspect things weren't going his way.

"And then there's *you*," Mal spat. "I've been tutoring you for years, but to no avail. Perhaps if your older brother Querul the Fifth hadn't died as a teen, the world may have been in a better state today, but I doubt it. He was more closely knitted to your grandmother and her love of the execution squads than you are. I suppose we have *that* to be grateful for," he added. "But the world is tired, Oren. Tired of your family, tired of your abuses, tired of your stupidity—"

"They could take naps," Oren offered lamely, nothing else coming to his mind. "When they're tired. I do. Every afternoon . . ."

Mal exhaled loudly. "Nearly half of our history has been dictated by your family, but no more. By nightfall, the world will find itself governed by a body of twenty-three experienced and wise professors from the University of Idumea. Tomorrow, the future of the world will be brighter because there will be no more Queruls or Orens in it!"

"What do you mean?" Now it was Oren's turn to tremble.

Now he was *sure* this wasn't going well, not at all.

The scribe scribbled so frantically that flecks of ink splattered around his desk.

"King Oren, today we are charging you with gross negligence and complete indifference toward the one million people of the world you have pledged to rule. You have done nothing to alleviate suffering, but instead increased it. You have not shielded your people from death, but brought more to them. You have not listened to their cries for help, but ignored them. We have not progressed under your rule, but have stagnated."

Oren wondered when he had done any of that. All he could remember doing was staying in the mansion and doing what kings do.

Although he'd always been a bit vague as to what *exactly* that was—

"I am here to inform you that you are not fit to lead this world," Mal announced, "and that in your stead will be placed a body of administrators and a chairman who will govern and protect this world in the way it was meant to be ruled, supported by the Army of Idumea. We will be here *for the people*. Oren, if you believe in a creator, now would be the time to begin a conversation with him."

Oren's tongue went limp as he watched the soldiers come around from behind the High General. He made a slight motion with his hand, and Oren could do nothing but watch the soldiers draw their swords. The scraping of the metal had always seemed to him a rather pretty noise, but today it seemed to scratch the inside of his ears.

Ten men.

There was a lot he knew he didn't know. It was as if the rest of the world had an edge up on him. Maybe they had extra eyes, because they always saw more than him. Additional ears, to hear things he never picked up. And maybe even more in the head. Mal always shouted at him, *Use your brains, Oren!* That always worried him. He knew he had a *brain*, so did others have more than one?

But there was one thing Oren *did* understand: the number of men in an execution squad. They used to be called killing squads in his grandparents' days. The name change was supposed to make people feel better.

As he stared at the ten approaching blades, he realized the change wasn't helping.

He hoped his cat would be all right. And the skunk—

---

A few moments later Professor Mal—now Chairman of the Administrators Nicko Mal—smiled grimly as the body of their dead king slumped in his throne. Ten sword blades thrust simultaneously was humanely efficient.

"Well," the High General tilted his head, "that was simple."

Mal nodded in satisfaction. "Yes, all of this was far simpler than I ever imagined. *Could* portend of good things," he muttered to himself, "or it could all prove to be disappointingly easy."

The High General glanced briefly at Mal's unusual musings before gesturing to a waiting servant at a side entrance. "Call in someone to clean up this mess. Then you and the others may have whatever you can carry from King Oren's private rooms, as agreed. But make sure that silk cloak he took is brought to me the moment it's found. Chairman Mal will be presenting it to the surviving family of that dead silk seller when he announces the change in government this evening. You—"

He pointed to the scribe, who had momentarily forgotten his duty and was staring at the growing pool of blood. He paled as he looked up into the terrible expression of the High General.

"—*You* will show me that record before it goes out to the copiers. I want to verify *every* word."

The scribe whimpered his response, and the servant dashed off to find the cloak.

Chairman Mal nodded. "Excellent, High General. I suppose that's why I'm keeping you on."

The High General scoffed. "As if any of this would have happened without my help."

Mal smiled thinly. "And why you'll also keep that mansion."

"You've taken care of his former *friends?*" the general asked, one eyebrow arched.

"Only the two sons of that mistress had any possible claim. And since they were never legitimately his, the claim is weak. So weak that a couple of bags of gold quashed it completely. She left that mansion for good years ago, and neither she nor her sons will be coming back to take it from you."

"The way seems to be wide open, Nicko," the general said plainly, "with only one man's blood shed. Indeed, quite efficient."

Mal looked around the throne room. "This is too ostentatious for a gathering room, wouldn't you say?"

The High General didn't even glance at it. "Perhaps better suited as an eating hall, or a—"

"Library!" Mal whispered, his smile growing. "I own nearly every book ever created in the world. And my personal writings . . . there's enough room here for those and more."

The High General sniffed. "Books. Thinking. This room won't know how to react to such behavior. Never saw it before."

Chairman Mal's grin chilled the throne room. "There are going to be all kinds of changes and progress made now, High General. The world will hardly know what to do with it all."

The High General looked askance at his new ruler, but said nothing.

Mal turned slightly to a slender older sergeant, formerly the head of the king's guard, who watched from a shadowed alcove.

The sergeant nodded almost imperceptibly back.

Stage One had begun.

# Chapter 2 ~ "I'm not about to argue who has the prettier hog."

The village school teacher sighed in contentment at how perfect her life was. She enjoyed her students, loved her village, and adored her home.

For a woman as smart as she thought she was, that utter sense of satisfaction should have been a clear signal that things were about to change.

But people usually aren't as clever as they hope they are.

It was Planting Season, 319, nearly two years after the loss of the king when a small woman left her tiny house on the perimeter of the inconsequential village of Edge. She rarely thought about the twenty-three Administrators who now ruled, and likewise those Administrators thought nothing of her at the northern edge of the world.

Well, except on days like this when they sent an unexpected message to her schoolhouse. All the teachers received it, and she was glad it came too late to read to her morning students. Six to ten-year-olds weren't old enough to hear about the killing squads during the era of the kings, but her teenage girls in the afternoon were supposed to be reminded that since the Administrators had come to power, the Army of Idumea had not convened one killing squad nor even carried out one execution.

It was a disconcerting announcement to make on such a lovely afternoon, but it did have the effect of immediately quieting her ten gossiping students, so Mahrree Peto felt obligated to send a thought of thanks all the way down to Idumea, eighty long miles away. Those stuffy old men liked to remind the furthermost borders of the world that they were in charge and "here for the people."

Mahrree didn't really care. They were too far away to influence—

Wait.

That wasn't entirely true anymore. As Mahrree wove through the maze of shops and stands at the market, now emptying for the evening, she remembered another announcement that came in the middle of Raining Season. The village of Edge of the World was receiving a fort. In fact, it was being constructed at the northern border of the forests, less than a quarter mile away from her home. She hadn't bothered to head over to watch its progress, like many of her neighbors had, but when the rector told the audience at the amphitheater two weeks ago that the commander of the fort would be arriving shortly, Mahrree heard the villagers around her grumble the same things she did in her mind: why did the Army of Idumea need a presence in Edge anyway?

"Remember, my beloved daughter—sometimes the world really *is* out to get you."

It was at the oddest times that the last words of Mahrree's father blew into her mind. They scattered her thoughts as if the cold winds that came down from the mountains behind Edge rushed into one ear and out her other.

Mahrree paused to consider the words as was headed to the village green and the outdoor amphitheater for the night's debate. She smiled sadly at the memory of her last conversation with him.

She was fifteen, thirteen years ago. He was thirty-seven. He had started coughing near the end of Weeding Season, and three moons later it was clear he was dying. His slender, small body was wracked with pain and chesty convulsions.

Mahrree's mother Hycymum could do nothing more but wring her hands and make yet another creative dish of something that he couldn't eat. Their rector came over every day to sit with his younger friend, and the village doctors tried every concoction they knew.

Someone even made the long journey to Pools, nearly seventy miles away, to bring the good teacher "healing waters" to cleanse him. Cephas Peto told his daughter he didn't know how water that smelled like rotten eggs could be healing, and that he was sure people in Pools and Idumea got sick just as often as people in Edge.

The healing waters, the prayers of their congregation, and the dishes of min-a-stroh-nee and fall-ah-fal his wife created didn't work, so on the 89th Day of Harvest Cephas beckoned to his daughter.

"Remember," he whispered to avoid another coughing fit, "my beloved daughter—sometimes, the world really is out to get you!"

Mahrree had laughed in spite of her sorrow. She expected something more sentimental or even profound. Her mother just shook her head and dabbed her eyes. She never understood the cutting sense of humor her husband and daughter shared.

Mahrree had gripped her father's hand and whispered, "So you're going to let it get you?" That's when her tears started.

"And remember, every story has a happy ending, if you just wait long enough." Then he told Mahrree his extensive collection of books was hers.

Half an hour later he was gone.

Thirteen years later Mahrree's sorrow was tempered because she still heard him. Not just words he said before he passed, but words he said *after*.

She never told anyone, but Cephas Peto still spoke to her and gave her advice. And as she strolled toward the village green she felt he was walking nearby, still watching out for her.

"The world is out to get me, Father? Doesn't sound like a happy ending just yet. But send on the world! After such a dreary Raining Season, I'm ready for some excitement."

She sucked in the surprisingly warm air and thought she could smell the deep brown dirt of the farms that ringed their village, just two roads of houses away from her home. White clouds streaked across the blue sky, and Mahrree predicted they would turn orange-pink with the sunset. The two moons, the Greater as well as the Little Sister which trailed the brighter moon, showed only half of themselves evening.

She was glad she had changed into her lighter tan cotton skirt instead of wearing the heavier woolen black one. She tucked her light brown shoulder-length hair behind her ears. Unlike most of the women in the village, she didn't wear her hair long only to tie it all up into a bun. Shorter hair was much more practical. And her father had said it looked better that way. But otherwise her features were nothing extraordinary, she thought. Symmetrical, feminine—she never was very good at judging beauty, nor did she see the purpose of it. Her grayish-green eyes were like her mother's, which her father loved, and her build and frame were as slight as her father's, which Mahrree loved.

In the common greens before her, where roaming sheep trimmed the new grasses, several groups of children were already playing Get Him!, Smash the Wicket, and Tie Up Your Uncle, which wasn't as violent as it sounded unless someone's real uncle participated. Their parents were filing into the amphitheater to listen to a chorus of broad-chested women from the south of the village, but first there would be a debate, and Mahrree was there to support one of her students.

"Miss Peto!" cried a 15-year-old girl who rushed up to her. "I thought you'd never get here!"

Mahrree smiled and calmly patted the girl's arm. "Sareen, you're ready for this, remember? You wrote out your argument—"

"But is it good enough?" she giggled nervously. Unfortunately for the girl, everything that came out of her dissolved into a giggle. "I mean, will they agree with me?"

Mahrree shrugged. "I don't know. Considering that your opponents are your own parents, and Rector Densal has agreed to let the audience decide the outcome . . ." She raised her eyebrows in a manner she hoped would convey that Sareen really didn't stand a chance at winning tonight's debate.

Every village in the world held debates before the evening's performances where people argued, sniped, and shouted, and occasionally reached a consensus. In Edge, one of the three rectors always moderated the discussion, since men who knew the Creator could better quell anger than the local magistrate who instead inflamed it.

While in the bigger, more sophisticated villages surrounding Idumea debates followed a more formal structure as was taught in the universities scattered around the world, Edge's debates were little more than a sharing-arguing-complaining of ideas, disagreements, and occasionally utter nonsense, as would be the case tonight.

Because tonight Sareen was going to tell the village she wanted to line her eyes with dark charcoal to make them "prettier."

Her parents thought that was silly.

But somehow Sareen managed to convince Rector Densal to let her debate that in front of everyone.

Then again, Rector Densal was rather mischievous for a teacher of The Writings and a leader of a congregation.

Sareen nodded confidently to Mahrree, let escape the longest, most tense giggle Mahrree had yet to hear erupt from her student, and she trotted into the amphitheater ahead of her teacher.

"I'm quite eager to hear how this will play out," said a voice behind Mahrree.

She turned around and smiled at the old man who stood there, rubbing his hands together. His white eyebrows bounced happily. "What do you think? Is she ready for her turn on the platform?"

Mahrree chuckled. "I think this will be one of the shortest debates we've had in a while. Her main argument is, 'My eyes look too small.' What's with girls these days, eh Rector?"

Densal chuckled back. "I don't know, Miss Mahrree—but we're about to find out!"

Mahrree turned to go into the amphitheater, but the small man gently caught her arm with his wrinkled hand. "If you have a moment, Miss Mahrree—I have an idea for another debate later this week, and I think you are precisely the person to handle this. But, on second thought, maybe it'd be too much for you . . ."

Not one to ever turn down a challenge like that, she turned back to him. "Oh, really?"

Mahrree prided herself, although she modestly knew she shouldn't, on her debating skills. She read everything she could find, listened to each idea, and wrote down any novel concept and the arguments for it and against it, laying out her father's collection of writings across her eating table in preparation for the debates. And her students, of course. She even ran them through the paces, turning the entire front wall of smoothed stone in the schoolhouse into a mass of words written in white chalk and black charcoal to represent the two sides and found it all great fun.

What students thought of it, that didn't matter as long as they learned to think. Although what Sareen was thinking when she decided to debate about charcoal and eyes, Mahrree wasn't too sure. After trying to help the poor girl created a rationed argument about enhancing beauty, Mahrree was ready for something a bit more demanding. "What's the topic?"

Rector Densal's eyes twinkled at Mahrree with just a bit too much liveliness, and she knew the old man was plotting something. "Well, if you don't mind, I thought I'd let the opponent surprise you with that," he smiled. "You see, there's a newcomer to the village who needs the opportunity to, shall we say, prove himself?"

Mahrree frowned but with a matching twinkle in her eyes. "And you think I should take him on in a debate? You must not like this person very much, then. You usually take in the lost and lonely, not hold them up for ridicule."

Rector Densal grinned. "Well, this is a special case. He's moving in just north of you—"

"Rector, there's only one ring of houses above mine before the barren lands, and no one's moved in . . ." Her voice trailed off as a horrible thought struck her. "The only thing *moving* in the north is the new fort," she said drearily.

Rector Densal nodded thoughtfully, as if that was the first he'd heard of it. "Why, that's right!"

"So you're proposing I debate . . . *the officer?*"

Densal began to smile as if Mahrree had just come up with a most brilliant idea all on her own, but before he could say anything she paled.

And Densal noticed. "Miss Mahrree," he said hurriedly, "remember— the army isn't what it once was. Many improvements have happened over the years, you know."

Reluctantly, she nodded. "I know, I know. I teach history, remember?"

Densal squeezed her arm kindly. "He just needs a way to introduce himself to the village, so I got to thinking . . ." and he winced at her in pleading.

"I suppose it was only a matter of time before the officer came down among us and did something official," she grumbled. "And you want me to help with *that*?"

Densal tilted his head. "Well, I know what Cephas Peto would do."

Mahrree groaned, but was intrigued that the rector would resort to using guilt as a tactic. Either he was truly devious or really that desperate. "I suppose my father would invite him over for dinner, share a few books with him, then go easy on him in front of the village," she murmured. "But Rector, that's not exactly my style, nor would it be appropriate for a strange man to be seen at my house!"

Oddly, Rector Densal chuckled at that. "No, I agree. I just want you to help him find his place here."

Mahrree smiled slyly. "You mean, *help put him in his place* at a debate? Ah, well why didn't you say so? I can do that quite well."

The rector waggled his eyebrows cheerfully at her and headed into the amphitheater.

Only once was he out of sight did Mahrree sighed loudly. "Debate the officer. From Idumea."

Her hands began to tremble.

---

It was warm in the afternoon of the next day when Captain Shin stared deep into the forest above Edge. The trees spewed out hot water and stank of sulfur and hid the Guarders. The enemy secreted themselves among the vents of noxious gases where the remains of deer decayed. The dense woods extended from the marshy eastern shore all the way to the western deserts, one hundred miles wide and at least one mile deep, rising up to the base of the jagged mountains.

That's where the Guarders lived, somehow, in that inhospitable forest. Or maybe they were somehow beyond it in the massive boulder field before the mountains, with rocks as large as feed barns.

Or if they weren't in the boulder field, they somehow managed an existence in the hostile terrain of the mountains that rose up as a menacing mistake of Nature. Land should be flat, not misshapen into peaks. Everyone knew that.

And at any time, according to the captured spy the High General interrogated, the Guarders would again begin their raids.

Instinctively the captain rested his hand on the hilt of his sword.

Shin glanced behind him to see where the new fort was from his current vantage point. It was across the barren swath of land that was a few hundred paces wide. The natural border lay before the farms and canals that ringed Edge, and on the other side was the forest that served as Nature's end to civilization.

Decades ago the villagers had been wise enough to not build anything right up against the territory of their enemy. Their foresight left plenty of room now for the fort, perimeter walls, stables, and feed barns the Army of Idumea would need to defend the northernmost border of the world.

The tall command tower, about four hundred paces away from the captain's position, was built higher than the trees with walls that were more glass than wood. The window panes were blow thin and clear by the glass makers in Sands just for the army. The command tower afforded a perfect view of the area—forest and village—precisely as Captain Shin had planned.

He turned to peer into the trees again, making notes with a sharpened piece of charcoal on a stack of thin papers. So far he had charted nearly two miles of the forest's border, beginning at the far eastern edge where the impenetrable marshes led to the seas. At times he could see almost one hundred paces into the forest, but other sections were so dense with pines that he couldn't see anything beyond what his arm could reach.

Today he was surprised to find a seemingly fresh water spring bubbling up from just inside the forest and trickling out to the barren fields in which he stood, the runoff disappearing into a narrow crevice in the ground. The spring's location would be suitable for watering the horses of the soldiers that soon would be arriving to patrol the forest's edge. But first he'd watch the deer he observed drinking from it, just to make sure he didn't find its corpse later.

Captain Shin jotted down another note about a high spray of hot water he saw about thirty paces into the trees. He paused when he heard shuffling footsteps in the grasses behind him.

"So, Captain Shin! Discover anything of interest today?"

"Always," he said distractedly, continuing to record his findings as the shuffling came to a stop. He glanced over to see a small old man craning to see what the captain was writing. He nodded in approval and looked into the forest himself.

"Can I help you with something, Rector Densal?"

The old man untied his thin leather jacket. His short cropped white beard and mustache framed his ready grin. For a rector, he had an alarming air about him, as if he was about to provide some *help*.

And *help*, from such an elderly man, always strained the definition of the word.

"Warming up nicely today, isn't it Captain? I love Planting Season! It always seems to promise a hot Weeding Season."

"Rector?" the officer said pointedly, but hoped it sounded patient.

The old man waggled his eyebrows. "I've come to help you, Captain." He crouched, faced the forest, and started to whistle. "Here Guarders, Guarders! Nice Guarders. Come out, and old Hogal will give you something sweet for your surrender."

The captain raised one eyebrow. "That's not helping."

Rector Densal stood back up. "Ah, well. Worth a try, my boy."

"That's debatable." Captain Shin rubbed his forehead. "Look, I don't mean to be rude, but I am rather busy. Was there anything else—"

"Yes, yes! I told you, I've come to help. You see, *dear Captain*, you've been here for about a week and a half now, right?"

"True," he said slowly, suspecting this line of questioning was to get him into a habit of agreeing before the real issue surfaced.

"And you've spent all that time either supervising fort construction, or making notes about the forest, right?"

The captain folded his arms.

"Well, the villagers are beginning to talk," the rector said more soberly, but still with a spark of plotting in his eyes. "And, my boy, they're a little worried. The army hasn't stretched this far north since the Great War. Sure, there was always a contingency in Mountseen, but we've never had more than a handful sergeants who sauntered through the markets during the day and drank in the tavern at night. But now we're getting an entire fort?"

"As directed by the Administrators," the captain reminded. "Never before has the Guarder threat been so clear."

The rector waved that away. "It's been over thirty years since there was even a sighting of Guarders here. Before you were even born, I imagine."

Captain Shin squinted at the old man. "I told you last week what the High General learned, Densal. You doubt the judgment of the High General?"

Hogal Densal waved that off with his other hand. "Of course not, but what I'm suggesting is, I doubt anything is going to come through those trees in the next few days. Have you seen anything yet?"

"No," the captain admitted, "but the Guarders are extraordinarily skilled at concealing themselves. The High General wants me to get to know this forest as well as I can."

Rector Densal smiled in a manner that immediately put the captain on guard. "Now, not having served in the army, I wouldn't know, but I suspect the High General *also* wants you to get to know the village. Maybe sent you off with an admonition to win the hearts and minds of the people, become part of the community so they'll more easily embrace the idea of a fort?" He waggled his eyebrows again.

Captain Shin sighed. "He did."

"Then that's how I'm going to help you, my boy!" He patted the captain's back in a fatherly manner. "I have a proposal: in three days' time you will come to the amphitheater at the village green after dinner and be the night's guest debater."

Captain Shin groaned. "Ah, no, no, no. I'm not going to—"

"Are you scared, Captain?"

"Of course not. It's just, what kind of debates would a place like Edge have? I'm not about to argue who has the prettier hog."

Rector Densal glared at him good-naturedly. "We do have other issues, you know. We may not be as sophisticated as Idumea, but we have a few thinkers among us. A few that might even make *you* think! I can assure you a most interesting time. Tell you what: you can even choose the topic."

The captain put a large hand on the small rector's shoulder. "I appreciate the offer, but it just wouldn't be fair to humiliate the revered rector in front of the entire village."

Densal shook a wrinkled finger at him. "First of all, it won't be the entire village. Maybe just five hundred. Everyone else is helping with the planting. Second, I don't take to the platform anymore. And third, what makes you think *you'd* win?"

The captain leaned closer. "I *always* win."

"Ha! Not in three days' time you won't. That is, unless you choose not to come because you're not up to the challenge .. ." He shrugged in what he likely thought was a casual *oh well* manner, but the stiffness of his shoulders suggested he hadn't practiced it enough.

Captain Shin glared, but he wasn't entirely annoyed. "That's the oldest trick there is, Densal. Daring me into accepting."

"Is it working?"

"Maybe."

Rector Densal grinned again. "I have just the opponent: the old school teacher. She delights in showing up overly-confident young men. She'll jump at the chance of humiliating an officer of the Army of Idumea. And when you *graciously concede*—" he ignored the captain's scoff, "—that she's the more skilled debater, I promise that Edgers will have a new respect for you. Acknowledge that they're still superior. They like those kind of reminders, you know."

The captain raised his menacing eyebrow again. "Concede?"

"After a good show, mind you," the rector assured him enthusiastically.

"Let the villagers see you, hear you, know you, and then pity you. You'll be one of them by the end of Planting Season."

The captain took in a deep breath, accentuating his broad chest.

The rector smiled and pointed at the large officer. "Good, good. Try to look handsome. That will help impress them."

The captain reluctantly smiled back. "Easily done."

Rector Densal rubbed his bearded chin. "Clean uniform," he gestured to the captain's pristine, tightly woven dark blue woolen jacket and trousers. "But maybe not the dress uniform—too intimidating. Clean shaven," he pointed to the captain's exceptionally smooth chin and upper lip, as all members of the army were to have, "and . . . don't wear the cap. Let the many *unmarried* women we have in Edge see that perfectly trimmed black hair of yours."

The captain groaned. It must have been a common trait in rectors—a result of the calling—to try to change the condition of every *single* person they encounter. "I'm not here to find any unmarried women, Rector."

"Even if they get lost? I think finding them would be your responsibility." Densal chuckled and rubbed his hands together. "Just let them admire such a cut of a man—that's a good way to win hearts, Captain Shin! The minds—they might follow later."

Captain Shin couldn't help but chuckle. "All right, Hogal. Three days. The old school teacher. Impress the village, and then let the naive woman think she's won."

"Wonderful, my boy! I look forward to it!" Hogal Densal slapped him on the back again and started to shuffle away.

Captain Shin turned again to study the forest. He didn't need to prepare for a debate. He never did, anyway. He'd just stand up there like he always did, his presence and size easily intimidating every opponent. Just a few well-stated comments and he'd have the debate all wrapped up. Right now he had far more pressing matters on his mind—a forest to know, a village to protect, and a High General to impress.

---

It was an intense staring match, but only one side knew it.

The two brown-skinned men wearing green mottled tunics and trousers stood motionless in a thick stand of pines. They were surprised—not that someone was at the edge of the forest, but that someone was actually peering *in*. No one had done that in nearly 120 years. They didn't expect the officer to see them, but it was the first time anyone had ever tried.

They didn't move or make a sound, but watched as the captain slowly continued his way down the tree line.

---

Eighty miles to the south stood the massive city of Idumea with its population of two hundred thousand. The seat of government resided near the center of it, with the headquarters of the Army of Idumea located a couple miles away at the new garrison.

From that garrison left the High General of Idumea, an appropriately imposing figure with a chest full of medals that glinted in the sun as he rode his horse to the Administrator's Headquarters. He traveled with only two lieutenants as guards, demonstrating to the people that scurried out of his way on the cobblestone roads that Idumea was so safe even the highest ranking officer in the world needed only minimal accompaniment.

The Administrative Headquarters had been finished the year before. It was a massive three-level edifice supported at the front by twenty-two white stone columns. For years King Oren tried to motivate his workers to complete the red and orange stone structure, but they failed to construct the pattern he had so carefully designed: burgundy stone winding through the orange rock background, as if an enormous pumpkin had sprouted red curling tendrils. When Mal took over he hired artisans to finish the project. Eight moons later the interior was finished with highly polished stone floors and exquisitely appointed offices for each Administrator and his aides.

But the High General felt that a large barn would have been more practical, and could have housed all the workers' horses as well.

Up the wide white stone steps he strode, nodding once in warning to the young pages dressed in short red coats who hurriedly opened the heavy doors for him. Once one of them was a bit too slow, but now that his arm was finally healed he wasn't ever going to make that mistake again.

Without breaking his pace the High General marched through the broad and crowded hallway, dispersing citizens and a couple of red-jacketed Administrators. He walked directly to the largest oak doors which again were promptly opened for him. His lieutenants struggled to keep up as the general plowed through the waiting room where he never waited. With another nod to the records-keeping men sitting at the large desk, the High General headed straight for the open doors of the grandest office in the building where he finally stopped at the broad and highly polished desk.

The occupant was waiting, and had counted down in his head the moment the highest ranked soldier, acting as the aggressive wolf he was, would stand in front of him.

Still, he said casually, "High General, I believe you're early."

"Is that a problem, Mal?" the officer said, clearly not caring if it were. He pulled several folded parchments from his jacket pocket and handed them across the desk.

Chairman Mal, dressed in his bright red jacket with tails, and a white ruffled shirt that matched his ruffled white hair, took the documents and opened them. "So the last fort will be ready on time?"

"I have assurances from the captain in Edge it will be ready ahead of schedule, Chairman."

"Good. Excellent," Mal nodded, but the High General didn't move to leave. Something else was on his mind, and Mal knew what it was.

The High General turned partway to his two assistants, made a slight motion with his hand, and the lieutenants left the grand office, shutting the door behind them.

Typical of the alpha wolf, Mal thought, sending away his pack so he could deal with the threat alone.

The general's tolerant pretense vanished as he leaned on the desk. "Now, as for those unexpected 'visitors' to my office this morning—"

"It's only three Administrators, High General," Chairman Mal said in a calming manner. "You know as well as I that the world still fears the army. But this is a way to demonstrate that the army is working hand-in-hand with the Administrators. Three of them on the Command Board of the Army? Why, it's a perfect balance!" Perhaps *calming* wasn't the correct term; maybe *goading*.

"Balance?!" the general growled. "It used to be just General Cush and I, and with the inclusion of three Administrators, I assure you there is NO balance! Get them OFF!"

Mal stretched his lips into a smile. "You and Cush are such large men, the two of you easily outweigh three slight Administrators."

The High General was not amused.

Mal nodded once. "You may add a colonel or a major, if you wish, to the Command Board."

"Oh, how generous," he sneered. "You've said the people still feared the power of the army, but maybe they should start fearing you. They may not see what you're doing, but I do."

"There was reason to fear the army in the past," Mal intoned. "People have very long memories, General. You know that."

"Especially when you send notices to the schools about killing squads, which we haven't seen since my father's time!"

Mal held open his hands. "Mere reminders of how much better their lives are now that the Administrators are in charge."

"I see," the High General's low voice rumbled like thunder. "Taint the image of the army to make the Administrators appear more competent. Can't be competent on your own, huh? The army's not to be feared, Nicko."

Mal's pacifying demeanor fell away. "Tell me, General—what's *not* to fear about ten thousand men armed with swords and long knives, and the knowledge of how to use them?"

"Use them to protect the world, not destroy it! My soldiers are disciplined and controlled. There's great comfort in that, not fear, especially now."

Mal squinted. "You sound worried, High General."

"Not worried," he said solidly, "just ready. As should be everyone in the world. Tell them, Nicko, what I learned from that spy. They're coming in numbers and with plans we've never before encountered. The people have to know they can trust the army to protect them."

"We don't know that, General. All we have to go on is what your captured spy alleges. How can we be sure he's telling the truth?"

The High General folded his arms. "I spent four days on him, Nicko. This was one determined, impressively well-trained Guarder. And when he finally broke, he confessed all he knew. Fortunately for him, they didn't tell him that much. They've been quiet for years, and now it's obvious why: they've changed their tactics, their training . . . maybe everything they do. We must have the citizens trusting the army, or we may have a disaster coming."

"Impressively trained, you say?" Mal said, his eyes twinkling slightly.

The High General missed it. "My men must win over the hearts and minds of the people before the Guarders strike. If we don't work together, you might see your world crumble. And then those that remain will be as eager to depose you as they were Oren."

"You best hope the Guarders are as fearsome as you believe they are," Mal said with quiet ferocity. "Otherwise I would never tolerate this kind of disrespect from you."

"Disrespect?!" The large man laughed, but without any joy. "Telling you the truth is disrespectful? Should I start calling you Querul the Third now?"

Mal clenched his fist, but knew his use of it would only amuse the condescending officer. Mal hadn't been able to make a move without the nosing about of the High General, his snide remarks and his pointing out the flaws and drawbacks to Mal's plans. While he wasn't always right, he *was* frequently enough to annoy.

Mal answered with chilling calm. "High General, three Administrators will stay on the Command Board to ensure balance in decision-making, and to prove to the world that the army and the government are completely united in all efforts."

The High General studied him in silent coolness before he said, "One thing I've learned about educated men like you is that they assume everyone else is gullible enough to believe them."

"It's not as if I control the reactions of the citizenry," Mal countered. "If they still perceive the army as a threat, that's up to you to resolve, not me. It's the history of your army that still fills their grandparents with terror. You can't deny history, Relf."

The High General's stony face hardened even more. "It's all in how you present that story, Nicko. You can't stay focused on what used to be, but see what it is now. Look at the color of the sky. People won't care what the weather was last week, or decades ago. They need to prepare to deal with what's coming now. Then what will you do? Convince them the sky is blue, no matter what they see?"

Mal leaned back in his chair. "Now why would a man like you be interested in what the children of Idumea are learning in school?"

"Why the change?" the general snarled.

Mal chuckled in a manner he'd practiced to be just to the side of oily. "Oh, my dear general—you've been at this for far too long. I promise you, six-year-olds being told that the sky is blue isn't some kind of tactic. You need to take a few days off, Relf," he said with a warm, sticky smile. "Take your wife and go to Coast or somewhere. Enjoy the salty air—"

The High General never shifted his cold glare. "I don't need to take a few days off, Chairman."

Mal's gaze chilled as well. "But you do need to leave my office. In two minutes I have a meeting with the Administrator of Loyalty that I want to get through as quickly as possible. Unless there's anything else?"

The High General straightened his jacket. "Nothing else, Chairman." He spun on his heel and headed out of the office.

Barely a moment later a tall sneering man forced his way through the doors, and Mal could only sigh.

"Of course he's expecting me! Now get out!" Administrator Gadiman shouted at an unseen page, who was likely cowering. Gadiman smoothed his red jacket and stretched out his neck while the Chairmen continued his long sigh. If Gadiman were an animal, his appearance would cause people to instinctively yelp, then proceed to stomp on him with their boots.

But for Mal, he was the perfect weasel.

"What have you for me today, Administrator?" Mal nodded to the stack of thick parchment files that held numerous thinner pieces of paper, tucked under Gadiman's arm.

"All kinds of potential!" Gadiman sniggered with his version of a smile that consisted of bared teeth and thinned lips. "Over in Marsh there's this group of cobblers—"

"I really don't have a lot of time for this today, Gadiman," Mal stopped him before he got too far.

"But they're organizing! So that they can share ideas and—"

"Gadiman," Mal said patiently, "I really don't think *shoe makers* will overthrow the government."

Gadiman leaned closer and whispered, "But what if they're not making shoes?"

"What would they be making?" Mal whispered indulgently back.

"They have leather," the pinched face said in a whisper. "Laces, rivet holes—*armor!*"

"We don't use armor, Gadiman," Mal said, feeling a stomping urge. "Not since the Great War. There's no need."

"There's a need," Gadiman pointed out, "if they plan to attack!"

"Shoe makers attacking the Army of Idumea?"

"Along with the tanners, who are supplying the leather, and the cattle ranchers who supply the cows for the leather," Gadiman said excitedly. "It's a conspiracy!"

Mal took a deep breath but regretted it, as the scent of the Administrator of Loyalty filled his nostrils and reminded him of rotting mulch piles. "That stack of files—," he pointed to Gadiman's arm, "cobblers, tanners, ranchers, and farmers? All organizing?"

"Farmers?!" Gadiman sat back up abruptly.

"Who supplies the feed to the cattle and the ranchers?"

Gadiman's mouth dropped open. "I didn't consider the farmers!"

Mal nodded. "I have a feeling there are a great many things you haven't considered. You have some more research to do, Administrator. Come back in say . . . a season?"

Gadiman nodded vigorously. "Of course! Of course, I will." He stood up and looked shifty-eyed around the large office. "About your *other* project, Chairman," he whispered, yet blew out such a great amount of breath that Mal could identify his dinner the night before, and it must have been most unappetizing, "have you given any thought to my participation?"

"I have," Mal tried not to inhale. "In the future I have no doubt I will be able to use you and your . . . talents."

Gadiman's face fell. "But I thought—"

"In *time*, Gadiman. We have all the time in the world."

---

The High General strode out of the Administrative Headquarters, his lieutenants on his heels. He headed to his horse, tethered and watched over by two young pages grateful they weren't in charge of holding open doors. Without a word he opened a pack secured to the side of the saddle wherein he kept thin papers, finer parchments, and even small vials of ink and quills. The High General believed in recording every bit of information that came his way, to be catalogued in his extensive filing system.

In the afternoon sunshine he wrote out a message on a small piece of paper, signed it, then blew on it until it dried. His lieutenants stood nearby, waiting patiently. He folded the message and sealed it in a thicker parchment envelope.

"Get this to the messaging office immediately," he said to one of the officers. "There's a rider heading out in less than half an hour. I want this delivered to the fort at Edge."

The lieutenant nodded, mounted immediately, and rode away as the High General watched.

"Weather's shifting again," he muttered under his breath, without looking up at the sky.

# Chapter 3 ~ "The sky really is blue, and they can count upon that fact."

Mahrree sniffed in the evening air and marveled how in early Planting Season it actually smelled green. She smiled as she shut the door to her little house to set out for the center of the village and the amphitheater for her debate. She normally didn't enjoy being outside with the dirt and bugs and rooty things, which was obvious by the preponderance of weeds and rocks in her small front yard. But on evenings like this, the air demanded to be appreciated.

Planting Season was her favorite because her students were frequently needed to help their parents in the fields every few weeks, affording Mahrree time to sit and study. She chose to become a village teacher of all subjects and ages, just like her father, although her mother frequently told her he would have been pleased if she became a wife, too. If it weren't for evenings like this that forced her outside, she would probably keep studying and forget to notice the greening of the world.

As she neared the common greens she passed playing and bickering groups of children, and headed straight for a gaggle of teenage girls preening themselves before the amphitheater's doors, hoping to be noticed.

When the children became teenagers, the girls stopped playing and started watching the boys. Even as a teenager Mahrree hadn't understood that behavior. Her friends had sat and giggled while she sat and thought about books from her father's collection, especially after he died. She knew her lack of attention to young men was why she was single at the overripe age of twenty-eight. The last in her group had married several years ago, and many of her ten morning students were the children of her childhood friends.

But none of the young men in Edge had intrigued her as much as accounts from explorers to the ruins, or speculations about the world beyond them that no one knew about. But when she mentioned such things to her friends, they looked at her as if she were a hairy insect. Studying history, then becoming a teacher, was far more satisfying than learning about the art of flirting.

Mahrree paused to watch three of her afternoon students smile coyly at the boys, who unsurprisingly didn't notice them. They had already divided into two teams for Track the Stray Bull and were deep in planning. The young men never seemed to have a hard time deciding who was the bull, but could spend most the evening trying to agree on a strategy that would take three more days to carry out. In the meantime the girls fluffed their hair, straightened their skirts, and eventually sat down to weave grasses together.

Mahrree strolled up behind her students and startled them with, "It will be much more interesting inside tonight. We have a new debater before the concert begins. I'm pretty certain the boys won't be falling out of trees for at least, oh, another half hour. By then the debate will be over, and you can rush over and comfort the fallen."

"Miss Mahrree!" the girls exclaimed in hushed embarrassment, as if the boys had heard her.

"You may find debating exciting, but . . . well, this is far more, umm," faltered fifteen-year-old Hitty. She looked at Teeria, who was a wise sixteen-year-old.

"Educational," Teeria said sagely.

Sareen only glowered. "I'm done with debating."

Mahrree nodded in understanding. "They were right though; you are already very pretty."

Sareen exhaled. "But they didn't have to say I'd look like a raccoon!"

"And your father adding that you might be tempted to go through the trash heaps at night, well, that probably wasn't called for either," Mahrree commiserated. "But tonight should be interesting. Rector Yung has arranged for the new officer of the fort to come—"

Something twanged in Mahrree's belly, as it had many times in the past few days. It was as if all the tension inside of her twisted yet again at the thought of facing a real officer.

And, as she'd done for the past few days, she shoved down the worry in-to a corner of her gut where it churned.

The girls rolled their eyes. "Sorry, Miss Mahrree," said Hitty, reciting her students' favorite rhyme, "but *this* will be so much more . . . and *that* will be so . . ." She rolled her eyes again as words of any real substance failed her.

Mahrree chuckled as she entered the amphitheater doors and went up the stone stairs to the wide rows of wooden benches filling with people. In inclement weather, the evening entertainments moved to the largest Congregation Hall usually reserved for weekly Holy Day services. But as the weather warmed, the diversions multiplied and the outdoor facility was necessary.

Now the written, developed, composed and practiced pieces that kept the citizens of Edge occupied during the long wet nights of the past season could be properly performed.

Over four thousand people could be seated on the long lines of wooden benches for large events, which was all of the adults in Edge and a few hundred of their children—far too many people for Mahrree to comfortably face. But on planting evenings like this, only about five hundred people would be there at the beginning. Once the sun set, many more would trickle in to catch the end of a concert or see the last act of a play.

As she walked to the front she saw her favorite old rector coming to meet her.

"I hope you're ready, Miss Mahrree," Rector Densal smiled as he shook her hand.

"I fear no one," Mahrree told him more confidently than she felt.

"Oh, I know you don't fear," Rector Densal said. "In fact, I hope you will find him *engaging*. I think he's precisely what you need!"

Mahrree looked at him, puzzled. "I didn't know I was in need of anything or anyone." She had a thought and sighed. "Have you been speaking to my mother again?"

Rector Densal laughed. "Not lately, but I do owe her a visit! Well then, maybe he's in need of you." His wrinkled face added new ones as he grinned and climbed the steps to the top of the platform to make general announcements before the debate.

Mahrree chuckled; everyone needed a bit of her.

She walked to the back of the platform and readied to take one of the sets of stairs that led up to it. She stooped to soak the tension out of her hands in the warm bubbling spring that gurgled next to her favorite young oak tree. This spring wasn't as hot as some of the others that were tapped and pumped into homes to be used as bathing and washing water. She'd heard that in Idumea some of the houses had water that was near boiling. But even though the ground was much more active near Edge, the springs that fed Mahrree's home were just pleasantly warm.

She went through her pre-debate routine: she stood back up, shook out her hands, rubbed her cheeks with her fingers, tucked her hair behind her ears again, smoothed down her skirt, and waited for the rector to introduce her. When she heard her name called she marched confidently up the steps and on to the platform, to the applause of the crowd. She waved genially to them as she had dozens of times before and waited for the next introduction.

"Today we have a newcomer to our community," Hogal Densal said to the crowd. "He's been educated in the university at Idumea, has been a member of the army for six years, and was recently assigned to the new fort being built in our village. I'm sure you're all just as eager to get to know him as he is to get to know you. He's heard of our debates and wants a chance at taking on our one of our favorite daughters, Mahrree Peto."

Mahrree steeled herself when she saw a movement to her right. A large and muscular man bounded up the stairs on the side of the platform. He wore the army's dark blue jacket with silver buttons fastened appropriately up to his throat, blue trousers, and, tucked formally under his arm, was a cap with brim.

He stepped on to the platform and paused in mid-stride when he saw Mahrree. He glanced over at the rector, then back at her. A small smile—or maybe a smirk—crept across his face.

Mahrree took a deep breath she hoped no one noticed and firmed her stance. She would not be intimidated.

However, she was unnerved that what she was feeling was not intimidation. And oddly, she suddenly wondered what her hair looked like. She tried to force herself to concentrate, but it wasn't easy since she couldn't stop staring at him.

He was considerably taller than her, but then so was everyone over age thirteen. His uniform was smartly pressed, and his black hair was neat and short and would probably feel thick if she ran her fingers through—

Mahrree blinked in surprise.

Where had *that* thought come from? It was as if the influence of her three teenage students had rushed into the amphitheater and overwhelmed her reason. Had they been standing next to her they would have pointed out his straight nose, his dark eyes, and even the tiny scar on the side of his mouth. One of them probably would have nudged her to notice his intense gaze. When she did, she was alarmed to realize he was studying her. He cocked his head as if trying to interpret the expression on her face. Mahrree shook herself a bit, not daring to guess how long she stared at him. He smiled broader and took a few more steps toward her.

From somewhere she heard the rector's voice. "Let us see how our children's teacher will handle our new captain!"

*Our new captain!*

Had her students been standing next to her, that's what they *would* have been cheering. Mahrree felt strangely weak before remembering she hadn't breathed for the past minute. She filled her lungs and smiled at her challenger.

"Well, *Mr. Captain*," she began, "What's the newest belief in Idumea? In the 319 years of our existence in the world, we have heard many strange things, but I'm sure what you will present to us will simply amaze us."

Her voice was sweet and stinging at the same time, and she felt her confidence return. Mahrree always saw the debates as two boys fighting for possession of a boulder. She pictured herself starting on the top, with her opponent down below where she could throw bits of gravel at his eyes—his unexpectedly dark eyes—which she chose not to look at. Instead she focused on a scar above his left eye and tried to imagine how it got there. A stick seemed to be involved.

"Perrin," was all the captain replied.

"What?" Mahrree was startled too quickly out of her scenario of a girl whacking him across the forehead.

He stepped closer to Mahrree. "My name is Perrin Shin. And you are?"

She knew that family name: Shin. She *should* know that name, but it escaped her for the moment.

As did, embarrassingly, her *own*.

"Uh, I'm . . ."

Maybe it was good her teenage students hadn't joined her that evening.

"Uh, Mahrree. Peto. Yes. That's me."

Eloquent. Poised. Like as a hog trying to jump a fence.

She thought she heard chortling from the audience. In the space just above her heart, a warmth filled her that she'd often felt before, and she immediately thought of her father. He would like this man, Perrin Shin.

"Well, Mrs. Peto—"

"Umm," she interrupted. "I'm *Miss* Mahrree."

Captain Shin sent a quick glance toward someone in the audience. Then in a low, deep voice only she could hear he said, "*I should have known.*"

Mahrree's previous flightiness flew away as she put her hands on her waist. There was nothing wrong with her age and her single status. Oh, let that be the debate topic he chose: the age at which a woman should marry! She'd won that argument many times with her mother. She eyed the captain and would have rolled up her sleeves of her tunic if they weren't already short.

In a much louder voice he announced, "There is a great deal of talk in Idumea. And the talk is, there's too much talk."

Mahrree smirked. Was he trying to be clever? Oh, this night was going to be easy. She watched him as if he was an infestation of approaching ants, and tapped her boot as if ready to stomp.

"There's too much talk," he repeated, "about issues we no longer need to discuss; theories and facts that the Administrators now believe have been decided and need no more debate."

Mahrree was suspicious and intrigued. "What kinds of issues?"

"Things such as the color of the sky; which is better, cats or dogs; the origin of our civilization; why the western ruins exist; what really happens when a volcano explodes. Small, simple things." He looked at her haughtily.

Mahrree knew the tactic: he presented her a list of topics, all of which he undoubtedly was well-versed in, and in an attempt to appear gentlemanly, he was letting her decide which she wanted. She had plenty to say about all of them, but the debate couldn't last all night.

Unfortunately.

"I had no idea all these had been decided," she exclaimed derisively. "Now, I agree that one or two of those things need no discussion, but to say we know the exact color of the sky? We could argue that all night."

One side of his mouth—the side with the scar—lifted into a half-hearted smile. "What color is it?"

"Blue. On some days. White on others. Blue with white, then white with blue. Gray. Black. Black with white dots—"

"Yes, yes, yes, the first debate many children engage in." He sounded bored as he cut her off before she could begin describing sunrises and sunsets. "Of course you'd bring that up. I've been told you spend your time teaching the simplest ideas to the youngest children."

"The earliest lessons are the most important, Captain," Mahrree pointed out, ignoring his insulting tone. "How children learn to think about ideas when they're young influences their ability to reason when they're adults. If they don't learn to think beyond the simplicity of what seems to be an easy question, then they'll fail to realize the deeper levels of every problem. That's why we begin the six year-olds with the 'what color is the sky' debate. The obvious answer is blue. But 'blue' isn't obvious; it's just lazy. From the beginning children need to learn that there are no simple questions, and no simple answers, so they can discover the best answers for themselves."

Many in the audience applauded, most likely the parents of her students.

She took a step toward the captain. "How have you begun to teach *your* child, Captain?"

The captain's half smile returned. "I am not a father, nor am I married, *Miss* Mahrree."

She gave him half a smile back and said quietly, in the same tone he had used, "*I should have known!*"

The captain only blinked at her insolence. "So," he continued loudly, "I suppose I'm not in a good position to judge whether such discussions are still useful. But the Administrators have issued a suggestion to teachers in Idumea. Instead of spending time debating the difficult nature of the sky with the children—"

"But learning *is* difficult!" she interrupted. "It's supposed to be! That's what makes it rewarding—"

The captain held up his hand to stop her.

And, surprising herself, she complied.

"The Administrators have suggested," he repeated steadily, "that the children be *told* that the sky is blue, since it almost always is."

Mahrree folded her arms. "Years ago I heard a revered scholar argue that the sky is not intrinsically blue. It's actually *black*. The blue that we see is merely an illusion—a trick of the sun, since once the sunlight is gone, so is the blue."

The captain squinted. "Blue is an illusion?"

"Very *much so*, Captain."

"Fascinating, Miss Peto," he said sincerely. "I'll have to look further into that. But such a concept is too complex for young children, and that's what the Administrators believe. To avoid confusion, children will be taught that the sky is always blue. This way they need not worry about getting the answer wrong on a test."

The worry corner of Mahrree's gut twisted. Much of what the Administrators had done in the past two years had been beneficial. They lowered taxes significantly—eliminated them completely for the first two full seasons—and had made suggestions to the manner of food distribution, herd growth, and farm development. None of that really meant much to her, since she knew nothing about them.

But this?

For some reason, the idea that the Administrators were now trying to influence the way parents and teachers taught their children filled her with traitorous thoughts of doubt.

"The sky is always blue? But that's not accurate," Mahrree protested.

"It's accurate *enough*," the captain said.

"Accurate *enough*?" she nearly wailed. "That answer simplifies the question inappropriately. This past Raining Season the sky was *rarely* blue. It was gray and depressing!"

"Just tell them that underneath it all, despite what they see, the sky really is blue and they can count upon that *fact*," said the captain indifferently. "Children are simple, needing only simple answers."

A few whistles of disapproval greeted his declaration. Peculiarly, a smile tried to escape his mouth.

And Mahrree saw it.

"You don't entirely believe that, do you Captain?"

He stiffened. "I'm reciting what the Administrators have said, arguing in their behalf."

"Why?"

The captain paused. "Because I'm the army's representative in Edge, and by extension, the representative of the Administrators. Their ideas in Idumea may be later applied here in Edge."

A flicker of concern flashed across his face.

And Mahrree saw that, too.

"The way children are being taught is changing," he continued formally. "Parents no longer have to concern themselves in choosing the lessons. Just as the Administrators have alleviated the citizenry of difficult decisions concerning farming and ranching procedures, they've also decided to alleviate parents of the burden of deciding their children's curriculum." He sounded as if he was reading from an official parchment.

Mahrree was glad she wasn't the only one disturbed by his message. The calls from the audience expressed a loud mixture of disapproval, intrigue, and confusion. Mahrree listened to hear what the overall concern was, and when she discovered it, she gave it to him.

"Why is it considered a burden to select what's best for the children to learn? That's the parents' duty. My job is to help the parents provide that teaching."

"Perhaps," he said mysteriously.

Everyone waited for an explanation.

He offered none but smiled vaguely at her. "Miss Peto, why do you find all of this distressing?"

She really wasn't sure, but it sat on her strangely. "Captain, what if the Administrators teach that which is against the beliefs of the parents?"

He narrowed his eyes. "Such as *what*, Miss Peto?"

She squirmed as she wondered just how close he was to the Administrator of Loyalty. "I don't exactly know yet, Captain. I'm just posing the question for the debate."

"And I answer for the debate," he said sharply. "I can't imagine any situation where the Administrators would recommend teaching anything that would be contrary to the welfare of the world. If anyone would be out of line, it would be misguided parents."

Now the audience squirmed, too.

Instead of responding to his insinuations, she remembered something else. "You mentioned a test of some sort. What kind?" She gave tests to her students occasionally, ones she made with their parents.

"A test that's been developed by the Administrators to make sure the children are learning what they should. A strong civilization needs consistently strong education," the official voice declared.

While evaluation seemed reasonable to Mahrree, something else wasn't. "No two children are the same. They all learn at different rates. How will the Administrators account for that in their testing?"

"This will be the first year of the test," he said. "I'm sure the Administrators are confident they can assess each child fairly."

"So this test won't allow for any answer to the *What color is the sky* question other than *blue?*" Mahrree already dreaded his response.

"I don't believe so." His face was unreadable.

That irritated Mahrree, among other things.

"So what if it's raining that day?"

"The children will have been taught that the correct answer *should* be blue."

"Even when Nature disagrees?"

"Nature agrees often enough with the Administrators." He smiled slyly.

Some in the audience laughed.

Mahrree's gut churned again. "And if it doesn't, will the Administrators change Nature?"

The captain's smile broadened. "They probably could."

More laughter.

"You have a lot of faith in this new government, don't you Captain Shin?" Mahrree said. And until five minutes ago, she did as well. So why did this make her so uneasy, the Administrators wanting to 'help' with education, changing the color of the sky to 'simplify' everything?

The captain's mouth twitched until carefully selected words finally came out. "The Administrators are still new—it's been only two years—so they're still trying to resolve the many problems left by the kings and their neglect. Change comes slowly, and that can be good. I do, however, have faith they are, indeed, acting in the best interest of the world so . . . yes."

Mahrree had started smiling halfway through his stumbling, diplomatic speech. "It took you a little while to get to that 'yes,' Captain," she noted, to some laughter from the crowd. "But after two whole years, I'd assume you'd have a firmer opinion by now."

Some in the audience 'oohed' in sympathy for him.

He had trapped himself and had to loosen the grip of his words. He analyzed her, seemingly searching for more than an escape route. To avoid his steady gaze, Mahrree tried to focus on the horizontal scar above his eye again.

"It's hard to judge something new, Miss Peto, and unfair to evaluate it until you see how it responds in different situations." He was sliding out of his trap. "Would you feel comfortable with me appraising how you think after this one brief encounter?" His smile was most disarming. No wonder he was a soldier.

"It *is* hard to judge accurately, Captain. I agree."

Some in the audience whistled in disapproval.

Mahrree tossed them a reassuring glance. She wasn't finished with this officer.

Hardly.

"But we must make some kind of initial judgment, in every situation, to assure our safety and create a basis for evaluation. Then we modify that judgment as new information arises. I made an appraisal of you the moment I saw you."

She thought she saw something like pleasure race across his face.

"And that's changed many times in the course of our discussion."

She said it sweetly, but his eyes looked almost pained.

"I now have another evaluation of you, Captain, but I won't share it until you have proven yourself."

Applause and even some laughter scattered through the crowd. The captain squared his back and stood a little taller. Mahrree hadn't realized until then that she didn't even come up to his shoulders. His very broad, sturdy shoulders, the influence of her teenagers pointed out.

"I intend to prove myself, very soon. I look forward to it," he announced.

"You're going to prove yourself to us? How *progressive* of Idumea," she sniggered, "they're now even sending us entertainment."

Several in the audience joined her in dubious laughter.

Admirably, the captain didn't even blink at the ridicule. "I have to admit, I'm intrigued that you seem to be against progress, Miss Peto. And as you know, Chairman Mal is all about progress."

The villagers looked at her in nervous expectation.

She knew about the Chairman's focus on progress. She *also* knew the captain was trying to show he sided with the Administrators, which would nudge her to some position opposite.

"Not every edict that came down from the kings was progressive, as I'm sure you'll agree, Captain. And I'm not yet convinced that every *suggestion* from the Administrators will be progressive either. Different, yes. Helpful? Ah, that takes time to evaluate."

"Be careful now, Miss Peto," Captain Shin simpered. "Someone listening might think you're not fully behind the *progressive* measures of the Administrators."

Mahrree squared her narrow shoulders and knew exactly how to push him off the boulder he was trying to climb. "Why? Do you have the power to create a killing squad to silence me?"

The captain's eyebrows shot upwards at her audacity, and she memorized the stunned look on his face. Three of those in a debate, and she would win the evening.

The audience tittered in loud nervousness, while a few men shifted their gazes toward the captain, their glares hardening.

"Miss Peto," he said earnestly, "I've never been involved in a killing squad, nor would I want to. They were done away with by the High General under Querul the Fourth, and the Army of Idumea has been a peaceful, protective service ever since. But Miss Peto," he said in a tone that dove straight into condescension, "let's avoid these emotional tangents and get to the real point: what's your definition of progress?"

She was grudgingly impressed by his ability to run her accusation right off the road.

Hmm.

She hadn't expected that. She rather thought he'd be as ridiculously thick as his neck. But he was a tricky one.

"Progress is change that improves everyone's lives," she decided. "Our way of living, thinking, behaving."

"And how do you know if something is progressive or not?"

"We test it," Mahrree said, "just as The Writings say: test all things, as we are tested. Oh, wait. I'm sorry." She batted her eyelashes. "I understand most people from Idumea no longer read The Writings. Too trite and unprogressive?"

She enjoyed watching his face tighten.

The captain nodded. "I have, in fact, read The Writings once or twice. I remember the Creator telling the first five hundred families that they should test all ideas and knowledge. So, how can you dismiss the educational suggestions of the Administrators without even *testing* it yourself?"

The audience chuckled nervously for Mahrree. He had a point.

She had one to match.

"I'm all for finding out the truth, Captain. You won't find anyone more determined than me. I'll see what happens first in Idumea before I suggest to my students' parents that we try any of it here."

"So you're not opposed to progress?"

"If I were, I would still be wearing animal skins and living in that same cave where the Creator first placed our ancestors when He brought them to this world 319 years ago!"

"You enjoy referring to The Writings, don't you, Miss Peto?" he said, folding his arms and evaluating her. "You probably know all of it, how the

Creator taught the women to shear sheep and card wool, and how He taught the men to smelt iron, make tools, cut down trees, and make planking for houses?"

She folded her arms in a similar manner and cocked her head. "I realize that in Idumea they call those of us who are still believers 'Writings Wretches,' but I do, Captain. I enjoy discovering the truth the Creator and His guides left for us."

Captain Shin held up a finger. "Can truth be found from other sources, Miss Peto? Can't we learn to do things without the guidance of the Creator? We've been without the influence of guides for almost 120 years now, and we seem to be just fine."

"Are you suggesting, Captain Shin," she glowered, "that losing our last guide in 200, his *murder* in the forest above Moorland, ending the words of the Creator to us, was progressive?"

The angry tension that filled the amphitheater told the captain what his response better be if he had any hope of winning any hearts and minds that night.

"Miss Peto, any man's murder is tragic," he said somberly. "And the death of the last holy man is beyond that. Of course I'd never suggest the death of Guide Pax was acceptable. But I *would* submit that we have carried on admirably since then, and those in this audience who still revere The Writings as deeply as you do, demonstrate that the spirit of the guides is still strong and viable. Perhaps the Creator now wants us to act for ourselves and progress to the best of our abilities without His direct guidance. Miss Peto, we didn't need a guide or the Creator to discover how to turn flax to linen, or discover silk.

"But, perhaps," he said with a growing smile that warmed his features and began to warm the audience as well, much to Mahrree's disappointment, "perhaps the Creator *did* influence that woman to do her wash under the mulberry bushes so that the silk cocoons would fall into her hot water and make such an absurd but useful mess. And it wasn't because of the guides that men discovered ways to combine different soils, gravel, and water to create mortar to hold rock together. Our ancestors discovered that themselves. They also learned how to turn the pines north of Quake and to the west of Trades into pulp and thin paper, allowing us to print far more books than if we had only costly parchment. *We* did all that!

"Miss Peto," he continued earnestly, "I believe the Creator gave us minds and choices so that we could become creators ourselves. He wants us to experiment, try, fail, and try again until we succeed. That's progress, Miss Peto, and I submit that the Creator is pleased with us when we experiment. In that light, the Creator is pleased with the Administrators when they experiment. These changes in education? Just experiments to see if we can progress to something even greater."

Mahrree couldn't do anything while the crowd wholeheartedly applauded the captain, except plot against him. In one little speech the captain, who was now smiling in triumph to the villagers, had taken her accusation of dismissing the death of the last guide to suggesting that the Creator would be pleased with the Administrators. She hadn't anticipated he could twist the argument so quickly.

She'd just have to twist it back.

"Captain Shin," she started loudly, "what year is this?"

The audience immediately silenced at the obvious question.

The captain turned to her. "It's 319."

"What year is it in Idumea?"

Now he squinted. "Still 319. Has been for the last six days."

"But it will instead be 313, if some professors at the University of Idumea have their way. Correct?"

The amphitheater waited silently.

The captain swallowed. "Perhaps."

"You see," Mahrree turned to the surprised villagers, "a few professors, one of them a brother to the Administrator of Culture, believe that our history should begin with the foundation of Idumea, and that the six years preceding that, when the first five hundred families were under the tutelage of the Creator for three years, then under the governance of His chosen Guide Hieram, be eliminated from our children's education. The Administrator of Culture wants our history to be taught that we began with the organization of Idumea, and that no mention should be made that the six men who founded it also *murdered* Guide Hieram."

Captain Shin paled slightly. "No changes can be made unless the majority of Administrators agree to it, Miss Peto," he said firmly. "That's why there are twenty-three. Had such a suggestion been made to King Oren, he would have foolishly enacted it and changed all the books the next day. But that can't happen under the Administrators. The suggestion is currently dying in a committee. That's *progress*, Miss Peto."

Mahrree couldn't help but smile slightly in admiration. He twisted that argument masterfully, too, judging by the applause of the villagers. He was nothing like the way she had imagined army officers. He was thoughtful, articulate, and hadn't once drawn the large sword he wore strapped to his side. If it weren't for that uniform, Mahrree would have thought him to just be an intelligent, insightful man.

"I'm glad to hear that suggestion is dying, Captain. And I strongly suspect it won't go anywhere because it would be most difficult to change the dating throughout the world. But I wonder if the question first arose because children in Idumea *struggled* and needed their education simplified. But here in Edge, our children are intelligent enough to learn all the truth, including how the world changed after the foundation of Idumea. I still question how any of those changes were progressive."

Captain Shin slowly shook his head as the crowd once again cheered, this time for Mahrree. "Indeed, Miss Peto, they grow them remarkably loud and brave in Edge. I suspect if you shouted, they could hear you in Mountseen."

Mahrree didn't know why the villagers laughed. Maybe it was the way he looked her small frame up and down.

It wasn't the first time an opponent tried to demean her. Back in upper school, before she went to college in Mountseen, many debaters—males, usually—would make some biting comment about her size in relation to her volume.

She never put up with that. Years ago she came up with a retort that was as sudden and sharp as, as . . . well, as the captain's two-edged sword which seemed to be about as long as Mahrree's leg.

She firmed her stance and yanked out her response. "The Writings, Captain Shin, tell us we waited eons for our chance on the world. Since this is my only shot, I decided long ago to go bold, or don't go at all!"

Oh yes, others rarely had a response for that. She sounded educated, enlightened, and patronizing all in one fell swish. It was a line she perfected when she was fifteen, and it always—

Captain Shin took a step closer, his brown-black eyes staring so deeply into hers that even her thoughts paused. He arched an eyebrow—which had the effect of making Mahrree's chest tighten and her tongue forget to move—then said, "Go bold . . . *where?*"

She swallowed.

No one had ever asked her that.

She didn't even realize until then that it was a potential question.

The audience tittered in anticipation while Mahrree blinked in sudden self-doubt, until the captain spoke again.

"And now, Miss Peto, how does one end the debates here?"

As grateful as she was to not have to review the logic of her life's motto just then, Mahrree fought the urge to bite her lip. She wasn't quite finished with him yet, but at least she found her words again.

"Against me? Usually one gives up and storms off the platform. You may do so now."

Everyone laughed.

The captain just smiled, making her wonder if he *could* laugh. "How else?"

"It depends. Either the rector overseeing the debate declares a winner or a draw, or the audience decides."

With that, Rector Densal stood up and turned to the audience. "Our debaters have given us much to consider tonight—far too many new ideas to consider before we declare a winner." He turned to the two of them. "And with that, I bid you a fair evening." He pounded his walking stick on the ground which signaled the end of the debate.

Shouts of "Declare a winner!" arose, but the rector held his hand up to his ear as if he'd gone deaf. The shouts dissolved into laughter and finally applause.

Mahrree waved politely, and then rushed down the back steps of the platform to the bench that sat under her tree. Usually she enjoyed meeting the audience after a debate, but not tonight. She felt oddly shaken, as if something was approaching to disrupt all that she knew. She remembered her father's words: "Sometimes the world really *is* out to get you."

Maybe the world was there in the form of Captain Shin.

She had to think carefully about him. Her mind was split in two: one-half influenced by girls that giggled about his features, the other half worried about his ideas of education and progress.

"An interesting evening, wouldn't you agree?" Rector Densal broke into her thoughts as he placed a wrinkled hand on her shoulder.

She stood up to greet him. "Oh, Rector, he seems to be a . . . a dangerous man, doesn't he? And he's our hope against the Guarders? If the rumors are true about their return, we might as well surrender now!"

Rector Densal's white eyebrows rose. "Actually, I thought him to be a pleasant-looking fellow and quite good-natured. And I thought for a few moments you considered him pleasant as well. Was I mistaken?"

Mahrree froze. She'd never been attracted to a man before, so she wasn't sure if she did. "But his arguments—"

"Consider this for a moment, my dear: did Captain Shin, at any time, state that the arguments he presented were his own ideas?"

She ran the debate quickly over in her head, but irritatingly found herself remembering only how he'd smiled at her. "I, I . . . honestly don't remember."

"Well I do. And no, he never said those were his ideas. He came for a debate, right? And he gave you an interesting time, correct?"

"Interesting or aggravating?" she snapped.

He smiled in unexplained satisfaction. "I look forward to three nights' time from now. Captain Shin asked to meet you again in debate, and I agreed. I hope that's all right."

He patted her arm without waiting for an answer—probably suspecting it would be "No!"—and slowly ambled away, leaving Mahrree standing under the tree still trying to formulate a way out of it.

A faint movement from the platform above caused her to look up . . . into the eyes of the captain. Each time she looked at him the world seemed to change, and it was most irksome.

He crouched to reduce the span that the ten steps created between them. "I want to thank you for a fascinating evening," he said with a smile that made the ground seem to shift under her feet. "We must do this again. And I understand we will be, very soon."

He seemed different somehow. More agreeable.

Mahrree slowly nodded, desperately searching her mind for some retort or comment besides the anemic, "Uh-huh," that she could manage. She shouldn't have been staring into his dark eyes.

"My great-uncle said my time here would be interesting. He was right, but he usually is. Good evening, Miss Peto."

And with that Captain Shin righted himself, turned, and walked out of Mahrree's view.

She didn't mean to whimper. It just leaked out.

# Chapter 4 ~ "All science is about proving a bias."

"I heard the debate was interesting tonight. I now wished I could've attended," Hycymum Peto said as her daughter sat down at her kitchen table to a mug of warm milk.

Mahrree fidgeted. She wasn't sure if it was because of what her mother said, or because of the new sheepskin coverings for the chairs that were dyed pink to match the curtains, tablecloth, dish cloths, and pink stain rubbed into the wooden cabinets.

"But you see, new linen arrived for my ladies' sewing night, and—"

"What did you hear about it?" Mahrree stared at the simple mug her mother gave her. It wasn't one of her expensive kiln-fired cups. Mahrree didn't mind being treated like a child that night; she felt more at ease holding the mug that cost fewer slips of silver, since she wasn't sure of her grip on anything.

"I heard the linens came from Coast and—"

"No, Mother," Mahrree said patiently. "I meant, what did you hear about the debate?"

"Oh. Ahh! Well, I heard," began her mother, pulling up a chair across from her daughter, "that a very handsome man has come to the village." Her voice was filled with the glee of a teenager, despite her forty-eight years. She began to wiggle excitedly, and the tremor rolled through her round body up to her plump face and through her brown and gray curls. "And that he took you on very handily."

Mahrree's head snapped up. "No one won! I *should* have, because he pretty much quit before I could finish him off, but he didn't 'take me on'!"

Her mother sat back and giggled. "My—so there *is* something there."

"Who told you that?"

"The Densals left just before you arrived. Hogal told me you did very well, but that he'd never seen you turn red so often. I told him you did that when you were little and looked at a boy, or you needed to relieve yourself."

Hycymum took a sip from her shiny cup. Her mother was often a rich source of information.

The most embarrassing kind, unfortunately.

Mahrree buried her face in her hands. "Oh, Mother—you didn't."

"Well, it's true," she said, unsure of why her daughter was upset. "So, was he handsome?"

"How should I know?" Mahrree wasn't truly lying, she was just asking another question. She reached for a piece of bread from the basket and noticed a layer of herbs encrusted on it. She never understood her mother's need to embellish everything, from her head to her food. Hycymum also insisted everything should be a *meal*. That meant taking three extra hours and twelve extra ingredients and stirring them into something no one would recognize anymore, then giving it a made up name like la-zhan-ya.

Then again, it was her job as the head cook for Edge's Inn, the finest establishment north of Mountseen, as its sign proclaimed. There wasn't much competition; Edge was the *only* village north of Mountseen, and the other inn—misleadingly named Inn at Edge—served food that they culled from Edge's Inn's trash heap. Or so Hycymum claimed.

"You know, the rector said the new officer comes from an army family. Something like that," Edge's finest cook vaguely waved her thick hand. "His father did something with someone . . . with the new Administrators. Maybe."

Mahrree sighed. The only way her mother would become interested in politics was if they started taxing polka dots or cucumber slices. "Is he related to a general?" she suggested. During the walk from the amphitheater to her mother's, Mahrree tried to remember where she had heard the name Shin before. There was only one man she thought of, but the captain certainly couldn't be *his* son.

Her mother looked up at the wood-planked ceiling for an answer. "General? Maybe. That's the highest rank, right?"

"Yes," Mahrree said slowly.

Her mother shook her head. "Doesn't sound familiar. Anyway, he's supposed to come from a good family. There."

Mahrree gave her a flimsy smile and took a taste of the bread. She couldn't define any one flavor in it. Not that it was bad, just *complicated*. Everything seemed unnecessarily complicated tonight.

"Anyway," Hycymum said again, "Rector Densal said the colonel—"

"Captain," Mahrree corrected.

"Whatever—was the kind of man your father would approve of." Hycymum put her hand on top of Mahrree's. "When you decide you want to marry him, I will help you pick your linens."

"Wha—, marr—, I—, MOTHER!" Mahrree spluttered. "What ARE you doing? I debated the man just once and you already have me, me . . . ?" She stood and circled her chair like a disoriented fly. Why was it that she could debate anyone in the village but could rarely get her mother to under-stand anything?

Hycymum looked at her sadly. "It's just that you aren't that young of a woman anymore. To find a man not intimidated by you is . . . wait. Oh no. What did you say at that debate? Oh, Mahrree! You didn't ruin your chances with a corporal by being *smart*, did you?"

"Mother!"

Mahrree tried to calm down by taking a deep breath. She chose not to correct the rank mistake again, but instead put on her kindest dealing-with-small-children expression before saying, "I came to visit you tonight because I wanted to be comforted. And I wanted to, to, oh I don't know anymore . . . What's so wrong about being smart? That's what Father encouraged."

"And he was much better at listening to you than I ever was." Her mother sighed. "You have a question about what to put on the table for a group dinner, I'm your woman," she said with a happy smile that dimmed. "But you have a question about why something is right or wrong, you needed to talk to your father. He kept me balanced."

Mahrree had often wondered why her parents got together. Then she remembered her father loved all kinds of foods. And he really did seem to adore her, her silliness and everything.

Mahrree took her chair again and the women sat in silence.

Eventually her mother spoke. "You would do well with a man to help you keep your balance. Yes, I know—you're very balanced. But a good man will help you *improve* the balance. I miss Cephas's knowledge, his always wanting to do right. Sometimes when I hear you speak it's like I'm hearing him. Maybe that's why I don't go to the debates too often."

And she had adored him, Mahrree thought. He could explain anything to her, and she absorbed it all. Mahrree seemed only to sloppily splash words against her mother. Of course she would miss him when she listened to her debate . . .

Mrs. Peto sighed. "Ah, that's not the entire reason I didn't go. I'd just rather look at cloth with my friends. I *am* sorry," she admitted with an apologetic grin.

Mahrree chuckled. Hycymum sometimes acted as if her head was full of bubbles, but at least they were honest bubbles.

"I'm sorry, Mahrree," she repeated. "I didn't mean to marry you off tonight. I just worry. I wasn't lonely for the sixteen years I had your father. I hate to think of you lonely for your whole life."

"As long as I have my students and you, Mother, I'll never be lonely!" Mahrree declared.

But tonight, those words seemed strangely empty.

---

Several roads away the old rector and his wife wearily entered their back door after a long evening of visits. Mrs. Densal lit a candle on their eating table, and her husband gasped.

The flickering light revealed a large figure in dark clothing filling the doorway between the kitchen and gathering room.

Mrs. Densal whimpered.

"It's unsafe to leave your doors unlocked now that Guarder activity has increased."

Hogal Densal expelled his lungs and shook his head. "Perrin Shin! Have you ever heard of knocking and waiting for a response?" He chuckled nervously and pulled out a chair, gesturing for the captain to join him at the table.

"Truly, Perrin! Frightening an old woman like this," Mrs. Densal scolded with a broad smile as the captain sat down. She turned to a cabinet, took out a plate loaded with a large piece of berry pie, and placed it in front of him.

The captain started to refuse it, thought again, and accepted the fork she offered.

"Thank you," he remembered to say before adding, "but I'm not here for your pie. I'm here for an explanation." He took a bite and glared at the old man while he chewed.

The rector's wife pulled out a chair to sit across from her husband who was practicing his best 'What have I done?' look.

"An explanation about what, my boy?" Rector Densal sounded genuinely unsure.

Perrin swallowed. "About tonight! About . . . umm," he waved his fork. "Miss Mahrree Peto?"

Perrin took another bite. "Yes," he mumbled, jabbing his fork at the rector. "Some old school teacher! That's what you said, Hogal. 'The *old* school teacher.'"

Mrs. Densal looked down to hide a smile.

Hogal put on a thoughtful expression. "Well, now, many of the younger children *think* of her as old. Perhaps that's what I meant—"

"I know what you're doing," Perrin said, shifting his gaze between the two of them. "And I'm not here to get married. I'm here to command the new fort. And to eat your pie. Delicious, as always." He smiled at Mrs. Densal.

She beamed, adding more creases around her ever-twinkling eyes.

"My boy, no one said anything about marriage. Dear, did you say anything about marriage?" Hogal asked his wife.

"Just so you both understand: I'm not the marrying type."

"Ah, Perrin," said Mrs. Densal, patting his hand. "Everyone is the marrying type. They just don't know it until they find their type."

"And it's my guess that Miss Mahrree may be your type," Hogal winked.

Perrin ignored that comment and focused on the pie. "And you already scheduled another debate?"

"Oh, she suggested it, my boy," the rector told him. "She's quite thoughtful. Just like her father, one of the wisest men I ever knew. And she might be considered pretty, too."

"Looks aren't everything," Perrin muttered as he broke off another piece, but something in his voice suggested they were part of the equation.

"She reads a lot. Tends to get a little outspoken, but I think you saw that," Hogal mused, trying to see any reaction on Perrin's face.

But Perrin kept looking at his plate, pushing bits of berries around with his fork.

"But at least she thinks," Mrs. Densal interjected. "It can be difficult to find young women who care for anything more than popular dress colors."

When the captain didn't respond, the elderly couple looked at each other and communicated silently.

The rector cleared his throat. "I'm intrigued about your presentation of the topics. First, you receive that message from Idumea—"

"He's always sending me weather reports," the captain said offhandedly.

"Curious that he should, considering that the weather we have in Edge one day is visiting Idumea the next. Reports should be going the *other* way, I would think. Or perhaps he's just drawing your attention to the color of the sky?"

The captain didn't answer, but took another bite of pie.

The rector smiled at the avoidance tactic. "You wanted her to choose the color of the sky topic, didn't you? Did you decide that before or *after* you laid eyes on her?"

Perrin shrugged without looking up. "I don't know what you're talking about." Another bite of pie.

"Of course not," Hogal said, with a slow nod. "She did rather well, I thought. Took you on quite handily. Knowing her, in about five more minutes she would have humiliated you. Maybe that's why you cut the debate short?"

Perrin stopped swirling around berries and stared at his plate.

"But you made great strides in proving to the village that you and the army are not lingering death tools of the kings," Hogal assured him. "You even earned a few smiles, nods of approval, and one hearty round of applause. Excellent work tonight, my boy."

Perrin just studied his nearly empty plate.

"You know," the rector said with a chuckle as he rearranged some of the dishes set for their breakfast, "I was just thinking, Mahrree doesn't live too far away from here. Just north and east. Rather along the way to the fort, I would think. It's rather easy to find her house. It's the only one without a proper garden. The woman cares nothing for maintaining her yard. She cares only for her books—and her students, of course."

When this failed to draw any kind of response from the captain, Mrs. Densal tried. "I was just wondering what color Mahrree's hair could be described as. It's too dark for blonde, and too light to be brown. I have the same question about her eyes. I'm not really sure what color they are."

Perrin stabbed his last piece of pie with more effort than needed and said, "Greenish-gray. But more green," then put the fork in his mouth. Something in the air suggested he decided not to add, "with little flecks of golden brown."

The rector and his wife exchanged triumphant looks. Rector Densal cleared his throat to begin again when Perrin finally looked up.

"Please don't do this," he said in a low voice. "I don't need to be made to look like a fool in love in my first major assignment."

"Oh, come now Perrin. How can we make the son of the High General of Idumea look like a fool?" Mrs. Densal asked. She looked at his empty plate and slapped the table. "I almost forgot!" She stood up, took a mug from the cabinet, turned to the cold cellar, and filled the mug with milk.

Perrin's hand automatically went up to his forehead in embarrassment as she placed the mug in front of him.

"I know what you're going to say: milk's for children. But you've always eaten my pie with milk."

Perrin slowly shook his head and fingered the mug. "I'm not a child anymore. And if I want to find a wife, I can do it on my own. *If!*"

He gulped down the milk.

Mrs. Densal smiled. "That's not what your mother said. By the way, I'm writing her tomorrow and I'll tell her how nice you looked tonight." She took a dish cloth, licked a corner of it, and rubbed one of the shining silver buttons on Perrin's chest.

He respectfully accepted her grooming, nodded a thank you when she finished, then pushed away his empty dishes and stood up, adopting a formal stance.

"I need to be getting back to the fort. It should be completed in the next few days, but there are many details that need to be addressed." Perrin leaned over and kissed the rector's wife on her forehead. "Thank you again for the pie, Auntie Tabbit. But can you *please* try to do something about your husband?"

The rector grinned and pointed at his forehead expectantly, his eyebrows bouncing up and down.

Perrin gave him a playful glare, put on his cap, and left out the back door.

The rector and his wife watched him close the door. Then Tabbit kicked her husband under the table. "Hogal, I said be subtle. Subtle! Do you know what that means?"

The rector feigned pain at her gentle kick. "But dear, he's twenty-eight, and we're in our eighties—we don't have *time* to be subtle. Did you notice he talked about marrying, at least twice?"

"It was three times, I'm sure!" Tabbit giggled.

---

Outside of the door, Captain Shin listened in on his great aunt and uncle. He shook his head at their banter and smiled as he left.

He walked the alley that ran behind the houses. One of the reasons he came to Edge was because of the Densals, but Hogal's idea of help was distracting him from his work. No other captain had been given so much responsibility. Then again, there was no other son of the High General, who was also the grandson of a High General. He had to make a good impression early, not only with the villagers but with the army and the Administrators.

Someday, once the fort was established and the threat of Guarders was again subdued, he could see himself looking around. By then he'd be about thirty, ten years older than most available females, but there still might be some close to his age.

Miss Peto seemed to be older. And fairly attractive. And smart. So why was she still single? Something must be wrong with her.

Then again, she might think the same thing about him.

*If* she thought of him.

He took another turn, then another. It wasn't as if her home was out of his way. He needed to walk past it on his way back to the fort. After all, it was his duty to learn every road and alley in Edge so he could defend the village against the raids that may be coming.

Still, he felt guilty when he found himself in front of her dark home. The tiny yard had no distinguishable pattern to the foliage, but maybe that was because the sun had set a while ago. The house was typical for smaller villages: large stones for the foundation, smaller stones mortared together for the main floor, and broad planked boards for the second level bedroom and attic, with a pitched roof covered in sun-dried tiles. It was small and neat with windows of thick wavy glass. In Sands the glass blowers were developing much thinner panes to import to Idumea, but no one else besides the forts needed to go to such expense. Neither did Miss Peto, he nodded in approval. He paused only for a moment to glance surreptitiously at the windows that revealed dark nothingness.

He walked slowly to the end of the road that led directly to the fort and stopped. Where she would be at this hour of evening? He felt concern for her safety—as a captain should—and turned to walk down past her house again.

Perhaps she *was* home, but had already retired for the night. Was she ill? That might be his responsibility, too. Maybe he should knock on her door and make sure that she was well.

But what would he say when she opened it? "Just making sure you're still alive"?

He reached the end of the road and immediately felt like a foolish fourteen-year-old. He turned again to walk past her home the third time and on to the fort. But again he slowed down as he passed her yard and looked in the dried weeds for any sign of trouble.

Strangely disappointed he picked up his gait, marched past the next house, and turned on to the fort.

---

From behind a thick evergreen shrub across the road, Mahrree finally felt enough courage to step out from her hiding spot and watch the dim figure of Captain Shin walk away. She'd seen him pass her house twice. What might have happened if she hadn't spent so long at her mother's? Was he attempting to find her house?

Or was he lost? That didn't bode well for the safety of their community, she thought with a wry smile.

She tiptoed across the cobblestones to the corner of the road to catch the last glimpse of him. Instantly she felt ridiculous about the entire thing. How would he even know where she lived? One part of her wished she paid closer attention to how her silly students stalked the young men outside the amphitheater. The other part wanted to slap her on the face and send her to the bedroom in disgrace.

---

Standing in the shadows across the road from Mahrree Peto's house was a slender man in dark clothing. He watched her as she went through her front door. Then he quietly slipped from his hiding place and slinked down the main road to the new fort, observing the captain's progress. The report he'd be sending would verify the captain's arrival and apparent intent to stay, as well as his defense of the Administrators' positions at the debates.

But the report would also describe his unusual behavior tonight.

The man smiled briefly. For someone of his age and stature, he shouldn't have been forced so far for this assignment. Once in the mansion, always in the mansion. Or so he'd assumed. He hadn't realized Stage One would mean leaving his well-deserved comforts to tail potential targets like a first year learner.

But *this* target—and those connected to him—was more important than any other.

The man knew his wisdom was needed, and so were his abilities. And now he was no longer resentful about his posting, especially after so many years of dull nothingness. Stage Two was beginning, and the north might *actually* be appealing.

Because Captain Perrin Shin was turning out to be interesting after all.

---

*Go bold,* Mahrree wrote on the scrap paper late that night.

She frowned at it.

It should have been *Go boldly,* right? She got it wrong all those years ago. But that indicated going somewhere, and what she'd meant was, *Be bold.*

But then it would have been, *Be bold, or don't be at all,* which was far more fatalistic than she intended.

She scowled at the paper. Things are so much simpler when one approaches them with the over-confident superiority of a teenage mind.

Now, as an adult, she finally realized just how simplistic and incorrect her old motto had been.

No.

No, *the captain* had pointed out how simplistic and incorrect she was.

With those deep dark eyes he'd looked at her with what she could only describe as patronizing curiosity, almost arrogant affection. The way one might regard a lamb tangled up in a laundry line.

Ah, look at the darling little creature, caught by her own stupidity. Let's see if she can get out on her own. Better yet, let's just end it right here, before she can extract herself.

Mahrree crumpled up the paper and hurled it furiously into the cold hearth.

Then she reluctantly stood up and, wishing crumpled bits of paper flew more accurately, trudged over to the wall where the small white mass lay apologetically, picked it up and tossed it into the logs waiting for a cold morning.

She blew out the candle and clumped up the stairs to bed.

Twenty minutes later, Mahrree couldn't stand it anymore. She got out of her bed, rushed down the stairs to her dark eating room, and relit the candle. Then she pulled one of the many books off the shelf, dropped it on the table, and thumbed to the back. She'd never before read the pages of supposedly "Interesting Facts" of the leaders of the world, but tonight she raced her finger across the words until she came to High General Relf Shin.

She swallowed hard as she read,

*Married, wife named Joriana. Son, born in 291,*

The same year as her.

*named Perrin.*

She had debated, challenged, insulted—and *been insulted by*—the son of one of the most powerful men in the world.

Her head hit the table in mortification.

---

Late that night two men sat in the dark office of an unlit building. Their meeting was private, secret, and the most important one in the entire world.

"Are you ready?" the first, older man with a shock of white hair asked.

"Does this mean you're *actually* about to begin?" said the second, middle-aged man in a bored tone. "It's been so long—"

"Question," the first man cut him off. "How will the world react to the return of their most feared enemy?"

The second man sighed. "Finally! I—"

"Now, now," the first man interrupted, holding up a finger in the dim room. "That's not the proper response. I want your speculation."

"You're going to be this exact?"

The first man's smile dimmed. "I've spent more than seven years preparing for this! And in the past two years the entire world has been placed under very careful controls. You think I'm going to throw out all research protocols and be casual now?"

His companion nodded. "Of course not. My speculation: if the return is impressive enough, then the people will panic and beg to be rescued. They'll likely cower in terror, as usual." He thought for a moment. "Perhaps there might be someone brave who decides to confront the conflict himself—"

"Ha!" the older man exclaimed. "Doubtful. That's precisely what I'm out to prove. Granted, someone may try that once or twice—I'm counting on it—but he'll realize there's no purpose in risking his life. Not unless the army's paying him, and even then he won't see it as enough. No one dares anything without the lure of a reward or fear of punishment." He eyed his younger partner critically. "But your naïve optimism is why I chose you. I need balance and I appreciate your perspectives, as inaccurate as they may be."

The middle-aged man squinted. "Now, while I agree that people respond to rewards and punishments, I also believe they can act because of other motivations—"

"Oh, come now!" the first older man sneered. "Don't tell me you're just like him. Next you'll try to convince me that humans have more noble traits than the rest of the animals."

The second man blinked. "You're still angry about that? That was what, four years ago?"

"Seven," the first said hotly.

"So that's what this is all about? *Him?*"

The first man glared. "No, of course it's *not all about him!* We're about to embark on the most extensive research project regarding the animalistic nature of humans ever attempted. He may have initially influenced it," the old man admitted, running a hand through his white hair, unconsciously ruffling it, "but what we will accomplish is far bigger than merely proving a point to *him.*"

The second man regarded him suspiciously. "So your purpose is to . . ."

"Demonstrate conclusively that men are simply animals, and can be broken as such." The older man rattled it off as if he'd been practicing for seven years. Which, he likely had.

"What about women?"

The first man waved that off. "Everyone already accepts they're only animals. Women have no more influence or thought beyond what their men accord them."

The second man smirked. "You were never married, were you?"

"No. I have better things to do. So, are you up to it?"

"Just one question: you *will* be objective about all of this, won't you? I'm a little concerned that your personal experiences—"

"Show me one man that's completely objective!" the older man snapped. "There's no such thing. All science—when you get right down to it—is about proving a bias. You know that as well as I do, so why should we pretend otherwise? I'll be as impartial and objective as any man *can* be, but if I didn't feel any passion for what I do, why would I do it at all?"

The second man nodded in reluctant agreement. "You may have a point."

"Naturally. Now," the first older man continued methodically, "there hasn't even been one incident, yet already some villages are reporting there have been sightings. You see," he leaned forward, "it's merely the *perceptions* of what is real that affect people, not reality. Just a *suggestion* of terror, and already they're trembling like a broken dog. I fear it may all prove to be too simple."

He sat back, almost sadly.

"But hopefully we'll be able to enjoy this study for a few years before the world crumbles into a cowering mess," he continued. "So, the oaths have been taken, all my men have moved into place—I've already received a very interesting report—and every fort will be in operation within the next few weeks . . . I can see you're intrigued, so I ask you again: are you ready? Because Stage Two is."

The second thought for a moment. "Who in the world will be tested first?"

The first smiled thinly. "I assume that question means you're willing to be my research partner. Take your pick. The world's under my control.

# Chapter 5 ~ "Tell me what you know about Guarders."

In the morning Captain Shin stared out again at the forest, his stack of notes in one hand, his sharpened charcoal in another, and his mind back at the platform staring at the memory of a school teacher with blazing eyes and a blistering demeanor. He shook his head to dislodge the distraction and glared at the forest.

It was no use. He should check on the builders' progress at the barracks, anyway. With a sigh of self-deprecation, he turned and headed back to the fort.

Just inside the forest, about thirty paces deep and sitting high up in a tree, two men dressed in mottled green and brown clothing waved good-bye to the captain. Then they winked at each other.

---

Chairman Mal sat at his desk going over files that morning from the Administrator of Loyalty—another list of citizens the sniveling man suspected of potential sedition, or at least weak senses—when the door swung open and a commotion of men poured into his office.

"Sir, I'm sorry, but he just won't—"

Mal held up his hand to calm the group, eight men in short red jackets subduing a scruffy creature. Mal's eyes fell upon the young man in his twenties, his hair filthy and mussed, his face smeared with muck, and his clothing disheveled—an unappreciated mutt left out in a storm. In his hand was a butchering knife.

Mal had no doubt he would have been lunging toward the Chairman if it weren't for the guards who'd finally caught up to him. Two were on each of his arms, holding him back, while another guard panted his apologies.

"Sir, he was so quick. Before we knew it he was through the outer doors—"

Mal nodded coolly. "To get through the outer doors is a serious breach, but you and your men made up for your previous error. He's not going any-where now, is he?" He stared into the blue eyes of his would-be assassin.

The young man stared back, full of fury.

"Relieve him of his weapon," Mal commanded, and a guard wrenched the knife from his fist. "Now, all of you may leave, for I'd like to have a few words with our guest in private."

"But, but . . . sir, he, he—" the head of the guard stammered.

"Is now unarmed, and knows full well that all of you will be standing outside the doors, your long knives and swords readied. Isn't that correct?"

The young man grunted in response.

Mal waved for the guard to leave, and reluctantly they filed out.

Only once the door shut behind them did Mal speak again, quietly. "Been wondering when I might see you, Sonoforen. Figured your gold may have run out by now, and with your mother dying last season, it was just a matter of time. Interesting attempt to disguise yourself, but I must point out, it was unnecessary. You don't look anything like your father and no one would think a moment about you. Disappointing. I had hoped you would have a little more forethought than Oren. Poor attempt at an execution."

"Well, you would know all about *executions*, wouldn't you, Chairman?" the young man seethed.

"Ah," Mal said easily. "So that's what you believe, is it? What are you calling yourself these days, anyway?"

"Batalk," he answered shortly. "My mother's maiden name."

"That's still too obvious, *Sonoforen* Batalk," Mal sneered. "And that was always your mother's name. Oren never married her."

"He planned to!"

Mal shook his head slowly. "Doesn't matter what he planned to do. You're not a legal heir to his throne, even though you're the oldest son. Neither you nor your younger brother. Where's Dormin, anyway? Covered in vines and waiting at the grand entrance pretending he's a tree?"

"Don't know, don't care." Sonoforen clenched his fists.

Mal smiled halfway. "Ah, the bonds of brotherhood. Did he bind you first, or did you bind him?"

"I'm here to take back my throne!"

"You may have it," Mal nodded casually. "Perhaps you noticed as you passed it on the way in, near the grand entrance? A reminder of the neglect and abuses of your ancestors. Get a few friends and haul it out of here."

Sonoforen slammed his hands down on the desk and bellowed, "I want to be king!"

Mal nonchalantly straightened up a few piles that were disturbed by the outburst. "I'm sure you do," he said in a jaded tone. "Someone like you believes the world owes him something, although he's done nothing to deserve it. Typical. So you thought killing me would let you become king? That this world which has embraced our government, rejoiced in our reforms, and sends us letters of gratitude each week would simply accept your killing me and restore you to a throne you have no right to? *Hmm?*" Mal shook his head slowly. "Astounding how you don't realize that it's that very lack of intelligence that destroyed your family's claim to rule this world to begin with."

Sonoforen breathed heavily, furiously, then, as the reality of what Mal said sank in, slower until even his shoulders sagged in defeat.

Mal sat back and evaluated him. Sonoforen had a modicum of intelligence. Not as much as his younger brother, but enough to make him a trainable mutt. "I understand your anger, boy, but I assure you—you're fury is not with me."

"You ordered the execution squad!"

"Is that what they told you? Oh, Sonoforen." He sighed. "You and I both cling to a shaky existence. Our futures are only as secure as we plot them to be. Sit down, son." He gestured to a chair near his desk.

Sonoforen considered the unexpected bone offered him. He sat down warily, never taking his eyes off the Chairman.

"Your father was betrayed *not* by me, his most trusted advisor," Mal whispered, "but by someone else close to him: the High General. Sonoforen, very few men know this, but Shin was planning a violent overthrow of your father. Fortunately I heard of it. I stopped him before he not only had your father killed, but the entire mansion staff along with you, your brother, and your mother. Shin was furious after that incident at the silk shops, and was ready to begin another war over it. I spent hours reasoning with him. One of my most trusted friends, Dr. Brisack, also helped me to talk sense into the man. I argued to dispose quietly of your father in some remote village somewhere, but Shin wouldn't hear of it. He wanted him—and all of you—dead. In the end, he agreed that your father's death would suffice, and that he trusted only someone such as me to now lead the world. Shin gave me the list of who should be Administrators and what kinds of laws we could enact. It was the only way to prevent war, Sonoforen. Your father died nobly, son, to save the world. I'm here only to try to keep Shin from total control. Your argument is not with me, but with Relf Shin."

Sonoforen remained motionless. "They told me that'd be your story."

Mal smiled kindly to show the dog who really cared for him. "And who is 'they'?"

"My father's servants. Ones I found not long ago."

"Think about this, son. I'm an old man, a university professor of animal behavior, and never held a blade in my life. Shin is more fearsome in his fifties than he ever was in his twenties, and is in command of more than ten thousand soldiers. Who, then, is the greater threat?"

Sonoforen sighed.

"It's a difficult balance I keep with the High General, Sonoforen. Right now I have just slightly more power than he does. Without my Administrators, the army would be ruling this world, and that is not a world either of us would want to live in."

Sonoforen squirmed. "Then he needs to die," he whispered.

Mal nodded once. "But that would be very difficult to do. Especially with the way you do things. What animal is waiting outside to swift you away from the scene of your crime? A goat?"

Sonoforen just stared at the desk.

"A sheep, then," Mal said sadly. "Sonoforen, Shin is a strong, cunning man. You'd never succeed. Not without help."

"I'd do anything," Sonoforen said, lifting his eyes to meet Mal's. "Work with anyone, do anything, to get my revenge."

"Are you serious about that?"

"He killed my father!" Sonoforen barked. "Denied me my throne!"

Mal's mouth pursed. "What kind of a relationship do you still have with Dormin?"

"None," Sonoforen murmured.

"Any other connections with family? Friends? Girls? Acquaintances?"

"Chairman Mal, if you're trying to figure out who I have waiting outside to help me the answer is . . . no one," Sonoforen muttered in embarrassment. "Not even an animal. My cat ran away last week."

"So you were just charging in here and hoping to . . . wing it?"

"You're point is well made, *sir*."

Mal clasped his hands together and rested them on the desk. A desperate, homeless mutt. Perfect.

"Sonoforen, how would you like to get your revenge? Not through a rash, ill-thought out plan, but in a rational, organized, and effective manner which will yield results that will not only appease your desires but will also lend me a great deal of research?"

Sonoforen blinked. "What *in the world* are you talking about?"

"First, we change your name to something less obvious. How does Heth strike you?" The corner of Mal's mouth went up slightly. "Then tell me what you know about Guarders."

---

Mahrree sighed for the twelfth time. Usually it was the six-year-olds in her morning class that couldn't concentrate for more than five minutes, not the eight teenage girls in the afternoons.

"If you really want to know that much about the captain, you should have come to the debate," she chided as Hitty asked yet another question about how many medals he had on his uniform. Mahrree hadn't noticed. "Now, we need to get back to our discussion—"

Hitty raised her hand again.

Mahrree groaned.

"Really, Miss Mahrree, this has to do with the discussion."

"Do you *remember* what the discussion was about?"

Hitty nodded. "The history of the Guarders."

"Good. Now remember, many of your parents contacted me this morning to make sure we went over it, considering that the fort will soon be ready. They'll be quizzing you tonight, so understanding the nature of the Guarders is not only vital to your welfare, but also to your passing this class. Be grateful, because we *were* to be discussing developments in sugar production in the south. So Hitty, I will happily answer any questions regarding Guarders."

Hitty put her hand down and tossed her straw-colored hair behind her, as she did every five minutes. "If the Guarders return, and they invade the village, with what hand will the captain fight them? My mother said he wore a very large sword."

The girls erupted into fits of sniggers as Mahrree practiced her best glare.

Hitty kept her face impressively still, but finally broke into a smile of embarrassment. "I'm sorry, Miss Mahrree," she whispered.

"His right." Mahrree sighed for the thirteenth time. "He wore his sword on his left side, so that he can draw it with his right hand."

"If his sword is large, then that means he's very strong, right?" Sareen asked in her usual giggle which made her brown curls bobble.

"Could you tell how strong he was, Miss Mahrree?" asked another dreamy-eyed girl. "You were closest to him. My mother said he was very tall and had a chest like an ox."

"Ooh, I hope she meant a *bull*," said another girl, to a variety of tittering.

Mahrree wondered why so many mothers—*married women*—had paid such close attention to him. "Believe it or not, I wasn't concerned with how strong he might be," she said sternly. "I was more concerned about his views on education and progress, which we'll be discussing next week. After we finish learning about *the Guarders!*"

Teeria nodded. "Because without the Guarders, there would be no new fort, and no Captain Shin." The rest of the class nodded eagerly back.

Mahrree could always count on Teeria. The girl was as straight and serious as her dark brown hair and somber expression. "You're right. Because of the Guarders, Captain Shin and a few *more* soldiers—"

Several of the girls sighed in anticipatory delight.

Ignoring that, Mahrree plowed on, "—will be living here. Edge, as you recall, was one of the four villages where Guarders were seen retreating into the forests one hundred nineteen years ago, in 200."

"Before or after the Great War?" asked Sareen.

"After. Right after. Remember, King Querul the First and Guide Pax were trying to find a way to bring an end to the fighting. All seventeen villages and the city of Idumea were entangled in the war that lasted five years. No one is sure of the population, but we were well over one million people, and the land was struggling to sustain that many people. Couple that with farms lying fallow because of the fighting, and herds being slaughtered for meat, meant people were dying. According to some estimates, we may have lost up to 200,000 people during those years."

The girls dutifully took notes on their slate boards as Mahrree spoke.

"Famine that King Querul vowed would never happen under his 'supreme guidance'," Teeria grumbled in disgust.

"Exactly. When he took power at the beginning of the war, he said he would unite the world and bring peace. But he tried to *force* that peace."

"That was the problem with all the kings, right?" Teeria asked.

These were the times Mahrree loved teaching. "Right again. The kings imposed changes upon us, without our consent. A leader may believe he's successful in forcing his will, but he rarely sees how his subjects are quietly plotting against him until it's too late."

"Like the Administrators," Teeria said. "Plotting to depose King Oren and surprising him. And the Administrators have promised to be here for the people to listen to what they want."

Mahrree recognized that phrase: "Be here for the people."

That's what Chairman Mal had posted on the notice boards two years ago, had shouted by his representatives in red jackets as they came to the amphitheater, and had repeatedly emphasized as he took over the government of the world. She'd always believed he was sincere. But since last night, that little bit of guilty cynicism had been tainting every thought of the Administrators. Where her doubt came from, or why it persisted, Mahrree didn't know.

"Yes," Mahrree said, hoping the girls didn't hear her hesitation.

Hitty wrinkled her nose. "But I thought it was the king that made the Guarders angry in the first place. Since the kings are gone, why are the Guarders coming back again?"

"No one's sure," Mahrree shrugged. "Maybe they don't know the kings are gone, or they don't care. In 200 Guide Pax came up with a plan. He and King Querul had realized those prolonging the war were only a small minority of the world. Pax suggested that they try to find a new land for those people to live. *Divide* the world to have peace."

"But we can't do that," another girl pointed out. "There's nowhere else people can live that's not poisoned."

Mahrree scratched her head. "Yes, that's what we've been told for over three hundred years. This plain where our seventeen villages and Idumea exist are the only habitable stretches of land anywhere."

Teeria squinted. "As usual, Miss Mahrree, you don't sound completely sure of that."

Mahrree shrugged again. "You know me and Terryp."

She loved nothing more than tales of Terryp the historian who served the first king and went on an expedition with Querul's soldiers looking for new lands near the end of the Great War. In the west he discovered vast regions of farmable land and enormous ruins of a massive civilization. But he came back from the expedition so crazed that the king vowed never to allow anyone else to suffer as much as Terryp did in the "poisoned" lands. Then all of Terryp's findings and writings were accidentally destroyed in a fire over one hundred years ago. Mahrree was always suspicious of just how honest King Querul was about the lands Terryp discovered.

Mahrree's students knew their teacher didn't have much faith in anything the kings had claimed, but they didn't know *all* the reasons why. She'd been told by her father years ago that King Querul the First took in several servants during the Great War and kept them secure in his compound.

By the time Querul the Fourth took over the mansion, the servants, who still believed the war continued for all those years, and that the only place of refuge was in the king's service, had multiplied to nearly three dozen. After eighty years those servants were finally released, and they were shocked to discover the world was something completely different than they had been led to believe.

Cephas Peto had a friend who helped those people, secretly relocated to the eastern village of Winds, learn to read and write and adapt to life in the real world. And Cephas had told the story to his daughter, years later, in confidence.

In rare, bleak moments Mahrree wondered if the world wasn't itself imprisoned in a compound and fed lies to keep them there. But such thoughts were so dispiriting it did no good to ponder them.

Besides, the Administrators were different, she loyally tried to remind herself. Maybe they might send another expedition to the west . . .

"Back to Guarders," Mahrree reluctantly continued her lecture. "Guide Pax traveled north from Idumea until he reached Moorland, about ten miles west of here. He bravely entered the treacherous forest hoping to find a way through it and up into the mountains. Maybe he could find a valley or another plain where the people who loved violence could live. He left with a dozen of the king's soldiers—his elite guards—and was never heard from again," she recounted sadly.

"The Creator's last guide, the last man worthy to add to The Writings and receive guidance from the Creator for us, was gone. Several of the guards with him were found later with blood on their hands and uniforms. That's when the awful reality was known—Querul's guards had betrayed the man they were to be guarding. Instead of helping Pax find a peaceful solution, they butchered him. We've called the tallest mountain where that occurred 'Mt. Deceit' ever since. The guards were captured by Querul and executed for their treachery, but that didn't convince their associates to stop their rebellion. Over 2,000 people during the next few weeks made mad dashes to the forests north of us, to escape Querul's fury. It would have been one thing to let the men—Guarders, as someone decided to call them—leave and finally end the battles, but no. Husbands and fathers forced their wives and children into the forests as well. The families had to abandon their homes, farms and shops, and flee to the wild north. Some of those men were even assistants to the guide. That's likely how he was betrayed—by his deceitful friends. They entered the forests near the villages of Sands, Scrub, Moorland, and even Edge."

"And all of them were part of the secret groups," Teeria said as she wrote on her slate.

"That's right. And the name 'Guarders' took on a somewhat ironic meaning. Now the only thing they guard is whatever they steal from us. King Querul—indeed, no one—understood that there was a secret society living among us. This society had their own connections and even methods of communication. Every village was affected with these spies and traitors, these people who Guide Pax was hoping to find a new home for and were to be divided away from the rest of the world. It seems they initially didn't want to go. They enjoyed continuing the war.

"But when Guide Pax was lost, King Querul was enraged," she told them as she slowly paced the classroom. "He demanded all of the traitors in each village be discovered and brought to Idumea for trial. That's when houses turned up empty, shops were abandoned, and farms were left alone. In the middle of the night for weeks on end, people darted in and out of trees in a race for the north, thieving as they went and damaging property wherever they could. There was even one family captured by law enforcers just outside of Edge. They had traveled all the way from Flax at the other end of the world, on the coast of the southern sea, just to escape."

The girls' mouths dropped open.

"That's an incredible distance!" Sareen said with a sad giggle. "Don't people *die* traveling that far?"

Mahrree shrugged. "One hundred thirty miles is a long way to go, but apparently not life-threatening."

"What happened to the family?" Hitty asked warily.

"The travel didn't kill them, but their treachery did," Mahrree said softly. "They were brought to Idumea, tried, found guilty, and executed."

The girls looked at each other, aghast.

"Children, too?" asked Teeria.

Mahrree pressed her lips together. She skimmed over these details when she taught the history to her younger group, but the teenage girls were ready to know the terrible truths. While Querul the First wasn't the greatest leader the world could have desired, his intention *was* to bring peace to the land. "King Querul felt the children were under the poisonous influence of their parents, so naturally they would grow up to be traitors too."

"Was that really necessary?" Teeria's voice was almost a whisper.

"Excellent question," Mahrree told her. "What do you think?"

Teeria glanced around the room at the other girls, likely hoping to see an answer on one of their faces.

Hitty tried. "If children are taught one thing by their parents, then . . . they usually stay with what they were taught. So . . . those children might have continued their parents' rebellion when they got older. I mean, if your parents are dead, wouldn't you be mad about who killed them?"

Mahrree was tempted to nod, but instead looked around for another opinion.

Teeria fingered her dark braid, thinking.

Another girl piped up. "But you could retrain those children, couldn't you? Teach them that their parents' stealing and fighting with the army was wrong. Then they'd change their ways."

Teeria turned to her, "Yes, but who would do that retraining to—"

Mahrree began to smile. That was the point she loved in teaching, when the girls turned from facing her and expecting to get the answers from the "authority," to probing the difficult questions among themselves. It was when they debated each other that the lessons were remembered.

*This* was why the what-color-is-the-sky debate was so crucial: people tend to trust whoever sets themselves up as the authorities, but at some point each person needs to look at what's claimed and test it. Is the sunset really pink, or is it more of an orange? What do *you* see?

Now none of the girls were facing Mahrree who was leaning, satisfied, against the large slate board at the front of the room. They were instead arguing as to whether children could be forced to think differently than how they'd been taught. If she had been alone, Mahrree would have whooped for joy. She would, later, in celebration of another successful day.

But right now she had a growing shouting match she had to gently calm. She learned years ago how to do so: with another question.

"Teeria," she said in a quiet but firm voice that cut through the arguing of the girls.

Eight heads turned to look at her, as if surprised she was still there.

"Teeria, if a group of Guarders were to steal you away from your home today and try to tell you that everything your parents, government, and even your teachers have been telling you is a lie, what would it take for you to believe them?"

Mahrree looked at all of the girls silenced by her query. "Any of you? What would they have to do to convince you that the truths are actually distortions?"

After a thoughtful moment, Teeria sighed loudly. "I really don't know, Miss Mahrree. Depending on how convincing they were, I might not be able to figure out what the truth is about anything. I might end up not believing *anyone* anymore."

Several of the girls nodded in agreement.

"So *that* would be worse?" Hitty wondered. "People who can't figure out what to believe?"

"Maybe the real question, Hitty," Mahrree said, "is what would it take to make *you* change your mind about everything you're sure to know to be true? That's the question for all of you, isn't it? Who do you trust?"

The girls thoughtfully stared at their desks.

"Parents? Friends?" Teeria suggested. "Neighbors? Teachers? Certainly the government could—"

Mahrree couldn't listen anymore, because her ears were stuck on the words "the government." Cynical thoughts once again flooded her mind. Did the Chairman and Administrators deserve her trust? They acted as if they already had it. As if they could just *take* it, not *earn* it. And no one was questioning that, were they? They collect our trust as easily as they collect our slips of silver twice a year. We wanted them to succeed so we trust them blindly. Foolishly. And they're *using* that. If people stop arguing, stop thinking, and are just willing to take—*to trust*—whatever the authority dishes out, they'll accept just about anything—

"Miss Mahrree?"

She looked around and, judging by the concerned looks on her students' faces, realized that she had been lost in her own thoughts for probably a bit too long. A common occurrence for her. "I'm sorry, what?"

"Teeria just asked you," Hitty said with a smirk, "Isn't that the job of the government—to tell us what is the truth?"

This was her test, as a teacher. Yes, there were many influences in the lives of these girls, but none so powerful as the one standing in front of them in that classroom. Even an Administrator wouldn't have a greater effect on the girls than Mahrree would have right now. They looked at her for her opinion and most importantly, her approval.

And she had to treat such moments so carefully. It would be arrogant to believe that every day the girls hung on her every word, but at moments like this, when the debate had steered itself into a question that could someday affect the future of each student, Mahrree knew that in a very real way, she controlled the world.

At least, she controlled the way her students would see it.

She knew the answer the Administrators would want her to give. Of course the government exists to give you the truth! And the sky is blue. Always! Trust us!

She also knew the answer the Creator would want her to give, and it was His approval she was more concerned about.

Mahrree slowly smiled before she began to recite, "'Test all things, as we are tested. Try all things, to discover the truths for yourself.'"

She could feel the tension in the room drain away as she continued to recite the words of The Writings. "'The truth of all things will manifest itself to those who sincerely want to know.'"

Her students smiled and visibly relaxed.

"Miss Mahrree," Hitty began soberly, tossing her braid with much less energy, "I was just wondering—have the Administrators executed anyone?"

A new wave of anxiousness filled the room.

"In the past two years, not that I've heard of, Hitty," Mahrree said with a reassuring smile. "Let's pray it always stays that way."

"The captain would never execute anyone," Sareen giggled nervously. "Would he, Miss Mahrree? I heard he claimed he was never part of a killing squad."

"But he would kill a Guarder, right?" Teeria said gravely.

Mahrree shrugged again. "You'd have to ask him. But I don't know why else he's here."

The girls covered their mouths and snickered at the idea of speaking to the captain. Mahrree groaned at their sudden return to silliness.

"Why don't you ask him, Miss Mahrree?" another girl suggested. "At the next debate!"

A lump appeared in her throat. She hadn't mentioned anything about another debate, but apparently they already knew.

"If it comes up, I'll try to remember to ask. Back to the Guarders." She cleared her throat, grateful for the diversion from the captain. "For years the villages on the outer rim of the world dealt with raids for goods, livestock, and occasionally people. Sands and Grasses in the west, and Trades in the southwest seemed to take the brunt of the attacks. Only occasionally would Guarders venture into Moorland or Edge. Our villages are much smaller and aren't as wealthy. The Army of Idumea fought those raids and killed many of the Guarders, but never eradicated all of them. The Guarders always raided at night, wore black clothing, and smeared soot or oil on their faces to keep themselves concealed. The last time any Guarders raided here was maybe thirty years ago, although there have been rumors that someone was seen lurking in the forest. It seemed that every time a new king came to power, the Guarders came to test his power. Once pushed back, the Guarders retreated back to the forests. That's why the forests are off-limits. Only fools would dare venture into them. If the poisonous gases, bottomless crevices, and hot water don't kill the stupidly curious, Guarders will."

"So why are the Guarders coming back now, Miss Mahrree?" Hitty asked again.

Mahrree sighed. "I can only guess they're testing the strength of the world. Remember, the Guarders now are descendants of the original 2,000 that left. All they know is that a king forced their ancestors away. I assume they came to take revenge each time one of the king's sons or descendants took the throne. How they know anything about us, I couldn't begin to guess."

One quiet girl with doe-like eyes, and a nervous demeanor to accompany it, timidly raised her hand. "Miss Mahrree?" she squeaked, "I think they're already back. My good stockings went missing from the line three days ago."

This was what Mahrree was hoping to avoid, the "Guarder snatched!" rumors. Oh, they flew on and off for years, whenever anything was pinched or lost—Guarders stole it! Yes, Guarders were now desperate for *stockings*. Children seemed to rely on that excuse, especially when a goat wandered away or the winds from the canyons were particularly strong and blew around items that were supposed to be secured into houses, sheds, or cellars.

Just as the winds were three days ago.

But adults were just as gullible. And manipulative. Anything questionable was attributed to Guarders. They were convenient to explain why a philandering husband came home late at night: "Thought I saw a Guarder! Had to investigate! I tracked him until he rushed off into the forest . . ."

Or why livestock vanished during the night, then mysteriously showed up later in someone else's barn. "Why, the Guarder must have had second thoughts about that cow, tried to return it, and mistakenly brought it to my place instead. Really, I can't imagine any other reason why she's here. Why *of course* you can have her back . . ."

Adults even thought leaving a candle lit in the window might frighten away potential thieves. If it looked as if someone was still awake, the Guarders wouldn't think of raiding the house, now would they? Mahrree thought it was all just a waste of tallow, especially since accidental late night fires caused more damage than the Guarders ever did.

But stories were powerful, and the less credible they were, the stronger they seemed to grow. People were more intrigued by gossip than truth. The rumors gave the Guarders more influence than they likely realized. If they knew the control they already possessed—even with being absent from Edge for decades—they probably wouldn't have stayed away so long. As far as Edgers were concerned, they were already here and causing havoc.

But Mahrree still hoped she might be able to keep the next generation from believing such ridiculous tales. Right now each girl was rapidly turning pale in fear that Guarders suddenly developed a desire for teenage girls' underthings.

"Gia, just how windy was it the night your stockings disappeared?"

The poor girl gulped. "Very?"

"And have you checked your neighbors' yard for your stockings?"

"No?"

"You might want to."

"But my older sister's uh . . . *unmentionables* are also missing!"

Mahrree sighed. "Is she still courting that boy next door to you? What was his name?" Mahrree rarely knew who the teenage boys were, since they were taught in another school, but occasionally their names were lovingly scrawled on the margins of her students' work.

Gia squirmed as a couple of girls tittered. "Um, yes?"

"Please don't answer everything with a question. Now, Gia—I may not know a lot about young men, but I do suspect that *unmentionables* flying in the breeze next door just might be a temptation for a hot-blooded boyfriend. And personally, I think he's a much bigger worry to your family than Guarders."

Gia turned purple as the other girls giggled.

One rumor put down.

At least temporarily.

"But where could the Guarders live?" Teeria pored over her notes on the slate, baffled. "How many are there?"

"If we knew, we could end all of this once and for all. When I was a girl we thought the Guarders retreated to the mountains and lived up in the higher valleys. But it seems they may have never left the forests."

Several of the girls shuddered.

"How many soldiers are coming to Edge?" Sareen giggled worriedly.

"You'll have to ask the captain that, Sareen."

"Hope it's a lot," she muttered with unexpected heaviness. All of the girls nodded in sober agreement.

"And I hope they're as handsome as the captain," murmured another girl.

Mahrree closed her eyes as the girls tittered again.

Teeria raised her hand. "Miss Mahrree? Just one more question." She looked over her slate examining her tight writing that extended to every corner. "Now, where was it . . ."

Mahrree smiled. Today had been a success, full of questions and many not easily answered.

"—because you know my mother . . . always ready to question me on everything . . . now I thought it was right about here . . ."

Ideally the girls would take those hard questions home and discuss them during dinner with their parents. That, Mahrree thought in satisfaction, would be the perfect way to end this day. Just one more hard question to mull over together—

"Ah, here it is." Teeria looked up studiously. "What my mother *really* wanted me to ask: exactly what color were the captain's eyes? Black or dark brown? She was sitting too far away to see."

---

That afternoon as Mahrree visited the market she fretted. But not about serious issues such as Guarders, or possible changes in education, or why she was suddenly distrustful of the Administrators. Oh no, she was far too silly to think about important things.

Everything had been going just fine until Teeria asked the question about the captain's eyes. Then Mahrree felt the same flustering heat as she had last night on the platform, and spluttered for a few seconds before blurting out, "Brown. Very deep, dark chestnut brown."

She didn't need eight teenage girls squealing and bursting into laughter to know she'd turned red. She hoped that her students were the only ones to notice that the captain rendered her somewhat senseless. Well, the Densals knew it, too. And so did her mother. But maybe that was all.

As she worked her way through the market, she realized it was maybe a few more people than that. More villagers than usual waved at her, and several mentioned they'd be closing up their shops early on the night of her next debate. She was sure she blushed redder every time someone mentioned it. Fortunately Rector Densal would be bringing her the topic soon so she could prepare.

The first thing she'd prepare was keeping her face from turning red.

---

Tuma Hifadhi ambled out of the small back office and into the room where twelve men sat waiting for him around a large, simple table. He smiled at them, his white teeth gleaming against the backdrop of his gray skin and hair. Years ago he was taller and darker, but age had stooped and faded him.

Yet it hadn't dimmed him; his bright grin lit up and wrinkled his entire face.

"So sorry to keep you waiting," he said to the men who were starting to rise from their chairs. He motioned for them to sit back down. "But I just received a most intriguing message. As you know, Edge has a new fort, and now a new captain to go along with it. And he spends his days just staring into the trees. My friends—" he waited for their eager exclaims to die down, "—I believe it's finally time."

"Do we start training now?" asked one middle-aged man.

Tuma shook his head. "Not yet. There's more he has to do before we can be sure. For now, we just watch. As always."

# Chapter 6 ~ "Miss Peto, it's obvious you have very little experience with men."

Mahrree had worked herself into a near frenzy of fretting by the evening of the second debate. She fretted she might run into him, although she never went as far as the new fort. It was to the northeast, and the school and markets were to the south, so she couldn't think of a good reason to wander over there, even if she did care.

She fretted that he might have walked by her house again and she didn't notice.

And she fretted that she was fretting about nothing.

It was all so ridiculous, and so she fretted about her being ridiculous all the way up until the start of their second debate.

As she walked to the amphitheater she kept checking the color of the sky, just to have something else to think about. It had hints of purple by the time the debate began.

Half an hour later she didn't have to worry about blushing in his presence again, because the second debate was nothing like the first.

Hogal Densal had decided they should discuss some of the new educational 'suggestions' being tried in Idumea. One of the more controversial was holding school all day, instead of just in the mornings for younger children and in the afternoon for the older. Mahrree argued that removing the parents from their daily work and discussion time with their children could weaken their family connections.

But the captain retorted that having such a break from the children could be beneficial to the mental and financial welfare of the parents. Even with families limited to just two children—a law enforced more diligently in the past few decades—parenting was still a great strain. With the children in school all day, both parents could spend more time laboring.

The tension mounted when Mahrree insisted that the Creator had intended for the parents to educate the children, and the captain contended that there was nothing wrong with letting the Administrators be in charge.

That's when it erupted into a shouting match.

"The Writings, which you *love to quote*," he simpered, "say everyone has the right to choose for themselves, Miss Peto!"

"But The Writings also say we're accountable for those choices, Captain! And everyone suffers when someone makes a terrible choice. The Second and Third Queruls held us petrified that we would say the wrong thing. The Fourth made us suffer from rising foods costs because of his fear of the chicken pox. Then Oren—why, he was like a neglectful parent who cared for only himself. What if parents follow the same pattern and become neglectful themselves? How do we know our children won't suffer from another ghastly decision forced upon them by their government?"

"Are you implying that the Administrators will prove to be as incompetent as Oren?" he demanded.

She knew her position was akin to running toward a crevice near the edge of the forest, but she just couldn't stop herself. "Any parent who thinks of his desires first will have children that suffer. I don't believe the Administrators intentionally *want* parents to neglect their children, but someone should warn them of the possibility. Perhaps some professor at the university—"

"All of the Administrators are former university professors, Miss Peto," the captain said smugly. "And none of them have come to the same conclusions as you. I wonder why that is? Might they know something more than a simple school teacher at the Edge of the world?"

The entire audience—more than one thousand strong that night—sounded a warning of, "Ooooh!"

The captain's fierce glare wavered for half a moment as Mahrree puffed up her chest in fury. She would not be demeaned, ever.

She would *be bold.*

Just . . . not mention that fact.

"It has been my experience, Captain Shin," she seethed calmly, "that a collective of men frequently put forth their untested opinions as fact, especially when their egos are in question. Be that collective an army, a government, or a band of boys arguing about who got to the swimming hole first. The results are inevitably an embarrassing display of clenched fists, shouted words, and bloodied noses. And still nothing is resolved to anyone's satisfaction, thus leaving open yet another opportunity for a *collective of men* to put forth more useless ideas masquerading as something constructive!"

His eyes were like rock as she spewed her venom, but he didn't flinch. "Miss Peto, it's obvious you have very little experience with men."

Many male villagers were bold enough to chuckle in agreement.

Until Mahrree shot them a look.

"I have enough experience with arrogant, ignorant men who value no one's opinions but their own," she boiled. "I've been gaining a great deal of experience in the past few days, *standing on this platform!*"

Several women in the amphitheater giggled nervously, and a few more brave men chorused another round of, "Ooooh!"

Captain Shin remained emotionless, refusing to take her insult. "Miss Peto, you know nothing of the Administrators who are endeavoring to lead this world to greater heights—"

"I agree, I don't," she cut him off. "I don't even know if they hold to The Writings, because I've never heard any of it quoted in the weekly edicts they send to the villages."

The captain shrugged. "So what if they don't? Can't they make decisions on their own without referring to an old text from an older time?"

"An old text?" she wailed. "Older time? It's for *our* time! It's the basis for our village, our families, our lives! If we throw out the guiding principles, what will guide us then?"

"Isn't that where faith comes in, Miss Peto?" he pounced. "The Writings talk all about faith. So have some faith in the Administrators."

"Faith means having trust in someone else's decisions for us," she declared. "I have faith in the Creator, because I've seen how His choices have benefited my life."

"You've benefited from the Administrators' control over food production," the captain pointed out. "I've seen the markets; there's no lack. I know people here complained as much as anywhere when the management laws were installed, but a year later we see the results."

"But farmers and ranchers no longer have a say in what they grow or how much they produce!" she gestured wildly. "They *might* be doing better without the meddling, but we'll never know now. They've lost their freedom!"

He folded his arms. "If losing freedom means a healthier world, then what of it?"

She spluttered and guffawed before she could make her mouth form words. "That's precisely what happened under the kings. We lost freedom, and lives, and even your precious progress!"

The captain took an aggressive step toward her. "No one has lost their lives under the Administrators, Miss Peto."

"Not yet!"

There it was: the first shocked look on his face, but Mahrree was far too furious to gloat.

"How can I have faith in someone if I can't trust their decisions, Captain? For that matter, how can I trust you? What kind of influence will you have in Edge?"

He scoffed. "Who's to say that the Administrators aren't making the best choices? Or that I won't? You just admitted yourself you don't know anything about them, and you certainly don't know anything about me. I find that admission quite remarkable, by the way, since you seem to think *you know it all!*"

"I know enough!" she shouted back. "I know that we've been forced to accept a fort in our village. I know taxes rose last year again, but for what reason? To arm that fort no one wants? We're just supposed to trust your decisions? The Army of Idumea's? Even the Administrators, who we don't know? To what end? Complete, blind obedience? Willingly accept that the sky is blue, and never question what it might portend when it's red in the morning, or clouding in the afternoon? Should we never think for ourselves and just become dumb animals?"

He leaned toward her, his left hand clenched into a fist. "Your emotions are clouding your logic, and you're imagining scenarios that may not lead to each other. You're too closed-minded to think clearly."

She firmed her stance. "I'm suggesting only one of many outcomes, but we never know what will happen when we blindly submit to untested leadership, Captain. When Querul the First took the throne, no one then would have suspected that generations later would have suffered from excessive control or be guided by idiots. I'm beginning to believe men simply can't handle so much power."

Captain Shin's mouth dropped open at her boldness. That was twice now. "So now you're insinuating the Administrators are no more trustworthy than the kings? I must warn you, Miss Peto, you are on very dangerous ground."

She knew it, but she stood firm even though she teetered on the edge. "What have they done to earn my trust? Kick out King Oren? What happened to him?"

"Died of a broken heart, from finally realizing how he neglected the world!" the captain retorted.

"So we've been told. But I've always wondered, just how many soldiers did it take to break that small, stupid heart, Captain?"

The captain's lips parted slightly, aghast at her presumption. Or maybe her insight. That was the third time.

She didn't care, but continued on. "Then the Administrators took over the city, and then the world. And what's next? For that matter, what have *you* done to earn my trust? Come to Edge with your arrogance to tell us we're closed-minded? Oh, well done!"

"Miss Peto," he said coolly, "if the Administrators were anything like Querul the Third, you wouldn't be allowed to say what you're saying tonight. You still have the freedom to express your mind, however emotional and illogical it may be, and no one is stopping you."

"Yet," she added coldly.

*Why am I saying all of this?* she wondered frantically, finally realizing just how close she was to disaster. *Where is this coming from?* As quickly as she could, she tried to backtrack from the crevice.

"Perhaps, Captain, we have nothing to fear from the Administrators, but I fear there may be a great deal to suspect about you."

She immediately realized that didn't sound like backtracking, but the words continued to pour uncontrollably from her mouth. "You have clearly demonstrated your arrogance and contempt for the 'simple' people of Edge. And you're our defense against the Guarders? Ha! I now fear greatly for all of us."

That's when Rector Densal jabbed the sides of the two large men sitting next to him. They jumped up and started for the platform.

The captain's face grew purple. "*You* fear for Edge—?!" he began as the men jogged the steps to the top of the platform. With big smiles, they stood between him and Mahrree.

It was like throwing water on fighting alley cats. They each stepped back but kept pacing and circling, waiting for an opening between the two large men standing there with fake grins plastered on their faces. The platform suddenly felt very crowded.

Mr. Metz, the personal assistant to Rector Densal and a large fellow, held up his hands and said in an excessively cheerful voice, "What wonderful words for us to consider! We thank Miss Peto and Captain Shin and invite everyone to stretch a moment before the musicians take to the stage."

Captain Shin was obviously not finished with her, but Mahrree wanted nothing more to do with him. To so easily dismiss The Writings showed his true nature, and it was ugly.

That had done it for her.

She didn't care about his accusing her of being a know-it-all—she'd heard that a dozen times before. But The Writings? Maybe he'd read them once or twice, as he claimed at the first debate, but he obviously cared nothing for the words of the Creator or the guides, which explained his ready devotion to the Administrators.

No matter how pleasant he appeared, his soul was grossly disfigured.

She stormed down the back stairs to her favorite tree, gave it a swift kick that she immediately regretted, and marched—or rather limped—back and forth trying to regain her composure. She considered soaking her throbbing foot it the warm spring, but couldn't imagine sitting long enough to do so.

She'd wanted to like him. She was afraid that some part of her already found him attractive, yet she needed solid reasons to feel anything for him. But now? There was nothing worthy in him.

She was also alarmed by her growing antagonism toward the Administrators. Where had that come from? Her father? Maybe his warning that the world was out to get her was his way of telling her a storm was approaching, but she didn't realize she'd be the storm!

She'd never before heard anyone say anything against the Administrators, but she'd spat accusations that she now realized had the possibility of reaching the ears of the Administrator of Loyalty. She'd also never heard of anyone in the remote northern villages ever catching his attention, but rumors abounded about his Querul-the-Third-tendencies down in Idumea. None of those rumors ever said Gadiman accomplished anything more beyond giving someone a threatening glare before another Administrator pulled him away. He was their token guard dog that no one really cared for, but needed to have around anyway, just in case.

Mahrree fretted all over again that she just might come across as the first real threat.

Until she remembered the captain's words: "a *simple* school teacher at the Edge of the world." Her worries vanished, replaced by livid fury.

A simple teacher, indeed!

Well, she had to admit as the pain in her foot forced her to calm down, she *was* a teacher. She'd never be fancy, so she *was* simple. And she *was* in Edge.

So while his words were accurate, his critical tone was meant to cut away all her confidence. But she wouldn't let it. She may be a simple school teacher, but simple things have a tendency to rise up in complex ways.

She felt enraged again, a raw emotion so powerful she didn't know what to do with it. Pacing wasn't enough. Maybe some trees somewhere needed all the bark peeled off.

She noticed someone standing in the shadows at the end of her pacing area, and he was wearing a blue uniform. Without thinking about the next move, she hobbled over to him. "Yes?" she asked, barely containing her disdain.

The captain's face was calm as he smiled, which made her all the more furious.

"Are you hurt?" He nodded at her foot.

"Only temporarily. Old debating injury," she explained bitterly.

To her surprise he grinned and held up his left hand. "I have one of those too." He made a fist with it.

It took all of Mahrree's remaining self-control to not make a match and show him what to do with it. His stomach was temptingly close.

His face sobered and he rubbed his forehead, near the scar above his eyebrow. "Look, I just want you to know that I feel awful about what happened up there," he said softly. "I lost my temper and I don't usually do that. Well, not with women. Something about . . ." His voice trailed off. He pressed his lips together before he tried again. "I just want you to know that your mind is much like mine. This got out of control. I *am* sorry."

Mahrree was stunned speechless, which was quite an accomplishment. She didn't expect any of that, so she had nothing to retort with. Later that evening she came up with a long list of responses, and even wrote them down. But all she could manage right then was a lame, "Thank you."

"I hope you feel better soon," he gestured to her foot. "Apparently we're on again in two nights."

Mahrree's eyes flared as he gave her a casual smile, put on his cap, and left quickly.

He'd been right, annoyingly. She had very little experience with men. They mystified her. She'd seen that behavior before in the little boys she taught. They'd have a terrible fight, hit and punch each other, then be friends again five minutes later as if the fight was part of the game.

Granted, the teenage girls were ridiculous too. They would just *perceive* an injustice and they'd give each other the silent treatment for an entire season.

But nothing was more astonishing than Captain Perrin Shin's casual smile and perplexing behavior. She had heard once of a man in the village of Moorland who thought he was two different people. He even went by two different names and carried on bizarre conversations that no one could follow.

"That must be it," Mahrree whispered to the air. "The man is not right in his mind. We *are* in trouble." She laughed weakly as she started to hobble for home.

It was better than crying.

---

The new lieutenant, a young man with dark brown hair, light reddish-brown skin, and a slight but muscular build, was disappointed the captain wasn't there to greet him. He was a bit anxious, and having the High General personally see him off yesterday morning didn't help ease his apprehension.

But for graduating top of his class at the Command School at the university, he was given the biggest responsibility available for graduating cadets: second in command of the new fort in Edge.

He'd heard the talk—it was *only* Edge. It was *only* the smallest fort in the world, likely to never see any action, and likely established only to give the High General's son an early command. But it was still a most coveted opportunity. He'd been studying for this assignment for the past six moons and was in frequent contact with the captain. Still, staring at the fort made it all a little overwhelming. He would've welcomed a familiar face.

Then again, he could hardly expect Shin to wait around on the off chance his lieutenant came a day early.

The master sergeant in charge of building, on loan from the fort at Rivers, assured him the captain would return after sunset. "He's doing what High General ordered him to do—winning over the hearts and minds of the people of Edge." Then he laughed at a joke the lieutenant seemed to have missed.

Lieutenant Brillen Karna set out to give himself a tour of the fort. The tall command tower provided unobstructed views of the forest and the mountains beyond to the north, and the village to the south. The large forward office with its vast windows and enormous desk would be an excellent planning area, and the adjoining office for the commanding officer held impressive views of the east, south, and west.

The officers' quarters and enlisted men's barracks were nearly completed, but the mess hall still needed a roof. The hospital wing was more progressive than any he'd seen, with thirty cots and dozens of dark colored bottles lining the shelves. The armory was waiting to be stocked with the swords, long knives, and bows and arrows that should arrive in the next week. The stables were nearly completed, the feed barns were already filled, and the wall that surrounded the entire compound would be finished in just a few days.

None of the land in the fort or the surrounding area showed evidence of danger. Just a few hundred paces to the north in the deep woods lay all kinds of traps—sink holes, small bubbling mud volcanoes, steam vents, and even occasional sprays of hot water.

Many of the recruits waiting to come from Idumea were already worried about living so close to the forests. Karna had assured them no one would enter the woods, but still the stories traveled faster than the wildfire that hit the forest several years ago. That the Guarders would have chosen such an inhospitable place to stage their new raids from was unfathomable to the lieutenant.

But in a way, Karna could understand the Guarders' warped wisdom. If the army dared to venture in the forest, they wouldn't escape without losing a horse or soldier to either the thin crust of the ground or a hiding Guarder. The army was limited to the open regions beyond the forest where they could sit and wait for the enemy. Until then, the soldiers would patrol the borders of the forest looking for signs from a people who never left any.

Karna turned from the noisy forest and admired the tall timbers that composed the outer walls of the compound. He was considering the captain's ingenuity to cut the tops into points when he saw someone in the distance walking with a determined gait to the fort. The sun was just setting, but the lieutenant was sure the large silhouetted figure was Shin. He followed quickly.

As Karna passed the stables, the sergeant inspecting them called out to him, "You just missed the captain, but you should be able to find him in his office."

The lieutenant made his way up the tall stairway of twenty steps that led to the command tower. Part way up he heard a splintering noise. He paused to work out from which direction it came.

When he heard no other sounds, he proceeded cautiously up the stairs. No one was in the forward office, so Karna ventured to the command office. The door was open and he saw Shin wrapping his left hand in white cloth.

"Captain?"

Captain Shin looked up at his lieutenant. "Karna! Good to see you again." He sounded slightly out of breath. "I didn't expect you until tomorrow, but I should have known you would be here early. Ever vigilant, ever ready," he said with a pained smile. "What do you think of the fort so far?"

Karna just stared at the cloth on Shin's hand which now had a splash of red emerging through it. "Uh, it's very impressive. The general should be pleased," he said. "Captain, are you injured?"

Shin's mouth twitched. "Not permanently, I hope. By the way," he said in an official tone, "be sure to tell the building sergeant that the quality of wood in this office shows evidence of structural inferiority."

The lieutenant then noticed a hole in the thin inner board that separated the office from the forward room. It was the size of a fist, and partly edged in blood.

Karna squinted and took a closer look.

"Something you want to say, Lieutenant?"

Karna swallowed hard and stood back up to face his new commander. "The reputation of the Shins is well known, sir. Stories abound about your—"

Shin held up his right hand to stop him. "I know what you're thinking."

Karna thought that was convenient, since he wasn't sure what it was himself, and didn't know where his nervous rambling was headed. All he could remember right then was how a shouting High General Shin could leave a class quaking in their boots. His son was more amiable, but evidently stronger and with an odd manner of testing the structural integrity of his office.

"Don't worry," Shin said. "I won't be requiring my number two man to practice his 'number two hand' hitting technique on the walls."

Karna noticed Shin's left hand was still in a fist, and growing redder.

"Mainly because I trust you only with a bow, anyway," Shin said with a hint of teasing. "This was entirely personal, Lieutenant. Not professional." Then muttering to himself he added, "Not in the least bit."

Karna dared to smile ever so slightly.

To his surprise, Shin grinned and winked at him.

"Uh, sir? You may not be aware of this, but the hospital wagon arrived early as well. Two surgeons' assistants came with it and were hoping to surprise you by stocking the supply room before morning, when they were to officially present themselves." Karna's eyes kept darting to the white cloth, now mostly red and occasionally dripping on the new wooden floor.

Shin didn't seem to notice the mess.

"Sir, perhaps it would be a good idea to go acquaint yourself with them *right now.* I'm sure they'll be quite eager to show off their skills in uh . . ."

Shin slapped him on the shoulder. "I see why my father recommended you. Observant, loyal, and with an eye for the obvious which is shockingly absent in most people. Perhaps I *will* go introduce myself before heading to bed. Claim your quarters tonight, Karna, get some sleep, and then be ready for tomorrow morning. We have an entire village to win over, and I seem to be making the job a bit harder each day."

Shin started out the door, but paused and put his good hand on the lieutenant's shoulder.

"And Karna, don't believe every story you hear about Shins."

---

The slender man in black chuckled to himself all the way back to the forest. It shouldn't be this easy. The targets shouldn't present themselves so obviously. He needed some challenge, didn't he?

Then again, maybe this was just the cosmos rewarding him for his decades of patience waiting for his skills to be required again. Not since the glory days of Querul the Third had he felt so alive.

It had been that stupid General Shin—the first one, appointed by

Querul the Fourth—that cut his fledgling career short. And now, in the marvelous twists of fate only Nature could create, decades later he was called back into service.

If only General Relf Shin had a clue, he'd be riding his fastest horse to Edge, panicked.

The man in black quieted his chuckling. No sense in giving himself away already.

---

Two men sat in the dark office of an unlit building.

"More reports are coming in," said the first older man. "A little spottier than I'd like, but not unexpected considering they have no idea to whom the reports go, or who's at the top. But so far I'm not displeased. However, I do have a question: why would he choose to stay in cold, dull Edge when he has the choice of any village? Coast. Waves. Flax. Somewhere warm that's far more interesting for a single man."

"Speculation," answered the second middle-aged man. "He's been ordered there. He upset the High General and now Father's banished him to the dreariest place in the world."

The first man shook his white head. "No, it seems he actually requested that posting. Now why would he do that?"

The second man shrugged. "Not enough evidence to form a proper speculation. But this development makes him far more intriguing. There's no obvious logic to it. Women in Edge wear far more clothing than they do in hot humid Waves," he said with a sly smile. "Maybe he doesn't know that."

The first man chuckled. "He does. He's one of the few that has been all over the world. But I agree—we don't have enough evidence."

"There's something more," his partner said. "According to the last report, he may also be interested in a woman."

"Oh, how lovely." The first older man smirked. "This wouldn't be the first time for him, you know."

"She's rather outspoken, too," the middle-aged man warned. "The report was that she's been quite vocal about the Administrators. Uh, in the *negative*."

But the older man shrugged that off. "Women have never posed a real problem."

"Tell that to the victims of Oren's grandmother," his companion reminded.

"She was an anomaly."

"So might be this teacher in Edge."

"No," the older man said confidently, "the only entanglement I foresee is the one she'll cause to Shin. She may make him softer than I was hoping, but that also may provide another level of observation. Will he behave more aggressively if he senses a threat to his latest interest?"

The second man pondered that. "But if he *secures* her as a  mate, won't his responses to a threat be more pronounced?"

"*Secures?*" his companion cringed. "Are you talking about marriage? Do you know how old he is? I realize you know very little about him, but trust me: he's not the marrying kind. He's the womanizing kind. Stories about him have been floating around for years. Maybe that's why he went north—he upset too many women in his last posting in Vines and had to get away from them."

The second man shrugged. "We have a similar situation developing in Grasses. A lieutenant there has a young woman he's been seeing. Here's a suggestion: we first test him by utilizing her, and then we can see what Shin may be up to. Perhaps we should send another to watch him more closely, stay on top of developments?"

The first nodded. "A few messages have been received about that captain at Grasses. Complaints from his parents, actually. Administrator of Loyalty has been disturbed. Not that it takes much to disturb Gadiman," the older man sighed. "But some messages will be sent in response. Now as for Edge, we can check on Shin later when the fort is settled. Until then, we have enough eyes in the  area. However, I see nothing wrong with sending that young  woman a subtle warning."

The second man nodded. "Whatever you decide—it's your world."

"Yes it is."

---

The next day Captain Shin forced himself to stare into the forest to record every potential hazard. That's what a disciplined soldier does: ignores all distractions and focuses only on the threat at hand. As he remembered that, he began to progress again along the borders of the trees. But he never saw another living creature, except for the ground that bubbled and groaned and occasionally rumbled underfoot. Land tremors were common here, he reminded himself as the ground shifted under his feet three times that afternoon.

He had to find the Guarders—that was his purpose in life. Nothing else.

Besides, she hated him now. And why wouldn't she? He was starting to hate himself for the way he was treating her.

# Chapter 7 ~ "You're just afraid of my blob and what it may represent."

There seemed to be nothing else in Edge to talk about except the very public argument the night before. And Mahrree heard about it everywhere—in school, at the market, even from her mother who had attended. She had told Mahrree she'd been there to see if the captain had the same look in his eyes that her daughter had the night of the first debate. She was sure that he did, when his dark eyes weren't shooting arrows at Mahrree, that is. Everyone had an opinion, and everyone was eager to share it.

Their debate two nights later could have been much more volatile, but Mahrree vowed that she would be the very model of poise and calm. She was sure to say nothing derogatory about the Administrators, which proved to be quite difficult, given the topic. She wondered if Rector Densal was *trying* to get her in trouble.

The topic was the mandates issued by Idumea over a year ago about herd and crop production. The Administrators decreed what each village was to produce and in what quantities. Many ranchers in Edge were upset that instead of raising cattle, they had to take on hogs and chickens as well. Some wheat farmers now had to plant more corn to feed those hogs, and some barley farmers were forced to now grow wheat to compensate.

It was all confusing, pointless, and out of Mahrree's realm of interest.

But she'd heard about the complaints in the market when the change occurred, and she spent the past two days interviewing families to find how to debate it rationally.

Each family was sure to point out that it was only the Administrators over agriculture and commerce they were frustrated with, but Mahrree saw through that. The more she realized how controlling the Administrators had become, the fewer ways she could find around it. The only option she had was to be excessively sweet and fully in control of her emotions—not exactly her strengths as of late.

"You see, Captain Shin," Mahrree said politely during the debate, "the concern was that Edge's ranchers and farmers lost their ability to choose what they should grow. They feel their experience has been—unintentionally, of course—ignored."

Interestingly, Captain Shin was also reserved in his observations, using such excessive diplomacy that he must have been borrowing some of the village's supply.

"Understandable," he said civilly, "and I'm sure they have a wealth of experience to share, which undoubtedly has made the markets here so thoroughly stocked, for which I commend Edge."

"We thank you, sir," she smiled kindly, "but we never had a problem with keeping the markets stocked. Perhaps other villages have struggled and therefore welcomed the Administrators' intrus—*suggested mandates*. But I'm afraid the question remains: why must Edge continue to conform when initially we were doing quite well?"

He nodded once. "Oh, I'm sure the Administrators haven't meant to cause anyone in Edge to feel disrespect—"

"And I thank you for that assurance," she nodded back.

"You're welcome. You see, the Administrators have only the best interests—"

"Oh, *COME ON!*" interrupted a loud voice from the audience. "I'm actually sitting and LISTENING to this?! Thank you! You're welcome! It's more entertaining to treat my cows for teat infection." And the young milkman began to act out the task with great exaggeration.

Yes, Mahrree thought as the audience howled with laughter, the captain had used up the village's supply of tact.

Captain Shin's ears turned red.

"Come ON, now!" the milkman called. "Less acting and MORE ACTION!"

The chant was immediately picked up by the rest of the audience. "Less ACTING! More ACTION!"

Mahrree guffawed at the rowdiness of the villagers. She glanced over at the captain whose eyebrows were furrowed in surprise. Obviously Idumea had never dealt with heckling, but in Edge it was a proudly honed skill. And tonight, every Edger was getting in some practice.

It was too much to continue the debate, and when Rector Densal held up his hands to call an end to the shouting, Mahrree was secretly relieved. The fake smile she kept on her face was causing her cheeks to cramp, and she didn't know how much longer she could stand looking at the captain. When she saw none of his ugliness, he was quite . . . tolerable.

By the time their fourth debate came around a few evenings later, Mahrree was ready. Her success at the last outing gave her the confidence she needed to take on the captain. Plus, she would enjoy defending her position, and she was going to turn the table on him.

She also considered that maybe she'd pushed him too far at the second debate. He was there to defend and represent the Administrators, and she accused them—and him, by association—as being as abhorrent as the kings. She could never get away with such naked incriminations in Idumea. It was only because the villagers knew her so well that the chief of enforcement hadn't sent any of his men to arrest her for subversion, or sent a report to the Administrator of Loyalty.

At least, she assumed no reports had been sent, because no one in a red jacket had arrived in Edge.

She was just Mahrree Peto, spouting off yet again. Edge was used to her. Captain Shin, on the other hand, still had no idea who he was up against at the second debate, resulting in his violent outbursts. But his restrained demeanor at the third debate demonstrated that he was learning.

The setting sun on the evening of their fourth debate caused the sky to turn pale green with bright yellow clouds near the horizon with darker blue-gray clouds behind. But Mahrree's focus allowed her to notice it only briefly when she strode to the amphitheater. She headed to the platform, first dropping off a large covered basket by Teeria and Sareen who flinched when they saw they'd be guarding it. Hitty abandoned her friends and moved several rows back to sit with her parents.

Mahrree didn't even realize that nearly two thousand people—nearly half of Edge—had come to watch the argument, because nothing could ruffle her that night. Not the captain, nor even the fact that she would likely lose, unless the captain proved to be a complete idiot. And if he *did* prove to be such an idiot, well, that would just make the evening that much more enjoyable.

The argument was to be the origin of their people. Even though Mahrree had told Rector Densal she wanted to defend the version taught in The Writings, he thought her skills would be better used posing all the fantastical ideas instead. She had to agree—she loved those stories that stretched children's imaginations by offering alternatives to explaining the world.

After the usual introductions, Mahrree took to the platform and launched into every alternative she'd read about, beginning with the theory that their lives were shot into existence by an arrow sent from another plane of reality.

Then she related the idea that the world came from a fortunate accident that occurred through a random sequence of unrelated events.

She continued with the belief that everyone existed in some lonely woman's head, and when she finally went to sleep they would all vanish.

She concluded with Terryp's theory that the world just appeared one day, and it was dragged behind enormous animals such as elephants, bears, turtles, and squirrels—depending upon the season—in search of peace and tranquility. Or a large stash of nuts. For some reason all of the animals, it was believed, craved nuts.

A few times Mahrree was amazed at the rapt attention of the captivated audience. It was as if most Edgers had forgotten about the tales, and perhaps, she thought sadly, they had.

Captain Shin just observed her with patient amusement.

When she paused to catch her breath after fifteen minutes, he asked, "But Miss Peto, what proof do you have that any of these theories is possibly true? Why would there be a giant squirrel anyway?"

"Why can't there be a giant version of something small? I see it in dogs all the time. Just because we can't see the giant squirrel doesn't mean it doesn't exist beneath us," she smiled mischievously. "But travel to the bottom of the world to prove to me there is no squirrel. Or anything else. Go." She shooed him.

His studious expression didn't change, even though the villagers snickered.

"Just because you and a few others imagine it doesn't mean it exists. You're suggesting you'll believe whatever someone can imagine."

"Only by taking our imaginations seriously, even for just a moment, can we expand our minds," she insisted. "I'll attempt to believe whatever I can imagine, until I can dismiss the idea as false or illogical."

"You simply can't entertain *every* imagined idea. That would be hundreds of thousands," Captain Shin pointed out.

"That's exactly what I try to do," she declared.

To the amusement of the villagers, Teeria shouted, "She does—really!"

"She never quits. We wished she did!" Sareen added loudly.

The captain shook his head slowly in sympathy as the audience laughed.

Mahrree nodded appreciatively at her students. "We *must* be imaginative, Captain Shin. The Creator is the most inventive Being ever, and since He created us, He expects us to think as ingeniously. Wasn't it you who said on our first debate that the Creator wants each of us to also become creators?"

Captain Shin glowered and nodded.

Mahrree beamed. "I believe the world holds all kinds of possibilities we've never expected. Ancient mysteries can be unraveled if we just take the time to ponder them. Our accomplishments in the upcoming years have to be imagined now before we can make them happen later. The sky's the limit.

And the color of the sky right now, by the way," she added impishly, "is a deep gray-blue darkening to *black* with white spotty stars and two larger spheres of the full moons."

As the captain rolled his eyes, Mahrree continued enthusiastically. "But maybe not even the sky's the limit! Maybe someday we'll even find a way to fly like the birds or even visit the Greater Moon. We just haven't worked out those possibilities yet, but we could if we started imagining it."

The entire audience burst out in dubious laughter, but Mahrree wasn't bothered. She didn't believe they would ever visit the Greater Moon either, or even the Smaller Sister, but she felt passionately about everything else she said.

And she thoroughly enjoyed the steady gaze of the captain as he tried to discern just how serious she was.

"In fact," she continued, "over the past two weeks I've given a great deal of thought to your argument about progress, Captain Shin. You said you'd never met someone so opposed to progress, but I believe in a *great many possibilities* in our progression. Already in 319 years we've accomplished so much. Our ancestors couldn't make melodies as intricately as we do now, or drawings or stories. I've even heard of people now carving objects out of rock."

Several in the audience gasped. Supposedly Terryp the historian had seen rock carvings in the western ruins 120 years ago. That was one of the things about the ruins that seemed so unbelievable: how could anyone carve rock?

But Captain Shin nodded. "We call them sculptors. There are a few in Idumea, and have been for quite some time. You can see their work on the Administrative Headquarters. Even one of Terryp's associates began experimenting with carving large stone and was fantastically successful."

The rare few in the audience who had actually traveled the distant eighty miles to Idumea murmured in agreement.

Mahrree smiled. "Thank you for making my point for me, Captain Shin. Until Terryp brought back those accounts no one here considered cutting stone. But now we have those who chisel stone for house foundations, and even sculptors in Idumea. Too often we make an assumption about an idea without contemplating if that assumption is correct. Cloth out of cotton plants? That seemed ridiculous generations ago. Now cotton is on everyone's body in the hot Weeding Season."

"Miss Peto," the captain interrupted, "as fascinating as the history of cotton may be to you," he said in a bored manner, "you're supposed to be making a case for where we came from."

Mahrree rubbed her hands together. "Oh, but I am, Captain! I'm first establishing that we shouldn't be quick to judge something. I believe we addressed this issue during our first debate?" She tapped her lips with her finger.

Captain Shin turned a slight shade of pink and gestured for her to go on.

She was having far too much fun. "My point is, perhaps our lives came from a possibility we haven't even yet imagined. The world surprises us each year with new creatures and plants we never knew existed, so who knows what else there may be?" She beckoned to her students sitting near the front row.

Scowling, Teeria and Sareen picked up the large covered basket Mahrree left them and walked it up the steps of the platform. Captain Shin folded his arms and watched. Mahrree smiled smugly as the girls set down the basket on a table already waiting for it. They backed away and then bounded down the stairs to their seats.

"Thank you, girls. I know how that difficult that was for you." Mahrree opened the basket cover and recoiled slightly, but forced a smile as she faced the audience. "We never know what the world may grow. I, for one, am *suggesting*," she emphasized to the captain who was straining to see into the basket, "that all kinds of matter could become something more. Something greater than it originally was."

She reached into the basket and pulled out a large platter with something on it. What that was, exactly, no one could tell.

Captain Shin grimaced as the stench of it reached him.

On the kiln-fired pottery was a mass the size of a loaf of bread. Mostly white, it also had striations of gray, green, and bluish-black. Its texture was bumpy and slimy, and a bit oozy. As Mahrree set the platter on the table, the mass jiggled ominously until a puff of something rose up from it.

The audience, almost in unison, said "Ewww!"

Mahrree grinned. "This, as you see it right now, is not what it was yesterday, or the day before, or even the day before that, as my students will attest. They've observed its changes with me. This is . . . well, we don't have a name for it yet."

Captain Shin dared to take a few steps closer to inspect, still keeping his arms folded. "What *is* it?"

"Last week it was my midday meal," Mahrree confessed. "I forgot about it at the school, and returned this week to discover that this . . . *blob* had grown. It seems the drawer I kept it in, along with some other items I had stored there for science experiments, produced this over the Holy Day."

The audience began to chuckle and shift uncomfortably at the thought of the unrecognizable midday meal.

Captain Shin looked at Mahrree. "So this, essentially, is your cooking? And you're *still* unmarried?"

Mahrree turned bright red as the audience burst into laughter.

"Don't worry, Captain. I wasn't ever thinking of inviting you over to share a meal."

The audience oohed in sympathy as Captain Shin backed up.

"I'll sleep better tonight with that knowledge. Thank you."

The audience howled again as Mahrree rolled up her sleeves.

"Now," she said loudly to draw their attention back to her, "as I said earlier, this is not what it was yesterday. It's changing and developing. Perhaps, if left to stew and ferment over many generations, it may just develop into something even more intelligent than . . . the captain here."

She gave him a sidelong glance and saw him take an insulted breath.

The audience chuckled.

"It would take several more generations, though," Mahrree continued, "before it became clever enough to become a teacher."

The audience broke out into applause and cheering.

Captain Shin remained immovable, keeping his arms folded.

Mahrree folded her arms similarly and turned to him.

His face was stern and set, but his dark eyes were bright and warm. She couldn't bear to look into them for long. The captain waited until the audience started to quiet down. Then he took a few steps toward her midday-meal-turned-science-experiment and jiggled the table slightly.

"Moves all on its own, doesn't it?" Mahrree pointed out. "Definition of something alive: begins, grows, moves, and dies. Just watch it for a moment and you'll see it doing something like breathing."

She was impressed that she could remain so poised. The blob had made her so nauseated that she'd been close to retching ever since she discovered it at school. Yet she knew it would be the perfect example for her class to test the Administrator of Science's recently released definition of "life." And when Rector Densal prepared her for the night's debate a few days ago by telling her the topic, she knew she had to cultivate the blob as lovingly as the illegal mead brewers watched over their hidden stills.

Captain Shin nodded, and she was sure he knew exactly what she was doing. "So you're suggesting that this is a form of life? You just recited the new definition of life in reference to it."

"I thought you might approve of my using that definition. It came from *your* Administrators after all."

There it was again, welling up in her chest: that inexplicable disdain for the Administrators. She had to be careful. She glanced around the darkening amphitheater, searching the area lit by torches for anyone wearing an official red jacket.

The captain opened his mouth as if to challenge that they were *his* Administrators, but she continued on, hoping to lighten the moment. "Interestingly, the definition of life fits even for this world we live in, doesn't it, Captain? We weren't around for its beginning, of which there certainly was one, nor will we be for its end—at least, I hope I won't be around to see the Last Day. Sounds a little frightening to me. But the world itself grows and moves, especially during a land tremor. Therefore, the world must be alive.

"But," she continued, putting a thoughtful finger to her lips, "it seems tragic that trees and plants aren't 'alive' since they don't 'move' unless the wind blows them. Perhaps the Administrators will amend their definition to grant life to things that can't move?" she said in a sugared tone. "Let our orchards, vineyards, and crops live? I may be only a simple teacher in Edge, but even my students realized that the university-trained Administrator of Science seemed not to recognize that 'moving' isn't necessarily an indicator of life."

Why did she keep saying such things about the Administrators? She bit her lip in worry as the audience chortled.

But the captain didn't look offended as he sighed loudly. "You're drifting off topic again. What do the trees have to do with your . . . blob here?"

"Glad you asked!" she answered brightly. "This, according to the Administrators' definition, is most definitely alive." She gestured to the disgusting mass. "So now I have one more theory to present about our origins. I will be so bold as to *suggest* that we may have even derived from something similar to this, thousands of years ago. Look at the colors—they change daily. Yesterday there was a lovely pink streak right along there, but now it's darkened to purply black. What if all of us derived from something like this lump of neglected midday meal? Under the right conditions, in the right temperatures, with the right elements, who's to say something like this didn't advance—*progress*—into something like us?"

Captain Shin stared hard at her with his deep dark eyes. They were nearly black, but still somehow warm. Mahrree tried not to look into them, but since he was only a couple feet away, he was impossible to ignore.

"I assure you, Miss Peto, I for one did not progress from something like *that.*"

"Can you prove it?" she dared.

The audience chuckled in expectation.

"Can *you* prove I progressed from that?" the captain challenged.

The villagers laughed.

"Prove to me that you *didn't!*" she snapped back. "In a few days, there might be a strong family resemblance."

Another "ooohing" sound arose from the crowd.

Captain Shin had been waiting for that moment; Mahrree could see it in his small smile. She had no proof that her blob was actually "progressing" and not just some aggressive molds multiplying under ideal circumstances. She was just presenting a debate.

So was he.

Even though she'd seen the captain in the congregation at Rector Densal's Holy Day services, after that second debate when he dismissed The Writings as a guide from another time, she still had questions about what he believed. Now she'd get to see what he knew.

"Miss Peto," the captain began, "and with all due respect to Rector Densal who selected this topic," he nodded to him and his wife sitting on the front row, "the question of our origins shouldn't even *be* a debate. None of us can prove any theory to be true. We each choose what to believe. So Miss Peto, if you truly want to believe your cooking will become something intelligent, which is its only hope since it's clearly inedible—" he paused. "Probably always was, too," he added as the crowd snickered, "I won't argue your belief."

"You're quitting?" Mahrree exclaimed. "Not even going to *try* to offer a counter argument?"

"Oh, no—I'll debate this matter. I'm just stating this is *not* actually debatable."

Mahrree smirked. "You're just afraid of my blob and what it may represent, aren't you? Always wanted a brother?" She jiggled the table.

She didn't anticipate the sudden rise of emotion in his face as he seemed to choke back a laugh. His eyes were so warm and bright Mahrree could feel their heat.

"Slide your 'blob' over, Miss Peto. I've got my own little demonstration for the table." He gave her an unexpected wink that only she could see, then turned and trotted down the front steps over to Rector Densal.

Mahrree turned away from the audience to slide her platter over to the side of the table, and so that no one would see the effect the captain's wink had on her. She must have gone purple. She quickly composed herself and turned to see the captain coming to the top of the platform with a large, heavy crate in his arms which he easily carried.

Yes, girls, Mahrree thought. He's as strong as an ox.

As a *bull*.

He set the box down with a thud on the table, and the blob quivered in fear. The captain shuddered at it.

"Can't you cover that up or something?" he asked in a low voice and winked at her again.

Mahrree couldn't have moved even if she wanted to.

Positioning himself behind the crate, Captain Shin turned to face the audience. "Miss Peto, and each of you, can believe whatever you wish about where we came from. Cling to whatever theory or even ridiculous suggestion that brings you comfort as you struggle in this difficult existence. There's no law to force you to believe—"

"Yet," Mahrree interrupted coldly, just as she had at the second debate when he pointed out she was still free to speak her mind.

The captain gave her a studied look, then turned back to the crowd. "Despite what I may have said at the second debate about The Writings, I do see them as a valuable work. And I *choose* to believe that the Creator brought our first five hundred families here 319 years ago. That gives me great comfort. And, I will *suggest*," he emphasized in a nod to Mahrree, "it is the most reasonable belief."

Mahrree craned her neck to see what was in the crate as he pulled off the top.

Dirt, and several different kinds of it.

She knew exactly what he was about to do, and tried desperately to think of a way to counter it. Someone had helped the captain with explanations about The Writings.

Captain Shin addressed the crowd again. "None of us knows exactly how we came to this world. Our ancestors, after the first year when babies began to be born, asked the Creator, 'From where did we get *our* bodies?' That's been one of *the* questions ever since, hasn't it?" He smiled. "The other being, 'And what happens after we die?' But that's a topic for another debate."

He paused and glanced back at the quivering mass.

"And, regarding where Miss Peto suggests life may come from, I'm not anxious to see her demonstration of what happens *after we die*. I might lose my appetite forever."

The villagers laughed as Mahrree gave the idea a thoughtful look, followed by a mischievous grin.

Captain Shin shuddered dramatically before resuming a more serious stance. "When our ancestors asked those questions, they weren't ready for the answers. Nor, even with all our progress and advancements, do I believe are we yet ready for the explanation of how we got here. Perhaps our ability to comprehend is still immature, or our faith is too weak to accept the truth. The answer may be a fantastic revelation that we would dismiss as bizarre as the idea that we emerged from Miss Peto's blob."

He glanced at her trembling concoction. "By the way, my brother would be much more handsome."

Mahrree smiled.

The audience chuckled, and several women clapped loudly in agreement.

Mahrree's smile darkened and she fought the urge to glare in his admirers' direction.

Captain Shin continued. "To help our ancestors understand something of the nature of our bodies, the Creator called them together in a vast field."

Mahrree sighed. Soon he would reveal just how much he knew, and how well.

"The Creator crouched in the middle of the field and scooped up a handful of earth." Captain Shin reached into the crate and pulled out a fistful of soil. "He held it up and said to His children, 'Consider, my beloveds, that you are of this earth. Your bodies belong to this world while you experience this Test. Your spirits have been with me for far longer than you can imagine; they are very, very old, but your bodies are very new.'"

Mahrree felt goose bumps on her arms. Never before had she heard someone say those words as the captain did. Usually people read The Writings as if reciting from a dull school text. But Captain Shin repeated the Creator's words as if he had actually heard Him speak them. Mahrree felt as if she was hearing Him right now. She glanced around the amphitheater and noticed he had the same effect on many of the villagers. They sat on the edges of the benches listening to his deep, rich voice.

"'My beloveds, to know where your bodies came from will not help you in your completion of the Test. Rather, it would serve only to confuse and even frustrate you. But know this: each of you is important and is here to serve a vital purpose. No matter your color or composition, each of you needs to help your family. And we are *all* family.'"

Mahrree held her breath as he recited, perfectly and powerfully, the words of the Creator.

"'Just as I designed this world for your habitation during this Test, so I also designed your bodies to house your spirits. You no longer have memories of your life with me before, but as I stand here now you have evidence that you did live with me. It is sufficient to know that I created all that is here on this world, including each of you.'"

Captain Shin shook out the dirt in his hand and took another fistful of the darkest soil in his box.

"Then the Creator held up a handful of dark brown earth and said, 'Suppose instead that all of you are as soil. Some of your bodies were created from earth as dark and rich as this. Already you have discovered this kind of soil will yield the greatest harvests.' I have to agree," said the captain, breaking away from his narrative. "I took this sample from the field of Mr. and Mrs.

Unabi, with their permission. The height of their pea plants right now is simply astounding. And from the looks of this soil," he said analyzing the darkness of it, "the Unabis were formed from that very dirt themselves."

The audience chuckled as the Unabis beamed with pleasure. Their white smiles seemed to glow surrounded by their dark brown skin.

Mahrree smiled outwardly but grumbled on the inside. He was smoothly winning over the audience. Every farmer or brown-skinned person of varying shades—which was about one-third of the audience—now felt a connection to her opponent.

Captain Shin then reached into the box and pulled out another handful of soil, redder and more claylike.

"Others, the Creator told us, were similar to this dirt. It is clumpier, moister, and yet still very useful earth." He balled it up in his large hand, clenching it a few times until he opened his fingers to reveal a lump of clay. "This sample came from the Dinay family's property whose pottery will be used by the fort. Seems to be sturdier than anything in use at the garrison in Idumea, and since soldiers tend to be clumsy creatures, we need plates and bowls that can handle a drop or two."

The audience chuckled in appreciation while the Dinays nodded that their goods would hold up well.

"Much like this red clay, many families like the Dinays have a similar hue. Still earth, just differently shaded, and still infinitely useful."

Another segment of the population of Edge, reddish like the clay, was now looking at Captain Shin with approval.

Mahrree moaned softly.

The captain dropped the clay ball into the box and pulled out another handful of soil, lighter and tinged yellow.

"Some of us, the Creator explained, could be considered derived from soil such as this one, yellowing with sulfur. Initially our ancestors didn't know what to do with this, until they noticed insects stayed away from it. Suddenly sulfur-tinged soil was desired for lining farms and gardens to keep out the pests. Then it was discovered that farming soils, even those as dark as the Unabis, became even more productive when just the right amounts of this was shoveled into it. Now this smelly substance is being experimented with in Idumea to create salves for skin problems. What we initially thought was useless now is exceptionally useful.

"My grandfather told me once that my great-great grandfather Shin, whose first name we never knew, was more this hue than any other. Over the generations his 'soil' mixed with others so that I can hardly see any trace of it in my own flesh. Yet as I look around tonight I see many with hair and eyes as dark as mine and skin tinted yellow as my great-great grandfather's. I may infer that you may be my distant cousins.

"There are those who lament the losses of our family lines—the records destroyed accidentally in that devastating fire after the Great War. But there are others who say it was an act of mercy. I don't know who my ancestors are, as do none of you, but I can assume all of you are part of my family. And, as the first line of The Writings reminds us, 'We are all family.'"

Mahrree might as well have conceded defeat right there. Telling another one-fifth of Edge that he was most likely a distant cousin solidly won their support. While his eyes were rounder than most of those he claimed as kin, many of his other features now seemed remarkably similar to those families.

Mahrree *should* have called for an end to the debate, because then she would have been spared what came next.

Captain Shin dropped the yellow tinted soil into the box and now took a fistful of sandy gravel, pale and crumbly.

"Then there were others of us created in a way similar to this . . . well, soil isn't an accurate designation. Still considered 'earth,' though. The other part of my family apparently is of this constitution. It took our ancestors a while to find a use for this. For growing crops or creating pottery, it was quite disappointing. Had no useful soil-augmenting or medicinal purposes either. It seemed like filler." He sifted the sandy gravel between his fingers. "Dry. Bland. Barren."

He glanced at Mahrree and stepped over to her.

"May I?" He took up her arm which was bare since she had rolled up her sleeves, and dramatically dribbled some of the pale dirt on her arm. "Hmm. Perfect match. No surprise there, since I took this sample from your front 'garden.'"

The amphitheater hooted with laughter, but Mahrree bristled in anger.

At least, she hoped she looked like she was bristling. She trembled slightly as his large rough hand held her narrow arm.

"I suppose I should have asked permission to take this," he apologized loudly over the laughter. "But I didn't think you'd notice a shovelful missing. Not sure if you'd notice *anything* different in your yard."

She yanked her arm away as the crowd roared again. With a huff she wiped off the dust and rolled down her sleeves.

Captain Shin smiled at the people packed into the amphitheater. More were arriving every minute.

"Our ancestors discovered that mixing this dreary substance with water and a few other elements could create a mortar to hold together stones. And suddenly this, too, had purpose and was necessary for our lives." He nodded at Mahrree as he dropped the last of the sandy gravel back into the crate.

"Over the years we've discovered that mixing soils creates other uses, just as blending our family lines has resulted in new and inventive mixtures. I asked Mr. Unabi if this soil," he again held up a handful of sample from Mahrree's garden, "could ever produce   anything besides spindly weeds. He assured me that with a few wagonfuls of his soil, other amendments like manure and sulfur, and a lot of hard work even this," he let it dribble out of his hands, "could become productive. I find that remarkable. And a far better science project for Miss Peto's students."

The villagers tittered in agreement.

Mahrree squinted.

"By combining what we know and what we are, we can transform nearly anything into what we need it to become. I think that was planned deliberately by the Creator. He knew we would need each other, especially if one kind of 'soil' couldn't do it all. This," he held up Mr. Unabi's black dirt, "would never hold as mortar."

Tossing the handful back into the crate, he continued. "Many of you, like me, would struggle to identify just what kind of 'soil' we are now. But we are all needed, all equal, and all capable of combining for intriguing results. I, for one, embrace the Creator's explanation. Our spirits are *from* Him. Our bodies are created *by* Him of the earth to assist each other. And we will be returned *to* the earth when we die. Then we have the promise that someday these bodies will be restored and perfected, never again to be separated from our spirits.

"There may be those who choose not to believe, and that's their right. But I receive comfort and peace from this belief, and I choose that this," he held up two handfuls of soils, the gravel and the yellow tinged, "is the constitution of my body, rather than to think that Miss Peto's blob," he jerked his head over at her sample, "is my future brother. This is not an issue for debate, but for belief. Make your decisions as to what to embrace, but let me embrace my belief."

The audience immediately rose to its feet and applauded thunderously.

Mahrree would have applauded too, but that wouldn't have been appropriate. Besides, his words couldn't have been *all* his. She stood with her arms folded and smiled faintly.

He glanced over at her and seemed just a little embarrassed, and Mahrree suspected why. She looked down at Rector Densal who grinned proudly at the captain.

Something was going on between them.

The rector looked after everyone: the lost, the lonely, and the clueless newcomers, because that was the kind of person he was. Hogal Densal would see a need and do all he could to fill it. He must have been coaching the captain for days to help him find a way to connect to every citizen of Edge.

Every citizen except *one*, who stood in obvious defeat on the podium.

At least she had the satisfaction of knowing it took the combined efforts of both the wisest rector *and* a university educated army officer to defeat her.

When the applause died down Captain Shin turned to Mahrree and leaned in so close she could hardly breathe. "Besides, Miss Peto, as much as you may love your blob—and I hope you and 'my brother' will be very happy together—"

Mahrree tried to ignore the sniggering in the audience as she blushed again.

"—you mentioned before elephants dragging the world. You and I both know that if one element of an idea can't be true, then none of it is. Elephants aren't real. Besides, you don't *really* believe that either."

It was his third and last wink that completely did her in. She turned red and couldn't form a retort.

When Rector Densal declared Captain Perrin Shin the winner, she wasn't surprised at all.

## Chapter 8 ~ "Uhhh, sometime I am available should be fine, when we, uh you, can make it."

Late at night, in the forests outside of the large village of Grasses, several men stood in a thick stand of trees. Two young men wore the village's garb, while the rest were dressed in dark clothing that allowed them to blend into the woods. They had been watching all evening, timing the patterns of the soldiers who rode by on horseback at regular intervals.

When all was clear, the largest man pointed to the two young men.

They nodded, then stepped out of the forest and started their brisk walk toward the village.

In the morning the fort would receive new recruits.

~~~

The captain in charge of recruits at the large fort of Grasses evaluated the two young men who stood at attention in the command office. "You'll need to pass the first three weeks of training before you can be officially called soldiers," he warned them. "Our colonel can't use men that can't run, ride, or fight."

"Sir, you and your colonel will be impressed," one of the young men answered confidently. "We'll qualify to be soldiers for the Army of Idumea. We already know how to do those things, and *more*."

The captain nodded once. "I'll hold you to your promise. So, why did you choose to leave Orchards to come north?"

The other young man shrugged. "We just find the north more appealing, sir."

"Well, then, welcome to the fort of Grasses. We have a long and prestigious history, dating back to the Great War. I expect you will help forward that. The lieutenant will see that you get uniforms and show you your bunks. Training begins at dawn."

~~~

As Mahrree walked to the marketplace to gather her evening's meal, her thoughts circled on just one thing: Captain Perrin Shin. The fourth debate had been several days ago and tomorrow would be their fifth. The closer it came, the more she thought about him—

That was a lie, Mahrree admitted to herself as she crossed a road and continued south. There wasn't any way she *could* think more about him. He seemed to be everywhere that week: walking past her school, in the neighborhoods, at the village green, around the amphitheater. And every day she heard reports of him from others, since everyone felt the need to tell her of their encounters with him. He even went so far as to go to Rector Densal's congregational meetings.

On the first Holy Day he attended, right after their second debate, he caused a mild panic. Everyone wondered why a uniform was there, although the gossip was that he was trying to appear penitent for his dismissal of The Writings.

Mahrree had seen him when she first entered the meeting. He was already seated on a bench on the right side of the building, with adequate space around him provided by the stunned parishioners who didn't want to risk getting too close. She stumbled over her feet for a moment, then made a bee-line for the other side of the building and sat down on a still-empty pew.

Her mother, saving a spot for her just two rows behind the captain, waved frantically for Mahrree to join her. Hycymum had deliberately chosen that spot, Mahrree found out later, so that they would have a *good view*. It was when she was shaking her head apologetically at her mother that Mahrree noticed positioning herself in just the right way would put the captain right in her line of sight, if she glanced to her side.

During the meeting she dared to peek over at him only twice. The first time a large woman leaned over and blocked her view. Mahrree had uncharitable thoughts about her for which she sent a quick apology upwards. The second time she *did* see him, but found herself so embarrassed she averted her eyes after only a brief moment.

When they broke into smaller discussion groups he sat on the same row as her. The way the row curved, however, gave her a clear view of him.

It also gave *him* a clear view of *her*.

She did her best not to look at him, but it didn't matter because everyone else was. It wasn't expected that an officer would be interested in an in-depth discussion of The Writings before the congregational midday meal. But from his comments it was obvious he had read The Writings and even memorized some sections. He also pointed out a minor detail to Rector Densal that clarified a confusing passage. The rector had beamed proudly at him, but maybe he'd already been coaching the captain.

That was when Mahrree finally stole a peek at him. He seemed to be looking in her general direction, leaning back in his chair with his arms folded and a studious look on his face. But she wasn't sure until he sent her a quick wink. She sucked in her breath and turned toward the front again. For the rest of the meeting she sat frozen in place, but something in her chest insisted on burning.

The day after their fourth debate was Holy Day again, and she sat a few rows behind him in both meetings so she could try to concentrate.

That wasn't the best idea, either.

Instead of avoiding his winks, she found it difficult to focus on anything else but his thick black hair and the details of his head. She had the curves of his ears and neck memorized by the time the midday meal began.

She could still recall the exact shape of his earlobes, and it gave her goose bumps as she walked to the market that evening.

"How adolescent!" she muttered in self-admonition. She approached the outer ring of shops, barely noticing the looks of confusion on the two women she passed as she declared their dresses, hats, or conversation as "adolescent."

Mahrree *did* think she heard one of them utter "—Guarder snatched!" so they likely deserved it.

And there he was again in her mind.

Now, there *were* many qualities he had worth admiring: his quick thinking, his ability to shift emotions, even the way he could stand straight and not appear to breathe for long periods of time. What that skill was for, she didn't know. Maybe for sneaking up on Guarders. But it was commendable and she could certainly admire someone's ability to . . . not breathe.

"How stupid," she told herself, and three men in discussion furrowed their eyebrows at her unsolicited criticism.

It was everyone else's fault, she decided as she worked her way through the crowds toward the baker's. Everyone else brought him up, repeatedly. Her teenage students asked endless questions about him, but they weren't nearly as annoying as her mother. Just yesterday she came over to ask what Mahrree and the captain did when they weren't on the platform, her eyes glowing with too much imagination.

"Nothing, Mother!" Mahrree had declared. "We never meet anywhere else. Now go back to your sewing group and tell them there's nothing to tell."

Hycymum just nodded and said, "We'll see about that."

"There will be nothing to see!" she called after her mother who was giggling as she went down the walk.

"She never listens," Mahrree grumbled as she paid for her loaf of bread. She pushed past the crowd at the baker's, not noticing the bewildered look of the baker's daughter to whom she gave her pay.

Normally the night before a debate Mahrree would be running different arguments in her head. But tonight she had nothing because Rector Densal had told her the topic would be a surprise for both of them. She tried to imagine what kinds of discussions he might spring on them as she wandered over to purchase some early greens, but her mind couldn't rest on anything for more than a moment. Every time her thoughts shifted, they shifted in only one direction. It was irritating to see him on every wall of her mind—

"Oy! Watch out, there!"

The shout behind Mahrree startled her out of her thoughts, and she turned abruptly to find herself in the arms of Captain Shin.

In the middle of the market.

With everyone watching.

At least, that's likely how it appeared to the surprised villagers, Mahrree realized in humiliating remembrance later.

In truth, the captain's arms *were* outstretched, because he had a jug in one hand, and a large bunch of flowers in the other, and a young child had just darted in front of him. That was what caused him to raise his arms upwards to avoid hitting the boy. He'd shouted the warning and then stepped awkwardly, losing his balance only to find himself within inches of Mahrree who had just spun around.

She also was unsteady on her feet as she turned suddenly, and found herself falling inexplicably toward him, her bread in one hand, her bag in another. With both of their hands full of goods, nothing prevented Mahrree's face from colliding into the captain's solid chest. She breathed in his earthy-yet-sweet-scent and her mind went blank. Blissfully, serenely blank.

And then he wrapped his arms around her.

It was only to steady themselves, she realized in *another* humiliated moment of remembering later. It was the jug in his hand clanking against her head with a dull thud that sent her into such a juvenile swoon, she decided even later. That was why she couldn't think properly for several minutes.

Instinctively she pushed away from him, trying not dwell on how firm his stomach was as she used it to brace herself.

"I'm so sorry!" Captain Shin exclaimed. "That child ran in front . . . I didn't want to hit him, but I hit you instead—"

Filled with sudden sympathy for his anxiousness, Mahrree cut him off. "Not at all!" She rubbed the side of her head vaguely. "No harm done. My bread's a little flattened, but I like it that way." It sounded silly as it came out of her mouth, but she couldn't think of anything else to say.

"Is that so?" he replied with an awkward smile. "I like flattened bread, too." His voice trailed off and he looked down at the ground, his lips twitching as if they had wished something smarter had just left them.

His discomfort comforted her.

She began to notice something different around them. All the usual market noise and talk had stopped.

The captain looked up slowly to face her, then simultaneously they both looked around.

The market was now a silent collective smile pointed in their direction. Mahrree estimated more than one hundred pairs of eyes were staring at them, and it was more unnerving than the thousands at the platform. She chanced a look at the captain.

His face was partly amused and partly pained. She had to fix it.

"So!" she said, a little too loudly but so that everyone around them could hear. "I thank you for helping me not to fall, and I'll see you tomorrow evening." She nodded to him formally and to those around her, and began her march toward home.

In the wrong direction.

No one else moved but instead watched her take seven or eight steps, then abruptly turn to her right and continue in a line that curved around the still smirking villagers. She didn't even dare look at the captain. She held her breath all the way, hoping she wouldn't make another wrong turn.

A moment later the marketplace resumed its activity and noise, and Mahrree released a sigh of relief as she reached the edge of the shops to begin her walk home. She shook her head as she slowed her pace.

Stupid! Adolescent! There was *no* possible way he could *not* have noticed her blushing. She still felt flushed and hot, despite the cool breeze coming off the mountains. She couldn't forget the feel of his arms around her, even if it was for just a moment.

She also couldn't forget that she couldn't remember where she lived.

Heavy footsteps pounding behind her made Mahrree glance back. To her surprise, Captain Shin was on her heels. Behind him several villagers were grinning and one waved. Mahrree groaned softly as the captain stopped next to her and continued walking along side. She didn't know what to do, so she kept up her pace.

"Umm," he started inarticulately, "I'm glad I ran into you, or rather, fell, I guess it was."

He hesitated and Mahrree peeked up into his face. She saw furrowed brows and a man at an unusual lack for words.

"What I mean is, I wanted to see you tonight before tomorrow's debate."

Mahrree didn't know how to answer. He sounded different when he wasn't in public. Tender and tense at the same time.

"I've felt badly about some . . . actually *many* of the words that have passed between us. You know, we haven't even been properly introduced? I don't feel we've presented our best sides to each other yet, and I'd like to change that."

Mahrree was pleasantly astonished. "You're right. We should have been properly introduced. This may be *only* Edge, but we do have some rules of etiquette that we occasionally remember. But oh, that first debate was *so* long ago—nearly three weeks now."

"I know, and I'm sorry. Please understand that's not my way. I just wanted to let you know that. And these are for you."

He stopped and thrust the flowers in her face.

She remembered that they looked much fuller and fresher when she first saw him. Their collision and his jog after her had decimated their blooms.

He blinked at them, perplexed.

"Presenting flowers to a woman when you meet her—that *is* a very proper thing to do." She smiled at the haggard stems. "You're learning. Next time you'll remember to keep the flowers wrapped in the scrap paper the sellers put them in, so that they don't lose their petals as you go."

"But the flowers were wrapped in an old Administrative notice," he said, his voice curiously hardening.

"Yes," Mahrree acknowledged, wondering if he was offended by the notice's second life. "We use them for flowers, for kindling, and even for emergencies in washing rooms when the wiping cloth hasn't been cleaned." Even as she said the words, she wondered why she bothered to add that last unpleasant detail.

But the captain wasn't offended. His face relaxed to a smile. "This village just becomes more interesting every day. Everything here astonishes me. No wonder I can't get anything right."

Mahrree laughed, surprising herself. "You like flat bread, Captain Shin. That must mean something."

Politeness. She should always be polite. That's what her mother drilled into her head when Mahrree was younger and said all kinds of things Hycymum didn't approve of to scare off young men. The young men that stopped trying to present her flowers many years ago.

Then she thought of what her father would do at a moment like this.

Before she knew it she heard herself saying, "Would you like to join me in eating my flattened bread? My home isn't too far from here. And I won't be serving blob. I had to bury it this morning in the back garden. It was becoming . . . a little more than I could handle." It was the only way she could think of describing the stench and the fact that it was beginning to eat away the kiln-fired platter at an alarming rate.

"Didn't look like your brother," she added impulsively. "Wasn't attractive at all." She was wincing before she even finished the sentence, realizing she should have stopped talking half a minute ago.

"Really?" He smiled. "I'm sorry. About the blob, that is, and . . . I'm afraid I already have an appointment elsewhere tonight." He held up the jug as an explanation.

Relief and disappointment simultaneously surged through Mahrree.

"Besides," he continued, "Edge would have a great deal to talk about if I was seen going to your home, wouldn't they?"

"Oh, oh, of course, Captain," Mahrree blustered in embarrassment. "Until tomorrow, then. And I thank you for the flowers."

"I *am* sorry," he repeated. He gripped her shoulder clumsily and stared deep into her eyes. "But can I make it up to you sometime?"

Mahrree waxed eloquent again in his dark brown gaze. "Uhhh, sometime I am available should be fine, when we, uh you, can make it."

He frowned as he tried to decipher what she tried to say. He must have assumed her answer was positive, because he said, "Then 'sometime' it is. And please, call me Perrin." Then he was gone back down the road.

Father would like him, but Mahrree didn't know why.

She turned back around and tried to diagram her last sentence all the way home. Once she got there, she put the haggard stems in a tall mug and tenderly watered them, smiling at the handful of wilting petals.

Her first flowers, ever.

---

At the fort that evening, the new spyglass that arrived was being tested. It wasn't sighted on the forest where the Guarders may be hiding and planning their attacks, but on a small house on the northern side of Edge.

---

It was going to be easy—the return of the Guarders—if this young woman was any indication. The man in black had been watching her ever since the first debate, and she didn't notice anything beyond her books. Except for maybe the captain.

He'd already searched her house—no one in Edge seemed to know how to work their locks—and found she wasn't hiding anything interesting. Oh sure, she had slips of gold and silver in her cellar, predictably stored under a bag of flour and a crock of oats. Everyone in the world thought their savings were secure in their cellars. They'd be shoving the hammered metals under their straw mattresses next. Every Guarder knew where to find the goods.

But thieving wasn't the point. If it were, they could leave every village destitute within a couple of quiet evenings.

No, the point was to leave *messages*.

That was *always* the point, although the messages changed frequently over the generations. He really didn't care what the message was now, so long as he got to be the deliverer. He'd been waiting a long time for such an opportunity, fearing that when the reign of kings died, so had everything else.

Instead, it was all reborn, just like the return of Planting Season. Except it was reborn with such calculation and planning that the man had been stunned. There's plundering and murdering, and then there's *this*. He hadn't quite worked out what all of *this* was yet, but it was certainly better than nothing.

He stepped out of the shadows of the kitchen and over to the mug of flowers on her work table. He sneered at it, amused. Usually the first blooms of Planting Season were hearty things, able to take a dumping of late, wet snow. They'd just shake it off and rise defiant from the cold ground. But these—these were just stems, with only a hint of "flowerness." What *did* the captain do to them?

The man in black glanced over to the door that led to the combined eating and gathering room. He heard her turn a page in some old book, oblivious to his presence.

He'd leave her a message, but it wouldn't be noticed.

He snapped off one of the traumatized flower tops and placed it deliberately on the other side of the table. But he knew what her reaction would be. She'd assume she had dropped it over there and simply forgot.

That was the thing about villagers: they saw only what they expected to see. It was said that Guarders left no signs, but that wasn't true. They left their messages everywhere, but like a soiled rag on the ground that everyone in a crowded stable feels is someone else's responsibility, it's bypassed, stepped over, or completely ignored.

Guarders never attacked without leaving a warning. That'd be unfair.

It was the villagers' faults for not noticing the warnings.

"Uhhh, sometime I am available should be fine, when we, uh you, can make it."

He noiselessly slipped out the back kitchen door, down the back porch, and into the night.

---

Mahrree went to admire her stems again before blowing out the kitchen candle, and noticed one of the flower tops on the other side of the table.

She smirked to herself as she picked it up, and immediately thought of what her father would say.

*Guarder snatched! Or rather, Guarder snapped.*

Mahrree chuckled quietly. "Oh yes, Father," she murmured. "Guarders are now interested in rearranging half-dead flowers. How unpredictable of them."

But something heavy lingered in the air, and she felt her father more distinctly. He was more than memory. When it was important, it was as if he had never left her side.

*Remember, my daughter—Guarders are unpredictable.*

Mahrree bit her lower lip. It wasn't as if someone in black had suddenly taken an odd interest in the stems. She knew what he really meant: she needed to be cautious. There was no cowardice in caution. It's not like she had anything of interest to the Guarders, but still—

She swallowed hard and glanced at her back door. Just to be safe, she latched the lock. But she was not about to needlessly burn a candle in the window to ward away any intruders.

"What else should I do?" she whispered to the quiet kitchen.

*Nothing for now. Just . . . be aware.*

Mahrree nodded. "Father? I was just wondering, what do you think of Captain Shin?"

The mood in the room lightened. *Perhaps a more important question is, what do you think of the captain?*

"I don't know what to think," she answered automatically.

*Oh, I'm sure you do, or you wouldn't have bothered to try to revive those stems. You just haven't admitted it to yourself yet.*

Mahrree shrugged, a smile of bashfulness lurking around her mouth. "So what do *you* think of him?" she asked again.

*Good man. I like him. Doesn't know beans from flowers, but that's all right—he's not a farmer.*

Mahrree chuckled as the influence of her father faded away. She floated the broken flower top in the water of the mug, blew out the candle, and went to bed.

# Chapter 9 ~ "Debate the merits of Perrin and Mahrree continuing the debates--"

Mahrree had been flustered ever since last evening's encounter when she was alone with him for barely five minutes, but now she was about to face Captain Shin again on the platform. She paced nervously before the young oak tree and warm spring, doubting that she could go through with it. Tonight there was a huge crowd, near capacity at four thousand, with more coming in.

She tried to calm her breathing. Rector Densal was reading an announcement from Idumea about an improved messaging system, but she couldn't concentrate on what he said. She considered running off or faking a sudden illness, but then she heard the rector call her name.

It was too late now. She took a deep breath and bounded up the steps as usual to wave to the crowd. Their typically polite applause was punctuated with cheers and some whoops. She'd never before heard them that enthusiastic.

She didn't have any time to worry as to what it might mean, because Rector Densal was now introducing Captain Shin. As he strode in on the other side, the captain appeared surprised too. He gave Mahrree a concerned look, walked over to her, and stood uncomfortably close and a little in front of her as if trying to shield her from the raucous crowd.

She felt a rush of gratitude at his gesture and wondered if it was a soldier's instinct.

"Tonight, we will do something different!" cried Rector Densal to the rowdy villagers. "Neither of our debaters knows what the topic will be for tonight, so there will be no unpleasant surprises left on a table. And, Miss Mahrree," he said, turning slightly to the platform, "I am truly sorry to hear of the demise of your blob."

Mahrree chuckled nervously. "It hadn't been looking well for a while. Nice addition to my back garden." She wondered how he had heard about the end of the mass. Only her students, who begged her to get rid of it after the fourth debate, and Captain Shin knew it was gone.

The crowd laughed and Rector Densal nodded his sympathies. He turned back to address the amphitheater. "For tonight, I've asked our good teacher's students for suggestions of what they should debate."

Mahrree cringed. Rector Densal had been talking to her students. That, at least, would explain his knowledge of the loss of the blob. Her stomach churned as she imagined what her students might have suggested as topics.

"Some of those debate ideas are here in this basket," he held it up high. "I will now ask Captain Shin to draw the first debate suggestion."

Mahrree searched the crowd as Captain Shin reached over to draw first. Her eyes finally settled on her teenaged students, all eight of them sitting together in a row. Grins and giggles burst across the girls' faces, and Mahrree grew hot with worry.

This could be a very, *very* long evening.

Captain Shin unfolded the small paper and his eyebrows rose.

Mahrree began to panic.

He cleared his throat and began, "Please prove that dogs are better than cats."

Mahrree relaxed and rubbed her hands. "I'll take cats!" she said with a grin and strode to her side of the platform to plan a strategy.

"I guess I'm dogs," the captain said to the audience.

A little boy named Poe in Mahrree's morning class clapped his hands. It must have been his suggestion.

The debate was won by Mahrree since she was convinced of the superiority of cats. Their independence, self-cleaning, and mousing abilities hedged out dogs' abilities to guard the house, be a companion, and come in a variety of sizes and colors. What tipped the argument her way was that the shedding and shredding of cats was slightly less annoying than the drooling, barking, and, worst of all, inappropriate sniffing of dogs.

Mahrree pulled out the next topic. "Resolve who is better: boys or girls."

As the audience "oohed" in eagerness, the captain bravely stepped up and said, "I'll start that one."

Mahrree's curiosity was piqued. "I await this opening line with GREAT anticipation."

He nodded at her, turned to the crowd and said, "To the young man or woman who suggested that topic I say, there is no woman without a man, and no man without a woman. Therefore, neither can be better than the other. They are, however, different, and each difference is necessary and complementary." Then he stepped back.

"Ah, come now, sir!" Teeria called out, disappointed her suggestion didn't elicit more of a response from the captain. "You can do better than *that.*"

The crowd teasingly repeated her complaint.

"Come now!"

"More!"

Mahrree stared at the captain. She didn't expect his response. Actually, she didn't know what to expect. But how could she take on what he said or even debate it?

He looked to her, waiting for her retort.

She smiled at him. Not a baiting, teasing, or chiding smile, but a genuine look of appreciation. He returned it.

She probably *could* find herself calling him Perrin, if the situation was right.

The crowd was calling her name, so she turned to the villagers. "All I want to say is, first there is no *man* without the woman. I rather prefer that order of words." Then she too stepped back.

The captain winked at her. Mahrree hoped she wasn't changing colors.

The rector stood up, to the good-natured whistles of protest from the audience. "Next topic is for the captain to select," he called.

The captain pulled out the slip of paper, read it, then looked around. "All right, who put this in here?"

Mahrree held her breath. Not the girls, not the girls, she silently begged.

"It states," he announced, "Debate the merits of the Jor house being painted that sickly shade of blue."

Mahrree exhaled and grinned. "Next!"

"Hey," someone yelled from the front. "I like that blue. What's wrong with it?"

"It looks like the cheese in my cooler when I forgot about it for a season," someone else shouted.

"Next, please!" called Captain Shin over the laughter.

The rector held up the basket again.

Mahrree took out the next slip and shook her head. "People, come now. 'Debate the merits of Mr. Arky being allowed to eat his dinner in any room of the house.' Is this *really* from the children?"

The captain took the paper. "I think we can handle this one."

Mahrree shook her head and said in a loud stage whisper, "You obviously haven't met *Mrs.* Arky yet."

"Let it be heard!" called a voice that sounded suspiciously like Mr. Arky, followed by howls of laughter from his neighbors.

The debaters looked at each other with small smiles and together called, "Next!"

Something in that moment made Mahrree's chest burn again. She didn't have time to think about it because Captain Shin was pulling out another topic.

They spent the next fifteen minutes discussing the qualities of stone versus wood in home construction. He defended stone and easily took that round, describing some of the ruins Terryp found in the deserted areas to the west that survived untold ages.

He won over the children, however, with a ridiculous explanation involving three talking and industrious sheep, and a wolf with an unusual lung capacity. Clearly, building with straw was the worst option of all.

Much to her chagrin, Mahrree found herself completely absorbed by his outlandish story—complete with surprisingly high-pitched voices for the sheep, and an even deeper-than-normal-for-him voice for the wolf as he threatened to "sneeze their houses down."

But even her chagrin faded rapidly as she watched him in action, his booming wolf roar drawing squeals of terrified delight from the younger children, and laughter from their parents.

She was falling for him.

While the audience murmured amused doubt about the authenticity of the captain's story, Mahrree pulled out the next slip. "Which is better, living in Idumea or living in Edge?" She burst into a grin. "I'll take Edge!"

To her surprise, Captain Shin sighed heavily before saying, "I'll take Idumea. If I must."

Mahrree spent the next ten minutes detailing every quality and attribute of Edge as the greatest next-to-smallest village in the world. Only Moorland was more sparsely populated since it sat at the base of the largest mountain, Mt. Deceit, and no one in the world appreciated mountains. She carefully avoided saying anything antagonistic about Idumea or the Administrators as she gushed about Edge's people, entertainments, music, food, rivers, schools, shops, services, houses, farms, orchards, and ranches. If she had time she would have gone on about each family she knew, but she could see the captain was waiting his turn.

At last she turned to him and said, "Now it's your time to dazzle us with tales about Idumea."

Instead he slowly shook his head. "Am I *really* supposed to follow your moving tribute of Edge with my feelings about Idumea? No, Miss Peto. You see, in Command School we took courses on diplomacy—"

"Is that something like Officers' Charm School?" she interrupted. She wondered if teasing was considered flirting.

The audience laughed and the sudden rise of emotion came over the captain's face again, just as in the last debate, as he fought back a laugh.

"Something like that."

"And how often did you have to retake the course until you passed?" she asked sweetly.

He waited until the laughter died down before he answered. "Just know that I passed."

He had to wait another moment for the audience to quiet again before he could continue.

"And in those classes we learned that sometimes no response is the best response of all. Look, Miss Mahrree," he said in a loud stage whisper he fully intended the villagers to hear, "I'm trying to earn some credibility in Edge. It wouldn't do me any good to regale you with reasons why Idumea may be considered superior. Let's just say that I look forward to experiencing all the qualities of Edge for myself. I've already enjoyed many."

The villagers laughed and applauded his non-argument, and Mahrree folded her arms smugly at her easiest victory over him yet. "I see you've been rereading your notes from your tactfulness courses as well. Then let's see how you deal with the next topic, shall we?"

He nodded. "I promise, you'll not defeat me so easily in the next round. Our score tonight currently stands at two for you, one for me, not counting the topics we've rejected. I'm not the kind of man who walks away when he's behind."

Flashing a grin that made Mahrree feel unusually weak, he pulled out the next slip. He studied the scrap long enough for    everyone to grow quiet with anticipation.

He gave Mahrree a quick glance before saying, a little coldly, to Rector Densal, "Any *other* requests?"

The rector shook his head as he peered into the basket. "I can't seem to find any more, Captain. I'm afraid that's the last one."

"Next!" he called.

"Oh, come now," Mahrree said, snatching the small paper out of his hands. "So sure you're going to lose again? You already know there's no more."

"Mahrree, trust me," he said. "Just don't pursue it—"

She looked at him suspiciously, secretly thrilled with the way he said her first name. The night was going so well she didn't want it to end yet. She flourished the paper and read in a booming voice, "Debate the merits of Perrin and Mahrree continuing the debates—"

The audience cheered.

"—forever as husband . . ." Mahrree's voice faltered and she felt a wave of regret and nausea wash over her. The laughter was already beginning.

At that moment Mahrree found herself in the same battle she'd be in countless times before—her brain trying to force her mouth to stop moving. But the message wasn't getting through quickly enough. Before she could stop herself, she was choking out the last words written on the paper.

". . . and wife."

The crowd leaped to their feet with deafening applause and shouts.

Mahrree was too mortified to look up. *Worse* than mortified, if there were such a condition. What must Perrin—Captain Shin think? That she put someone up to this? Why else would she insist on him reading it?

She let the note drop out of her hand, glanced up quickly with a forced smile, waved, then turned and hurried toward the back of the platform and rushed down the stairs.

Several calls of, "No! Come back!" followed her, but there was no way she could allow anyone to see the condition of her face. Besides, what more could she say?

In the background she could hear the rector's words faintly in the din. "And I suppose with that we conclude tonight's debates."

Mahrree went straight to her usual bench under her favorite tree and hoped no one would join her. She sat down hard and stared at the ground, breathing deeply and trying to understand why the phrase "husband and wife" had both startled and thrilled her.

"I am so sorry, really," she heard Captain Shin's voice above her head.

She moaned softly. He was the last person she wanted to see. She shifted her gaze slightly and saw his boots in front of her.

"He had no right to do that to us."

"It's all right," Mahrree whispered. "I don't think Rector Densal knew what that paper said."

"Well, yes I do believe he did," he said, a bit sharply. "I know his hand-writing and I'm *very* sure he composed it." He held the note in front of her down-turned eyes.

She looked at it closely in the dim light. The writing was a little shaky and not that of a teenage girl. None of the i's were dotted with flowers.

Surprised, Mahrree looked up at the captain. "Why would he do that?"

She had expected him to be angry, but his face was soft and sympathetic. "Because he told me yesterday over dinner that he's an old man who's worried he'll never see you happy. He said he promised your father years ago that he would help you, and I guess this is his way. His help is . . . well, not exactly *helpful*," he said as if he had a lot of experience with that.

"Indeed that was entertainment!" interrupted Tabbit Densal, coming up to the two of them. When she saw the look of distress on Mahrree's face she turned to Captain Shin. "Please don't be too angry with Hogal," she begged, and looked at Mahrree apologetically. "He really thought you'd debate it."

Mahrree exhaled, stood up, and said, "How? Anyway, I'm glad you enjoyed yourself, Mrs. Densal. But I'm afraid that will be the end of the debates for a while. I'm falling behind on my students' work and must spend more time at home."

"Come, come," said Mr. Metz, joining them. "I haven't had so much fun in years! How often do we all get to watch the progress of a courtship?"

Mahrree closed her eyes in agony.

"Sir, you presume too much and have gone too far!" the captain said sternly. "I'm afraid I may have been neglecting some of my duties as well. Our debates must end now."

Mahrree's heart dropped to the level of her knees. She felt a gentle hand on her shoulder.

"Try to have a good night, Miss Peto," Captain Shin said in a low voice that sent a new wave of goose bumps down her arm. He briefly squeezed her shoulder and vanished into the dark.

She excused herself and hurried home, grateful no one else tried to stop her. She didn't even dare look out her windows that night to see if anyone walked by her house unnaturally often.

---

At the fort the spyglass remained trained on the village, and a new hole appeared in the wall of the office.

And the cuts on his hand from his last fit of fury had just scabbed over.

---

The small man in dark clothing sat in the privacy of the trees and finished composing the message to be sent with the next delivery. He smiled, imagining how the news would be received.

Captain Shin was a fool in love, and the entire village knew it. There was quite a bit that could be done with such information. It just might be enough to get the man in the dark a better posting.

But if it didn't, that was all right, too. The north was more appealing every day.

# Chapter 10 ~ "Not at all coincidental, is it?"

The next morning at school, Mahrree's young students bragged how she had decided the cat and dog issue once and for all. She was impressed they carefully avoided discussing any other points of the evening.

But her teenage class in the afternoon was uncharacteristically silent. During their mid-lesson break, Teeria came shyly up to her. "Miss Mahrree, I hope no one ruined anything for you last night. I've asked around and no one admits to writing that last debate suggestion. We don't know who did it."

Mahrree squeezed her arm. "Thank you for your efforts. I know none of you wrote that. And I also don't believe there *was* anything to be ruined, so no worries there, all right?"

Teeria looked disappointed, but smiled and nodded before returning to the other girls who anxiously awaited her report.

After school Mahrree went to the markets and quickly bought enough provisions for several days. To make sure she missed Edgers' looks of apology, amusement, or pity, she didn't make eye contact with anyone. She purchased enough food that she could hide in her house until the memory of the last debate was overshadowed by someone else doing something ridiculous or ridicule-worthy.

Then she made good on her word last night and spent the rest of the day catching up on her students' work.

Except that took less than two hours, because the parents did all of the grading and reviewing.

So she found herself that evening sitting at her table in her kitchen after dinner wondering what the night's entertainment would be, before realizing she couldn't show her face in public for at least a few weeks. Instead she looked around her the bookshelves that lined the dining area and leaked over to the gathering room. She needed to gain more knowledge before the next debate that . . .

. . . would most likely never happen.

Brushing aside that discouraging thought, she came up with an idea to keep her mind occupied. She walked over to a shelf and pulled down the copy of The Writings she had since she was a child, along with a stack of blank pages. She tried to read The Writings at least once a year, but had never done so as intently as her father. Now it was time. Tonight she would take notes of the thoughts that came to her as she studied.

That should chase away any thoughts of . . . what's his name.

*Page 1, verse 1:*

### We are all family.

It was always easy to recite the first line.

*Verse 2.*

### We have always been a family.
### We have always been progressing.
### We have always been.

How was it that we have always *been?*

A thought came to her: What if you choose to *not* insist on understanding, but choose instead to just *believe?* Can you just accept that you had no beginning and have no end, but that you are now in the middle?

Mahrree wrote that down on her paper. She could understand 'middle.'

But I'm an adult, she thought. I should be able to understand all things by now. But then she considered, how much did Hycymum not yet understand? The six-year-olds in her class, how much did they not comprehend beyond the number one hundred?

Why should she be any different?

A new thought rushed through her and she wrote it down: I do not know what I do not know that I do not know.

The next morning when she read that again it still made sense, sort of. She'd spent three hours the night before studying—*really* studying—The Writings, and had five pages of notes to prove it. In the past she'd breeze through the more mundane descriptions of the first three years their people were in the world. But last night she finally began to see the first five hundred couples that came to the world, highly intelligent and innocent, as real people: her ancestors. She didn't know which specifically her "first parents" were—no one knew anymore—but they were there, somewhere.

And so Mahrree immersed herself in the comfort of their ancient world of 319 years ago, since her current world was quite discomforting.

The Creator had stayed with them for their first three years, teaching them everything they would need to know to be successful in their Test. He told them their lives would be unlike anything they had ever experienced before.

It would be glorious and terrifying.

They would find love and loneliness.

They would learn what they could become and what they already were.

It would not to be a test of theories and knowledge, but a test of application and will.

The Creator had promised the Test was designed to allow all to succeed. He'd even give them notes, show them the way, and provide a way for them to communicate with Him.

All would struggle. All would fail. Some would give up, declare the failures as signs that the Test was unfair and refuse to fix the errors of their ways.

But failure wasn't a fault of the Test, the Creator had told them. The Test, personalized for each who came to the world, may not be *equal* but it would always be *fair*. Failures didn't need to be permanent; they meant only that the lessons had not yet been learned correctly, and needed to be tried again until they were.

Mahrree always thought those words were the most comforting in The Writings.

There had even been some who had so little faith in their Creator that they refused to take the Test. Mahrree could never understand that. To not even *try*? How could one not even want to attempt the adventure, to explore this existence on a new world the Creator designed for them?

True, she had no memory of that life before. No one did. And that, according to The Writings, was the reason those who didn't want to try refused to come. They couldn't imagine the Creator would leave them enough clues, through whisperings or writings or miracles, to make the correct choices.

Mahrree found that tragic. So many people now didn't believe. It was almost as if those who didn't choose to come to the world—those who followed the one they now called the Refuser—had come nonetheless, intent on pulling away those who had once believed.

As Mahrree read the details of her ancestors' first weeks on this world, she put herself with them. She could almost see them as they discovered the wonder of grinding small bits of matter into a powder, mixing it with liquid, adding a rising agent, and then heating the combination into something that smelled wonderful and was called bread. What faith they must have had in the Creator to be the first to put it into their mouths!

She smiled as she considered how unusual it must have been to pull food from trees, from plants on the ground, and even from under the dirt, and

then begin the cycle all over again by deliberately returning parts of the vege-
tation to the soil. She imagined that if the Creator told her to bury the pit of a
peach, she would have raised her eyebrows at Him in surprise. She most likely
would have done it, but wouldn't have had much faith in her meager gardening effort.

And it was such thoughts that troubled her and stopped her reading.

Would she have had as much faith as her ancestors? Imagine being the
first woman to give birth to a baby! The Writings recorded she was taught all
about the process by the Creator, as were all the other women expecting at the
same time. But still, nothing could have been more bizarre and alarming than
the stages of expecting—then delivering—the first child! Mahrree had known
about the process since her cat gave birth to kittens when she was four years
old, and still it seemed unreal.

Then again, what could have been more amazing than that first tiny
baby? He must have been held by every set of arms in the world.

Other aspects of the first families' experiences were amusing. Mahrree
loved reading about the ancestors' wonder at first smelting metals from rock.
The Creator had to rein in their eagerness to keep them from burning every
object they found, hoping to see what may be hiding deep inside.

Other ancestors were truly courageous. The man who first sat on a horse
was one of Mahrree's heroes, since she would never voluntarily mount one.
And his wife, who was the first to set a broken arm, was as equally gallant.

She read in wonder about the first five hundred families creating melodies, then chords, then instruments that were blown and strummed and beat
to express those tones. She concluded that not only had the Creator chosen
His bravest to begin the world, He also chose His most creative as well.

To express how one sees the world by stretching hides, then covering
them with carefully placed colors derived from flowers and earth turned into
liquids in order to create the first paintings must have required pure genius.

Mahrree also admired their writing. The Creator gave them language
and then ideas for recording it, but allowed a few of the first ancestors to put
all the suggestions together to devise their alphabet. What inspired the shapes
of their words always intrigued Mahrree. She wished they had spent more
time writing about how they created writing, then printing with wood blocks.

That was Mahrree's pattern for the next few weeks. She found herself in
a race to finish The Writings before school let out for the Late Planting
Season break. Some nights she spent four and five hours trying to get to know
her ancestors, wishing she knew which of the names mentioned may have
been her family line. She suspected the women who first wove together fibers
from plants and sheep to replace animal skins must have been the ancestors of

her mother. She imagined the history recorders and story tellers must have been directly linked to her father.

The night she came to the passage about the first guide, Hieram, sacrificing himself for the world's families to fight the growing rebellion in the land, she felt familiar tears of regret and gratitude. It was three years after the Creator had left them, and six years since He first placed them in the world. All had been well until six men decided they wanted to do things their own way. Even as his murderous brothers came at him, Hieram continued to shout about following the Creator's will for them.

Mahrree wondered, as everyone must have at some time, if she would have died as willingly as Guide Hieram. Would she give up her life trying to save her people from their own destruction? She hoped she would, but she suspected she would have hidden in a cave like everyone else. But *perhaps* she would have been brave enough to witness what happened and insist on recording the truth, as the next guide Clewus has done.

Some passages she read quickly, while others kept her rapt attention for an hour. She nearly forgot all about Captain Perrin Shin.

Nearly.

Sometimes she reflected on him, and instead of feeling pangs of loss at not seeing him lately, she felt an unexpected calm.

Each night she read the histories that the guides recorded and the miracles each saw in his day. Mahrree wondered why no one talked about current miracles. She assumed they still occurred, but that no one noticed them for what they were. She knew she felt the Creator's influence her life. Her father was gone, but she felt him near when she needed his guidance. Wasn't that miraculous?

She read about the conflicts of their people as they expanded and multiplied. Neighborhood arguments evolved into violent village debates. Those erupted into full-out battles which spilled into neighboring villages. Everything seemed to explode in the middle age of their history. Even knives became daggers that grew into swords. It seemed as populations exploded, so did their tempers and pride.

It wasn't as if one village battled with another to avenge a murder or the taking of someone's daughter. They came to blows over minor things. A missing sheep. A misunderstanding about a repair on a chimney. Three mugs of cream that weren't delivered on time.

Chaos over next to nothing.

But the damage done wasn't next to nothing. By the time the people reached one million, Querul the First, who named himself king in 190, vowed to control the growing violence. He believed that uniting the villages under his rule would unite their desires. But the forced unification only made the turmoil grow.

With sadness Mahrree read the accounts of the growing disputes and population, and finally the Great War that started in 195 that destroyed so much over the next five years. She'd always skimmed through those passages, but now with the fort in the village she felt she should try to understand the mindset of going to battle to force peace.

Three hours later she still didn't follow any of the logic.

As she read those passages, she wondered if Captain Shin could explain it to her, but she couldn't imagine ever asking him. Although she'd seen him in Rector Densal's congregation—and the rector had apologized copiously to Mahrree on Holy Day after the fifth debate—she hadn't spoken again to Perrin.

Captain Shin.

He did the same as she did the last two Holy Days: slipped into a back bench unnoticed just as the meeting started. They were always on opposite sides of the hall, and she glanced over at him only three or four times each Holy Day.

But she never caught him looking at her.

One afternoon Mahrree stared at The Writings, her entertainment every night for the past two and half weeks. She tried to imagine a way to approach the captain and ask him a question or two, but she couldn't think of anything that wouldn't have sounded contrived. She came to a depressing conclusion that day.

Her first real romance was over before it had even started.

---

Captain Shin stared at the smashed nib of his quill and winced. It was the third quill he'd destroyed that afternoon. He looked down at the parchment and made a face. He'd have to rewrite the entire second page of his report. The huge blotted out section, and the ferocity with which he had blotted it out, gouged a hole through the thick parchment and stained the large oak desk underneath.

It was the word "armory" that did it.

He *started* writing "armory," but embarrassingly it turned into something else. That's when he set out to obliterate the mistake to make sure no one saw that *her* name had leaked into his writing.

Again.

He rubbed his forehead in frustration and looked out the large windows of the command tower to the west. The sun wouldn't be setting for at least another hour. He had to eliminate the distraction. Commanders of forts facing dangers of invasion couldn't afford to be so preoccupied.

He tossed the ruined quill on the desk, put on his cap, and headed out of the command office into the large forward office.

"Lieutenant, I'm just—" He stopped short when he realized Karna wasn't alone. He was looking over some pages with Sergeant Major Wiles. That Captain Shin didn't hear the slender old man, newly assigned to the fort, come up the stairs was also evidence that he was far too unfocused.

"Captain," the sergeant major nodded with a sly smile revealing a few missing teeth in his craggy mouth.

"We're just going over the progress reports, sir," Karna held them out to him. "Did you want to review them?"

"Later, men. I, uh, there's some business that I need to attend to in the village. I'll finish the report to Idumea in the morning. I know I said I'd be here all evening, but there being pressing matters . . ." He didn't know how to end his rambling.

Wiles smiled gappily. "We're on schedule, Captain. The High General will be pleased with our progress. Go on, take care of those *matters*."

Karna smirked and looked down at the pages in his hand.

"Yes, thank you. Hold down the fort, men." Captain Shin started down the stairs.

"Sir," the sergeant major called down after him. "Would you like me to get someone to repair the two holes in your office wall, or do you suspect there may be a third joining them tonight?"

Shin stopped halfway down the stairwell and closed his eyes. He'd forgotten both of the soldiers had been at that last debate, his new sergeant major arriving just the evening before. Then both of them had been in the forward command office to hear when his frustration with the results of that last debate manifested itself with another fist through the planking.

He massaged his left hand, the gashes finally healed over.

The sounds of Karna snorting a laugh into his sleeve traveled down to him.

Shin answered nothing, but continued down the stairs.

"Good luck, son!" Wiles called after him. "He's gonna need it," he muttered loudly to the lieutenant who snorted again.

Shin marched out of the receiving area of the command tower and out into the busy compound of the fort. He automatically returned the salutes of several soldiers making their ways from the mess hall to their evening shifts. Shin headed straight for his quarters, taking off his cap as he entered his room.

"Not in the uniform," he murmured as he unbuttoned his blue jacket.

---

It was the 39th Day of Planting, just before the weeklong school break, and Mahrree saw she had only four pages left in The Writings. That filled her with satisfaction at completing her goal, and disappointment that the end had come so quickly.

Tonight she would read about the decision of Guide Pax and King Querul to divide the people to establish peace—which didn't happen—and she would read Pax's last prophecies recorded just before he disappeared. One of the assistants of Guide Pax left some notes in a bag that was found when the king's search parties went looking for them. The notes mentioned traitors among them, but little else to describe what happened.

Mahrree knew it was useless to guess, but she couldn't help wonder what happened to the Guarders once they left. Where exactly did they go?

To the north, the violent forests and the massive mountains were impassable—everyone knew that.

To the east and south was the great salty sea as far as the eye could see. Only a few brave men ventured into those waters in their canoes to fish.

To the west were yet more dense forests, and beyond, in the northwest, a massive desert that bordered the village of Sands.

As vast as the sphere where the Creator placed them may have been, it was obvious that only one small segment of it could be inhabited. The rest was just there for . . .?

Mahrree shrugged, the thought too big for her mind to comprehend.

And why had the Guarders been quiet for so long, but now attacking? It seemed reasonable that they needed the livestock and goods and perhaps even the gold and silver they stole, but where did it all *go*?

A sudden thought entered her mind, bearing the mark of her father. She pondered it for a moment, until her chest grew hot and her breathing increased. A new understanding began to form in her mind.

She shoved back her chair and raced to the bookshelf to pull down several texts of history she used to teach her students. She plopped them on the eating table and flipped the pages, already knowing where to find the information. On a piece of paper she made two columns, and under the heading of the first column she wrote a number. Then she turned a few more pages and wrote another number under the second column. For ten minutes she did that, flipping pages, double-checking the dates, and skimming the text for additional insights. She found a few more, made additional notations, then sat down heavily on a chair.

It was so obvious that she was stunned that she—and no one else—had never noticed it before. But there it was: the Guarder attacks had two distinct patterns. The first were their major attacks on the villages, *always* just one year and a season minus a week after a new king took power. Just after he rearranged his advisors and told the world that he could, indeed, keep them safe. And always, the Guarders were repulsed and the new king appreciated for his ability to stop a full-out invasion.

Then there was a second pattern, more subtle, but still amazingly *coincidental.* Outbreaks of rebellion in the world were few and far between, especially since the terror-filled days of Querul the Second and Third. But they did happen, seven recorded times since the Great War. Each time the village or region was complaining about poor treatment by the king, always—*always*—they were hit by Guarders within six weeks of their uprisings.

About eleven years ago, when Mahrree was a student in Mountseen, a riot occurred in Sands after King Oren levied a high tax on glass sold from there. A Guarder raid hit the large desert village, destroying much of the glass-making shops.

The professor of her history class speculated that the Guarders may have thought that Sands wanted to further rebel against the king, so likely they were coming to join with them. But the villagers mistook the Guarders' intentions and attacked them instead, resulting in so much violence.

But Mahrree had been suspicious, even then. To her the attack seemed more like a vengeful act, rather than a mere misunderstanding. And now, as she traced the timing of subsequent and earlier attacks, the pattern was clear, albeit completely unbelievable.

"A new king. A show of Guarder force just over a year later," she murmured at the numbers on the page. "The king and the army put it down. An uprising by the citizenry, then a Guarder attack . . ."

She bit her lip in concentration and disgust.

"Not *at all* coincidental, is it? Guarders weren't coming to show their support for the rebellious citizenry. They were coming to *punish.* Because they were *sent.*"

As soon as she muttered the words out loud, it was as if all the warmth in the room was sucked out.

"And who sent them?" she asked the coldness around her.

*I'll give you one guess.*

Mahrree closed her eyes in fury. "The kings! Somehow they controlled the Guarders, all this time!" She looked around, panicked, as if anyone might have been able to hear her words. Her house was quiet, but still a heavy lump grew in her belly. "Father, might that be true?"

*Remember, my darling daughter, sometimes the world really is out to get you.*

She couldn't do anything but stare at the dates and notations on the paper in front of her. The possibility of kings staging the attacks on their own people was simply overwhelming.

"But why?"

*You've already pieced most of it together.*

Mahrree nodded slowly. "To show they were in power, that no one could prevail against them. To remind the citizenry who's really in charge."

*Very good.*

Another thought came to her, in a sideways motion slamming against her mind, and it truly confused her.

"But . . . not *all* of them. *Not all of the Guarders?* So what does that mean? Some are entrepreneurial thugs? Setting up their own independent raids at discount rates?" she asked with mystified sarcasm.

She felt her father smile, but he answered her nothing. There were no more answers to give her, yet. But that was all right. She wasn't sure she could have handled any more anyway.

"So the attacks *were* convenient," she whispered to the air. "But now, the kings are gone. We have the Administrators, who have improved and changed so many things . . ."

The air around her developed a cynical quality. Her father was still there, creating a distinct edginess in Mahrree. Cephas Peto was the most thoughtful, gentle, intelligent man she'd ever known, but he also had a strong skeptical side to him that occasionally arose when he told his daughter that things were just *not quite right,* but he couldn't put his finger on it.

The air around her now was thicker and heavier than a humid Weeding day afternoon, filled with his doubt.

"Father, what do I do?"

*Nothing now. Just know. Just watch. But do nothing.*

Mahrree wrung her hands with worry, fury, and fascination. "It was you, wasn't it? Placing those suspicious thoughts about the Administrators in my mind during the debates? Making me say such things? Antagonizing Captain Shin?"

The cynical heaviness in the room lifted slightly, replaced by an apologetic yet amused air.

"Why did you do that? Do you realize how much trouble I could have caused?" She couldn't help but smile. Her father must have completely enjoyed those debates. Nothing as scandalous had occurred since he argued that the sky was intrinsically black, and that all other color was merely an illusion.

"But you would never influence me beyond what would be sane and safe, would you?"

Something in the air came closer to her until it was a warm presence just above her heart, where she frequently felt her father.

"I thought you liked Captain Shin. But if you do," Mahrree whispered to her gathering room just beyond her eating table, "then why did you let me say such awful things to him? About the Administrators?"

If the cosmos could chuckle, it did.

Slowly the presence of her father slipped away, and the air in the room returned to its normal dry, cool Planting Season feel.

Mahrree stared down again at the dangerous page of dates and numbers. Maybe . . . maybe she *wasn't* the only person who looked at their history and made those connections. Others may have too, but didn't dare say anything. Or maybe they tried to, but someone like the Administrator of Loyalty knocked on the door and—

She picked up her notes and tossed them into warm ashes of the fireplace. A small fire flared up to consume the evidence. There was nothing—absolutely nothing—a simple teacher in Edge could do about any of that. Except to know, wait, and watch.

Mahrree sighed.

Maybe the Administrators *were* different. It had been over two years since they took power, and the latest hearsay was that Guarders had been spotted in several locations. The pattern was different this time. So maybe it *was* a genuine threat, and the presence of the fort was necessary. Perhaps the twenty-two administrators and their chairman *did* know more than one lone woman at the Edge of the World.

Mahrree grumbled to herself over that most aggravating idea.

She took a deep breath and looked again at the remaining pages of The Writings. Her stack of notes awaited her last entries. She closed her eyes to clear her thoughts of Administrators and Guarders and captains and anything else distracting. Even though she'd read the pages often, she was sure there was something new to learn, if only she—

There was a knock at the door, but she ignored it. She mischievously thought it was a Guarder coming to explain his side of the story, or maybe an Administrator who had already gathered the ashes of her notes. But she knew she'd never meet any of those stuffed red jackets since no one in the government ever bothered to travel all the way up to the Edge of the World. And she certainly wasn't about to head down to Idumea for a chat.

At the door was most likely someone telling her they were retrieving their goat that was nibbling the weeds in her yard—

The knocking came again.

She opened her eyes and, feeling a mixture of annoyance and amusement, decided it was one persistent Guarder. Hoping that whoever it was wouldn't take long, Mahrree reluctantly got up and went to the door. When she opened it she could only stare.

There stood a hulking man filling her doorway, dressed in black trousers and a tunic that matched his dark hair. For the briefest of terrifying moments, Mahrree *did* think it was a Guarder, until she noticed the man's worn brown leather jacket.

And the flowers wrapped appropriately in an old Administrative notice.

Mahrree couldn't move or speak.

It was Captain Perrin Shin.

# Chapter 11 ~ "So I've actually rendered you speechless?!"

"It feels like a year since we've last spoken." Captain Shin's voice was low and earnest. "I never thought two and a half weeks could feel so long. I thought maybe the custom here was to bring more flowers to renew an acquaintance?"

Mahrree blinked, then blinked again to make sure she saw everything properly. Yes, that was him standing in the doorway. And that was her still holding the door open, strangely paralyzed.

The captain leaned toward her, waiting for a response.

She recovered just enough to stiffly answer, "Yes, hello. Yes, it has been some time."

She simply couldn't think of what to do next. It wasn't every day a man stood at her door. Actually, a man was never at her door unless he was there to clear a clog in her water pumps or scrub out her chimney.

They both stood there uneasily for a moment until he slowly presented her the flowers. "Am I doing this right?"

Mahrree felt a slight knock to her mind and said, "Oh! Of course. Yes, thank you. I'll take those." She did, thinking they could replace the dried stems still in her tall mug, but continued to hold open the door dumbly.

"So . . . I suppose I'll leave you now. Unless you'd like to talk? I have 'some time' tonight," he hinted.

Mahrree rolled her eyes. "Please Captain, do you have a jug you can hit me with? I can't seem to think straight right now."

He grinned in such a way that Mahrree finally understood the meaning of the phrase *feeling faint and fancied*. He held up his other hand. "Actually, I do. New berry juice to share with you, not the Densals. And it's Perrin, remember?"

She smiled back. "I'm trying. Really. Please come in."

"You *are* trying," he teased. "And now I see it's berry juice that gets me in the door, not flowers. I thought maybe mead was more appropriate," he explained as he entered the gathering room, the area shrinking in relation to his height, "but one's never sure of the strength, and in case I brought the wrong thing I didn't want you to think I was trying . . . um, uh . . . " He rubbed his forehead, looking for a graceful exit.

Mahrree squinted, trying to figure out where the rest of the sentence may have been headed. When he didn't say anything, she decided a polite host should help. "I don't enjoy mead. I saw enough students at the university in Mountseen drinking the wrong distillations. I couldn't understand why they'd voluntarily give up their ability to think clearly."

Perrin smiled. "Exactly! I was always the odd man out when everyone else enjoyed their days off in a stupor. But I wanted to be ready when the call came. As they say in the army, you don't want to be caught with your trous—" He stopped, searching her face to see if she knew the phrase he nearly uttered.

Her curious and innocent look must have told him she didn't know his meaning.

He wasn't about to explain. "Caught off guard," he salvaged. He sighed and looked around him for the first time, staring at the number of book-shelves in the room.

"Really, I'm sorry about not letting you in right away," Mahrree explained as she set the flowers down on the eating room table. She should have put them in the mug in her kitchen, but she didn't dare leave, just in case the captain vanished while she was gone for two minutes. Besides, she wasn't ready to replace the dried up stems he gave her three weeks ago. "I was just so surprised to see you there. I wasn't expecting . . . but I am glad you've come. Please, sit down." She gestured to a stuffed chair her mother bought for her when she moved into her small home.

But he didn't move. Instead he cocked his head to look at the shelves, reading the titles carefully burned into the leather spine bindings. "How did you get so many books? They must have cost a small fortune!"

"It cost my father a small fortune," Mahrree told him. "I inherited them when he passed away. Mother didn't want them, except for the one about embellishments through the ages. I must confess, I haven't read all of them yet, but I plan to."

"May I borrow some? So many of these titles are old. All I could find in Idumea were new writings and ideas. But I find there's more truth in most of the old writings. Don't you agree?" He turned to Mahrree with the eagerness of a young student.

Something in her chest burned again. "Of course. Borrow whatever you want. Take home an armful before you leave."

"Trying to get me out the door already?" Perrin asked.

She didn't notice the twinkle in his eye. "No! Stay as long as you wish tonight."

His eyebrows rose in astonishment at her insinuation.

She still missed the teasing in his eyes. "No, that's not what I meant!" Mahrree backtracked in a panic. She knew this was why she usually didn't talk to men. "I'm not implying any impropriety—"

As soon as she said the words she was even more mortified.

"Oh, no, *no*—what I *mean* is . . ."

"Stop!" Perrin laughed. "Stop!"

He actually laughed, and it cleared Mahrree's mind completely. It sounded like bells.

"I know what you mean, don't worry." He extended his hand as if to take her arm, but pulled it clumsily back instead. "Ah, but you're so easy to tease and fluster! I can't help but wonder, why? When we were on the platform I found it very difficult to shake your confidence. You gave me the greatest challenge I've had in many years, and that was in front of thousands of people. But when we're alone," his voice quieted, "you can't seem to string a coherent thought together."

"That's not exactly a compliment, is it?" Mahrree said, pursing her lips.

"You're doing better now, recovering some of your intelligence."

She saw the teasing twinkle in his eye that time. "I'm just better able to deceive you now. I'm still incoherent, but I can mask it when I have a few moments to prepare," she confessed.

He sighed. "I don't think you could *ever* deceive me. But I'll confess I've deceived you." He looked around for the stuffed chair. He gestured to Mahrree to sit in its match across from it, and he sat down after she did.

"How have you deceived me?" Mahrree dreaded to hear. She wondered if her father would still like him. She felt a warm touch just above her heart again and she braced to hear just about anything.

As long as it wasn't about a wife in Idumea . . .

He placed his elbows on his knees and leaned forward, putting his hands together. "I've deceived you by not being completely honest. I've been testing you, I guess."

"Testing? Why?"

"I came to the village because I requested this assignment. You see," he leaned forward in his chair closer to Mahrree.

She could almost smell him, but she didn't dare get closer, especially if what he was about to say would make her hate him.

"You see," he repeated hesitantly, looking into her eyes, "I worried about the ideas I saw emerging in Idumea. I wanted to find a place that would reinforce my belief in The Writings. Yes, I do believe in The Writings despite what I said at that second debate. I hope I proved that in the fourth. In many ways, your mind is the same as mine. But The Writings and beliefs are dying in Idumea, and new suggestions are spreading. The 'suggestions' will be 'mandates' soon enough, I'm sure." His tone hardened as he looked down at his hands. "You see, the Administrators—"

He stopped abruptly again and looked up into her face, as if fearing he'd just revealed a secret.

Mahrree held her breath as a fantastic idea filled her. Suddenly everything in the last half hour—the last several weeks!—was making sense. He's skeptical too! Just like Father! She waited in eager anticipation to hear his evaluation of the Administrators.

She wasn't about to get it.

"I looked for a village as far away as I could," he instead continued on a safer path, "hoping to find a place where I could continue believing. My great-uncle has written me a lot about Edge. When the need arose for the new fort, I had my reason to leave and the general approved my request. I guess I've been testing to see just what the people here think. What *you* think." He looked down at his hands for a moment. "My mother says I have a tendency to 'stir the pot'," he said with a small chuckle. "She's always warning me about behaving." He looked up at her again. "I realize I haven't always been honest, and I certainly wasn't fair with you. I'm sorry about that. Can you forgive me?"

Mahrree was stunned by even more than his apparent skepticism of the Administrators.

"I never imagined . . . you actually *want* to be here? That was all *you* at the fourth debate? Stir the pot?" Then she remembered something else. "Who's your great-uncle?"

"You don't know? Our one-time matchmaker: Hogal Densal. He's married to my mother's aunt."

"Of course!" No wonder Rector Densal puffed with pride whenever he saw the captain.

Perrin's dark eyes softened. He seemed so different this evening, but also familiar somehow. "He likes you, you know. I'm sure that was obvious a few weeks ago. In fact, he's the one who suggested I debate you the first night. He said he'd make my time here interesting." He chuckled again. "I actually thought the teacher would be an old spinster."

"So, I'm not old?" Mahrree ventured with a small smile.

"No!" he exclaimed. Then more calmly he said, "No, no, no. Not at all. I was quite surprised to see someone so, so—" He turned a little red.

Mahrree grinned to herself. She flustered him!

"—so, so . . . young and capable," Perrin finally finished.

Mahrree tried not to look disappointed. She was hoping for something a little more than that, maybe even something bordering on romantic, but "young and capable" would have to suffice.

Perrin appeared frustrated with his words as well. "I've missed our debates," he continued. "Much more than I expected. These past few weeks have been the longest I've experienced since initial training for the army. I've worked my new soldiers, mapped the region, planned patrols for the forest borders, *and*," he looked down at his hands again, "ruined more than one report because your name keeps cropping up in my writing. Not exactly efficient—"

"Wait," Mahrree stopped him.

He looked at her expectantly.

"Wait, how many patrols can a few soldiers on horseback watching the forest have?" she asked.

Perrin looked disappointed, then surprised. "What do you mean, *a few soldiers?* The full one hundred arrived last week."

"One *hundred?*" Mahrree was shocked. "The most we ever had in Edge was five! I thought maybe a dozen, but what do you need with one hundred men?"

"You didn't see them come in?" He sat back in his chair and gestured disbelievingly with his hand. "It was a great parade. One hundred men in uniform, twenty-five of them on matched horses—I thought all of Edge came out."

He was like a ten-year-old who just figured out how to do a back flip but no one saw him.

"I, I was, uh, at the head of it all," his voice quieted. "Really quite something to see." He looked at his hands which didn't know what to do but slap gently against each other.

"I heard the children in school mention something about a parade, but I didn't pay much attention to it," she admitted. "I heard some noise out in the road last week, but I just thought it was the musicians marching as they practiced or something. But why one hundred men? And where are they staying?"

He frowned at her. "The fort is quite large. We took over the old farm and orchard area to the north. Completed the barracks and mess hall just last week. You *really* didn't notice one hundred new soldiers?" he persisted. "We marched up the road just one house away from here."

"I've been busy at home," she said dismissively. "Why so big? What are the Administrators expecting?"

"Guarders," he said solemnly.

Of course he'd say that. Mahrree saw her chance. He wasn't in uniform so she could ask him about the real threat of Guarders, and there really wasn't anything he could do—officially—about her doubts. "If I may ask you something, in confidence, *Perrin?*"

His eyes brightened. "Anything, *Mahrree.*"

"Honestly, is there really that big of a Guarder threat? After all these years? Especially here in Edge? It just seems so . . . so *convenient* sometimes."

All the light dimmed from his eyes. "Guarders. You're asking me about Guarders."

"Yes, Guarders," she repeated, not understanding his reticence. "I've lived here all my life and have heard of only two people who supposedly ever saw Guarders, and one of the witnesses had been drinking old grape juice. Guarder activity hasn't been close to Edge since Querul the First's soldiers chased them to the forest. *Perhaps* they're still there, but they never come into the village. I've even walked along the forest edge to see the bubbling mud and have never seen anyone."

"You also didn't notice when one hundred men plus twenty-five complement, a dozen full wagons, and twenty-five horses moved in less than a quarter mile away from your home," Perrin countered.

Mahrree paused. "You make a good argument," she murmured. Mahrree was never one to look too far beyond her books. She was a woman of the *word*, not of the world.

"Still," she continued, "doesn't one hundred soldiers, or rather, one hundred-twenty-five seem excessive?"

The previous brightness in his eyes still didn't returned. "If you knew what I knew . . . but I can't tell you all of it." He sat up straight and looked like a soldier at attention.

Mahrree assumed it was an instinctive stance.

"The Administrators, when they came to power, initially attempted to send out scouts to look for new lands to settle." Perrin's voice was careful and calculated. "They were headed to the ruins King Querul's soldiers had visited many years ago, hoping to discover if the area was still poisoned—"

Mahrree sat up eagerly at the mention of Terryp's ruins, but had the wisdom to not interrupt.

"Their findings were most disappointing. They never reached the ruins. All of the forests surrounding the world on the north and west show evidence of increased Guarder activity. One of their spies was apprehended and brought to the High General for questioning. There's no doubt: they *are* moving closer to the smaller villages. We have every reason to believe they're planning to raid places even like Edge, thus we've implemented a presence to discourage such activity."

Mahrree sat at attention, trying not to show her disappointment that the scouts never reached Terryp's land, or that he provided an army-issued explanation that sounded rather rehearsed. In her most official voice she said, "I thank you for your report, Captain."

Perrin's lips parted in surprise but he quickly closed them. "Uh, old soldier's habit, to make reports. Sorry."

"And how old a soldier are you?" Mahrree prodded with a smile, even though she already knew from that one interesting fact in the back of the history book.

"As old as you," he smiled.

Mahrree wondered how he knew her age.

He leaned back in his chair and studied her, resting his head on his fingers.

But Mahrree didn't notice. She had to try one more time now that the official report was out of the way. "Do you *really* think these mysterious peoples of violent tendencies, whom we've heard very little from for one hundred nineteen years, are suddenly coming to invade us here in Edge?"

His studied look vanished and he shrugged. "Sounds a little far-fetched when you put it *that* way, but yes, I suspect they may."

"'Suspect' and 'may,'" Mahrree jumped on his hesitation. "Yes, you really *are* convinced. Is there not any other reason those men, I mean *your men*, are here?"

He leaned forward. "For what other reason could there be?"

"I really don't know," Mahrree admitted, suddenly feeling chilled, "but as you spoke even the air seemed to change. Didn't you feel it?"

Perrin sighed. "Conflict always brings an odd feeling. Even preparing for a conflict that never comes changes the air around it. I don't like it, Mahrree, but I like even less what a full battle would mean to this village. Or to you."

Mahrree swallowed. Something in the way he said her name, then said "you," felt very intimate.

Then she remembered something. "Ruins! You mentioned something about ruins, Captain. Will they be sending another scouting mission? Once the Guarder threat is put down again?"

Perrin looked a little annoyed and Mahrree didn't know why. "The ruins. That's what you want to talk about now? The ruins."

"Oh, yes! I've always been fascinated by those who lived here before we did. Just imagine—they've already gone through and completed The Test! Terryp had spent so much time—"

"Terryp?" he interrupted her and squinted in surprise. "I remember you mentioned him at the fourth debate, but just how much do you know about Terryp?"

Mahrree rolled her eyes. "The greatest historian of the Middle Age? The one who studied the great ruins beyond the deserts west of Sands? I think I know all there is to know about Terryp. More than just his stories, his *discoveries!* When I was a girl I used to fantasize about his expedition after the Great War. My father and I would hypothesize about what he discovered, what might have been on his map, and why Querul didn't want that information known—"

She stopped in worry, realizing she was saying too much in front of a man who swore to serve the king until the regime change just two years ago.

The corner of Perrin's mouth went up. "As a girl you *fantasized* about a *historian* who's been *dead* for a hundred years?" He chuckled. "You're just full of surprises, aren't you?"

Mahrree relaxed at his changed demeanor. "I found Terryp far more interesting than the stories of girls in distress awaiting rescue. Where's the adventure in that? Sitting around in a tree hoping some dashing soldier would look up and see her cowering in fear from Guarders?" She scoffed. "But ruins—ah! Now there's something worthwhile—"

"Mahrree!" he said abruptly and pressed his lips together.

She stared at him, startled by his outburst. "What?"

"Can we discuss ruins at another time?"

"I suppose so, but what would we discuss instead?" She was mystified, and a bit put off.

"I have been thinking about the debates—"

"So have I!" Mahrree grinned. "I was thinking, when we have time maybe we can start them again. I have some new arguments for Mrs. Arky to counter Mr. Arky with about eating anywhere in the house. The number one reason has to do with ants. Oh, but I shouldn't tell you that. Don't want to give away—"

"*Mahrree!*"

The solemnity in his voice startled her. He looked at her with such intensity that he clearly wasn't thinking about the Arkys.

Or ants.

"Just . . . let me say this, all right? No more interruptions?"

By the way his jaw clenched, she decided she best just listen. She gave him a brief nod to continue.

He took a deep breath. "I haven't been able to get the debates out of my mind. Or *you* out of my mind."

Mahrree bit her lower lip.

"I didn't know what I would find in Edge, but I was really hoping to find . . ." He paused, stared at his hands, and shook his head.

Mahrree was completely bewildered by his behavior. She *really* didn't know men.

"Honestly, Mahrree, it was only a little ways into that very first debate that I thought to myself, 'I could, I could . . .'"

He could *what?*

"Icouldloveawomanlikeyou," he rushed. He slowly looked up into her face with something like anguish.

Mahrree sat stunned as she ran the words, or rather *word*, over in her head to break apart the syllables. I *think* he said it, she mused. It was too much to hope for, but she hoped anyway. She smiled encouragingly. "So you could, could you?"

"Mahrree, what are you doing to me?" He stood up abruptly but then sat back down again.

She'd never seen him like this. The confident captain was nowhere to be found. Instead sat, stood, then sat yet again an agitated—and now almost pathetic—man.

"I'm sorry, what am I doing?" she asked sweetly, but not innocently. She thought briefly that her teenage students would be proud of her composed reaction to this most unexpected conversation.

He put his hands together and rested his elbows on knees. One leg began to bounce nervously. "I feel like *I* can no longer create a coherent sentence. Maybe we need an audience." He stood again, walked around the chair, and used it as a buffer to stand behind. He put on a look of resolution and blurted, "Mahrree, I don't want to get married—"

Definitely unexpected.

Her heart dropped through the floor.

"—to a woman who cannot think or take a challenge. The only kind of woman I could ever marry—"

Her heart lifted back up to just above her belly.

"—is a thoughtful woman who can hold her own in a conflict. I need someone who believes just as strongly as I do."

Her heart hovered. He meant *her*, right? He was talking about *marrying* . . . and suggesting *her* . . . in the same sentences?

How did they get *here*!?

But another thought struck her and she knew what she had to say, yet couldn't believe she'd utter the words until she did. "But Perrin, I don't think I believe the same as you," she said miserably. "So many things we debated, we were on opposite sides, except for the fourth debate. Rector Densal gave you *my* position. Otherwise—"

"No, no, no!" he cried and came around the chair to sit back down to face Mahrree. He leaned forward earnestly and was so close she could breathe in his earthy sweet scent.

She struggled to concentrate.

"Don't you remember?" he pleaded. "I've told you twice now, your mind is closer to mine that you realize. We're so alike. You defended every argument the way I would. I argued ideas, but not always *my* ideas. I've never believed the sky is *only* blue. In fact, the more I think about it, the more I'm convinced that it truly is black, and that the blue is an illusion. And that fourth debate, that's when you finally heard how I *really* feel. I told Hogal I wanted that position so that I could try to prove to you that I do believe in The Writings. I agree with you on everything. Except dogs. Dogs are far better than cats."

Sometime during his speech Mahrree's heart leaped to her throat making it very difficult for her to breathe. So she just hoped for what might come next. And hoped she wouldn't lose consciousness waiting.

Perrin gathered her small soft hands into his large rough ones.

The effect caused Mahrree to lose all ability to speak, had she been able to breathe.

"Mahrree, what I want to say is," he began, staring at their hands together, "why I am here is . . ." He looked up into her face. "You can see the direction all of this is going, right?"

Mahrree was sure she could, but she didn't feel it was her place to make this any easier. She smiled and shook her head. Besides, her lungs still couldn't function and everything was starting to go gray.

He took a deep breath, closed his eyes, and said, "Mahrree, may we continue our debates forever as husband and wife?" He peeked to gauge her response.

At least, she thought he did. Her eyes were too full of astonished tears to see him clearly. She nodded vigorously.

"Really?" Perrin asked, immense relief in his voice. "You don't want to have time to think about it?"

She thought briefly. She *didn't* want to think about it? Inexplicably, she felt no reservations—none at all. Instead she felt a great surge of peace and thought of how her father would approve. Somehow he was behind all of this, she was sure. Mahrree shook her head just as vigorously as she had nodded it.

"So I've actually rendered you speechless?!" Perrin grinned.

"Yes! Yes, you have!" Mahrree shouted.

"No, no, I haven't, I see," Perrin laughed. "But I think I know a way to keep you from speaking." He stood up and pulled her up too. He released her hands and moved his up to hold her face.

Mahrree panicked. She'd never kissed a man before, besides her father. And judging by the spark she saw in Perrin's eyes, she was fairly confident he was *not* expecting a quick peck on the cheek. As he bent closer to her, she trembled.

"WAIT!" she exclaimed. "Wait, I don't know what I'm doing."

Perrin stopped just inches from her face. "*What?*"

She squirmed. "I really don't know how to do this. I've never kissed a man before." Mahrree suspected this conversation wasn't going right.

Perrin relaxed, probably expecting to hear something worse. "Well, neither have I." He smiled and cocked his head. "Understand," he began patiently, but she took a nervous step back anyway as he kept his hold on her, "I haven't exactly spent the last few years doing this every day either. But I do know a few things," he continued. "And, well, I'm trying to kiss you for the first time, and, and . . . you begin with a *warning?*" Frustration grew in his eyes, dimming the spark.

"I thought you should know!" she whimpered.

He narrowed his eyes and spoke slowly. "I am trying to make you stop talking, for just . . . one . . . moment."

"*I know!*" Mahrree bellowed and bit her lip nervously. The longer she looked at him the worse she felt. She was going to lose him—she could feel it.

Perrin released her face and stepped back to study her. "This . . . this is . . . unexpected."

Mahrree cringed and wrung her hands. A first kiss was supposed to be instinctive and genuine—not, not *this*. She looked up at Perrin and realized he was as nervous as she was. How long had he been preparing for this moment, and she had knocked him off his course? She had no preparation at all!

He pressed his lips together and continued to analyze her.

Mahrree knew then that she'd ruined it all. Just as she had a most wonderful future in her grasp she was losing it because . . . because she was afraid that she didn't *know* how to do something? Stupid, she told herself. What was she—

She didn't get to the end of her mental chastisement.

Perrin stepped forward suddenly and wrapped his arms around her before she realized what he was doing. He mashed his mouth against hers before she could think about how to do it. She could think of nothing clearly, but in the stunned confusion of her mind was a sense of surprised bliss.

A few seconds later he pulled away. Keeping her in his grasp, he whispered, "Now, was that so difficult?"

"I'm not sure," she admitted. "It happened so fast. Can we try that again?"

"For my future *wife*, anything!" He grinned. "I have a feeling life with you will mean anticipating the unexpected, then finding my expectations exceeded in every possible way."

"That wasn't entirely coherent," she gently pointed out.

He sighed. "That's just what you do to me. As long as it's only you who knows what power you have over me, I should still be able to maintain my reputation."

Sometime during their long second attempt Mahrree decided that kissing him wasn't going to be difficult at all.

The rest of the evening they sat huddled together on the small sofa planning, discussing, and laughing. It felt surprisingly natural, as if they had always been this way. They decided that after such a public courtship, their marriage ceremony should be small and private with just Mahrree's mother, Rector Densal who would perform the ceremony, Tabbit Densal, and Perrin's parents, since the High General was planning to be in the area in about three moons to inspect the fort. To make up for the small ceremony, they decided to have a large celebration afterwards as was tradition in Edge, where everyone came with a dish of food to share along with a piece of useless advice.

Perrin left Mahrree's home that evening—to be his home as well in a season, they decided, since it was relatively close to the new fort—at an appropriate hour and with a stack of books.

Noticing the neighbors across the road sitting on their front porch to enjoy the surprisingly warm night air, he announced loudly, "Thank you for your information and time, *Miss* Mahrree. I'll enjoy reading these books."

Mahrree's neighbors, a middle-aged couple she'd known since she was a child, just smiled and nodded at him.

Then they winked at each other.

---

Lieutenant Karna was in the forward command office going over the next day's work assignments awaiting the return of the captain. Frequently the old sergeant major trotted up the stairs and raised his eyebrows in questioning.

"No third hole in the office . . . yet."

Wiles would chuckle all the way down the stairs.

The fourth time Wiles came up the stairs, looking a bit tired from his journeys, he plopped down on one of the chairs by the large work desk. "Whew! Now I know why I never married and had children." He took off his cap to smooth his thin, gray hair. "Waiting up for them is exhausting."

Karna grinned. "Wiles, I can just let you know when he comes in."

Wiles smiled slyly at him. "Getting rather late now, Lieutenant. My guess is, it's been a successful evening, and he's not coming in until morning."

Karna shook his head. "The captain's not that kind of man, Sergeant Major. I know him. And he'll be back up here before he retires for the night to brief the night shift."

Wiles sniggered and put a boot casually on the corner of the desk. "You haven't been in the army as long as I have, Lieutenant. I see now why Chairman Mal *himself* said my wisdom was needed up here." He puffed up his narrow chest. "I suppose if I weren't so wise, I'd have been given a position somewhere warmer. But, the High General agreed with Mal, and so I'm here to teach all of you boys a thing or two. Here's your first lesson: no man is exactly as he presents himself. There's the public man, and then there's the private man. Shin puts up an excellent public front. I've heard he handled himself quite well at those debates, and so far the village seems completely enamored with him. So likely is that lovely young woman. But privately, Shin's a man with *needs*, Lieutenant. And when an animal feels a need . . ." He raised his eyebrows and leered. "Now, you just run along to your quarters. I'll brief the night shift. Shin will be back in the morning—"

"Shin's back right now!"

The voice booming up from the stairs made both of the soldiers jump in their seats. Wiles put his foot back properly on the ground before Captain Shin strode up to the office. He was wearing a black tunic, trousers, a leather jacket, and a small smile that refused to be suppressed.

Karna shot Wiles a look of, *I told you so.*

Shin casually picked up a piece of paper from the desk and glanced at it. "Thought I wouldn't be back to do my duty for the night shift, Wiles?"

"No, sir!" the sergeant major said. "It's just that . . . I, uh . . ."

Shin looked up him. "Leave the two holes in the wall, for now. Rather like them. They're only through the first layer of wall anyway, and not the second. And no, there won't be a third hole. Karna," he turned to his lieutenant who had a cautious smile on his face. "If you wish, in about three moons you can move into my quarters. They're a little larger."

Karna grinned. "And why won't you be sleeping there anymore, sir?"

Shin tried to keep his smile down, but failed. "I think *my wife* will prefer that I spend my nights at our home instead."

Wiles clapped his hands loudly and stood up. "Knew it! Well done, Captain." He shook Shin's hand and slapped him on the shoulder.

Karna chuckled. "Sir, that's . . . that's good news. Rather sudden, don't you think?"

Shin's smile faded a little. "Uh, well, perhaps. That's why the three moons' time, Brillen."

"I can't wait to hear what the village will say," Karna said. "Marrying one of their own? That's certainly a way to win hearts and minds."

Karna and Wiles laughed together as Shin reddened.

"Well, the High General will certainly be impressed," Wiles hinted.

Shin went a deeper shade of burgundy. "The High General . . ." He stared at the floor.

Wiles and Karna shared a look of concern.

"When do you plan to tell him?" Wiles asked quietly.

Shin blinked and looked up. "Soon, soon. Listen, we'd really like to keep this quiet for a while. I told only the two of you so that you can . . . understand. But please, let *us* reveal it when the time is right."

"Of course, sir," Karna answered.

Wiles nodded slowly. "Captain, I'm glad you told us. Now that she's someone important to you, she *may* become someone important to the Guarders."

Shin let out a low whistle. "Hadn't considered that either."

Wiles patted him on the back. "We can take care of that, Captain. Soldiers need to start patrolling in the village, too. We'll simply put your future home on the routes. In fact, as an early wedding gift, show me right now where she lives." He pulled out a clean sheet of paper and a piece of sharpened charcoal. "We can put her road on the routes. Don't worry, I won't say anything to the soldiers until you want us to. But we'll keep her safe."

Shin smiled. "Thank you, Wiles. That'll make me feel better, until I'm living there." He started sketching out a rough map of the northern village. "She's on the second ring of houses, just off the main fort road. Barely a quarter mile away from the fort."

"That's convenient." Karna nodded at the map.

"And she hasn't even seen the fort, yet," Shin said, shaking his head and chuckling. "And didn't even know the soldiers came in! Have to give her a tour sometime, I suppose." He made a notation for her house.

"Doesn't she have a mother, Captain?" Wiles gestured to the map.

Shin nodded. "I've only heard about her, but yes. I better put her mother's on here, too. Just so Mahrree feels she's protected. Good idea, Wiles. Now, according to the Densals, Mrs. Peto is on the third ring, on the other side of the fort road . . . one of these two houses. Both have elaborate gardens, so I'm not sure which." He paused, wondering which house to mark.

"You're not sure which house is your future *mother-in-law's*, Captain?" Wiles scowled good-naturedly.

Shin paled at the phrase *mother-in-law*.

Karna covered his grin with his hand, while Wiles chortled. "We'll just put that entire road on the routes and mark both houses. Now that I think about it, isn't that aunt and uncle of yours along the same area?"

Shin eagerly made some more notations on the map, further west. "Densals, right there. Again, good idea, Wiles. Thank you."

Wiles smiled as he took up the map. "Just doing my duty, sir. And again, congratulations. You're going to make many people happy. Now I'm glad I'm all the way in the north. I'm beginning to see the appeal."

Karna laughed as Shin glared affably at the old sergeant major.

# Chapter 12 ~ "We've done this kind of backward, haven't we?"

Mahrree thought she'd never fall asleep that night. She didn't feel the bed under her, the small one she'd have to replace. The elevated wooden frame it sat on, so that she could store lessons in crates underneath, would also need to be lengthened to accommodate Perrin's size. But she couldn't dwell on that for too long, because so many things raced through her mind as they had nonstop for the past three hours since Perrin left.

Since her *future husband* left.

Every time she had that thought, she grabbed her pillow and screamed into it. If anyone had been passing by and heard her, they would have been alarmed, and then perplexed to hear her laughing right after. Mahrree didn't know how to appropriately express her excitement, but she decided it didn't matter, as long as she was able to compose herself by morning before she faced her students, especially her teenage girls. Although they never said a word, they'd regarded her with pity for weeks.

She couldn't reveal her news, though. She and Perrin had agreed to keep their engagement to themselves, just for now. Neither of them was quite ready to deal with the village's reactions, which undoubtedly would result in a bit of teasing with some leading comments. And Edgers' comments could also be a bit *unrefined* at times.

One thing that kept Mahrree's mind occupied that sleepless night was how to expand the house. She had a 'singles' house which she adored. When Mahrree was eight she watched her father and other villagers build it years ago for an elderly widow. She was impressed that even with his slight build and small frame Cephas could move the large rocks and position them in just the right way to make the smoothest interior walls. She often looked up from her reading at the table at the rocks she knew her father had carefully placed. Her bookshelves fit perfectly against his structure. As Mahrree now lay in bed and looked up at the pitched eaves of the roof, she smiled as she remembered helping her father carry smaller pieces of wood up for the cozy bedroom.

The villagers would come again to add on another room since she was adding a new family member, because cozy also meant cramped. Perhaps she would add a study for Perrin. Her land was small, but it might as well all be taken up by house. If she ever wanted a garden she could rent out space in the farms that surrounded the village as a buffer from the forest. She wouldn't need to worry about Guarders because she would be protected by her husband.

*Her husband!*

She grabbed her pillow and screamed again into it with delight.

Only then did she realize she hadn't completed reading The Writings.

*Dear Creator*, she thought. *I am so sorry! I fully intended to—*

A great warmth of comfort enveloped her with the message,

> *You can finish tomorrow, then begin again to take notes on what your children should know.*

The thought struck her so unexpectedly that she nearly fell of the bed. Which children? Her school children or . . . ?

The idea was too wonderful. She'd stopped thinking years ago that she would ever have her own children, and now the idea energized her so much she could barely stay in bed. She had to finish reading The Writings in the small hours of the morning.

But before she could get up, the lateness of the hour and the exhilaration of the evening abruptly collided in her brain, and soon she fell into a shockingly restful sleep.

Then Mahrree found herself sitting before a large wooden home, made of pine planking that had weathered into a soft gray. The entire area was ringed by tall mountains she didn't recognize, and around her were a dozen or more children running and laughing. She was sitting in dry dirt, and felt the heat of the sun beating gently down upon her. She looked around, perplexed and intrigued.

She was in a very large garden, and she was pulling weeds. Willingly.

And she was inexplicably happy.

She woke up from the dream laughing.

---

In the middle of the night, in a large house in Grasses, a father woke up in bed to find a figure standing over him, holding a jagged blade. Before he could cry out, the blade plunged into his heart.

His wife, in bed next to him, didn't hear it. She was already dead.

The man holding the jagged knife, dressed in black and with his face darkened with soot, nodded to his companion that the room was secured. Together they crept down a hallway and flung open the door. They sheathed their knives and pulled out thick wooden clubs.

Then they walked up to the bed where the young woman slept.

---

In the early morning Mahrree rushed to her table to finish reading before school began. She quickly thumbed to the last four pages, but instead The Writings fell open to the very last page, and she found herself staring at the final words of the Creator, revealed to Guide Pax:

> *Before the Last Day even the aged of my people will strike terror in the deadened hearts of the fiercest soldiers.*
>
> *On the Last Day those who have no power shall discover the greatest power is all around them.*
>
> *On the Last Day those who stayed true to the Plan will be delivered as the destroyer comes.*
>
> *I have created this Test, I have given this Plan, and I will reward my faithful children.*

Mahrree stared at the last passage for several moments, unable to move. The words, which she'd read dozens of times before, now struck her with such unexpected force that she wondered why she never felt the power of them before. She didn't just read them, she *felt* the reality of them—as if they were said directly to her—and she thought she could actually see that day right before her, if only she knew how to focus her eyes properly.

She was glad that she couldn't.

It was almost a full minute before she could finally do something, and it was just to say, "Hmm."

Eventually she closed The Writings and smirked guiltily. How fortunate she didn't punctuate last night's glorious evening with such a dreary exclamation mark. She sighed, shook off the ominous feeling, smiled, and opened the book again to the beginning.

*We are all family.*

Her new one would be starting soon.

She shrieked again for joy.

---

That morning in Grasses, the large fort was in complete upheaval. Hundreds of soldiers ran throughout the village looking for more victims, law enforcers brought reports to the colonel that at least half a dozen homes had been hit, and the fort's surgeon worked tirelessly to save the life of a young woman who had been beaten by what appeared to be wooden clubs.

Her intended, the lieutenant of the fort, sat in an adjacent room, weeping quietly.

The captain of the fort joined him, sent by the colonel, but he could only sit and stare in disbelief. Both of his parents were dead, and now his younger sister was lying near death. Later he collapsed, overwhelmed by grief.

The colonel frantically got off brief messages to every fort in the world and to the garrison in Idumea, with a promise of more details to follow. But for now, everyone in the world had to know as quickly as possible.

The Guarders were officially back, and more violent than ever.

---

It was the last day of school, and Mahrree found it even harder than her students to concentrate as they pored over their final writings to present to their parents that afternoon. The day moved excruciatingly slowly. She'd had only a few hours of sleep and couldn't think of anything else but Perrin. He was to return that evening to join her for dinner, and she worried over what to prepare for their first meal together, even though at this time of year it was rarely anything different than bread, cheese, and early greens.

The only sound in the classroom was the scritching of quills on parchment as her eight students wrote. If she put her quill to any parchment, she feared she would juvenilely practice writing "Mrs. Mahrree Shin." So instead she just stared at the door and daydreamed about a tall, muscular, and not-unpleasant-looking captain.

Until he stood right there, having abruptly opened the door.

Mahrree blinked to make sure she actually saw him.

Captain Shin stared back. "Miss Peto, five minutes please?"

Her heart sank. He wasn't the laughing, affectionate man that left her house last night—he was far too serious and intense. Maybe he'd had a change of heart and was there to tell her it was all just a big mistake.

"Good afternoon, Captain Shin!" eight girls chorused together in a singsong voice.

Captain Shin looked over to the girls seated behind their desks, noticing them for the first time. "Good afternoon, girls. Ladies. *Young* ladies." His eyebrows furrowed over figuring out which label was appropriate.

Mahrree blushed as the girls erupted into giggles.

Captain Shin's severe demeanor softened a little with a faint smile in their direction. Then he turned back to Mahrree, again completely somber. "Miss Mahrree? *Now?*"

Mahrree nodded and stood up, feeling weak and confused. If he was going to call it off, why would he do it right now? She followed him outside the door, her stomach twisting in dread. He didn't stop in the grassy area in front of the small school building, but continued over to a storage shed partially secluded by blossoming apple trees. He opened the door to the shed and, while looking around, cocked his head toward the door indicating that she should go in.

Completely baffled at his behavior, she complied. He didn't shut the door—there wouldn't have been enough room for him among the rakes and buckets if he did—but looked around the grounds once more before finally turning to her.

She wrung her hands in worry.

"Ah, Mahrree!" he breathed, releasing all tension from his face. He stepped closer and wrapped his arms around her, pulling her into him.

"Wait a minute," she giggled in relief. "You just pulled me away from my class for a *hug?*"

"And this, too." He kissed her so ardently that she would have forgiven him of anything.

"Mmm, good thing today is the last day of school." She chuckled as he finally released her. "Can't have you coming by and doing this every day. People will start to talk."

He chuckled too, but rather mirthlessly, and suddenly turned grim. "And I came to give you this as well." He pulled something long from the inside of his uniform jacket. In the dim light of the shed she wasn't sure what it was until he put it into her hands.

"It's a rod of iron," she said tonelessly. "Is this some kind of army thing? I know occasionally men give their intendeds jewelry, but—"

"Mahrree, just minutes ago a messenger arrived from Grasses. The Guarders have attacked."

Mahrree bit her lower lip.

He put his arms around her again, and she sank into him. "Not only that, but they attacked the intended of the lieutenant there. He was to marry the sister of the captain."

"Oh Perrin . . ."

"They killed the captain's parents and brutally beat the young woman," he said quietly. "Grasses' commanding officer wrote that the surgeons aren't sure if she'll survive."

Mahrree clutched the iron rod and tears squeezed out of her eyes. What had she just agreed to last night? Becoming the next victim?

"I want you to hold on to this rod and keep it next to your bed," he whispered softly, holding her tighter. "They attacked at night, which is their typical pattern. I really don't think anything will happen here, but I'll sleep better at night knowing you have some sort of defense."

"They're really real, aren't they?" she whispered into his chest, all doubt fleeing. She knew she'd be lighting extra candles and keeping them in a few windows all night long. Suddenly she understood why the simple-minded and gullible of Edge did that: not to ward away Guarders, but to make it harder for them to see what was lurking around outside in the dark. The reflections of the light on the wavy windows obscured everything on the other side.

She wondered if she had enough candles.

"Yes, they *are* real," Perrin said in a low, dreadful tone. "And very effective. They hit at least six houses last night. Probably more. Grasses is large, and they were still surveying the area when they sent out the message. The captain's family lived in the middle of the village, not on the outskirts. The Guarders had to venture quite a ways to get there, and it seems they chose that house deliberately. None of the Guarders was captured."

Perrin squeezed her tighter. It was getting hard to breathe, but she didn't mind.

Abruptly he stepped back. "I need to get to the fort. Lots to do right now. I'm running extra drills in sword work this afternoon. Suddenly all of the soldiers are taking it much more seriously." He smiled, but it wasn't genuine. "We really have nothing to worry about. Guarders aren't anywhere near Edge, and my sergeant major is arranging for patrols in the village. The first begin tonight, and your road is on it. You'll be fine, Mahrree."

She didn't think so. She looked into his face, pleading for him to take her with him to the fort, but not daring to say the words.

"My five minutes are up, and your students will be talking. I'll see you in just a few hours for dinner, then I'll be there all evening. We should take measurements of your windows and doors," he decided. "I'll have the fort blacksmith create some reinforcements to make entry more difficult."

He paused.

"Maybe we should move up the wedding. We really don't need three moons, do we?"

Mahrree felt a flush of panic. Maybe he didn't need that much time to prepare, but she certainly did. "We shouldn't move it up just because of this. Besides, your parents can't come any earlier, can they?"

He sighed. "My father's schedule is usually set at least half a year in advance. There's no way he could change it. Unless we went to Idumea—No!" he declared immediately. "Absolutely not. We'll just keep to what we decided last night. You'll be fine."

He kissed her again and hastily darted out of the shed, leaving her to hold the rod.

Mahrree stared at the crude weapon, and her belly aching with worry. She couldn't exactly walk into the classroom holding the iron. She tried slipping it into her sleeve, but it was too long and extended beyond her elbow. She slipped the rod down into her skirt and secured it in the ties for her stockings. If she sat down just right, she wouldn't stab herself. She giggled uncomfortably at the position of the rod, then giggled again at the look on Perrin's face when he first kissed her. Then she giggled again out of sheer nervousness.

She couldn't remember *ever* giggling before she met Captain Perrin Shin.

Mahrree stepped out of the shed, knowing she had to get back to her class before they started asking too many questions. But she couldn't push away the heavy thoughts about the fort at Grasses, or the realization that this time it *was* real. She could see in Perrin's eyes that even he was surprised. The attack wasn't controlled by kings as a convenient show of force, but was instead something much darker and threatening. It followed her like a black cloud as she walked gingerly back to her class, hoping the rod wouldn't slip.

When Mahrree opened the door she saw eight eager faces.

"Well?" Teeria said.

Mahrree couldn't even muster a smile. "The answer to your question a few weeks ago: Yes, Captain Shin would kill a Guarder to protect the village. Protecting all of us is his duty."

"Nothing *else*, Miss Mahrree?"

"You have essays to write, girls."

---

When evening finally arrived, Perrin stood at the door and knocked formally with his foot, since his arms were full of books.

Mahrree, who'd been jittery as she walked through the market that afternoon, even though she knew Guarders attacked only at night, was anxious to see him. But she was slightly disappointed he was out of uniform again. He seemed a little more vulnerable without his sword. But at his trousers' waistband she saw what looked like the handle of a knife sticking out above his hip.

She smiled and announced loudly, in case any neighbors were in earshot, "Ah, Captain Shin! Have you finished these books already? My, my. Do come in to get some more."

Perrin rolled his eyes at her terrible acting and walked in. He dropped the books on top of the table and Mahrree gasped.

"What's wrong?"

"The . . ." Mahrree began to laugh and covered her mouth. "The . . . *bread!* You dropped the books on the bread. You flattened it again!"

Perrin looked down and saw that what he thought was bundled cloth actually contained a fresh loaf of bread from the bakers. The top was squeezing out under the pressure of the books and split open like a wound.

"Uh," he lifted up the books and looked around for another place to put them. Since most of the surface of the table was covered in student writings, he settled for a chair.

Mahrree removed the cloth from the squashed bread. "Well, you said you liked flattened bread, remember?" She smiled as she held up the misshapen loaf. "Now it's time to see how honest you are."

"I promise to be as honest as I can be," he said solemnly. Then with a wink he added, "From now on." He kissed her and tore off a large piece of bread. "Now I can get more into my mouth at one time," and he shoved it all in his mouth.

"Oh," Mahrree snickered. "That behavior isn't acceptable, even in Edge! It's fortunate for *you* that I didn't share my bread with you that night before the fifth debate. I would never let you back into my house again. This day is filling up with all kinds of surprises about what it will mean to be your wife."

"I'm sure you'll surprise me with your fair share as well," Perrin garbled with a full mouth. "Any blob for dinner?"

After dinner—a safe assortment of cheeses, fresh greens, dried beef, and flattened bread—they stepped out on to the back porch. Mahrree shut her back door, and Perrin's hand rose and brushed against hers.

Oh dear, Mahrree thought. She forgot about that. People who are intended tend to hold hands.

In public.

To show they are . . .

She really wasn't quite sure *why*, but he likely expected her to grasp his hand, which she did.

"Uh," he said, staring at their hands together. "*No.*"

Mahrree blushed in embarrassment as he gently pulled his rough hand away. It continued to rise to point to the metal locking latch on her door. "I was trying to point to that. Are you going to lock it?"

Mahrree's embarrassment vanished and she chuckled at the old lock. "Are you serious?"

"Do you really not remember what just happened last night? In Grasses?"

"No, I remember," she said, much more subdued. "Quite vividly. Tomorrow you tell the rest of the village?"

"When the rest of the details come in, yes. So lock your door, Mahrree."

She wondered if he practiced that authoritative tone, or if he just naturally sounded commanding by lowering his already deep voice. However he did it, he was chillingly effective.

Mahrree opened the door again, removed the iron key hanging on an old nail by the door, and shut the door again.

Perrin was rubbing his forehead earnestly when she looked up at him. "Do *not* tell me you keep the key to your door on a nail *by the door!*"

Mahrree fumbled with the lock, since she'd worked it only a handful of times. "Then I also won't tell you that this key is identical to everyone else's in this half of Edge, since the same blacksmith made all of our locks years ago and knew only one way to do so."

Perrin groaned.

Before Mahrree could pocket the key, he caught her hand. "Now, unlock the door."

"But I just—"

"Humor me," he said in the official monotone he used during the debates. "Unlock the door."

Mahrree exhaled in exasperation and unlocked it. "See? I *do* know how to work it—"

"Now," he ordered in full commander style, "walk into your house, up to the front door, and lock *that* door."

Mahrree's mouth dropped open. If he dared to interrupt her one more time . . . "What makes you think that door isn't—"

"I noticed it when I came in tonight. Besides, if you don't lock your back door, then you likely don't lock the front, either. Go. *Lock it.*"

He has a point, Mahrree thought grudgingly as she stepped back into the house. She decided she couldn't be angry about his cutting her off, because, well, her front door *wasn't* locked.

She quickly made her way to it, fought the rusted lock for a moment to get it to twist, then hurried to the back door.

Guarders *are* back. Edge *isn't* the same. The world *is* changing, today.

She closed the back door behind her and dutifully locked it as Perrin watched.

"Remind me to oil your front lock when we get back," he said.

"How did you know—"

"I could hear your grunting to turn it all the way out here." His commanding voice had faded away, replaced by a decidedly amused tone.

Mahrree cringed as they started out the back gate.

"Also understand," he continued, much more warmly, "that I'm not really the type to hold a woman's hand."

"Of course," Mahrree said, slightly relieved that she didn't have to engage in that juvenile behavior, but also mysteriously disappointed.

"It's because I'm a soldier," he told her. "I need to keep my sword hand free."

"But you're not wearing your sword," she pointed out.

"Then it's my knife hand."

"I see," she said. "So is your left hand ever free?"

"Sorry," he said, and seemed like he meant it. "But that's my two hand."

"Your what?"

"You really don't know anything about soldiers, do you?" He smiled.

"And who would have taught me?"

He chuckled. "First lesson, right now." He stopped in the alley and held up his right hand. "Sword hand. If no sword, then knife hand." Faster than she could follow the movement, his hand slipped under his jacket and shirt and came back out with a knife that had been tucked into his waistband on his hip.

She'd heard of long knives. But this massive blade had ambitions to be a short sword, and she marveled that he was able to sit down without slicing any important anatomy.

"First thrust, with the blade."

He lunged at an imaginary threat, and Mahrree instinctively leaned back. He relaxed his stance.

"Most people think that's where it's all at—in the blade. That kind of thinking works for you. They're watching the blade, not the *two* hand."

He held up his left hand and formed a fist. She'd seen him do that before, during a debate.

"First thrust, then comes the second hand with its accompanying hit. One, *two*." He lunged again with the knife, then followed up with punch at his invisible enemy.

Mahrree winced.

He smiled at her proudly and held up his hands. "I need them both. Sorry, but I *am* here to defend Edge first, and be your intended second. That's just the way it is. I know it's not ideal, but can you live with that?"

Knowing that she likely didn't fully comprehend what that meant, she shrugged back. "Yes, but you know we do have law enforcement too," she reminded him. "They're supposed to defend Edge. You're supposed to defend *the border* to Edge."

He scoffed at that. "They bring drunks home, break up fights between cats, and occasionally catch a thief. If your enforcers are anything like those I've seen elsewhere in the world, half of them don't dare to use the wooden club they carry, while the other half look for any excuse to wallop something. I, however," he said with a return to the official voice, "will truly protect Edge. All of it, and from threats bigger than mouthy teenagers."

Mahrree couldn't help but grin. He really meant it. Someone more cynical—rather like her just a few weeks ago—would have thought he was too well indoctrinated in Command School, but he truly believed it. He *would* protect Edge.

His eyebrows furrowed. "Why are you smiling like that?"

She wasn't sure what response he'd expected from his little speech, but smiling obviously wasn't it. "I'm just glad I have you by my side tonight."

He squinted suspiciously at her, but she squeezed his ample arm. "Now, we were planning to go somewhere, remember? You're going to show me just how brave you are, Captain Shin. Right?"

His squint disappeared as he winked at her. He replaced his knife in his waistband and they left the alley for the main road.

They headed east, receiving stares and a few waves from several people sitting on their front porches to enjoy another warm Planting Season evening. It wasn't going quite as they'd planned. They had hoped everyone would be at the amphitheater. But tonight's entertainment must not have been as amusing as Mahrree and Perrin's awkwardness in trying to walk together without looking like they were walking *together*.

They felt a bit deceitful not telling anyone about their engagement. But now with the knowledge that the Guarders had attacked, it seemed necessary to leak the news ahead of Captain Shin's announcement to Edge tomorrow evening about the raid in Grasses, just so that the neighbors could help keep a careful eye on Mahrree's house.

Mahrree noticed that Perrin kept a hand close by his side where the long knife was secreted. He not only looked around at the neighbors, he was looking in their bushes as they walked.

There was one simple way to let the entire world know about their intentions without Perrin or Mahrree having to say anything to anyone.

Mahrree took a bracing breath as she led Perrin up the gravel path along a garden that was perfectly symmetrical in its pattern of flowers, color, and rock. She raised her hand to knock on the elaborately painted door. The lavender of it matched the lavender flowers growing in the lavender stained pots on either side.

She turned to Perrin with her hand still in the air. "Are you ready—*truly ready*—for this?"

"No, truly not," he admitted. "But I wasn't entirely ready for last night, either, and the results were satisfactory." He squeezed her other hand in encouragement, but quickly released it and looked around for any threats. Or maybe witnesses.

Mahrree knocked loudly on the door and held her breath.

The door swept open a moment later and Hycymum Peto stood there with a look of astonishment on her face. She glanced at her daughter's face, then Perrin's, and squealed so loudly that she made the captain jump. "Oh! Happy day! It is, is it not, a VERY HAPPY DAY?!"

"Yes, Mother, it is," Mahrree said hurriedly and pushed Hycymum with gentle force into the house. With her free hand she grabbed Perrin's arm and dragged him in. "Shut the door before the Arkys come running from next door," she commanded, and he obeyed.

Mahrree had once watched a fat cat scrabble unsuccessfully to climb a massive boulder, much to her amusement. She was wise enough, however, not to laugh as her short round mother tried to embrace Perrin the boulder. He remained stiff, unrelenting, and—smartly—silent as his future mother-in-law affectionately mauled him in her joy. Only once did he glance at Mahrree with a long-suffering look that said, *Yes, I still want to marry you.*

It took nearly an hour to calm Hycymum down, then another half hour to convince her that a small private ceremony was all they wanted. They readily agreed, however, to let her organize the celebration meal after. Hycymum was satisfied only when Mahrree also agreed to let her decorate the addition to their home.

But Mahrree stopped short of letting her embellish the fort, for which Perrin gave her a most grateful look.

For most of the evening he just sat silently on the lace covered sofa with a pained smile on his face, watching the two women bicker and compromise.

As he walked her home that evening in the growing dark he had only one comment. "You take after your father, don't you? I'll have to thank him for that when I get to the other side."

"I suppose I should have warned you more about her." Mahrree bit her lip. "I guess I didn't tell you enough last night."

He nodded. "There are probably a few things about me you should know, too."

"Such as, what *your* parents are like?"

"Oh, you won't have to worry about them—they're great."

"Hmm," she said, unconvinced. Her pace slowed a little. "Your father is the High General. So was your grandfather."

His pace slowed even more. "Yes. Is that a problem?"

"I don't know. Is it?"

He stopped completely and looked around at the dark neighborhood.

Mahrree watched him anxiously. Despite the shadows she could see concern in his face.

"We've done this kind of backward, haven't we?" he said. "We probably should have discussed a few more things before we, um . . ."

Mahrree nodded. "Well, I've never become engaged before. I think we did that part right. It's the 'getting to know you' part we kind of skipped."

He nodded back, took her arm, and started walking back to her house. "Uh, Mahrree, considering everything, I'd understand if you now think that maybe you don't . . . it's not too late to change your mind, about . . ."

"You're right," she cut him off. She didn't want him to say it. "It's not too late for us to start getting to know each other."

Then she was struck with a terrible thought.

"Unless *you*, uh . . ."

Perrin chuckled quietly. "No. I can't understand why, but I've never felt more sure of a decision than this. I don't think anyone else could stand being my wife. Just remember to lock the doors."

Mahrree sighed and giggled. She realized giggling was now just a part of her life. "I'll try, and I feel the same way too. You may be the only man in the world who can tolerate me. You dealt with my mother quite well."

"In my negotiations class we learned when it's time to step away from the conversation. Silence seemed to be the best tactic."

She laughed. "Just remember that."

"I have a plan," he announced cheerfully. "Tomorrow night, when I come back from the fort, we'll resolve this. Make a list of questions. I'll make one too. Everything we need to know. Then we can start negotiations."

"Yes, sir!"

"Oh, I like the sound of that," he said as they continued to walk to her home.

"Oh, and I didn't," she laughed. "That's the last time you'll hear me call you 'sir'."

"Fair enough. I don't think I could order you around. You wouldn't obey anyway, would you?"

"Only if you're right. If you aren't right, well then, we go to negotiations."

"I should probably tell you I received my lowest marks in that class. Got the highest marks in command, tactics, training—but negotiations? A little worse than Officers' Charm School, as you called it. Let's just say I do better with a sword in hand."

"If you're as stubborn as I am, then tomorrow night you should maybe leave that sword at the fort again."

# Chapter 13 ~ "Love is just a cover-up. Always is."

Two men sat in the dark office of an unlit building.

The first older man smiled. "Enough information coming in for you yet?"

His partner scoffed a chuckle as he sifted through the pages on his lap. "And this is just from the first day! So many people, so many different reactions. You were right about not killing off the girl. Watching how others deal with the uncertainty of her future will yield volumes of information."

The first man nodded his fluffy white hair. "Well, enjoy yourself. By the time the situation in Grasses reaches a conclusion, we should have enough details to keep us occupied for half a year. And no one will be bothered by letters from that captain's father complaining how the new herd production mandates lost him his ranch. Moving to a village isn't so bad, now is it? Being near his son? Oh wait—I guess it is *now.*"

The first man laughed callously while the second man just nodded.

"Ah, my friend—just show me another research project as fulfilling as this promises to be."

The second man held up a finger. He put down the stack of papers and reached over to retrieve a document he had placed on a shelf behind him. He leaned over and handed it to the older man.

He held it up in the dim light and squinted. "What is this? Looks like a map of some sort."

"You just said, show you another project . . ."

Out of his shirt pocket the older man pulled out a warped piece of glass he used to make the markings on the page appear larger. "A map of Edge?"

"Yes. I have some more news for you to further improve your day. If you thought the raid was a triumphant success, wait till you hear this: Captain Perrin Shin intends to marry!"

The first man was stunned silent for nearly a full minute. "Marry?"

"You always say he surprises you . . ."

"That can't be right! For as long as I've known Perrin I've known he's not been the marrying type. Before he even arrived at the university his reputation preceded him. Graduating men went to that eighteen-year-old for advice on women, but he'd never share his secrets. I have no doubt he left Vines because the women were chasing him out."

His partner squinted. "And that's why he requested the transfer out of Vines?"

The first man pointed. "He's got himself in trouble, he has! Perrin's become sloppy. Now he has to marry some senseless village girl to cover for his mistakes."

"He hasn't been there long enough to have to force a marriage," the second man concluded. "According to the message that came with the map, he's marrying the woman he debated in the village amphitheater. The rather vocal one? Trying to win hearts and minds, all that."

"*Win hearts!*" the first man disparaged. "That's not Perrin. *Break* hearts—that's Perrin. He's a bull in a pasture full of cows, ready to—Ah, I see it now. He's actually in trouble in *Vines*, and using some hapless girl in Edge to cover for it. If he's already married, no one else can lay claim to him as father of her child."

The second man sighed. "Does it really matter why he's marrying?"

"It does!" The first man pounded the padded armrest of his chair. "Every action people take is in response to something else."

His partner shrugged. "Have you considered that maybe he fell in love?"

"Love is not involved here. Love is just a cover-up. Always is. I realize you're married, but you must confess that at the basest of emotions, it's the physical drives that deluded you into thinking there was an emotional counterpart. Animals don't love."

The second man held up a finger. "But many animals mate for life. Wolves and falcons, for example, create a bond that—"

"*Bond*, yes," the older man interrupted. "But love? That's the word we attach to 'bond' to create romantic nonsense so that women feel better for giving in to men's basest desires."

"And to think you never married," the second man said, almost sincerely. When the older man only glared at him, he continued. "So I'm assuming Captain Shin hasn't told Father and Mother about his intended. According to the message, he's been so obvious the rumors should have flown all the way to Idumea by now."

The first man nodded. "I'll keep my ear tuned to the wind. And this map?"

His partner smiled, anticipating the reaction. "Notations of where Captain Shin's intended, her mother, and Shin's great aunt and uncle live. So that patrols can watch their houses *more closely.*"

The first man threw back his head and laughed. "Wonderful! Fantastic man we have up there in Edge, to get such vital information so quickly."

The second man cringed. "I still have my doubts about him, considering his age—"

"But I told you, didn't I? Didn't I say he'd be the best fit?"

The second nodded reluctantly. "True."

"So many new questions we can test now," the first man mused. "Where to begin? He's losing his edge in Edge. And I thought he'd be so much more of a challenge. Well, perhaps it's time to see just how sloppy Shin is."

The second man shook his head. "I don't think we should start anything new until we see if the girl in Grasses survives. The captain and the lieutenant are taking the news harder than I expected. I'd hate to miss any details by beginning something with Shin."

The first man shrugged. "You may have a point about Grasses. That situation could provide an intriguing contrast once Shin is married: the reaction of an *intended* losing his woman, versus the reaction of a *husband* losing his wife. Since you mentioned wolves, it's been my observation that wolves become protective of their mates once they are acquired, and act more aggressive when they sense a threat to their pack. Perhaps our next question will be, Might Shin be a wolf?"

---

Early in the morning Captain Shin stood with his hands on his waist at the edge of the forest. He stared hard into it, trying to discern if the rising sun might expose different sections. The view would be different, though, just a little ways—

"Captain? You sent for me?"

Shin pulled his gaze from the trees. "Lieutenant Karna, yes. I want you to stand right here and record what I call back to you."

He picked up some paper and charcoal from the ground and handed them to the younger officer. "I have an idea," and the captain started walking toward the forest.

"SIR!" Karna exclaimed as his commander continued into the woods. "Sir, *STOP!*"

Shin stopped and turned, about ten paces in. "Karna, it's just *trees.* I've been watching the spot for past twenty minutes. The ground's stable, there's no quaking or sulfur—"

Karna looked around him frantically, hoping someone from the fort would notice his panic. "Sir, you *cannot* do this! The first rule of the Army of Idumea explicitly states that—"

"'—No officer, enlisted man, or citizen of the world is to enter the forests for any purpose.'" He sighed impatiently. "Yes, yes, yes, I know. My grandfather Pere wrote that rule. But Karna, consider this: the Guarders are adept at making themselves hidden at night, lurking in bushes, wearing all black. But that won't work in the forest. Brillen—"

The young lieutenant's eyes darted back and forth, hoping someone older, braver—or just ornerier—would realize that the captain was violating the first rule.

"Brillen?"

Karna looked back at Shin.

The captain was inexplicably calm. "Think about it—wearing all black *in the forest*? You know how easy they'd be to spot? And I doubt they move carefully in the trees. They know we can't go in here—it's been forbidden for over one hundred years. So why would they practice moving quietly in here? Bushes rustle, leaves and sticks snap—we could track them, *in the forest*, Lieutenant! We could find their hideouts."

"Sir, please," Karna glanced over at the fort again. "You're making me very nervous."

Shin marched out of the trees to his lieutenant, who began to breathe easier as soon as the captain's boots hit the grasses. "There's nothing inherently wrong with the trees. I *know* it, Brillen," he whispered earnestly. "I can prove that—"

"Captain Shin!"

The bellow made both officers spin around.

Sergeant Major Wiles was jogging toward them, shaking his gray head. "Captain, did I just see you—or maybe it was a remnant of last night's mead—but I could have sworn I saw you come out of the forest."

Karna bobbed his head back and forth toward the disobedient captain. It was Karna's lucky day. Old, brave, *and* ornery had arrived just in time.

Captain Shin sighed as if he was a child caught stealing a sweet from a confectionary shop. "I was just trying to prove that—"

"—that the son of the High General can get killed by Guarders too?" Wiles shouted.

Shin puffed up. "Look, Sergeant Major, I don't need you to—"

Wiles waved an official parchment in his face. "Just arrived last night. You didn't read it yet, did you? Allow me: 'From General Aldwyn Cush, Advising General to High General Relf Shin. Restating the importance of soldiers and officers, now that the Guarders have attacked, to STAY OUT OF

THE FORESTS—'"

Shin rubbed his forehead. "All right, all right . . . yes I saw Cush's message. But if I had the chance to prove that—"

"Prove nothing, Shin!" Wiles shouted at the commander. "Or I'll send a report to your father and have you shipped back to Idumea before your future bride can finish wiping her tears."

Shin folded his arms. "You can't do that!"

"No, but your father can! The same messenger that's leaving this afternoon to carry your good news to him can also bring news from me about his son's blatant disregard for the number one rule of the army."

Shin growled under his breath.

Wiles sighed and put a grandfatherly hand on his arm. "All of us are upset about the attack in Grasses," he said in a soothing tone. "Fourteen houses hit? Ten deaths? Twenty-two injured? Stolen goods? It's horrible. But this isn't the way to fight it, Perrin. Don't make me report you to your father, son. You wouldn't look very good in a private's uniform. Now more than ever it's more important to keep you, and *everyone*, safe."

Karna nodded so vigorously his cap shifted on his head.

Shin looked longingly into the forest. "All right, Wiles, Karna. Today you both win. I'll sit here and wait for the world to come get me."

Wiles shook his head and tugged gently at the captain. "No, you'll come back to the command tower and fill out those reports General Cush wants."

"Never knew a man who loves his reports more than Cush," Shin muttered as the three men started back for the fort.

---

In the forest, about forty paces back, two men dressed in green mottled clothing with sticks strategically attached to their tunics glanced at each other.

Then they continued to hold still, their shoulders sagging slightly in relief, and watched the fort and village beyond.

---

That night Perrin and Mahrree sat together on her small sofa after dinner, each with a list of questions. Mahrree had a few unofficial questions as well, waiting to spring at the right moment. Perrin still wore his long knife, and brought an extra one to place in a secret drawer in Mahrree's eating table. When he showed it to her before dinner, she was dumbfounded. "I never noticed that drawer there before!"

"Where did you get this table?"

"It was here when I moved in. The widow's daughter didn't want it and said I could keep it."

"And what did that widow's husband do professionally?"

Mahrree thought for a moment. "I never met him, but I think he used to be a soldier."

Perrin nodded. "Not just a soldier. An officer, I'll bet. I noticed it the first evening I came here. Every officer has a secret drawer. Did you notice how silently it opened? Now if there's any threat, you can pull it open and retrieve the knife."

Mahrree shuddered. "And do what with it?" She stared at the shining blade that was longer than her hand. While it was shorter than Perrin's mini sword, the point was so sharp she couldn't even discern where it ended. "Give it to the Guarder and ask him to peel me some potatoes?"

Perrin's eyebrows furrowed. "On second thought, just keep it in the drawer for me to use. Maybe I should place guards at the house instead, until the fort's smith can finish the iron reinforcements for your doors and windows—"

"Oh, please don't! I'd be too embarrassed to have such attention. You said yourself there have been no more sightings of Guarders, and that they made off with plenty of gold. Except," she paused, her forehead wrinkled in thought, "what do they *do* with it? Not as if they can saunter into Quake and buy a loaf of bread with it. So do they trade among themselves? Use it for jewelry? Set it on their shelves and say, 'Wished I'd stolen that in a different color?'"

Perrin shrugged and noiselessly slid the drawer shut.

"Perhaps that will be the only incident for the year," she decided. "What more could they want?"

He merely smiled at her and said, "Let's eat and get to negotiations."

Mahrree was quickly learning not to keep a hungry soldier waiting for dinner.

The first on her negotiation list was: Will we have to someday move to Idumea? Soon after she accepted his proposal she began to worry about having to leave Edge where she'd spent almost her entire life. The two years she was away at Mountseen for college, her mother sent so many messages in worry that Mahrree walked home nearly every week to prove she was fine and to ask her to stop writing.

Perrin's face contorted as he answered her question. "Yes, someday I may need to return to Idumea. You should know," his face turned into a genuine grimace, "it's expected that I become the next High General." He added in a hurry, "But not for many years. Still want to marry me?"

Mahrree chuckled at his pitifully desperate look, and also out of her own apprehension. "How *many* years?"

"My father doesn't retire until seventy. He's only fifty-three now."

"Whew," Mahrree breathed.

"*Unless*," Perrin added slowly, "something happens to him. My grandfather Pere died suddenly of a heart attack at sixty-five. That pushed my father's promotion up rather faster than we anticipated. He was only thirty-nine at the time."

Mahrree did the math and gave Perrin her best brave face: lips pressed together in a weak smile, chin held high, eyes strong and proud. "That's still a few years," she said optimistically.

He grinned and pointed at her face. "Not bad. The smile is a little forced, though. Try to relax it more. You'll need to pull that face out frequently in the next few years if negotiations tonight go well." He sighed. "I really should have told you this before, but I just assumed you knew. I thought *everybody* knows about the Shins and High Generals. But Mahrree, High General is my parents' wish for me. They think it's a tradition now. My grandfather Pere was appointed in 280, then my father in 306 . . . It's not my wish, though. My great grandfather Ricolfus was the first Shin officer, and he earned only the rank of Lieutenant Colonel.

"Of course," Perrin's face darkened, "he didn't make it to general because he died from a fever. Not the most distinguished way for an officer to go." His voice trailed off and he stared at the fire in the hearth.

Mahrree squinted, wondering what kind of death would be considered "distinguished." Probably something involving sharpened metal, shouting, and blood.

Perrin shook away the thought. "It doesn't *have* to happen. I don't *want* to become the next High General. I love the army, I've enjoyed organizing the fort, training the men and preparing for what may come. I can't imagine doing anything else. But to be honest, I hate Idumea."

Mahrree blinked in surprise. "Really? Why? I mean, not that I want to live there *right now*, but I've heard lots about it—"

He was shaking his head as she spoke. "I used to like it when I was younger, but over the years I've changed my mind. That's why I didn't defend it at our last debate. I agree with you—Edge is far better. *Anywhere* is better than Idumea. Imagine: two hundred thousand people all living in the same confined area. The village of Pools where I was born will soon be engulfed by Idumea. Singles like you don't live in their own houses. They share buildings, up to four levels high, and each have their own little compartment. Children can't run on the roads like they do here or they'll be hit by the hundreds of wagons, horses, and carts that pack every road. It's far too crowded. And the entertainments they have! Well, some are interesting, like the acrobats and the bear tamers, but some of the things they put on the stage . . . " He rolled his eyes.

Mahrree pondered his critique. "I've heard the pools are quite beautiful—"

"When they don't erupt!"

"They erupt?"

"Last year one of the larger pools boiled until a huge amount of water erupted out of it. Destroyed three of the most expensive homes in the area."

"I had no idea—"

"And don't get me started on the shops."

Mahrree paused, trying to understand how they jumped from the erupting pools to shops in one breath. But as she looked at Perrin she saw irritation that she decided she better let him express.

"You want a hat—" he started.

"Actually, no. I don't really wear hats."

He stared at her perplexed, but then smiled. "I meant, *if* you want a hat. *If* you want a hat, there isn't just one shop in the region; you have your choice of over a dozen shops."

"And how many hats do you buy each year?" Mahrree squirmed. The question wasn't on her list, but then again, she didn't think something like that *would* be.

His irritation slipped away, replaced by amusement. "I don't buy the hats," he chuckled. "My *mother* does."

"Ah," Mahrree understood. "You've suffered having to be her porter one too many times?"

He nodded. "Yes. On my father's command. And, Mahrree, I want to thank you now for not wanting to buy hats. That means I can cross off number eight on my list."

He started to do so but stopped.

"I mean, my mother would try on one, ask me what I think, then try on another that looks just the same . . . I tell her they all look fine, but does she believe me?"

Mahrree giggled. "How long ago was that?"

"After I finished upper school. My mother wanted to spend some time with me before I left the house. She really needed a daughter."

"Wait, so it's been more than *ten years*?" Mahrree asked. "And you still haven't got over it?"

He gave her a playful glare. "I was *eighteen*, Mahrree. How many eighteen-year-old young men do you see enjoying women's hat shops with their mothers? Some things just stay with you."

She kept laughing. "So I need to worry about your mother wanting to go shopping?" she hedged, finally relieved to hear something about her, number three on her list.

"Oh, no. Not here in Edge. Everything is several years out of date, so she says. But don't worry about her. She's great."

"That's the fourth time," she pointed out, "that you've said that about your parents. I've been counting since you arrived. You can express your opinion on anything—even hat shops!—but you can't tell me anything more about your parents other than, 'They're great'?"

He squinted. "I don't think we've reached that number on your list yet, have we? We were talking about Idumea, remember?"

"You like to do things in order, don't you?" she probed. "Make your list, have your plan, stick with it. No deviations?"

"Something wrong with that?" he asked stiffly.

"Only if you're inflexible when you shouldn't be. As a teacher I often take the lesson plan and toss it for the day when a student comes up with a really good question. Plans need to be flexible."

"I'm not inflexible." His shoulder twitched.

Mahrree smirked. "Really."

"Go ahead. Ask me anything. Deviate from your ordered list." He fought the twitch, almost successfully.

"All right . . . but first, anything else about Idumea I should know about? Or any more opinions about Edge?"

Perrin's face softened. "Only that I think Edge is the most perfect place in the world. I've already written to my father that I want to serve here as long as possible. I could probably be promoted up to colonel without having to transfer. We can be in this house for many years. And I've found *everything* I could wish for here."

"Mmm, really?" Mahrree leaned against his arm.

"Oh yes." He put his arm around her and kissed her head. "I've been to every village in the world, and I have to say that I've never been as happy as I am here." He sighed in satisfaction. "The fishing is absolutely amazing."

She slowly pulled away to look at him.

"Must be something about being the first village the river runs through," he continued with a faraway look in his eyes. "Or maybe it's the way the warm waters from the springs feed into it. Must help with the growing the fish to such enormous sizes."

Mahrree put her hands on her waist.

Something glinted in his eyes.

She pursed her lips and pouted.

He grinned and pointed at her face. "Oh I like *that* look. You don't have to practice that one at all." He gave her pout a quick kiss.

She laughed. "And I assure you I will remember *that* look in your eyes! You won't fool me again."

"What look?" he said, confused.

"That one, right there. I'm on to you, Perrin Shin!"

"Good. You're paying attention. My father always says more is expressed with the eyes than anything else. You could have been trained as the first female officer."

She snuggled into him. "Would be a disaster *for men*. If I were an officer, no soldiers would ever listen to anyone else but me forevermore. My logic and intelligence are simply overwhelming."

Perrin scoffed good-naturedly.

"Yes," she sniffed in feigned arrogance, "every woman knows the reason we're not allowed any power is because we'd take over the world. I'd be High General in less than a year, Chairwoman Mahrree a season later."

Perrin chuckled. "You may be right. You can certainly exaggerate like an officer."

"Speaking of the High General, tell me more about your father," she said. "That's my number two question."

Perrin's jaw moved a little and she thought she heard a small groan. "He's the general—"

"Something I don't know."

"Uh, he's fifty-three. Oh. You know that as well. Uh . . . he's a good man. I'm told I look a bit like him. He's very honest. Trustworthy. Um . . ."

"This is really hard for you, isn't it?"

Perrin shifted uncomfortably. "I respect him, Mahrree, more than any other man. But he's always been . . . Let me put it this way: my first words were 'ma' and 'sir.' He's always been 'sir.' Kind of hard to describe a man like that. 'General' pretty much sums it up."

"So" Mahrree began, "if *we* have a child . . ." She skipped to number five on her list and braced for the response.

"I will not be 'sir.' I want to be a different kind of father. I like children. I think that's what I first found attractive about you. If you're a teacher you have to like children, right?"

Mahrree laughed. "Usually. Then there are days you're grateful you don't have to spend any more time with *that* boy or *that* girl! But yes, I do want to have our own child. Maybe even two?"

He hugged her. "Sounds great to me."

Mahrree grinned in delight, until another thought came to her. "Uh," she hesitated, "I see a pattern in the naming in your family. Your grandfather Pere's name became Perrin for you. I understand that—I was named for my paternal grandmother Morah. But I'm just wondering . . . I see potential for Relf, but . . . how *important* a family name is Ricolfus?"

Perrin smiled, understanding her concern. "You can see why Pere short-ened Ricolfus to Relf. Don't worry—there need not be a Ricolfusin in our future, or even a Relfette. I don't hold with traditions just for tradition's sake."

"Thank you!"

He chuckled. "We can come up with names that our grandchildren will cringe at. And actually, the question of children was my first one, so I can scratch that off. About being a father, though, I have to warn you—"

"I know, I know," Mahrree said. "You won't change cloths, you won't give them baths, and if the baby spits up on you, I clean you up first. When the child finally has something interesting to say, that's when you'll become involved. I've heard plenty of men at the congregational midday meals state the rules of fatherhood."

Perrin was silent for a moment. "Really?"

"Really, what?" Mahrree asked.

"Really they don't *want* to give the baby baths? I thought that sounded like fun."

Mahrree sat up and looked in his dark eyes. There was no glint. "You're serious?"

"Well, yes. What's the point of having children if you don't experience the whole thing? It'd be like preparing for a fishing trip, setting up camp, sitting by the river, but then never dropping your line. What's the point? And it's not a successful trip unless someone gets soaking wet. Besides," he continued, suddenly sheepish, "Hogal once argued with my father that children aren't here to be our legacy, or honor us, or even entertain us. They're here to educate us—"

Mahrree just stared at him.

"—in how to be more like the Creator." He shrugged. "Leadership is actually service-ship. I supposed I could use a bit more education, especially in that regard."

"So," she said, now confused. "What were you going to warn me about?"

"That I have no idea how to change the cloths, so I'll need some help the first few times. Now what's *that* look for?"

"Someone will have to teach *me* first," she murmured.

"What?"

"Nothing. Perrin, have I told you yet that you are absolutely *the* most perfect man in the entire world, and that I love and adore you beyond words can express?"

A grin slowly grew on his face. "I'm sure I would have remembered. That's a good line. Feel free to remind me anytime."

Mahrree felt the opportunity was also perfect. "Can I ask you another question, not on either of our lists?"

"After calling me the most perfect man in the world, how can I deny you?"

# Chapter 14 ~ "Keep a closer eye on this one."

**M**ahrree had him right where she wanted him. "Perrin, the other night when we were talking, you started to say something about the Administrators."

The spark in his eyes dimmed. "So?"

"You don't entirely trust them, do you?"

His eyes softened, but the spark didn't return. "The army and the government rarely see eye-to-eye. You have enough history books on your shelves to know that."

"I'm not talking about the past, Perrin," she said with sweet determination, "I'm talking about now."

He searched her face. "I haven't told you yet, but you are the *most* beautiful woman I've ever seen. And I'm not just saying that because I want you to marry me," he winked. "You're truly exquisite."

He slipped his thick fingers through her light brown hair, gently twisting the ends around.

"Your little nose, those incredible pink lips, your green—No, wait—gray eyes. But there's some brown. *Your eyes*—"

So desperate he was to avoid discussing the Administrators that he was about to attempt—Mahrree suspected and feared—poetry.

"Your eyes remind me of a . . . of a field of green after a rainstorm, when the mushrooms pop up, all brown and beige—those poisonous one, you know? The ones that—"

He must have noticed her mouth twisting in amusement.

He sighed in exasperation. "Clearly I'm not skilled in romantic talk."

"Fortunately for you, neither am I," she laughed. "Comparing a woman's eyes to lethal fungus?"

He smirked. "So exactly what color are your eyes?"

"Might as well ask me the color of the sky."

"Well, anyway," he tried again in his attempt to sidetrack her, "you must have turned many men's heads over the years. They just couldn't turn yours, and for that I'm most grateful you think me perfect. You're perfect for me."

"Thank you," she blushed. She recognized his diversionary tactic, although he did seem sincere about his compliments and she enjoyed his flattery.

Besides, it gave her an idea.

She'd read a few silly love stories when she was a teenager, trying to understand her friends and their longings for admirers. Most of the secretive tales were slid from girl to girl under desks where teachers wouldn't notice, and were so sappy that she was surprised the well-worn pages weren't stuck together from the goo. She'd taken to skimming pages of uncomfortable details, hoping her eyes would fall on something interesting or even useful. She was always disappointed. But it was strange how bits and pieces of things she really didn't want to read were the parts that were so difficult to purge from her memory.

And yet, she considered, a couple of those bits just might come in handy right about now . . .

"That someone like you would even *notice* someone like me," she sighed. "Can I do something I wanted to do the first moment I saw you?"

"Perhaps," he said slowly. "Depends on what that is."

"Well, at first I wanted to hit you with a stick—"

"You wouldn't have been the first female." He rubbed the faint scar on his forehead.

"Really? And what did you compare her eyes to?"

"They weren't like yours, all brownish-gray, with green, and bits of gold like straw—" he tried again.

"Hmm. I think you just described the colors of horse manure," Mahrree decided.

His face lit up. "Yes!"

He realized his mistake a second too late.

"I mean, no!"

But Mahrree was already laughing. "The affect you have on women."

Perrin growled quietly, but smiled. "I do believe her eyes were blue."

"All the more reason you insulted her by declaring her eyes to be the color of manure."

His growling grew louder. "I didn't—" He gave up before trying. "Go ahead and believe I have no influence with women."

Mahrree had a worrying thought. "She . . . uh, wasn't *pretty*, was she?"

The lines around his mouth did the closest thing possible to a swagger. "What would you expect from a girl who falls for me? But I must confess she was quite *unappealing*. Of course, what kind of a judge of beauty was I when

I was only eleven?"

Mahrree didn't mean for her relief to come out in such a loud exhale.

He chuckled. "Weren't you about to do something a minute ago?" he reminded.

"Oh, yes. What I *really* wanted to do at that first debate was this." Satisfied that her only competition was seventeen years ago, she slowly ran her fingers through his black hair.

He closed his eyes partway. "And here I thought Hogal was being silly about my not wearing my cap. Anything else you wanted to do?"

"Actually," she blushed again as she stroked some of his short hairs on his neck, "do you remember the second Holy Day meeting? I purposely sat a few rows behind you."

His eyes opened. "Oh, I remember. I was watching for you to come in until Hogal motioned that you were already behind me."

"I did that on purpose," she confessed. "I didn't want you to see me turning red whenever you looked at me."

"I love watching you blush." He slid a finger over her cheek. "That's why I started winking at you. Gave me hope that maybe you thought of me as much as I thought of you."

"And here I was hoping you hadn't noticed the effect you had on me."

"Oh, I noticed," he said earnestly. "So what about that Holy Day meeting? I swear I could feel you staring at my neck."

She grinned. "I have no idea what Hogal talked about that day. Actually, I was staring at this." She ran her finger over the curve of his ear.

His eyes closed partway again. "Mmm—anything *else*, Miss Peto?"

"Yes," she leaned in closer until she breathed gently on his ear. She never thought she would've been grateful to remember a few painfully awkward passages from *How to Sway a Boy in Six Simple Steps*.

Perrin's eyes closed completely and goose bumps rose on his neck.

Mahrree almost smirked. Well, what do you know—the stories were correct. He was quite literally swaying.

"I also wanted to say this," she whispered, her lips brushing against his ear in accordance with Step Five.

"Yes?" he breathed in anticipation.

She couldn't remember Step Six anymore, but she didn't need it. "I recognized your diversionary tactic, Captain. So I'll try something else." She kissed his soft earlobe.

More goose bumps.

"Tell me, Perrin . . . what does your father think about the Administrators?"

His throat gurgled as if he were being strangled.

Mahrree pulled away and smiled sweetly.

Perrin blinked and exhaled, as if to jar himself from wherever his mind had been. "Yes—definitely NOT an interrogation technique my father ever considered." He sighed. "That was just cruel, Mahrree."

"Hmm, interrogation . . . maybe women *should* be in the army," she mused.

"Not you!" he pointed at her. "Shouldn't mess with a man's mind like that, giving my thoughts whiplash—"

"Well?" She ran her hand along his solid neck.

He rubbed his forehead and groaned. "Mahrree, Mahrree . . . you don't need to worry about any of that—"

"The condition of my civilization? The attitudes of my future husband and father-in-law toward our leaders?" she scoffed. "Next you'll say something inane like, 'Don't trouble your *exquisite* little head with such details.'"

He smiled partially. "You're something else, you know that? How could I fall in love with anything less?"

"Again, thank you. I think." She furrowed her brows wondering what "something else," meant. "But Perrin," she shifted into debate form, "when you came over last night, you said you would be honest with me in everything *from now on*. We're here tonight trying to be sure this union will succeed, and if you begin by going back on your previous declaration of honesty, how can I trust anything else you tell me? I'll be honest with you first—until a few weeks ago I believed the Administrators truly were making great strides in improving the world, but then you told us about the suggestions in education. That struck a bit close to home for me. It may be silly, but I've always loved debating about the color of the sky. It's far more than an exercise in assumption and observation. So now that the Administrators are suggesting that we don't need to teach *how to observe*—even now my belly is clenching at the idea, and I'm not sure why. If you have *any* light to shed on my discomfort, I'd like to have it."

He paused. "Mahrree," he eventually whispered, "my father is trying very hard to keep civility in our world. For me to express to you anything he suggests would—"

He hesitated again. "He's the *High General*, Mahrree. There are certain things that *must* be kept in confidence—"

"Do you trust me, Perrin?"

"Of course."

"With everything? Because I can't go into a marriage knowing you're keeping secrets from me. Important secrets. I don't believe in that."

He pursed his lips as he considered, and she was so tempted to kiss him that she did.

He chuckled as she pulled away. "You have a point," he said. "And incredible influence over me, but don't let anyone know that. All right . . . I understand your feelings about secrets. But you also must understand my position in the army. How do you feel about *hints?*"

"Hints?" she said, suspicious.

"These *are* negotiations, Mahrree," he reminded her. "One side gives a little, then the other side gives a little. You need to meet me halfway on this."

"Are hints all that I might get?"

"It's to *protect* you, Mahrree, not aggravate you." He became startlingly sober. "If you know too much, you're vulnerable. I already love you too much to put you in danger. Can you accept that?"

She was so thrilled with the way he readily confessed, "I already love you too much," that for a moment she didn't register the rest of his sentence. Her startled mind caught up a few seconds later. "Danger? All right. I guess I can accept that."

Perrin nodded once. "He sends me weather reports."

Mahrree frowned at the odd sentence. "Uhh . . ."

He smiled. "Specifically, the color of the sky."

"Really?" she beamed. "I think I like your father already."

"Good, because not a lot of people do. The citizens still have the wrong impressions about the army. My grandfather Pere was a remarkable man," he said with genuine admiration. "He cleaned house when he took over as High General, and even reined in some of the tendencies of Querul the Third's very threatening widow. But that family worried that the world would embrace the army more than they appreciated the kings' leadership. So they spread rumors. Despite my grandfather's efforts, and now my father's, the army is still seen as something to be feared. But Mahrree, I promise you—danger does not come from the *army,*" he said meaningfully. "And while they all respect him, very few people appreciate my father, especially a particular *former professor.*"

"Ah," Mahrree said, understanding his allegations. "Wasn't he your professor as well?"

Perrin nodded. "He doesn't have the best of feelings toward me, either. You know how I love to debate? When I was younger, I wasn't as disciplined as I am now—"

"You think you're disciplined *now?*" she teased.

He laughed. "More than I was. As a twenty-one-year-old . . . well, let's just say I was well-known, and not in the best of ways. Nicko Mal doesn't believe in debating, only in shutting down and humiliating. Well, I don't believe in being shut down or humiliated, as you've discovered. It was not the best of combinations, but the class was never boring. Mal and I bickered about so many aspects of human-animal behavior . . ."

He paused again. "I'm not proud of that. I was arrogant and high-minded. The problem was that Mal was too, but even more intensely. Sometimes nothing happened all class hour except for us conducting a shouting match while the rest of the class watched the entertainment. I don't know why I let him get under my skin so frequently. And the worst part is, I tried to use The Writings against him."

"Against him?"

He shrugged guiltily. "I had been studying them, and at times I was filled with righteous pride for all I thought I knew. Guess what: 'righteous' and 'pride' don't go together. I'd throw phrases from The Writings at Mal as if they were balls of mud, leaving both of us filthy. It took me a few years to realize The Writings aren't meant to be used as a vengeful weapon, but as a guiding tool. The Creator isn't trying to punish us; He's trying to warn us. But I wasn't mature enough to understand that seven years ago. So I'd counter every comment and argument Mal made by quoting some passage at him, with a tone that removed all tenderness and replaced it with malice."

"I think you're being a little hard on yourself." She patted his firm chest, and he didn't seem to mind that her hand remained there. "I'm sure he realized you were immature. I know I've said some things I've regretted when provoked in just the right way—"

He smiled faintly. "Sorry about that."

"And Nicko Mal is a mature man, right?"

He pondered. "Interesting question. Supposedly he is, but you know I've often wondered, why did he let me so annoy him? He truly hated me. I could see it in his eyes. Even just last year when I ran into him—" His hand that wasn't around Mahrree suddenly clapped on his leg to signal an end to that memory. "Well, all of that was long ago. We've both moved on, I'm sure. It's just that . . ." he struggled to find the most diplomatic way to say it. "Chairman Mal's not entirely forthcoming about everything."

"I see," Mahrree said slowly. "That was vague enough to be misunderstood, but clear enough that I get the idea. When was the last time you received a weather report from your father?"

"Right before our first debate. He wrote, 'Children of Idumea know the sky is blue, thanks to improvements suggested by our Administrators.'"

"Clever. Should anyone else happen to read that, they'll not hear the sarcastic tone with which it was undoubtedly penned."

"And my father is the master of the sarcastic tone," Perrin acknowledged.

"Now I understand more of why you accepted the 'color of the sky' debate."

Perrin turned a little pink, much to Mahrree's surprise. "The moment I saw you, I thought to myself, 'This just might be a woman worth getting to know.' Then I cursed Hogal for making me think I was about to debate the village spinster," he chuckled. "But I needed to know how you thought and felt. That night you argued everything precisely in line with my own beliefs. A woman who claimed that the sky wasn't even blue, but inherently black? Well, some part of me knew right then I wanted to spend the rest of my life with you, and I believe I cursed Hogal a second time for his setting me up like that." He pursed his lips as he remembered.

Again Mahrree couldn't help herself, planting a kiss there which Perrin heartily accepted. She pulled away just inches from his face. "We'll have to tell Hogal that we forgive him," she whispered.

"I think asking him to perform the ceremony might accomplish that," he whispered back. "There *will* be a ceremony, right?"

She grinned. "Negotiations seem to be leaning toward that end, don't they?"

He kissed her again in answer.

---

After two hours of exhaustive discussion, covering what they figured to be at least three moons' worth of courting information, Perrin and Mahrree left out the back door again, and Mahrree locked it without his prompting. Hogal had told Perrin when the performance at the amphitheater would be ending, and the captain of the fort needed to make an announcement while the villagers were still there.

The plan was for Perrin to go to the fort, change back into his uniform, then take a horse to the amphitheater in time for the announcement. Mahrree would meet him there, and would, in the meantime, walk to the center of the village.

Alone.

That was what bothered Perrin as he stood on her back porch. "It's just not a good idea, Mahrree. Alone?"

"As I've done for years," she reminded him.

"But it's already dark," he gestured to the obvious evidence.

"I know. But you've trained your soldiers for this, right? Already they're patrolling the village. Look. Two more, right there on the main road."

At that, Perrin stepped back to her back porch and out of all possible view of his soldiers.

Mahrree elbowed him. "Someday they're going to find out about us."

He took her by the shoulders and pulled her close to him. "I suppose they are." He kissed her. "And I suppose they should know something *right now*."

Abruptly he stepped off the porch, pulling her along by her arm. He walked so fast to the back alley and over to the main road that Mahrree had to trot to keep up with him.

"Privates!" Perrin bellowed at the soldiers walking away from them.

Obviously startled, the two young men jumped, spun, and faced their commander. The swords strapped to their sides caught up a moment later, slapping awkwardly against their legs. Remarkably, the soldiers didn't wince but saluted smartly.

Well, one started to wince, likely thinking the dark night hid his pained expression. But the torch he carried gave him away.

Mahrree stifled a chuckle and Perrin grumbled quietly as they neared. "All right, I'm *still* training many of them," he whispered to Mahrree. "Clumsy things." In a louder voice he said, "Men, I need you to escort Miss Peto to the amphitheater. As I'm sure you're aware, this isn't a time for anyone to be walking unattended."

"Of course, sir," one of the young men answered briskly.

Oddly, Mahrree felt like laughing. Seeing the slightly-terrified-but-completely-obedient response of the soldiers to her future husband was rather impressive. For some reason it hadn't occurred to her that men in blue uniforms *would* snap to attention in his presence. Maybe because *she* didn't. It struck her as rather comical, in a daunting sort of way.

Fifteen minutes later Mahrree arrived safely and successfully at the amphitheater. She was not successful, however, in engaging the soldiers—large boys of not yet twenty years old—in any kind of conversation. They just marched stoically on either side of her answering her questions in the briefest of ways, and she tried to remind herself she wasn't their prisoner on the way to visit the Administrator of Loyalty.

They followed her to the back entrance of the amphitheater. She stopped at one of the sets of stairs that led up to the platform and dismissed them.

Or tried to. "As you can see, I'm here now so . . . shoo. Off with you. Well done, privates."

They tipped her caps to her, but didn't move. "We're to remain here, ma'am. Captain's orders. He wanted to introduce many of us tonight to the villagers."

Mahrree glanced around and saw that many more pairs of soldiers were coming to the amphitheater, also carrying torches. There must have been over seventy of them, and she understood why. Edgers would be understandably nervous to hear that Grasses had been attacked. When they left the amphitheater, seeing dozens of soldiers ready and waiting to help them home—even lighting the way—would be most comforting.

Mahrree smiled. She was marrying a most clever man. And thinking of clever men—

She heard the horse trotting toward her in the darkness before she saw it. The gray beast came all the way to the back entrance, and was reined to a stop by Captain Shin. She couldn't help but grin at him in his full uniform, with his sword strapped securely to his side. Yes, he would protect Edge.

But he only tipped his cap in formal response to her. "Miss Peto. Glad to see you arrived safely," he said as he got off the horse and handed the reins to one of Mahrree's soldiers.

Mahrree immediately erased her goofy grin and adopted an equally reserved demeanor. "Yes, thank you, Captain. Your men did quite well."

Keeping their intentions to marry secret for just one more day *was* difficult. No wonder her mother wailed in grief when they told her to not spread the gossip until after tonight's announcement. Even Hycymum didn't know what was coming, but she was in the audience, eagerly waiting.

Captain Shin nodded briefly to Mahrree and surveyed his assembled soldiers. "As I instructed, post yourselves at the exits," he told them. "We'll be escorting as many we need to, for however long we need to, tonight. Win their hearts and minds, men. If Edgers don't trust us, we've already lost the battle."

As the soldiers dispersed, except for a dozen assigned to that exit, Captain Shin glanced back at Mahrree and winked at her.

She covered her mouth with her hand to avoid smiling in front of the remaining soldiers. Captain Shin wasn't making this any easier.

A roar of laughter, then loud applause came from the platform beyond and drifted down to those waiting behind it.

"I've seen this play before," Mahrree told Captain Shin and the soldiers. "By the laughter, I can tell it's the final scene, and should be over in just a couple of minutes. You best get into position, Captain."

"Thank you, Miss Peto," he said stiffly, then walked to the stairs and waited for his cue from Rector Densal.

Mahrree slipped around to the front of the platform and subtly took a spot at the end of a nearly-full bench. The villagers were too involved enjoying the play to notice her arrival, and when the actors left the platform, all of the audience stood to applaud.

Rector Densal quickly made his way to the platform and held up his hands. "Thank you for your attendance this evening," he called as loudly as he could. "Please—we have one more item tonight. If you would all just sit back down. Five minutes, that's all—"

His voice was drowned out in the crowd's noise of gathering up blankets, children, and bags, and jostling to be the first to get out.

Mahrree wrung her hands worriedly in her lap, until she saw Captain Shin stride onto the platform and march right up to the edge of it. The movement caused a few people to stop and look up.

"Hey, it's Captain Shin! Back for more punishing debates?" someone called loudly.

"What, wanting more humiliation, Captain?" cried out another voice.

The evening's performance had left Edgers in a particularly jolly and stupidly brave mood, Mahrree thought sadly.

But all that was about to change.

Captain Shin just stood solidly at the front of the platform. Large. Forbidding. And intriguing. More Edgers were stopping their movements to watch him for any.

All he did was nod once to his great uncle, who made his way back down the stairs. Then the commander of the fort repositioned himself with his feet slightly apart, with his hands behind his back, and with a fixed glare on the crowd of nearly four thousand.

Mahrree felt goose bumps rise on her arms as she watched her future husband, stern and imposing, make men more than twice his age suddenly feel the need to sit down and hold very still. Within seconds, the entire audience was silently taking their seats again.

Incredible, Mahrree thought. He may not ever want to be a general, but he certainly carried the blood and bearing of generals.

Then again, Mahrree realized, she'd never *met* a general before, so she wasn't sure exactly how one would convey himself.

But Edgers hadn't either, and they were fascinated by the officer standing in front of them waiting for them to come to order as if they were a classroom of disruptive teenagers.

As the amphitheater hushed to silent anticipation, Captain Shin stood stock still for yet another agonizing ten seconds. Mahrree almost chuckled. Classic debating tactic—work the crowd, get them begging for you to say something, *anything*. She'd have to keep a close eye on this one, she thought to herself.

"Villagers of Edge!" Captain Shin's deep voice finally boomed to the crowd.

Everyone shrank on their benches.

"I am here to inform you that the night before last, the village of Grasses experienced an attack by Guarders."

The gasp wasn't just audible, but tangible.

You *should* be scared, Mahrree thought in satisfaction. And grateful my future husband is here.

She had to stop thinking things like that. It made her want to smile, and that was rather inappropriate right now.

Captain Shin waited for the hushed murmurs to quiet before he continued. He reached into his jacket and pulled out a piece of parchment. "A short time ago I received this update from the colonel commanding the fort in Grasses. The Guarders were, unfortunately, very effective in reaching into the very center of Grasses. In total fourteen houses were hit, thirteen citizens and soldiers lost their lives, and more than thirty were injured."

Not one Edger said a word. All of their mouths were hanging open far too wide.

Mahrree just sighed. Perrin already shared those numbers with her, but they still sounded so awful. She couldn't remember an attack in the past thirty years that caused so much damage in one place.

"You may be comforted to know that nine Guarders were also killed, by the Army of Idumea," Captain Shin continued, sounding both terrifying and consoling. "Members of that same army are now standing outside this amphitheater with torches ready. Should you feel the need to be accompanied by a couple of strong soldiers armed with swords and long knives, please feel free to take my men home with you, with my compliments." He smiled ever so slightly.

The audience ate that up, breaking into grins far broader than they should be for such a subtle touch of humor. But they were eager for any kind of break to the instant gloom that overshadowed them.

"You will also notice that, effective immediately, the Army of Idumea will be patrolling your roads and alleys to keep you safe and the Guarders in the forests—*where they belong.*"

Mahrree didn't expect the crowd to break out into applause, but they did, even adding a few cheers and whoops. Perhaps they didn't know what kind of response was appropriate, Mahrree considered, so they tried a little bit of everything.

Captain Shin's eyes wandered over the grateful crowd, stopping briefly when he met Mahrree's. She winked at him in encouragement. He did nothing but look at her intently for just a moment longer before turning his attention back to the villagers.

"I recommend," he said loudly over their noise, which rapidly quieted again, "that you now gather you things, your children, and make your ways home in large groups. The army will assist you as needed. I also recommend that you remember how to work the locks on your doors. Now is not a good time to become an easy target. Good night." He shifted his stance just a little, and suddenly the audience rose up as one body and made a mad—but orderly—dash for the exits.

Mahrree let the village stream past her so she could observe the captain as he watched the crowd with falcon-like alertness. It wasn't until that evening that she realized just how duplicitous he could be, but in a good way. He was both intimidating and compassionate. Unapproachable, but concerned. A few people paused at the platform to call up words of thanks to him. He'd nod curtly and offer half of a brief smile before scanning the area again. Mahrree could tell no one was quite sure how to react to the captain, who wasn't there tonight to be the object of their teasing, but to be the preserver of their safety. And they were glad he was.

Once Captain Shin was sure the villagers were well on their way home, he walked down the stairs in the front and over to his great aunt and uncle. Mahrree could only catch glimpses of the three of them in conversation as Edgers hurried past her. But suddenly both Tabbit and Hogal Densal looked over at Mahrree. Not sure what Perrin had said to them, she just smiled and waved hesitantly.

That time Perrin did wink at her, and put a hand on each of the Densals' shoulders. She saw his lips form the words "We'll be at your place in about ten minutes, then."

The Densals just stared at each other as the captain gently pushed his way through the thinning crowd to Mahrree, and then he—

Well, she wasn't sure *why* he did it. Maybe it was to appear to Edgers that he wasn't an entirely terrifying authority figure, but also just a gentleman. Perhaps it was to give Edgers something else to think about rather than the fact that Guarders were indeed active again. Or maybe he thought Hycymum Peto wouldn't be effective enough in the morning.

But for whatever reason it was, he smiled at Mahrree and offered her his arm.

She raised her eyebrows at him in surprise but happily linked her hand into the crook of his elbow and allowed him to escort her out of the amphitheater, to the astonishment of everybody.

---

Tuma Hifadhi, the old faded man, shuffled over to his front door and opened it.

"Hew Gleace! What can I do for you?"

The man in his fifties smiled at Tuma. "I have news that I thought you'd be interested in."

"About our captain?"

Hew nodded. "A few mornings ago he walked into the forest!"

Tuma's eyebrows shot upwards.

"Then he walked right back out again," Hew said, disappointed.

"Ah," Tuma smiled, "but why did he enter the forest, Hew?"

"It seemed he wanted to discover something, or prove something."

"Interesting, interesting. And why did he leave again?"

"Pressure from his officers. They both escorted him back to the fort."

Tuma rubbed his chin thoughtfully. "*In* to discover something, *out* because of pressure."

He pondered for a moment.

"Hew, increase the patrols above Edge. Keep a closer eye on this one. *In* to discover something," he muttered as he turned around and shuffled back into his office. "*In* to discover."

---

"I think it's safe to say the entire village knows," Mahrree said to Perrin two nights later as they ate dinner. "I found these slipped under my door this afternoon." She slid a few small notes across the table to him.

He picked them up, made a face at the writing where each 'i' was dotted with a flower, and said, "One of your students? She has interesting ideas for debate topics, doesn't she. Baby names? People debate about that?"

"I don't know. Never had that experience. They were from Sareen, I'm sure. I heard giggling by the door moments before I heard the knock."

Perrin put down the slips. "I think your evaluation is correct. I've been getting looks from everyone in the village and the fort. You know, *the look?*" He made his eyes large, accentuated with raised eyebrows.

Mahrree laughed. "Yes, I know that look. I received quite a bit of it at the market this morning."

"Your mother is a most efficient . . . news-spreader," Perrin decided.

"We call them gossips. And they all visit Edge's Inn when my mother's working."

"I was trying to be diplomatic."

"Well done," Mahrree nodded in approval. "But I think you walking me out of the amphitheater the other night in front of nearly the entire village *may* have contributed to chatter."

"Well, the news had to get started somehow," he said dismissively as if he just did her a tremendous favor but really didn't need so much thanks.

Mahrree rolled her eyes. "So is the gossip why you snuck in the back door today?"

Perrin shrugged. "Just a slighter faster way to get to your house."

"So you're not taking the back alleys just to avoid my neighbors? Because you realize they'll soon be *your* neighbors."

"I suppose we can be seen together in other places, too," he said.

"Well, we can't avoid it forever. They'll be making faces at us for just a few days, then the novelty will wear off. Edgers are skilled at finding new targets. Everyone already knows I adore you—I'm sure my mother has made that clear."

He grinned. "And I guess I should admit that my soldiers have been giving me subtle smiles. I suppose I can't blame that on your mother."

Mahrree laughed. "You might! She has connections everywhere. She's a good resource. You may have to start talking to her just to know what's going on in the village."

"I'll try," he bravely promised.

"I'm going over to her home tomorrow to learn how to . . . um, *cook*," she confessed. "You could come over after your shift. To my mother's."

"Is that really necessary?" he scowled, not too diplomatically.

"You want to risk eating blob? She's going to teach me how to make bool-yon and dim-sun and jel-a-ton."

He squinted. "What *are* those?"

She shrugged. "Not sure myself. I never eat at the Inn. I can't understand her menu. Please?"

"Of course," he smiled when he saw her sincere worry.

"Thanks. And since I spent the morning learning more about *your* family, it's only fitting you spend an evening getting to know mine."

"Of course," he repeated offhandedly, picking up a chicken leg. He stopped. "Wait. *What?*"

"I had visitors this morning for a couple of hours," she said as she slowly buttered a slice of bread. "Does the name 'Auntie Tabbit' sound familiar?"

"But," he blinked rapidly, "we told Hogal and Tabbit everything after the announcement at the amphitheater. What more could there be to discuss?"

"Oh, there's *lots* to tell about the most—how did Auntie Tabbit phrase it? 'The most adorable little boy with the biggest brown eyes ever to be seen.'" Mahrree batted her eyelashes at him.

"Oh no," he whispered.

She laughed again. "It wasn't that bad."

He rubbed his forehead. "Understand, they never had children. I was the closest thing they had. Kind of their grandson, I guess, especially after my mother's parents died. I only saw them a few times when I was younger and they traveled to the forts where my father was posted. Whatever they said, please realize that—"

But Mahrree was still laughing. "They just told me how sweet you were when you were little, that's all. Goodness, you look like you're afraid they revealed some horrible secrets about you."

He watched her intently. "It's just . . . you know . . . never quite sure how *others* will remember incidents from your past."

"Maybe I need to ask them for more details?"

"That's not necessary," he assured. "So what else did they talk about?"

"Actually, I heard a few more interesting things about your parents," she said with a deliberate look.

He paled. "Oh no."

"Relax, will you? I feel a bit better now. Tabbit obviously loves her niece. She went on and on about Joriana this, and Joriana that. But I must admit, it sounds as if she's a bit more *sophisticated* than anything in Edge," she hinted.

Perrin nodded. "I told you that. Sort of. But don't worry, she's great. She'll love you."

"Hmm," Mahrree said, unconvinced. "Tabbit said that too, but we'll see."

"So, did Tabbit or Hogal say anything about my father?"

Mahrree nodded gravely. "Your father wants to be buried standing up and at attention when he dies."

Perrin snorted.

"According to Hogal," Mahrree clarified.

"That sounds like Hogal. He and my father . . . well, Father doesn't read The Writings as often as Hogal thinks he should, and Hogal is too narrow-minded to give Father any really good advice. That's pretty much how every conversation between them goes."

She cringed. "Should be an interesting wedding ceremony."

"Don't worry—they're more civil than they used to be. Now it's just a thing the two of them go through. Neither really agrees with the other, but they respect each other, and for that I admire them both."

Mahrree bit her lower lip.

"My parents are great, really." Perrin nodded and took a bite of his chicken to avoid discussing the matter further.

---

The professor lecturing in basic command tactics stumbled over his words as he saw the door to the classroom unexpectedly open. Each of the first year command students looked over at the door and sucked in his breath.

"Don't mind me," the white-haired man in the red coat smiled amiably. "Just had a few minutes, was feeling nostalgic, and I decided to sit in again on some of my favorite classes. See what's changed in the few years since I've taught here. Please, go on."

The professor paled, looked back down at his notes to see where he was, and began haltingly, trying to ignore that Chairman Nicko Mal was taking an empty seat on the side of the room.

Slowly the faces of his students, the future officers of the Army of Idumea, turned back to the professor and dutifully took notes.

Chairman Mal continued to wear his thin smile and nodded at points the professor made about planning and preparation. When the class ended, mercifully only five minutes after the Chairman arrived, the young men stood at attention, saluted their professor as he exited, then gathered their books while keeping the Chairman in their peripheral vision.

He was watching one new student, a young man who entered mid-term, but had caught up to be on track with the rest of them. As the soldiers filed out of the room, Mal gestured to the remaining young man who would shape up into a useful dog, with the proper training.

"Lieutenant Heth, the uniform suits you. You look much better than you did several weeks ago in my office."

"Thank you, sir," the former Sonoforen began. "I appreciate that you—"

Mal held up his hand to stop him. "Don't be sloppy," he hissed in quiet warning.

Heth paled and nodded. "Yes, sir. What can I do for you, sir?"

Mal stood up and clasped his hands behind his back. "Just checking on my future officers. Like to step in every now and then, question a few here and there. Make them know what I expect and see that they're up to the challenge."

Heth straightened even more. "I assure you, Chairman, that I am up to any challenge you may issue."

Mal nodded. "Very good, Lieutenant. In about two years, once you've completed your education which is being provided for you at an extraordinary cost—which I'm sure I don't have to remind you—I shall have some exceptional challenges for you. Until then, know that I will frequently check on you, as I check on all my *special* cases."

Heth's eyebrows furrowed, either at the news that he could expect future visits, or that he wasn't the only one. "Yes, sir."

"Any news on your brother's whereabouts?" Mal whispered.

"None, sir."

Mal nodded once. "You have another class to attend, soldier. Best not be late."

Heth saluted, grabbed his books, and headed out the door to his next class.

Mal waited in the classroom for the next batch of students. Just a few moments later several young men filed in, each hesitating at the door as he recognized the Chairman. One young man stopped completely, then cleared his throat and nodded almost imperceptibly to Mal.

The Chairman nodded back, smiled that the message was received so quickly by the smarter dog, and left the room, much to the relief of the professor that was about to enter it.

---

Lieutenant Heth enjoyed stretching his legs and taking in the sights of Idumea. He allowed himself a break since he was ahead of schedule in Command School—because of a "tutor" and a few pages of test answers. With the right papers signed by the right people with the right *extensions of the truth*, even a failed assassin could find himself with a new name, history, years of enlisted army service, and the honor of the pre-commission title of lieutenant for his "exemplary past work."

He loved Idumea, where reality never interfered with one's ambitions.

He strode around the grand city purposely taking the long route to make sure no one could discern his final destination. With his cap pulled down, he walked casually up to the grand gates of the place he used to call home.

Two more soldiers, dressed just like him, manned the gates but made no motion to open them for him.

Eight years ago they would have given "the Little King" anything he wanted. No one outside the mansion called him that, though, because he wasn't legitimate. His mother said it was because she wasn't in any hurry to marry Oren.

Then one night when he was seventeen, his mother roused him and his thirteen year-old brother from their sleep, told them to pack lightly, and whisked them away to her aunt's house in Scrub. She said everything was their stupid, senseless father's fault. But he loved his father. Sure, he was a little slow, but that wasn't enough reason to kill him, was it?

Lieutenant Heth strolled past the mansion's entrance remembering how he and his brother used to shoot arrows at each other in the long grand hall. Dormin was far sneakier than any boy should be and was never hit. But if they met in that hallway now, Heth would pierce his traitorous brother in the heart. His skills with the bow were improving every day.

Heth stopped past the gates and sighed, looking up through the iron bars at the two-story stone mansion where the High Traitor now lived.

*He* didn't deserve those bedrooms or that grand staircase where Heth had frequently taken the mattresses from the maids' rooms and slid down the stairs.

*He* killed his father and didn't care that his mother died poor and bitter in Scrub.

*He* poisoned his brother into believing the lies the rest of the world told about their father and family. Dormin was the most devoted idiot High General Shin didn't even know he had.

As Heth looked longingly at the tall chimneys rising out of the mansion, he remembered the last conversation with his brother.

"You've got it all wrong, Sonoforen," Dormin had tried to tell him after they buried their mother more than eight moons ago. They walked through the burial grounds, alone, to the small house where their aunt had let them stay.

"Our father really *was* useless. I've read all the books and talked to some who served under him. He was just a stupid man, completely ill-equipped to lead anything more than a goat to a pasture."

"How dare you!" Sonoforen had exclaimed. "He was our father! The fifth in the line of great leaders!"

Dormin sighed and scratched his head. "You sounded a lot like Great-Grandmother there. And she wasn't just occasionally scary, she was downright evil. Have you heard of the killing squads? They were *her* idea, Sonoforen. Honestly, I'm glad we're out of there. The only thing I wish now was that I didn't look so much like them. You're lucky you got Mother's face. But me? I'll never be able to go near Idumea. Too many people still remember what they looked like."

Heth had stared at his brother who was broader shouldered and a bit taller than him, much like their father, with similar straw-colored hair and gravel-pale skin. "What have they done to you? Who's poisoned your mind?"

Dormin smiled sadly. "Every history book in the world. You should try reading some time. It's a very humbling pursuit. Next I'm going to crack open The Writings. For as much as Great-Grandmother hated them, I simply must know what's in there."

"I'll never understand you." Heth shook his head. "You sound like you don't even miss the life we had."

"I don't!" Dormin exclaimed. "Not after I discovered what our comfort did to the rest of the world. Sonoforen, if I could fix any of that, I would. And *we should*. It's our responsibility to reverse all that—"

"I'm planning on it," Heth had promised darkly.

"Really? How?"

Heth didn't answer him, knowing his brother would only punch holes into his idea.

"Oh . . . no. No, you can't be serious."

"I didn't say anything," Heth shrugged.

"But I know you. When my dog attacked your cat, you killed my dog," Dormin said bitterly.

"No one but *you* would have ever called that animal a *dog*," Heth said steadily. "More like a deformed rat. It deserved to die."

Dormin took a couple steps away from him. "Yes Sonoforen, you're definitely the offspring of our great grandparents. You're going to do something you think is noble, then justify it in some easy way. Going to try to kill Chairman Mal or someone?"

"And when I do, don't come back looking for a bedroom in Idumea!"

"Oh, I won't, Sonoforen. I'll stay as far away from you as possible, just like I avoided Great-Grandmother."

That was the last time Sonofor—*Heth* had seen him. He left that night heading south with a butcher knife in this waistband and a determination to rid the world of a certain professor.

But now he had better plans. What Dormin the Doormat was doing now, Heth didn't care. He stared at the mansion he was going to retake and smiled. Someday when he would be hosting a grand dinner there, and his starving brother would come limping back to beg a chicken wing to nibble on, Heth would greet him with a bow and arrow.

Or maybe a jagged dagger.

In either case, Dormin would never spend the night in the mansion again.

# Chapter 15 ~ "You have deep dark secrets?"

The next several weeks flew by for Mahrree. Between learning to cook, letting her mother decorate her home—within reason—and overseeing the building of the new study, Mahrree suddenly found herself just four days before her wedding.

And the reality of it all was weighing heavily.

It wasn't that she was regretting the decision, she considered that evening as she laid out dinner in the eating room. It was that everything would be changing. She was used to having things her way, but this past week, after Perrin started moving in his things, it finally hit her that she would have to start doing things *his* way, too. After eight years of independence, she was going to have to live with someone else. That was going to take a little getting used to.

But her fluttering moments of doubt were always blown away by her excitement that she was about to be united with the most intelligent, powerful, and—all right, she'd admit it if she had to put the title on him—handsome man ever to be in Edge. Not that she ever bothered with such designations, but since she ran into Teeria's mother at the market who placed that label on her future husband, Mahrree decided it would be impolite to disagree with her.

She was still smiling to herself as she set his plate down on the table, and then heard an *almost* silent step behind her. The first time that happened she cried out in terror when two strong arms wrapped around her from behind. Until she realized it was Perrin. Since then he'd been sneaking up on her at irregular intervals, hoping to elicit that same blood-curdling scream that sent him to the floor laughing while she ran to the washing room to relieve herself.

But she'd improved in detecting tiny noises. That he made it through the back door and kitchen without her hearing was quite impressive. But the wood floor squeaked under his massive frame, proving why he could never succeed as a Guarder.

She spun around. "Nice try!" she declared as she threw her arms around him.

"Wow, you're getting good at that," Perrin grinned as he kissed her. A minute later he pulled away.

"You have news again, don't you?" she asked worriedly. He always kissed her longer when he had an update from Grasses about the captain's injured sister.

"I do," he said soberly. "Received the message this morning. They think they're finally losing her. She's growing weaker and unresponsive."

Mahrree's eyes filled with tears. She'd never met the girl, but she felt as if she was her own little sister. She and her lieutenant should have been married three weeks ago, but that didn't happen.

Despite the constant attention of the surgeons, her brother, and her intended, she never improved. A few weeks after the attack it was obvious the greatest damage was done to her brain, and she'd never be the same again. Still the fort at Grasses had hoped, and Perrin and Mahrree had written frequent notes of encouragement. But the captain's sister never showed more than the occasional flicker of recognition. All of them suspected this might be the end, but to hear it from Perrin sucked away the last hope.

"Oh, Perrin . . . I'll send another letter."

"I already sent a message," he said quietly. "The captain and the lieutenant sent us their best regards about our marriage." His voice grew gruff as he held her closer. "I hardly knew how to respond to that beyond, 'Thank you, and we'll be remembering you.' So unfair. They may be attending a burial while we're celebrating our wedding."

Mahrree brushed away a tear. "It's awful. Any more news about the sightings in Moorland?"

"More than just sightings," he grumbled. "They made off with over fifty cattle."

"Cattle can be tracked."

"Right into the forest?" he said bitterly. "Where no one can go."

"*Why not?*" she whispered traitorously.

"Because the first rule of the Army of Idumea expressly forbids it," he whispered back.

"Your grandfather didn't know things like this would happen."

"But the Command Board does, and it won't allow such radical changes. We've discussed this before, Mahrree," he said heavily. "And considering who's coming soon, will you please promise me you won't mention such ideas again?"

"I'm sorry. You're right. I'm just feeling a little . . . nervous, I guess. With them arriving tomorrow—" She felt his entire body go rigid. "Perrin? Are you all right?" She stepped out of his embrace to look at him.

"Tomorrow. They're really coming tomorrow, aren't they," he said tonelessly.

"Perrin?"

He broke off his stare at the wall to look at her. "They're great!" he said with forced brightness. "Really!"

"Then why is your voice so high?"

"Looks like dinner's ready. I'm starving!"

By the next afternoon, Mahrree paced the floor of her house. Her home would be the Shins' first stop on their way to inspect the fort. She checked the windows frequently looking for Perrin to arrive and calm her nerves, anxious about impressing her future in-laws.

Her back door flew open and Perrin strode into the kitchen. "I just received a report that they've been sighted. They will be here momentarily," he informed her.

His official tone and dress uniform took Mahrree's breath, but not in a good way.

He saw her dread and tried to smile. "Really, they're great."

"You keep saying that," Mahrree whimpered. "Why?"

But she wished she could have taken that back when she saw tension had taken over his entire body. If his black hair could stand at attention, it would have.

He clapped his hands suddenly, smiled, and said, "I know what we need—a distraction." With a spark in his eye he tossed his cap on the table, walked up to her and caught her in an eager kiss.

He was right. It was exactly what they needed.

But then he abruptly pulled away.

"Hmm. Normally that works. But now I feel tense *and* a bit guilty. Maybe it's because I know my mother is coming."

"It was working for me," Mahrree protested. "Try again?"

He grinned at the offer and obliged her. She felt his broad shoulders finally start to relax until the unmistakable sound of horses and a coach could be heard rumbling down the road.

He tensed and stepped out of her arms. "They're here," he announced the obvious as he brushed down his dark blue dress jacket with extra patches and medals, as if trying to wipe away his deeds of the last few minutes.

Mahrree handed him his cap and told him what she'd been practicing all morning. "You look perfect, Captain. The fort is an amazing piece of crafts-manship. Your men are obedient and disciplined. Everyone in Edge adores you, especially since you're my intended. They *will* be impressed."

He put his cap on and smiled as they heard the coach rattle and clank to a stop in front of the house. "And they'll be impressed with the power you have over me." He winked at her and stepped confidently to the door and out into the front garden.

Mahrree followed, but stopped in the shadow of the doorway.

By the road Captain Shin stood at attention as a soldier held the horses, and a footman—an armed soldier likely chosen because he could move so stiffly—made his way to the coach door.

Mahrree had heard stories about a massive black cavern on the edge of the forest near Moorland. Stones thrown into it were never heard to hit the bottom. It even sucked in animals, sunshine, and joy—or so the stories went.

The enclosed coach standing in front of her home had the same effect.

Nothing like its size or workmanship had ever been seen before in Edge, and Mahrree noticed people down the road cautiously coming out of their houses to glimpse the black beast. Somehow, even after days on the road, there didn't seem to be a speck of dust on it, as if dirt didn't dare touch the brass trimmings on the doors and wheels.

Even the four dark brown horses, perfectly matched and fitted with brass-studded harnesses, had an air of aloofness about them. They snuffed in impatience, tossing their manes, and eyeing a few young boys who dared to sneak closer for a look.

Mahrree gulped and wished she could shoo away the boys. They had no idea what was in that coach. And the occupants of that coach, she realized in dread, were about to come into her house.

The footman, after some odd stepping that Mahrree assumed was some kind of formality, finally opened the heavy coach door with a strained flourish.

The little boys by the horses ran back to their homes, and Mahrree wished she could have joined them in ducking into their front doors to peek out the windows with their mothers.

The cavernous coach belched out the general who smartly saluted the captain of Edge. The general wasn't quite as tall as his son, but made up for it in a little additional girth. Perrin bore a remarkable resemblance to his father. Mahrree felt a bit of guilty relief that the general seemed to have a full head of graying hair under his blue cap, and was aging handsomely. So then too might her future husband.

But everything else about the general was as intimidating as his ride.

His uniform was packed with so many medals and patches Mahrree wondered that any of the dark blue still showed through. His ornate sword hilt glinted in the sunlight and even the air around him seemed to still, as if afraid he would inhale it. His dark eyes were like rocks, and his face was etched with what the originator of the description "rugged" was undoubtedly imagining.

Mahrree had intended to leave the doorway and join Perrin, but the general was more unapproachable than she expected. She waited for the official façade to fall away and the general to hug his son, assuming that might be her cue to appear. But he didn't.

"Captain Shin!" The general's voice was more severe than Mahrree imagined. "The cobblestones in this area are much rougher than on the village main. Do you see that as a problem?"

"Only if you do, sir. However, the citizens seem to be fine with the condition of the roads. And it's only the state of the fort that we can control, sir."

"That answer will suffice, Captain. At ease."

"Oh, come now, Relf!" said a woman's voice from the coach. "Is that any way to greet your son?"

With more oddly crisp movements, the footman helped Mrs. Shin from the blackness and she held out her arms to her son.

She was slender and nearly as tall as her husband, her brown hair twisted into a bun and positioned under a fancy felt hat with a wide brim. Mahrree almost giggled when she saw it, remembering Perrin's admission to hat shopping, and wondering who helped her pick out her hats now. Her gown of tightly woven cream-colored linen would have won Hycymum's wholehearted approval. Mrs. Shin was the very definition of Idumean poise, elegance, and beauty, even after three days of riding in a hot coach. Why her son chose someone like Mahrree . . .

Mahrree whimpered softly and felt underdressed, even though she wore her best Holy Day skirt. She unconsciously tried to smooth the light brown cotton.

The general nodded his permission to his son, and Perrin walked up to his mother and gave her a big embrace.

"It's so wonderful to see you, Perrin," she said sweetly as he set her down on the ground. "But I want to see someone else even more."

"Absolutely, Mother." Perrin turned to the doorway with a big smile and held out his arm to where Mahrree stood, pretending to be brave. "This is Mahrree Peto. Soon to be Shin."

"Welcome to Edge, Mrs. Shin, General," Mahrree said with a flimsy smile and an impulsive curtsey. She knew they did those back in the time of the kings. What people did now when they were terrified to meet someone, she didn't know, but hoped it was sufficient.

General Shin only nodded in her direction, but Perrin's mother walked up to her quickly and gave her a hug. "You have no idea how long I've hoped my son would find you," she whispered.

Perrin sent Mahrree an 'I told you so' look.

Mrs. Shin pulled away and Mahrree knew she was on inspection. Mrs. Shin smiled as she examined her quickly, head to toe. "Very nice. Very nice indeed. Should be a beautiful grandchild."

"Mother!" Perrin shouted, offended at her assumption.

She glanced at him over her shoulder. "Don't worry—I trust your integrity completely and don't expect to visit my grandchild for *at least* nine more moons."

Perrin looked at his mother as if he had never seen her before.

Mahrree released a nervous giggle.

Mrs. Shin turned back to her. "Come, my dear, let's get acquainted while the men out there talk about duller things." She waved to her son and nodded to her husband who tipped his cap. "What a charming cottage," Mrs. Shin exclaimed as Mahrree led her to the gathering room.

Mahrree always thought of a cottage as something half the size of her house. Maybe the Shins lived in something twice as big?

They sat on the small sofa and exchanged shallow pleasantries for a time, but Mahrree could see something else was concerning Perrin's mother. Was it her dress, or her house, or the fact that Mahrree didn't own a single hat?

After a few minutes Mrs. Shin said, "Mahrree, you seem to be a wonderful woman. I can see why Tabbit told me I'd approve, and I am so happy you love my son. But there's something I really should explain to you."

Mahrree nodded apprehensively. "Go ahead."

Mrs. Shin studied her hands. "Being married to a man in this army will not be easy. As much as he may adore you," she looked into Mahrree's eyes, "you'll always come second. His duty to his government and our civilization comes first. They're simply more important than you," she said sadly. "I'm sorry to put it in such a blunt manner, but you should be prepared, so that you . . . in case you—"

Mahrree knew what she hesitated to say. "In case I want to change my mind?"

Mrs. Shin nodded uneasily.

Mahrree sighed and now looked down at her hands. "I've heard that before, Mrs. Shin, from your aunt Tabbit shortly after our engagement. It was on her mind, too. He's told me before he's here first to defend Edge. I come second. I don't like that, but I understand it."

"No, my dear. You don't," she said sorrowfully. "The first time he's taken from you in the night and you hear nothing from him, you'll realize you weren't ready for that."

Even though she couldn't imagine changing her mind about marrying Perrin now, Mahrree wished she had more time to think about it. But she knew how she felt, and didn't all married couples have troubles now and then?

"Mrs. Shin, I appreciate that you want me to be warned and I'll accept any advice you can offer me on how to be married to an officer named Shin."

Mrs. Shin smiled and squeezed her hand. "I think you should consider this—*really* consider—at least for the night. Mahrree, please understand: the man you marry this week may change dramatically. The first time he has to take a life, you will feel some of his own life leave him. It's Nature's way. It's the Creator's way. Even if it's necessary, a good man will feel it. It's the evil men who feel nothing."

Of course that was why he was here, what he'd been training for. Conflict. But somehow Mahrree never imagined it would be her husband directly *in* it. She just thought he looked striking in his uniform riding a horse and brandishing his sword. That he would actually use that sword on another person or bloody that uniform—.

She shuddered inside. She had known it the entire time, but being caught up in the excitement of planning a wedding made it easy to ignore the important factors that she convinced herself were inconsequential. Still, she couldn't imagine any other future.

"You can still change your mind," Mrs. Shin said gently. "As much as I want him to be married, I don't want either of you to regret that marriage."

After a silent moment Mahrree said, "Mrs. Shin, I can't imagine ever wanting to be with anyone else. And I've imagined a lot over the years. If it's not him, then it's no one. I prefer him to nothing."

Mrs. Shin sighed and patted her arm. "That's a good answer, but I still want you to give it until tomorrow. I'll call on you in the morning, and we can talk some more. Until then, some men outside think we're discussing only trivial wedding details, so we best not disappoint them."

After five minutes of wedding talk—primarily Mahrree explaining with some embarrassment how Hycymum was embellishing the light blue dress she made for the wedding with darker blue and gold highlights that she thought would match Perrin's uniform, and Mrs. Shin nodding politely as if making a wedding dress match an army dress uniform wasn't the most peculiar fashion idea she'd ever heard—Perrin knocked gently on the door frame.

"Mother, the general says it's time to be moving on to the fort. Apparently you've made arrangements?"

Mrs. Shin clapped her hands on her knees. "Yes, I have! Mahrree, will you please accompany me outside?"

Mahrree gave Perrin a confused look, and he returned it.

Mrs. Shin led Mahrree outside and right up to the waiting general.

She changed her mind about her first evaluation—he *was* tall.

"Relf, this is Mahrree," Mrs. Shin announced, "your soon-to-be daughter-in-law. Since it's such a fine day I think it most appropriate that you should walk her to the fort for the inspection. This will give me some time to spend with my son. We won't be far behind you. We'll send the coach on ahead."

Perrin and Mahrree's eyes grew large as they stared at each other. Perrin opened his mouth to say something but his father was faster.

"Miss?" he offered his arm to Mahrree and she took it without thinking. "Shall we go, my dear? You may lead the way." But the general stepped first anyway.

Mahrree glanced back to see Perrin's face contort in concern. His mother took his arm and patted it gently as his future bride was led away by his father.

The general's voice brought her back around, not allowing her any time to panic that she was now walking with the most powerful and terrifying soldier in the world. "I was told in the coach ride from Idumea that I'm to make my acquaintance with you today, because my wife needs to speak to her son about his marriage. Apparently there are things *she* knows that a man who has been married for thirty years simply doesn't know to tell his son."

His tone was formal but Mahrree thought she heard just a bit of Perrin's sense of humor in it. Mahrree laughed gently, but stopped and glanced at the general to see if that was appropriate.

He didn't look angry or make any movements toward his sword, so she took that as a good sign.

She desperately tried to think of something to say, but it was if the shelves of her mind marked "conversation starters" were filled only with cobwebs and a surprised spider who never expected to see someone there. She'd never imagined this scenario, hanging on the arm of the High General of Idumea trying desperately to think of how to impress him by not sounding like an idiot.

There seemed to be an unusually high amount of traffic on the main road to the fort. Word of the massive black coach must have got around. It was as if every soldier, villager and supplier of goods was coming or going to catch a glimpse of the High General and the very uncomfortable younger woman with him. She'd never realized how often someone like him had to return a salute or tip his cap, and she wondered if his right arm was stronger than his left from how often it went up and down. She opened her mouth hoping something suitable would find its way out, when the general spoke.

"I understand you're a teacher." His deep voice sounded like gravel when a herd of cattle stampeded across it.

He likely *caused* stampedes, Mahrree mused, merely by walking past a ranch and muttering, "Puts me in mind for steak."

"Yes, sir," she answered, relieved for a topic. "I've been teaching for seven years now. Two different ages."

"And you enjoy this work?"

"Yes, very much. I find it most rewarding."

"Then you're not the kind that's interested in cloth or decorating?"

Mahrree chuckled. "No, sir. Do you think Perrin would want to marry a woman who was? All you need to do is look at my garden to see how little I care about such things."

"Yes, I'm sorry about your yard. It looks as if someone's sheep was carelessly let into it. I'm sure it usually looks . . . lovely." The way he stumbled on that last word made it clear that it was not part of the general's regular vocabulary.

"Truly sir, it is never 'lovely.' And it was a goat. I love books and ideas. The person in my family interested in decorating is my mother."

The general nodded. "Yes, I'm aware of that. She sent me a letter recently."

If words could hang suspended in the air like thick black clouds, these words did.

"No!" Mahrree whispered, louder than she intended. She glanced up again at the general.

He wore a barely discernible smile. "Yes, apparently Captain Shin told her that forts aren't in need of decorating, and any changes to the plans would have to be approved by me. Hence the letter."

Mahrree closed her eyes in agony.

"She sent me a sample of cloth with a new pattern called 'plaid' that she claims is 'very masculine' and she believes would be appropriate for the barracks and Captain Shin's office."

Mahrree opened her eyes. The fort was still torturously far away. This was the longest quarter mile she had ever walked.

But there was still more. "Mrs. Peto is under the impression that the large observation windows should have the option of being covered. And pillows for troops should be . . . 'attractive,' is how I think she phrased it."

Mahrree had an image of her mother trying to teach dirty and exhausted soldiers how to place their tasseled pillows so they looked 'gently lived in.'

"Oh General, please say no more! I can't even *begin* to tell you how sorry I am. I, I . . ." she stammered.

"As long as I know I needn't be concerned that you will attempt to carry on her efforts?"

"Never, sir! And I will do my best to keep my mother in check."

The general actually smiled—barely. "Miss Mahrree, I don't know that we can ever keep our parents in check, nor our children."

Sensing they now shared a tiny bit of common ground, she confessed, "My mother actually wanted you and Mrs. Shin to stay with her during your visit. She has a nice home, just a little crowded—"

And Mahrree couldn't, in any situation, imagine the High General of Idumea agreeing to sleep under a blanket painted with daisies that coordinated with the daisy rug, daisy curtains, and daisy pillows.

"—I told her you will be staying at the guest quarters at the fort, but she's insisting on having you over for dinner one evening. She's a most creative cook, but if that doesn't fit into your schedule . . ." Mahrree held her breath, waiting for the answer.

"We dine with her tomorrow. That was in the last letter she sent."

"Oh, sir," Mahrree murmured wretchedly, "how many letters has she sent you?"

"I think eleven. I may have lost count."

Mahrree checked the distance to the fort again. If she made it there alive without dying from absolute humiliation, she could handle just about anything.

"I suppose I should tell you," the general continued quietly, "that I was rather startled when my son wrote that he wanted to marry. I didn't think there was someone who could ever be considered his equal, especially not someone raised in Edge."

Mahrree squinted, trying to figure out if she had just been complimented or insulted. It felt like both.

"Of course, his mother said the fact that he found someone who would put up with his obnoxiousness only signified that miracles are still occurring in the world."

She looked at him sidelong and saw another faint smile.

Compliment.

Maybe.

"I assure you, sir, ever since we announced our engagement many in

Edge now also have a greater belief in the Creator. My mother, for one. All the girls I grew up with, the men I've insulted over the years . . ."

The High General smiled more distinctly. "He's an exceptional man, Miss Peto. In many ways."

"I'm discovering that he is, sir. I'm very fond of him."

"And apparently he thinks highly of you, as well."

"I hope he does, sir."

The High General nodded once. "Well. Then. I suppose that's *that*, then."

Mahrree wondered what 'that' was all the rest of the way to the fort.

---

Captain Shin stood at attention with the rest of his soldiers, facing High General Shin. Their backs were to the forest, the tall timbers of the fort providing an impenetrable shield. For the past fifteen minutes the men had stood with their chests out, chins up, and eyes focused on a distant nothing while General Shin walked up and down the line inspecting each man, questioning a few on tactics, and seeing just how long a slight private could endure the large officer's hard gaze before swallowing nervously.

Two minutes.

Very commendable.

"But know that Guarders will stare at you for far longer than that!" the High General shouted at the soldiers. "But you are the might and strength of the Army of Idumea!" He stepped away from the line and turned to face the northeast gates, thrown wide open to reveal the forest behind.

Perrin smiled inwardly. He knew what was coming next, and he was going to enjoy watching the effect.

In a voice louder than any man should possess, High General Shin bellowed to the forest as he paced slowly before the assembled men. "Guarder spies: I know you're out there! I know you've watched this fort rise from the ground at a remarkable speed and with meticulous care. I know you've watched these exemplary soldiers march into it and now realize that the Army of Idumea is a fearsome and powerful force, not to be lightly reckoned with. We have no quarrel with you. Our ancestors are dead and gone, as are yours. We have no desire to raid your lands, as you raid ours. We have no desire to steal away your people, as you have stolen ours. We have no desire to fill your women and children with terror, as you fill ours. But we desire to protect all that we love, and I assure you, we will kill every man who stands in our way!

We stand here ready. Strong. Trained. Armed. Organized. Not to attack, but to defend. Defend our land, our people, and our freedom from your terror. You want a fight? We'll give you a fight. You want a surrender? We'll accept your surrender. You want to destroy us? We'll destroy you first! We don't fear you. We're prepared. It's you who should fear, for today I stand before the greatest fighting force the world has ever produced. Soldiers of the Army of Idumea, let the Guarders hear you roar!"

Perrin received reports later that the residents of Edge came running out of their houses and shops when they heard the tremendous noise from the north.

Captain Shin, standing in the middle of it, heard nothing, because the sound was completely deafening.

He winked at his father as the soldiers cheered and chanted and taunted any Guarders that might be within earshot. The general's speech wasn't for them, though. It was for the soldiers of Edge.

Relf Shin winked back at his son. Inspection passed.

---

In the forest about thirty paces in, but in view of the open northeast gates, two men dressed in mottled green and brown clothing sat in the middle of a stand of scrubby oaks.

"Nice speech," one said as the yelling finally subsided.

"I've heard it before. At Grasses."

---

That evening as Mahrree washed her plates at the basin she tried not to think about her walk with the general. Although it started uncomfortably, she had to admit that it turned out fine when he said it would be agreeable to call her daughter-in-law and told her how the desert village of Sands has rock gardens. Mahrree looked up from her chore. Through the thick wavy glass she saw the blue smudge of Perrin hop over the low back fence along the alley and come to the back door.

He walked in and looked at her blankly before announcing, "Passed inspection—*both* of us!"

"So that's what that shouting meant? I was starting to run for the long knife in the table."

He grinned, took her arm, and led her to the eating room where they both sat down. "And now," he said, "I want to know what my father said to you. I had no idea that was coming. I don't think he ever spent time alone with any other woman besides his mother and his wife. He looked more uncomfortable than you did. But whatever you said made a good impression on him. He approves of you whole heartedly. So . . . what did you talk about?"

"About my not making window coverings for the fort," she related soberly. "Apparently my mother has become quite the letter writer."

Perrin's face distorted as if he smelled something nasty. "Oh. Well. That's a promise easily kept. Anything else? Any deep dark secrets from my past that he shared?" He smiled in anticipation.

Mahrree's eyebrows rose. "You have deep dark secrets? I think I may get more information from your mother. But no, nothing very interesting transpired between us. Just civil conversation."

Perrin looked disappointed.

"But what about you and your mother?" she asked.

He took her hands in his and seemed to consider if he should tell her. "My mother told me how to be a good husband," he finally said.

"She talked to me as well, about what it's like to be married to an officer," she hinted.

Perrin nodded to affirm the same conversation. "Have you thought about what she said?" His face showed even more concern than before his parents arrived.

She glanced down at the table. When no answers could be seen in the grain of the wood she looked up at him. "Really, Perrin—how bad could it ever be?"

He attempted a smile. "My parents have lasted this long and not killed each other."

She returned the smile. "Yet."

He sat up straight and put on a mock serious face. "I've got it: I promise you Mahrree Peto-soon-to-be-Shin, I will never kill you. How's that?"

She sat up straight too and mimicked his look. "And I promise I will *probably* never try to kill you either, Perrin Shin. Maybe we could get Hogal to add that to our vows?"

---

The next morning Mrs. Shin arrived to check on Mahrree. "Well?" she asked hesitantly as she stood at the front door.

"Since I am about to become his wife, I think it best that you start telling me all of his deep dark secrets. He confessed he has a few."

A smile grew on Mrs. Shin's face. "Maybe after you hear about what kind of a troublesome boy he was, how he got all his nicks and scars, you may *still* want to reconsider. Your chances of having a son like him may be very great. But then again," her voice warmed considerably, "he is also a great son."

After the first three stories Mahrree grabbed some paper and a quill. The details were fascinating and worth recording.

That evening she prayed for daughters.

# Chapter 16 ~ "Expectations? *I* didn't expect this!"

Two and a half weeks later, two men sat in a dark office of an unlit building.

"Question," began the first man, "now that the fort in Edge is fully operational, the wolf has secured his mate, and the Grasses situation finally ended with a—what was the description? 'A *heart-wrenching* burial'—"

"The letter from Chairman Mal to the officers expressing sorrow about the circumstances was a lovely touch," the second man nodded.

The older man held up his finger. "That *was* considerate, wasn't it? As I was saying, I believe it's now time to propose a new question: Is Shin too comfortable with his little successes in Edge? First the fort, then the woman . . . seems like he needs a challenge."

The second man smiled. "Comfort is never a good thing. People become complacent, which would be terrible for the captain. So here's a supplementary question: Does growth come from discomfort?"

"Ah, intriguing!" The first man rubbed his hands together. "Growth or failure? My speculation: When faced with discomfort he will fail, and magnificently. How could any man fulfill the expectations of a father like Relf Shin?"

His partner rubbed the closely-trimmed beard on his chin. "Then I speculate opposite of you, since Shin always surprises you. I believe he will prove to be a most protective, and even aggressive, wolf to protect his new pack."

The older man cocked his head. "Oh, *really?* You don't know Shin like I do."

The second man chuckled. "And I don't think you know him as well you think you do."

The first man's eyebrows went up. "And I think you've heard one too many stories about the great young Perrin Shin!"

The second man sat back, startled by his partner's adamancy. "Are you sure you're not taking this a little too personally? Nicko, one could surmise you're not entirely objective about—"

"Objective? I assure you that no one has more objectivity than I do!" Nicko Mal shouted. "I have a point to prove to Captain Shin, so I'm setting things in motion. Perrin's going to learn about discomfort!"

---

"This is the last crate, right?" Mahrree asked as she eyed the large wooden box that was placed—*dropped*—in her front garden.

"No ma'am, sorry," the sergeant said as he went back to the wagon. "This one," he grunted as he pulled it out, "is the last crate. Where do you want it?"

Mahrree gestured to the other three crates already on the dirt. "Right there. My husband will move them in." She tried not to grin when she said "my husband." After two weeks of marriage, the newness of it all was still so delicious.

The sergeant dropped the smaller, heavier crate on top of the larger one. "Hope you like books, Mrs. Shin, because I think that's all that's in this one."

"And I thought I already had every good book printed in the world."

"You can use the crates to make new bookshelves," the sergeant suggested as he brushed down his uniform.

"Want to stay and help build them?"

"No, ma'am!" the sergeant shook his head. "I need to be getting back to Idumea."

"What an excuse. Tell Mrs. Shin thanks for packing all of this. I think." She glanced behind her and looked at the new study that had just been completed earlier that week. Maybe it *wasn't* big enough.

The sergeant tipped his cap and chuckled as he went back to the wagon he spent the last three days driving to Edge. "Again, congratulations on the marriage, Mrs. Shin. Hope you find wedded bliss to be all that you imagined."

"It has been for the past two weeks," she grinned. "Until now."

The sergeant just laughed. "I've known Captain Shin for many years—you're a perfect match for him, Mrs. Shin. Good day to you."

Mahrree waved as he clucked the horses to head to the main road. She smiled at the crates. It was going to cause an argument, she was sure. This was the second delivery of Perrin's things, and he had more books and maps than she expected, but she really didn't mind. The past two weeks really had been bliss.

Their wedding on the 38$^{th}$ Day of Weeding was exactly what Perrin and

Mahrree had hoped it would be: intimate with just the Shins, her mother, and the Densals. Although Perrin said it wasn't necessary that his mother, new mother-in-law, and great aunt sobbed the entire time. Even Hogal shed a couple of tears. At least Mahrree remained composed, too excited to cry.

The meal afterwards was exactly what Hycymum had hoped it would be. It seemed the entire village came out to the village green and brought a dish of something to share. There were enough donated leftovers that Perrin sent the remaining food up to the fort, which endeared him even more to his soldiers but not the cooks.

Even High General Shin was heard laughing a few times during the dinner, and judging by the amazed look on Perrin's face, Mahrree surmised that didn't happen very often.

Since then, they'd been getting used to living with each other. Perrin made the mistake on their third day of issuing her an order, to which she responded by putting her hands on her hips. "You want 'forward progress?' That's not the way, *Mr. Shin*."

And more than once he had to remind her, "Your house? You said this was *our house* now, remember *Mrs. Shin?*"

While the past two weeks really had been bliss, anyone listening in on their conversations would have thought there was already trouble in Paradise.

They argued.

Constantly.

Over who decided what's for dinner and when, and who cleaned up afterwards, what they did that evening, and where Perrin's things should go in the house.

They started arguing even before the wedding, when Perrin came by on his day off to build a new bed for them that took up nearly the entire upstairs bedroom and threatened to burst into the adjoining attic. Mahrree had skeptically evaluated the massive timbers Perrin had hauled up there with the help of a winded Lieutenant Karna.

"I was actually imagining a *standard sized* bed—"

Perrin raised an eyebrow at her. "I'm not a *standard sized* man, Mahrree. The new bed will fit."

"If we jump onto it from the small desk—"

"We need a big bed. You don't want me kicking you at night, right?"

"Well, no, but I would've preferred that you tell me your plans for my--"

He raised an eyebrow again at her.

"*Our*," she corrected herself, "*our* bedroom. I don't even know where to get a mattress and ticking big enough—"

"You can't," he grinned. "Has to be special ordered, from Rivers. Should be here tomorrow evening."

"You already bought the mattress?"

"You'll love it, I promise. I slept on something similar when I was posted in Vines. It's rather pricey, but the most comfortable blend of straw and down—"

"But you didn't even ask my opinion?"

"Think of it as a gift. That bookshelf has to go, by the way. Down into the new study—"

"Which I just found out you paid for! We were going to split the cost evenly, remember?"

"I was never going to let you do that. You paid for the house years ago, so the least I can do is pay for the new study and the bed."

"But that's not what we agreed!"

"Well, I came up with something better!"

It was the slow, dragging noise coming up the stairs that stopped their bickering. "I could use some help here," Karna said as he struggled to bring up two more large timbers.

Mahrree and Perrin glared at each other as Karna dropped the beams in the room with a resounding thud. As he wheezed, Mahrree discovered something about the way she and Perrin functioned. Their glares were shifting into something just as intense, but no longer angry. She realized Karna was speaking again.

". . . down in the wagon is still plenty of lumber, so if the two of you would just kiss and make up already, I'd appreciate it."

Something was happening in Perrin's eyes, and Mahrree had the same thought. *Karna, if you'd excuse us for a moment, that's precisely what we'll do right now.*

"Honestly," Karna continued his complaining as he tried to catch his breath, "I'm a little worried that the larger officer's quarters might not be mine at the end of next week, the way you two keep *debating* things . . ."

*No problem there, Lieutenant,* Mahrree thought as she watched the gleam in Perrin's eyes take on an additional level of sharpness. A small smile was forming on his lips. Maybe it was because they were standing in what was about to be *their* bedroom, but she felt her breathing start to increase as she held his deep gaze.

It was *precisely* the debating that did it to them. It was the arguing that opened some gate, started a flow that wasn't to be diverted, like the force of the canal water channeled from the river. Once the current hit you, it was nearly impossible to stand against it.

That's when she decided it was likely a good idea Karna *was* there. Even at their age, it seemed they needed a chaperone.

Still, she was too preoccupied with watching Perrin's face to notice Karna was saying something again. There was a flood-like intensity in Perrin's eyes now—

"I said, *Ahem!*"

Perrin blinked, and so did Mahrree. They looked sidelong over at Lieutenant Karna, almost sheepishly.

He tried not to smirk, probably worried it wasn't appropriate, but he did give them both a stern, evaluative gaze. "I see," he said slowly, as his captain and Miss Peto turned pink in the realization that he was in the room. "I misread the previous situation. That's poor soldiering of me. I now see that it's exactly *the opposite*. Shin, aren't there more timbers to bring up here?"

Perrin nodded once and turned back to gazing at is future bride. "That's right. Brillen, go get them for me. I have one or two things I'd like to *argue* here first, so take your time."

Mahrree giggled and Karna scoffed loudly. "Uh, no Shin. I think I need to remain here to protect Miss Peto from *potential danger*. You go fetch, sir." He shook his head and sat down on the wood he'd brought up. "If you two aren't the strangest couple," he mumbled. "But apparently perfect for each other."

Mahrree laughed in embarrassment as Perrin glared at his lieutenant, eventually shrugged in reluctant agreement, then jogged down the stairs to retrieve more lumber.

Karna ended up staying the entire day to help his captain more quickly construct the bed frame and also, he claimed, to make sure Miss Peto was kept safe by an *objective* member of the Army of Idumea.

By the next evening the massive bed frame was finished, and the enormous mattress, which was heavier and bulkier than Mahrree could have imagined, arrived. It was dragged up the stairs and hefted into place by Perrin and Karna. It *did* fit—barely—with plenty of room underneath for storage crates.

"Well?" Perrin asked as he beamed in pride at his creation.

"I have to admit, it's not too bad." Mahrree eyed the massive timbers turned into simple furniture. Apparently the blood of the High Generals had never been tainted by craftsmen with artistic leanings. She wondered if, left to their own devices, the Shin men would have opted for clubs torn off of trees instead of elegant swords with ornate hilts. "Certainly sturdy."

"If it would make things easier, Miss Peto," Karna leaned against the wall, "I could step into the hall to let you two *debate* this in private. But I have to warn you—I'm staying within earshot, and I can report you two to Rector Densal if I must."

Insulted, Perrin scowled at him, but Mahrree laughed. "Thank you, Lieutenant. It *is* getting rather late, so I'll let the *two* of you get back to the fort now."

It was quite the opposite of sleeping on the small sofa, as she had for the past few nights while the bedroom had been under construction. But once she got over the feeling of being lost on the massive mattress, she had to admit it was the most comfortable night she'd ever had.

"I should start keeping track of my wins against you," Perrin smiled smugly when she told him over dinner the next day that the bed was, indeed, adequate.

It was on their wedding night that the debating began again. The evening started off promisingly when Perrin carried Mahrree easily up the stairs to their bedroom and set her down on the new bed.

He smiled and she giggled nervously.

He removed his sword—part of the dress uniform, he assured her that morning when she saw he was wearing it for the ceremony—and stood it sheathed next to the bedroom door. Then he undid the top button at the throat of his dark blue dress uniform while his bride, trying to give him a flirty look, apprehensively bit her lip instead.

He smiled confidently at her, stepped up to the bed, and pulled out the chair from the small desk and slid it over next to the bed.

Mahrree stared, bewildered, at the chair which now blocked the narrow passageway in their bedroom.

Perrin squeezed past the chair to his new wardrobe which was wedged into a corner and pulled out one of his regular uniforms that he'd placed in there the day before.

Mahrree furrowed her eyebrows. This really wasn't what she thought would be happening next. "Uh, what are you doing?" she asked as he positioned his regular trousers on the chair at a precise angle.

He flashed the grin that always unfocused her. "Getting ready for bed, *Mrs. Shin.*"

She got up on her knees to watch him as he eyeballed the angle of the chair to the bed and shifted it slightly.

"And so the surprises begin," she murmured.

He ignored her comment as he placed his every day boots slightly skewed at the end of the bed and checked the angles.

"Perrin, remember how I said you were the most perfect man in the world?"

"Mm-hmm," he said, shaking out his jacket.

"Right now you're being *a little odd.* I know you like to have things a certain way, but—"

He put the jacket over the back of the chair just so and winked at her. "You married the commander of Edge. I've trained myself so that every time I undo my top button, I remember to prepare my clean uniform for my next shift."

Her eyebrows went up. "Trained? Did Professor Nicko Mal experiment on you, too, as part of your animal behavior course?"

"He only manipulated horses and dogs. Never humans."

"Are you so sure? Perrin, you can't have the chair *right there*. Now there's absolutely no room left."

He nodded once. "Sure there is. I measured for the chair. And as the commander of the fort, I have to be ready for anything. Each night I place my uniform in such a way that I can be dressed and out the door within fifteen seconds."

"You can't be serious. Perrin, it's our wedding night. Wiles's on duty, Karna's there, your father's even at the fort! Should something happen, I seriously doubt any of them would come bother you *tonight*."

"Mrs. Shin," he said gravely, "Guarders don't care when someone gets married, or gets injured, or has other plans. They'll attack whenever they want. If I'm needed, they'll send for me. I pledged my duty to the army before I pledged myself to you. You know that, Mahrree."

She slumped in resignation. "So the chair's going to stay there?"

"The chair stays there," he said firmly. "Tonight and every night. With my uniform waiting on it."

"On the side of the bed *I* usually sleep on."

He raised his eyebrows. "No, that's the side *I* sleep on."

"You could sleep on the other side."

"I've practiced getting out of the bed and getting dressed in the dark on *this* side."

She squinted. "You practiced getting dressed in the dark?"

He folded his arms. "Yes. It will be easier for you to get used to sleeping on the other side of the bed."

They stared at each other for a moment before they both began to smile.

"Leave it to us," said Perrin as he stepped up to the bed and took her face in his hands, "to spend our wedding night debating." He kissed her.

"I'm done arguing," she whispered. "Are you?"

"This is my side of the bed," he whispered back. "If you can accept that, we can stop arguing. Besides, you owe me one."

"What? Why?"

"Our first debate. Hogal told me to win over Edge by going easy on you."

"But you quit."

"I was to concede. To win you over."

She giggled. "That you did. All right, as my wedding gift to you, you can have your side of the bed."

"See? Already we've got this marriage thing figured out," he said as he pushed a lock of hair off of her face. "Just always agree with me, and our marriage will be perfect."

"Don't count on it!"

"Just stop talking and kiss me."

That's what Mahrree was trying to do when he suddenly said, "Like the back of a turtle."

She paused in mid-pucker. "What?"

"I figured it out. Your eye color," he said, just inches from her face and staring deeply—analytically—into her eyes. "Like the back of a turtle— grayish, brownish, greenish. Maybe if the turtle were more of a honey color, though, then—"

"Are you trying to be . . . romantic?"

"It's our wedding night," he explained, and Mahrree thought she heard just a touch of nervousness. "I thought it would be appropriate."

"First mushrooms, now turtles? Your descriptions of my eyes are starting to sound like one of my mother's more unusual recipes. Forget the sweet talk, Perrin. I've realized we do better when we argue."

"No, I really don't think—"

The only way to shut him up and prove her point was to kiss him.

"Hmm," he mumbled as he kissed her back, "I have to admit, you just might be on to somethi—"

Fortunately the forest was quiet that night and ever since then, but even so she begged him to demonstrate how he could get dressed quickly in the dark. He refused.

"I don't do any kind of performance unless I'm in the amphitheater. But when the time is right, you'll be glad I can move so fast. No one's faster than me."

So for the past two weeks of married life they deliberately argued about everything, just so they could get to, well . . . *resolving the issue.* That was the most discreet way to refer to it.

As she stood staring at the crates that afternoon, she wondered how she could use them to start another debate. She got so caught up in the details of her planning that she didn't even realize she'd been daydreaming in her front yard for several minutes. When she finally came to herself, she was sure she was blushing. She glanced around to see if any neighbors could read her mind or see her reddened face, and went back quickly into the house.

Perrin wasn't due back from the fort for another hour, so she had some time to figure out where to place the rest of his possessions. When Perrin unloaded the shipment yesterday, he hadn't realized he had so many things stored at his parents' home. Much of it he tossed to the rag bag and kindling pile; he wasn't sentimental about his lieutenant's uniform or any of his clothes or school writings from when he was growing up.

But Mahrree knew that he was most anxious about the shipment arriving today. He had a collection of old books and maps that he treasured because no one else did. His rescuing old writings from the trash heaps of the garrison was one of the many things she loved about him, and every day she discovered something new. All in all, being married was one amazing, intriguing surprise after another.

"But surely, this will be the last surprises," she smiled as she looked at the many waiting crates. "After this past season and a half, how could anything be more exciting?"

---

It was at the beginning of Harvest Season, two and a half moons after their wedding, that an urgent knock came at their back door late one night. Perrin scrambled from the bed into his trousers, landed into his boots and threw on his jacket in just seconds.

"Wow," Mahrree whispered, duly impressed.

He barreled down the dark stairs, somehow simultaneously buttoning his jacket while fastening his belt holding the sheathed sword around his waist. Before she could get her bed clothes covering on to follow him, she heard the back door slam.

She was all alone, and the sky was black.

---

"Ambush, sir! Two of the soldiers on patrol by the forest. Suddenly they were cut down," the private hurriedly related. He and the captain mounted the horses the private brought with him.

"How long ago?" Captain Shin demanded as he wheeled his horse around and kicked it into a run toward the fort.

The private followed. "Unsure of when the initial ambush happened, sir."

"Unsure? How can you be 'unsure'?"

"Well, one of the wounded thought they were hit maybe . . . ten minutes ago, by now."

Captain Shin tried not to swear under his breath, but a few words slipped out anyway. "Unacceptable! Is anyone in pursuit?"

"Just about the whole fort, sir. Lieutenant Karna has sent everyone out in fours. He's stationed himself at the edge of the forest."

"Ten minutes," Captain Shin whispered to himself. "*Ten minutes!*"

---

Mahrree heard the two horses galloping away. She made her way down the dark stairs and sat on the little sofa to wait his return. In all the years she lived there she never noticed before how shadowy and silent the house could be late at night. She secured each door and sat down again, suddenly feeling cold although that night was the warmest all year.

---

"Lieutenant!" Captain Shin barked a few moments later as his horse stopped abruptly in front of Karna at the edge of the woods. "Report!"

"Captain, they're everywhere!" Karna cried, slightly panicked. "Nothing's secure! Reports of at least four, maybe up to six groups. Guarders, we're sure."

"And how are you sure, Karna?" Shin slid off his horse and drew his sword. He looked up into the dark forest searching for movement and heard shouts coming from the west.

"Uh, well, who else would it be, sir?"

"Descriptions!" Shin demanded. "Give me descriptions!"

Karna nodded quickly, remembering. "Dark clothing, dirtied faces, and from the wounds on the soldiers, jagged blades."

"Condition of the wounded?"

"Surgeon thinks they'll survive, sir."

Captain Shin growled and looked at the trees.

"Now what, sir?" Karna asked.

"We find them. No more wounded, and certainly no fatalities!" he announced, marching straight north.

"Captain! Where are you going?"

"Where the Guarders are. Wiles," Shin called to the sergeant major, jogging up from the fort. "You will replace Lieutenant Karna as point commander. Karna, you and I are going to put a stop to this, right now."

"But sir," Wiles exclaimed. "We've been through this before! You can't go into the forest!"

Karna nodded in agreement.

"Says who?" Shin challenged.

Wiles held out his hands helplessly. "Your father, for one. The rules of the army state—"

"There are *rules?*" Shin stopped, turning to face the two men. "Rules for when to attack? How to cut my soldiers? Who's allowed where?"

"Well, sort of . . . *expectations*," Wiles spluttered.

"Expectations? *I* didn't expect this!" Shin shouted. "Did you, Wiles?"

Wiles swallowed hard and shook his head in surprise at the accusation.

"I will require no one else to enter the forest," Shin promised, "but Karna, you're with me now."

"Yes sir," the lieutenant said feebly and jogged up to the captain. He drew his sword and together the two men disappeared into the trees.

Wiles stood frozen in place.

Eventually he covered his mouth with his hands.

"Not supposed to enter the forest . . . not part of the plans . . ." he mumbled. "Never drilled for that . . ."

He stared, horrified, into the darkness.

An uneasy private stood loyally nearby, trembling at the shouts for help he heard coming from the west. He didn't notice that the old sergeant wasn't staring worriedly at the origin of the shouting, but at the point in the forest where the captain had gone.

---

High in the dark trees sat two men in green and brown mottled clothing. Their eyes grew large as they saw the two uniformed officers boldly striding into the forest.

Well, *one* strode boldly, the other just slinked behind.

The men in the trees exchanged glances, watched the captain and lieutenant slip quietly past them below, and looked at each other again. One smiled and the other nodded.

It wasn't going to be a dull night.

---

Mahrree's neck was cramped. The pain was why she opened her eyes and realized it was morning. She'd fallen asleep sitting on the sofa, but Perrin hadn't returned.

She looked around her quiet gathering room. A gnawing worry in her belly reminded her she was still alone. Her mother-in-law had been right about her "not being ready."

She cleaned up in the washroom, dressed, made breakfast, ate, and tidied the house. She set the washing to soak, did some reading, and looked up and down the road frequently. School was out for a week for the early harvest, ever since the last day of Weeding on the 91$^{st}$, so Mahrree had nothing else to do but wait.

It was going to be a dull day.

# Chapter 17 ~ "Some rules are meant to be broken by the right men."

Karna was never so happy to see the sunrise, or so Perrin deduced by the look of relief on his lieutenant's face. But the light only revealed just how deep they were in the forest that growled around them. For the past several hours they'd been following shouts that moved west.

At least, he assumed it was west. Perrin judged direction based on the slope of the forest. Down had to be south, up was north, so he was facing west with sun rising behind him.

Already they had surprised one Guarder—and themselves, to be honest—and chased him toward the edge of the forest where several soldiers captured him. Now they were about fifty paces behind another two Guarders, visible at the edges of large grassy patches and moving toward Moorland.

But Moorland, ten miles to the west of Edge, didn't know a battle was coming. Because the village was so sparsely populated, they didn't even have a fort yet, just a converted barn and a dozen soldiers recently sent there to help since the village lost a herd of cattle to the Guarders. Perrin wasn't about to leave them overwhelmed.

In the distance he saw one of the men in black turn up and north. Through the trees the figure trotted, skirting past a swath of dead pines standing in dirt that was—oddly—white. In the middle of the soil—or perhaps it was now white rock, Perrin wasn't sure—and among the blackened tree trunks was a gaping hole which belched out hot water, sending it nearly ten feet into the air. Steaming, the water followed a channel in the ground and disappeared into another crevice a few hundred paces away.

Perrin signaled to Karna behind him, and wordlessly the two officers, keeping to the trees, jogged north as well. Captain Shin kept his eye on the black figure that popped in and out of the tree shadows, while making sure that he never touched the white ground that reeked of sulfur.

He kept his other eye *on* the trees, though, trying to figure out why he felt so comfortable picking his way through them when he should have been terrified.

---

"What should we do with him, Sergeant Major?" the younger sergeant asked cheerfully as he and his men stood just beyond the tree line.

Wiles stared in amazement at the Guarder bound by rope around his wrists and ankles.

The man in black glared back at Wiles.

"How was he captured?" Wiles asked, barely above a whisper.

"Captain and Lieutenant chased him right into our waiting arms!" a corporal announced, grinning at the three other men.

Wiles gestured lamely to the bound man. "How did you—*Why* did you—"

"Captain Shin ordered us," explained a satisfied private. "Said to me, 'You grew up on a ranch, right? Use your rope.'"

"So you . . . you *hog-tied* him?" Wiles said in disbelief.

"Actually, it's called calf tying," the private clarified, sniffing with authority.

"Granted, we don't teach that in training," the sergeant said proudly, "but we ought to."

The soldiers laughed, their fear gone now that their enemy was immobile.

But Wiles's anxiety had increased so much that he couldn't move. "But . . . but Guarders are *never* captured."

The wooden expression on the Guarder's face told Wiles the reminder wasn't necessary.

"Until today," the sergeant winked. "Rather like Shin's thinking. He wants him held for questioning. And if the captain interrogates as well as the High General, well I have high hopes for the future of the Army of Idumea."

Wiles didn't notice the proud chuckling of the three soldiers as they gazed at their prize.

"Interrogation?" Wiles muttered and turned a sickly gray.

The Guarder's glare turned brittle as the two men shared a look.

"Didn't drill for this," Wiles said under his breath. He slowly walked backward, oblivious to the look of surprise the soldiers now wore. "Not according to plan . . ."

---

At midday meal Perrin didn't return. Mahrree wanted to believe she was ready for his absence, but she knew that was a lie. She'd lived alone for years, so why was she worried now? Her belly churned in dread and fear.

Perhaps this was one of those days her father had warned her about. The world really *was* out to get her.

Or her new husband.

---

Captain Shin and his loyal lieutenant paused to look around.

All they saw now were pine trees, so close to each other it seemed that at any moment they might break out in a fight for sunshine. But that was all right. Just ten minutes ago two more Guarders had been stunned to find themselves chased out of the forest. Then the captain took some emergency food rations from the soldiers and hauled his weary lieutenant right back into the thick of the trees again.

Karna sighed.

Perrin smiled to himself. There was a lot associated with that sigh. "Tell me, Brillen. It's your job, you know. You're my third and fourth hands, as they say, so I rely on you to keep me informed and on task."

Karna made a "Pfft!" sound, which was likely the most insubordinate noise he'd ever uttered.

Perrin grinned and turned around to face his second in command. "You have something to say, Brillen?"

Karna froze, stunned. His face registered frustration, agitation, and now uneasiness as he realized his "Pfft!" was audible.

What he finally said surprised the captain. "Why do you call me Brillen, sir?"

Perrin blinked. "Why not? We're not around the other soldiers—why shouldn't I call you by your first name?"

Karna licked his parched lips. "It's not protocol, sir."

Perrin grinned again. "I'm not exactly protocol."

Karna threw his hands in the air. "Really? I hadn't noticed!" he exclaimed in a rare show of sarcasm.

Perrin folded his arms, fascinated. "I've never seen you like this, Brillen. Normally you're so by-the-book I could use you as a reference guide. Getting annoyed with your commander isn't exactly protocol either. But I heartily approve. Keep it up!" He slapped the lieutenant on the shoulder.

Karna took a deep breath and twitched his complimented shoulder. "Permission to speak freely, sir?"

"Only if you call me Perrin. It's only fair, Brillen."

"Sir!"

Amused, Perrin said, "Sir?"

Seeing the lieutenant couldn't come as far as Perrin was hoping, he patted his shoulder again in a conciliatory manner. "Go ahead."

Karna cleared his throat formally. "Sir. As your third and fourth hands, it is my duty to inform you that . . ." He gestured lamely to their surroundings. "We're breaking every rule in the book!"

"I know."

"Your FATHER'S book!"

"I know."

"Your GRANDFATHER'S first rule!" Karna's voice a full octave higher now. "First rule states, 'No man—'"

"Goes into the forest, blah-blah-and-ahem, yes I know," Perrin said dully. "So that's what's bothering you?"

Karna gestured again with his arms outstretched. Obviously the captain had gone blind and stupid in the last several hours.

Perrin smiled in understanding. "I'm not showing disrespect to my grandfather, if that makes you feel any better."

Karna squinted dubiously.

Perrin glanced around to make sure they were still alone. The immediate forest was remarkably still. "You see, my grandfather was an excellent man, Brillen. Do you mind if I call you Brillen? Better get used to it, because you're also my second mind, and I can't refer to my own thoughts in a formal manner, so neither will I refer to you formally. As I was saying—" he continued, ignoring the baffled expression of his lieutenant, "—my grandfather was an excellent man. Better than most people ever knew. Yes, he set that first rule, but in order to keep the world out of harm's way. He didn't want the common man, woman, child, or soldier risking their lives unnecessarily by stepping into the forests. Hence, the law."

"Which you have broken. Which you tried to break several weeks ago," Karna reminded.

His mouth opened and his eyes narrowed as a new understanding came to him.

"Which you intended to break for a long time now, haven't you, sir? You came to Edge *precisely* to enter the forests!"

If he feared his allegation would offend the captain, Karna was going to be surprised.

Perrin merely shrugged and raised his eyebrows in reluctant confession.

"You did!" Karna nearly shouted, forgetting to keep his voice down to avoid calling Guarders to their position. "You came here deliberately to break the law! Sir!"

Seeing the worry in his lieutenant's eyes—he'd have to report his commander as noncompliant!—Perrin put his hands on Karna's shoulders. "With my grandfather's approval, I promise."

"Oh, that's convenient to claim," Karna snarled. "He's dead!"

Perrin blinked at the outburst, and Karna slapped his hand across his mouth. "That sounded so awful, sir!" His voice was muffled. "I'm so sorry."

Perrin just shook his head and chuckled. "Don't be—I'm quite enjoying this new display of independence from you, Brillen. And don't cringe like that to your name, just get used to it. You see, while my grandfather made the rules, he also had an interesting perspective about them: some rules are meant to be broken by the right men. A rule may not be a good one, and begs to be violated so that it can be replaced by a better one."

"Again," Karna said, but this time more carefully, "that's convenient reasoning for violating the law."

"But that doesn't mean it's wrong," Perrin suggested. He looked off into the distance as if he could see beyond the twenty paces of dense fir trees. "Sometimes the right man must go where no one else has dared to. He may be the only one that can go over the wall, break down the door, or go into the forest and see, once and for all, what's *really* happening. That's because he's the only one who can actually *do* something about it."

Karna was silent for a moment, then eventually said, "Go over the wall, sir?" He glanced around, not seeing any walls.

Perrin blinked out of his thoughts, ignored the last question, and glanced over at the lieutenant. "My turn to ask a question—why'd you follow me in here?"

Next to any other man, Brillen Karna wouldn't have looked so short. He steeled his stocky frame before giving his answer. "Because I was following your orders!"

"Fair enough. But you could have rejected my orders. No one would've blamed you."

Karna raised his eyebrows. "Obviously you didn't see the look on your face last night. No one would have survived had I opposed you. Sir," he remembered to add.

Perrin chuckled. He wasn't sure why he felt so at ease in the trees. That should have alarmed him, he knew. More than the idea that he was, in fact, *in the forest.* "Well, I'm glad you're with me. We've already had success and I'm confident we'll have more. If we ever get our bearings again," he added in a mumble. "The only thing I'm sure of is 'downhill.' Everything downhill must be 'out'."

Karna mumbled something, too, as he gave the trees an agitated glare.

"What was that?" Perrin asked.

Karna's troubled *he-heard-me* look returned. "I . . . just, uh . . ."

"Spit it out, Brillen. And stop grimacing."

Karna gulped. "Maybe I mentioned something about following your father's orders is more difficult than anticipated. Sir."

Intrigued, Perrin put his hands on his waist. "What orders might those be? From his book about command?"

"From his instructions to me, just before I left to come here."

A corner of Perrin's mouth lifted into a subtle smile. "Which were . . . ?"

"'Keep my son out of trouble.' Sir."

"He really said that to you?"

"Along with a few other bits of instruction. Warnings. Threats—"

"Sounds like the High General," Captain Shin chuckled. "He's the one who recommended you to me, you know."

Karna looked surprised. "Because I earned the highest marks in his class, sir?"

"Or I suppose he thought you'd be the best man to remind me of my duty."

Karna sighed heavily. "Obviously I'm failing at that."

"Oh, not at all," Perrin assured him. "I'm just ignoring your reminders." He laughed at Brillen's scowl.

---

The two men dressed in mottled clothing with fresh green branches tied to their tunics sat so high in the trees that they couldn't hear the conversation, but they were fascinated all the same.

Why was the captain so comfortable in the forest?

The men formed some speculations, then observed in amazement as the two officers made their way further into the trees.

---

Two more.

There were *two more* Guarders, tied hands to feet, and lying helpless on their sides. There was no need to gag them because they weren't about to say anything. Their glares spoke volumes, though.

Wiles could barely move as he stared at the next two prisoners.

"Men are doing quite well, aren't they?" said a master sergeant as he folded his arms in victory. "In my fifteen years in the army I've never seen anything like this. None of this is going according to army protocol, but then again, why should it be the Guarders dictating how we battle them? Captain Shin's quite the innovative young officer, isn't he? Said he'll just keep chasing Guarders downhill through the trees, so we best just keep catching them!"

Wiles felt his chest tighten and grow hot.

The master sergeant frowned at him. "Wiles, are you all right? You're sweating."

"It's hot," was all Wiles could reply.

"Not really," his companion said as he looked up to the sun. "Today's much cooler than yesterday . . ."

Wiles continued to stare, almost apologetically, at the Guarders.

The Guarders didn't even blink at him.

"So," said the master sergeant, unsure of how to respond to the sergeant major's unusual lack of enthusiasm for their success, "do we leave them here—guarded, of course—or do we lug them back to the fort? Shin's still in the trees with Karna, sure they can find a few more volunteers for questioning. Wiles? Sir?"

Wiles's shoulders dropped and he rubbed his chest absent-mindedly. Without another word he turned and trudged back to the fort.

---

Hours later, Captain Shin wondered again why the army proudly insisted that the buttons on their uniforms "glisten in the sun." It was just a signal that said, "Come get me!"

He paused at a trickling stream below a large cavern, took a handful of mud, and smeared it over the dried dirt that was flaking off of his buttons.

Lieutenant Karna crouched next to him and recaked his silver menaces as well.

Perrin envied him; the darker hue to his skin allowed Brillen to blend in better with his surroundings. Perrin was tempted for a moment to rub some of the mud over his own gravel-colored face, until he had another thought.

He looked over at Karna's jacket, smiled mischievously, and smeared mud over the yellow patches and white insignias on the shoulder and chest of his lieutenant. Conquering the forest was doable. You just had to become part of it.

Karna raised his eyebrows in dismay at his jacket, but then he scooped a handful mud and eagerly slapped it on the captain's shoulder. For good measure he rubbed it in to dull the golden shoulder braid. Smiling, he mouthed, "Tell wife sorry."

Captain Shin winced as he looked at his much more functional, yet filthy, jacket.

His wife.

He hadn't considered her much since they entered the forest. His focus had been singular, his resolve unswerving. She didn't need his concern. She'd lived alone for years, and probably hadn't even noticed he was gone. Might not even realize until dinner time.

As he started to creep up the shrub-filled hillside, trying to catch sight of the Guarder they'd been following, he felt a gnawing in his stomach, and it wasn't just from hunger.

Of course she would miss him. She was probably searching the fort right now, trying to find out where he went. It'd be ridiculous if she did, but Mahrree was the kind of woman who didn't care what kind of behavior was expected. She'd do whatever struck her as right and logical.

Perrin shook his head to clear it. He couldn't afford to think of her right now. The best thing he could do was bring her home his filthy uniform, with him still alive inside it.

Shin and Karna continued to crawl up the side of the crevice which produced such an awful stench—a mixture of sulfur and decay—that the two men wore constant scowls. But the forest really *was* traversable, Perrin considered, even if occasionally repulsive.

Given enough time he could map all of its secrets.

First, uphill was in, and downhill was out—usually. There were dips and valleys he discovered that flouted that rule, but he'd find them all.

Second, he noticed that wherever there was danger—gaping chasms, sprays of hot water, stenches of sulfur—the trees didn't grow. Instead, the ground was barren and white, making it easily identifiable. Contrary to everything he'd been taught, the trees were the *safest* parts of the forest.

But convincing the soldiers to overcome their generations-old fear of the woods would be an immense hurdle. But not impossible.

Perhaps this was why his grandfather had pulled him aside when he was twelve and gave him the lecture of, "Some rules are meant to be broken by the right men. Perrin, you will be one of those rare 'right' men . . ."

The Guarder they tracked was now at the top of crevice, and the captain and lieutenant crept among the shrubs below it toward the west side. The Guarder, dressed completely in black, was obvious in the sunshine as he squatted between two white rocks and looked below him for signs of activity.

Shin stopped and held out his hand to halt Karna. Even with their attempts to blend in, the scrubby brush and low rocks around them didn't offer much cover.

The Guarder saw someone, below and to the east on the other side of the crevice.

Perrin squinted in the sunshine and noticed another man in dark clothing climbing up to meet his companion.

The first man gestured in the general direction of Shin and Karna. The second man nodded and turned to look toward the officers.

Perrin held his breath and hoped Brillen did the same.

The second man broke into a run and raced up the side of the crevice.

"Been spotted," Shin whispered down to Karna, and he heard Karna quietly draw his sword. Perrin drew his too, but continued to crawl between the bushes toward the top of the cavern.

"There!" he heard the man at the top of the cavern shout.

The second man now reached the first and together they began to rush down the other side of the crevice toward Shin and Karna's position.

"Stay down, under that bush!" Perrin whispered to Brillen behind him.

As the lieutenant scrambled, Perrin crawled between more bushes and rolled away from the crevice.

Within moments the two Guarders arrived at the spot where the captain had been. They stopped and looked frantically around.

Shin leaped to his feet, swung his sword, and caught the first Guarder with the flat side of the blade. He didn't want him dead; he wanted him for questioning.

The man flailed as his footing shifted on the loose gravel below him and he fell backward. His companion caught his arm as the first man began to slip on the edge of the cavern.

"No!" the first Guarder shouted as he lost his footing and began to slide into the crevice.

Karna leaped to his feet but stared in amazement at what happened next. So did Perrin, whose sword was raised to deliver another blow he had hoped would render the Guarder unconscious.

The second man nodded once to his companion and deliberately let him go. Without a sound the Guarder fell into the groaning cavern below him.

While Shin and Karna stared in shock that the Guarder let his friend drop to his death, the man drew his jagged dagger and lunged toward the captain.

Perrin dodged out of the way and slashed the Guarder's arm with his sword as he passed.

The Guarder spun around, furious to have been cut. Making a strange guttural noise, he charged at the captain. Shin sidestepped the Guarder who overshot his target, barely stopping himself at the edge of the crevice.

Instinctively Perrin reached out to grab the man and caught his arm before he fell in.

"What are you doing?" Karna yelled. "Let him fall!"

"I want answers!" Shin yelled back.

The Guarder turned to Shin, delivered a frosty glare, and slashed at him with his dagger. Perrin released the man's arm to avoid being cut, and the Guarder fell back purposely into the crevice where his companion had just vanished.

"No!" Perrin cried, looking over the edge.

There was nothing more to be seen but blackness.

Karna rushed over and shook his head as he stared down into the seemingly bottomless pit. "Why did they do that? They just . . . they just *quit*. I don't get it, Captain!"

"Neither do I, Brillen. So many questions to ask them—maybe that's why. They don't want to give any answers."

"So . . . so what's the point of all of this? Why attack us if they're just going to commit suicide? They had a good chance at killing one or both of us—"

"Your confidence in me is overwhelming, Lieutenant," interrupted the captain.

"I'm sorry, sir, that's not what I meant. It's just that . . . I don't get it."

"We've established that," Perrin said impatiently. "I'll tell you what's happened: the two highest ranked officers of Edge are standing miles away from the fort in unfamiliar territory staring into a crevice which no longer holds any danger for us. What we need to be doing, Lieutenant, is finding the rest of the Guarders and our men!"

---

Mahrree spent the afternoon standing in the vacant land next to the main fort road. And she wasn't alone. Dozens of people came and went, none approaching closer than Mahrree had, and all speculating as to what was happening. She watched the trees and tried to see her husband among the soldiers, but she didn't dare approach the fort to interfere. There was a constant stream of horses and soldiers riding back and forth, with accompanying shouting, so obviously something was going on.

"Looks like a full exercise to me," decided a villager.

"As if you would know. This is more than just an exercise," said a larger man in his fifties. "Right Miss Mahrree?" He'd known Mahrree since she was a child, when he and his wife moved next door to the Petos. She'd always be Miss Mahrree.

"I don't know, Mr. Arky," she confessed. "I haven't seen the captain since all of this started."

He cleared his throat. "You haven't? You mean, this might *actually* be the first Guarder attack in Edge in thirty years?"

Everyone within hearing distance took a step closer for Mahrree's response.

She knew she had to make it a good one. What she said would travel throughout the village in less than an hour. Their perception of the situation was more real than anything they might be seeing. But all Mahrree could think to say was, "I really don't know. As I said, I haven't seen the captain for two days."

The news unsettled her as much as it did everyone else around her.

She walked home, lonely and worried, when the sun finally set in the blood-red sky.

As Mahrree blew out the candles that night she felt a bit light-headed with silly fear. In her hand she kept the metal rod Perrin gave her, but she slept in fits and starts.

By morning she was so irritable her stomach couldn't hold any food. She made it through the day but found herself napping on the sofa in the afternoon. She surprised herself by wishing her mother was around, but Hycymum was treating herself to a stay at Waves, a grueling wagon ride four days away. When someone undertook the extreme discomfort of traveling, it was a sign they thought they were aging and wanted to see the salty sea before they died. Now that Mahrree was married, Hycymum thought her time must be growing short and took the "old person" trip, even though she was only forty-eight.

Mahrree was alone. That shouldn't have bothered her, but it did.

She couldn't confide in any of the other teachers or even to Tabbit Densal that suddenly she was scared sick. It was so unlike her.

---

Captain Shin was lost—*really* lost. It was so unlike him. The last several hours of the afternoon hadn't been for nothing, though. They'd already chased another Guarder into the hands of waiting soldiers. That would be four men the captain would interrogate with his most pressing question, "What do you want?"

The night before, he and the lieutenant had found their way to the edge of the forest between Edge and Moorland. They wolfed down some rations provided by ten soldiers who had been tracking their progress, and the captain and lieutenant even got a few hours of sleep while the soldiers took turns keeping watch. But Perrin's rest was disturbed by dreams of his bride fighting off Guarders in their bedroom. Even with the unprecedented Guarder captures, Shin still felt he was losing the battle.

Battle.

It didn't feel like a battle but an absurd game where only one side knew the rules and the other side tried vainly to figure out the players and the objective.

For the last several hours he and Karna had been tracking another lone Guarder, but Perrin had lost sight of him. Maybe he was as disoriented as the two officers. The trees were so thick Perrin glimpsed the sun above him only occasionally. Yesterday, when he was quite sure he had his bearings, he noticed that the moss here grew on only one side of rocks and trees—the northern side.

Forest secret number three. Until he could be sure of his location again, he navigated by tiny green growth.

Had this been happening twenty years ago, after the forest fire, he would've easily seen how to get out. But the pines that grew to replace the fallen timber competed for every available inch. Making their way through the trees was not only disorienting but painful. Perrin and Karna had scrapes over their hands and faces, and more than once the useless ribbons and decorations on their uniforms snagged the protruding needles.

Several times the captain stopped to listen to the forest around him. Sometimes it was intensely still, not even the birds calling. Other times it was so noisy it sounded as if the entire ground below him was making ready to open up. But usually Perrin heard nothing that would help him. He'd look to Karna for ideas, but the lieutenant would just shrug.

The Guarders were out there; Perrin was sure of it. He could feel them but not see them. His only comfort was hoping they were as frustrated as he was, lost in the pines.

---

By evening Mahrree forced herself to eat something and felt a bit better.

Perrin had been gone for two full nights and days now, and she couldn't just sit and pine for him. She thought about walking into the village but felt so alone without him. Then she considered heading up to the fort and asking what was happening, but she was strangely embarrassed by that.

As she went to bed early that night she wished she had let Perrin get that puppy he had seen last week, just to have something else in the house. She lay in bed awake for hours, wondering where he was.

---

Somewhere near Moorland. That was Shin and Karna's best guess. They camped—or attempted to—in the forest approaching the small village, and hoped their dozen soldiers were on duty. All day they'd been on the tail of a Guarder, but they could never quite catch up to him. He knew the forest better than they did, but just *barely*. By the time the sun started to go down, the Guarder in the distance was looking around disoriented, and Perrin felt a little more confident when he realized the man was lost, too.

When it grew dark the officers lost sight of the Guarder again, knowing their chances of finding him in the night were nil. And their chances of finding their way out of the forest, even less.

It was going to be another long, uncomfortable night lying in the dirt trying to rest. He tried not to think about his hunger since their rations ran out at midday meal.

He tried not think that he'd led his lieutenant to the middle of the unknown, and that he wasn't sure where they were going in the morning.

And he especially tried not to think that his new wife of just two and a half moons was going to bed alone, for the third time.

# Chapter 18 ~ "Then they did the strangest thing . . ."

The surgeon jogged over to the knot of soldiers at the edge of the forest. "Well, what kind of trouble have we got ourselves into now?" He was already opening his travel pack in eagerness to initiate it.

None of the men had seen the surly doctor looking happy about anything before. Then again, besides the two injured soldiers the first night of the raid, nothing beyond a few cuts had yet occurred at the fort, and a man with more than thirty years of army service needed to be useful. The surgeon's eyes glowed in anticipation as he yanked off the sleeve of the wounded corporal.

"Seems it's just a nick in the arm, Surgeon," said the master sergeant. "From that last Guarder they've tied up."

"I'll be the judge of that." The gray-haired man sighed in disappointment as he examined the gash. "Not very deep . . . suppose I don't need to stitch it, then."

The corporal closed his eyes in relief that his head wasn't about to meet a wooden plank to render him unconscious for the procedure.

"Still," the surgeon cocked his head, "it could stand a thorough cleaning. Decades ago Guarders attempted to poison the knife blades." A grim smile crept across his face. "We don't want infection setting in now, do we?"

The corporal looked at the master sergeant in pleading, but he could only shrug in apology.

"This will do the trick," the surgeon announced as he opened a bottle from his pack containing clear liquid.

The corporal's shoulders sagged as he saw it was only water.

But it wasn't.

"Yee-OW! What is THAT?" the corporal cried as he yanked his arm away.

"My own brew," the surgeon's grim smile developed a baleful quality as he gripped the young man's wrist again. "Burns away any infection. You'll be arm wrestling again in no time."

"Gonna burn off my whole arm!"

"Nonsense. Besides, this wrap I'm applying will make sure your arm doesn't fall off."

"That could happen?"

"Strange things do," the surgeon said without a hint of humor.

The master sergeant shook his head in assurance at the corporal, but the soldier didn't know who to believe.

"There," the surgeon said as he tied the wrap. "You'll be good as new in a few days." He sounded disappointed, but turned to the master sergeant. "A word?"

The master sergeant nodded and the two men walked a little distance into the vacant field.

"I'm also here to inform you, sergeant, that you are now in command of the fort." The surgeon was never one to beat around a bush. He'd plow right over it.

"What?!"

"The captain and the lieutenant are still in the forest, correct?"

"Yes, but Wiles—"

"—who is third in command has been relieved of duty."

"Why did you do that?"

"I didn't do it," the surgeon grumbled. "He did it to himself. Something's snapped in Wiles's mind, and he's completely useless. I suspect he's traumatized, but there hasn't been a case of real trauma since the Great War. Maybe he's unstable, I don't know. He's doing nothing right now. As fourth in command, you are now point commander here, and at the fort. Should Shin and Karna not return . . ."

He cleared his throat and paused.

"The High General will have our uniforms, then our heads," he declared plainly. "Maybe Shin's unstable too. Why else would he take such a risk? Sergeant, we both know this is disastrous. You and I need to maintain a semblance of calm and command while our two officers find new ways to die and the sergeant major stares at the walls."

The master sergeant swallowed. "But . . . I retire from the army in just two more moons," he said as if it mattered.

"Well then," the surgeon slapped him on the back, "you're going out as a commander. Congratulations."

---

Wiles rocked himself on the chair like a terrified child, trying to think.

The fort had only a handful of new recruits left in it, tasked to run food, medical supplies, and rope to the rest of the soldiers waiting along the trees for more Guarders. Even the surgeon walked slowly up and down the edge of the forest waiting to be needed, or just wanting to see some action.

Wiles hadn't ordered any of that; the master sergeant now standing in charge at the northeast gates likely had. He'd even started lessons in hog tying, or calf roping, or whatever it was they did to immobilize the Guarders that they hoped to catch next.

All Wiles could do was sit behind the big command desk in the office and slowly sway. None of this was right.

That was what occupied Wiles's mind—how completely contrary to any protocol, rule, or past action all of this was. There were supposed to be stages and order, but instead there was chaos and complete loss of containment.

"*Containment,*" Wiles whispered again, closing his eyes in dread. For two days he hadn't eaten or slept, too obsessed with the word. "When he finds out we lost containment—"

He could barely bring himself to admit his fear, but he had to. His training demanded it. The oaths demanded it.

There was only one solution, for him and for the captured Guarders.

That was the other problem. Guarders were never captured alive. Until now. And there was only one way for a captured Guarder to behave.

Wiles added a quiet moan to his swaying as the sun slowly set in the west.

---

The night had been unbearably long for Mahrree. As exhausted from worry and illness as she was, she couldn't rest. Then the next day was as insufferable as the previous two. She couldn't eat, she couldn't sleep, she couldn't think of anything else but Perrin.

Mahrree had to face the truth. Being married to an officer was sickening.

---

"And I used to think the miles they had us run each week for training was useless," Karna whispered to Shin as they hiked over yet another wooded rise.

The sun was high again in the blue sky, but it didn't help with spotting anything in the dense trees.

"Been running and walking so much the past few days, I think I'm going to be sick when all of this is over. I mean, really, when was I ever going to need to be in such good condition when, as an officer, I would spend all my time on a horse?"

Shin chuckled. "And who told you that you would be spending all your time on horseback?"

"Hmm, a fat, balding general named Cush. I believe you know him."

Perrin smiled at Karna's contempt. The lack of sleep and food was making the lieutenant bolder. Maybe the entire army would find itself braver if it took to the forests.

"Known Cush since I was a child," Perrin said as he scanned the bushy distance for their quarry. "Cush petitioned my father heavily for the position of his advisor. I think it was so that he could spend his time behind a desk. That's where he's the most comfortable."

Perrin nudged Karna and pointed into the distance. The forest dipped from their position on a hillside, allowing them a clear view of the tree-covered slope rising on the other side of the small canyon at the base of the mountains. They saw a slight movement several hundred paces in the distance.

"And Cush sitting behind a desk makes all the horses at the garrison comfortable as well," Karna said, pointing to where a tree shimmied ever so gently. It may have only been a bear scratching an itchy backside—they'd already seen two—but the officers decided to believe it was something more significant.

Perrin nodded. "That Guarder can't go too much further. The forest narrows just before Moorland there. See that rock outcropping? Very few trees—he'd expose himself too much. I'm guessing he'll backtrack again, looking for anyone else. I wonder if he realizes he's going in large circles."

"I'm glad he is. I almost used to this terrain now. I'm sure we've seen that tree before."

"That's because it's a *forest*, Brillen. There's only about a million more trees just like it!"

Karna smirked and was about to respond when they both heard a shout. They looked into the distance toward the south where the woods ended.

More shouts came from the tree line, and a slight movement of tree branches suggested someone else was running into the forest. Either that, or that the winds were picking up again.

Shin and Karna looked in the direction of the man they had been following for two days, but saw nothing. Perrin groaned in frustration and signaled to Karna to follow him. They darted through the trees down the hillside and toward the edge of the forest to the shouting.

In a small clearing just a few paces from the edge of the woods stood a Guarder. His arm was wrapped around a terrified private, and his other hand held his jagged dagger against the young man's throat. Three soldiers were facing him, their swords drawn, when the captain and the lieutenant appeared behind them.

"I said don't move!" the Guarder shouted, twisting himself and his hostage to face the filthy captain and lieutenant. "Guarantee me safe passage, and the soldier goes free."

Captain Shin held up his hands calmly, but the Guarder shifted in agitation, causing the private to whimper.

Karna drew his sword but Perrin kept his hands up.

A few more soldiers charged into the clearing and stopped abruptly when they saw the situation.

"All right," the captain said. "You may go free after you answer a few questions."

"No questions!" the Guarder in dark dirt brown clothing with a darkened face cried. Frantic, he shifted his grip, and the soldier tried to pull his arm away from his chest. But the Guarder held the knife closer to his throat. "Nothing! I'm leaving now, and I'm taking him with me! I refuse to be captured!"

Shin took a cautious step toward the man and put his hands on his waist. "And how far do you intend to take him?" he said levelly. "How am I supposed to get him back?"

"That's not my problem!" the Guarder shouted at him.

"Yes it is," Shin said coolly. "Because I have eight soldiers with swords pointed at you. I think you have quite a big problem. But if you answer a few questions, I'm willing to let you go free." Perrin raised his hand in warning to Karna who he could tell was ready to protest the offer.

"Get out of my way!"

"Why are you here?" Shin took another slow step forward. "What do you want from Edge?"

"I said no questions!"

"Because if there's something you need—food, supplies, whatever—we might be able to help you."

"Get out of my way!"

Shin stepped closer.

The Guarder pressed the knife against the private's throat.

"Where do you live?" Shin said. "Why have you come here?"

"Shut up! Just shut up!"

Shin shook his head. "You don't really want to do this, I can tell. Your heart's not into it. That's good." He took another step. "You don't have to, either. You can just drop the knife, and I'll guarantee your safety. Just tell me how I can help—"

"Don't you understand shutting up?!"

"Never been good at it," Perrin admitted, taking one more step. "Just never know when to quit . . ." He saw the man's finger twitch on the handle of the knife.

Karna repositioned his grip on his sword.

"Just drop the knife and—"

The captain recognized the Guarder's movement seemingly just a moment before it actually happened. Shin drew his sword in an instant and thrust it into the Guarder's side just as he began to cut into the private's throat.

Karna's sword struck the Guarder from behind a moment later, and the Guarder and the private both dropped to the ground.

The Guarder was dead.

The private only thought he was as he whimpered and held his bleeding throat.

Shin rushed over to lift him up. "You're all right, soldier. Just nicked your skin. Calm down," he ordered as another soldier arrived with a cloth to tie around his neck.

Perrin looked over at Karna who was checking the dark man for a pulse.

He looked up at the captain and shook his head.

Shin sighed and rubbed his face thoughtfully. "We have one more, Lieutenant. It isn't over yet," and he scanned the thick trees for any sign of their last Guarder.

Karna nodded, stood up, and gestured to the other soldiers. "Sergeant, take the private to find the surgeon. The rest of you stay along the tree line. The captain and I may have one more for you."

A corporal pointed at the still body. "What do we do with that, sir?"

Captain Shin looked down at the Guarder. "He's of no use to us now. Leave him for the buzzards and bears. Karna, now, before we lose the last one."

Shin took off in an aimless jog into the trees with Karna right behind him. Perrin noticed that this time his lieutenant was much keener to follow him.

Perhaps, just perhaps, all the soldiers would see the need to follow him into the forest.

After a minute they stopped jogging and looked around. The forest was absolutely still. Shin glanced behind them as Karna tried to look into the distance. There was no evidence of anyone anywhere.

"Do you think he heard what happened?" Karna whispered.

"How could he not?" Shin whispered back.

"It's going to get dark soon," Karna said.

"We have a little time yet. We're not leaving until we have to."

"Understood, sir." Karna's voice was a little shaky.

Shin turned to him and saw his lieutenant's light brown skin had gone pale. "You all right?"

Karna shrugged. "Never did that before."

"What, run into the forest? We've been doing that for the past few days now." Shin surveyed the area again.

"That's not what I meant," he said quietly.

"I know, Brillen," Perrin whispered back. "I've threatened many men, but I've never been deadly." He smiled grimly.

"Which one of us did it, do you think?"

Shin shook his head. "Maybe both of us. Does that help?"

"We each claim half a death?"

Perrin cringed and went back to examining the still trees around them. "Why are we here, Karna?"

"I've been wondering that for awhile, sir."

Shin turned back to him. "Really? You don't remember why you wanted to become an officer?"

Karna sighed. "I wanted to serve, to protect the citizens. I never wanted to . . ." He shrugged lamely.

Perrin sighed back. "I know, I know. None of us want to. But that's part of the serving and protecting. Did we have any other option?"

"I suppose not. You *did* try to negotiate with him."

"Always my greatest weakness," Perrin admitted. "I've gone over a dozen scenarios in my head, but none of them end with him still talking. Maybe you should've conducted the negotiations."

"You had a *dozen* options?" Karna scoffed. "I still can't think of one!"

"So that's it, then," Perrin said. "We did what we could, he forced our hands, and he lost the game. What more is there to say?"

Karna shook his head. "Nothing, sir. I still don't feel any better, but there's nothing more to say then . . . let's go find that other Guarder."

Perrin nodded and the two of them ventured deeper into the woods, keeping an eye on the sun that was close to setting.

Two men in mottled green and brown clothing sitting high in the trees watched as the two officers quietly walked below them. Neither of the men breathed or made a sound. When the captain and lieutenant had carefully picked their way past, the two men in the trees looked at each other.

One raised his eyebrows at the other.

The other man nodded back and broke into a big smile.

Then the two men saluted the captain.

---

Mahrree's evening and night dragged. When she went to bed that night it was with a heavy heart and a fluttering belly. Anatomically, that put them at direct odds with other, so she hardly slept at all.

In the early morning she heard a noise from the kitchen. She instinctively picked up the iron rod and crept down the stairs. Her weary and anxious mind played tricks with her depth perception, so the steps seemed to shift up and down. Growing more terrified by the moment, she thought she would become sick before reaching the bottom. Then she heard a noise come through the kitchen door which halted her in her tracks.

"Perrin!"

He stopped, looked up at her on the stairs and tried to give her a smile, but his heart wasn't in it. He looked terrible. His black hair was disheveled, his face was scratched and stubbly, his sleeveless undershirt was stained by dirt, sweat, and what Mahrree feared may have been dried blood, and his jacket, which already hung over a chair by the eating table, was caked in what looked like mud.

Still, she sighed and closed her eyes, feeling an immense wave of relief.

Then she felt another wave of *something else* that she chose to ignore.

She opened her eyes and tried not to stare at the filth on his used-to-be-white undershirt, but she couldn't stop herself. "Oh Perrin! I've been so worried! It's so good to—"

That's when the *other* wave she was feeling refused to be ignored any longer. No matter how she fought it, she became sick all over the lower half of the stairs.

Perrin stood rigid in surprise.

Mortified, she winced at him as she wiped her chin.

"I have to admit," he said unemotionally, "I've received better welcomes than that. I'll get something to clean it up. You just stay right there." He turned to the washing room.

"But Perrin—"

"Just stay!" he called back. "There's no way you can make it down without, well, *slipping* or something." He sounded as if he might be sick as well.

Mahrree slumped down on the still-clean steps, exhausted, embarrassed, and feeling much, much better.

Perrin returned and tossed some washing rags up to her. "I think we can meet somewhere in the middle. How long have you been sick?" His face reflected some worry as handed up to her one of the two tin buckets he brought. He squatted to begin his unpleasant task at the bottom stair.

Mahrree laughed weakly as she started to mop up. "Ever since you left. You know how people say they're worried sick? Well, I think proved that statement to be true. Oh, but I'm so sorry. You look awful. You finally come home and then I do this to you—"

"It's all right—part of our vows: Together, make the best times out of the worst." His voice sounded a bit sharp.

"Perrin?" Mahrree stepped down a stair.

"Yes?" He didn't look up from his work.

"Perrin," Mahrree said more forcefully.

He glanced up. "What?" His eyes were as clouded as the morning sky.

"What happened?" she whispered.

He was quiet for a moment. "We'll talk when everything is . . . cleaner. Both of us," and he gave her a half smile which improved his mouth, but not his murky eyes.

An hour later they sat at the table for breakfast. Perrin, now washed and shaved and in a new undershirt, gulped down his food as if he hadn't eaten properly in days.

Mahrree still felt dizzy, and watching him made her lose whatever appetite she had. She nibbled her toast just for show.

"So," she started when he'd finished half his breakfast, "what happened?"

"Just what I told you would happen," he said brusquely between bites. "Guarders."

Mahrree was taken aback by his abrupt manner. But maybe since he'd been an officer for the past four days and nights, his mind was still stuck there. "Really?"

He nodded, focused on his plate. "It seems they've been watching the fort for some time. Knew our patrols. Ambushed some of the men during the first night."

"Oh no!" Mahrree breathed. "Are they . . ."

"Recovering," he said tonelessly. "Some nasty gashes."

"Is that why your clothes—"

"No," he cut her off. "Soldiers were already at the surgeon's when I got there." He tore off another bite of bacon and studied the table.

Mahrree wondered how skirt around his formal tone, but felt she was talking to a stranger. "So whose . . ." She couldn't say the word "blood" without feeling queasy. She hadn't seen more than some superficial cuts on him so she knew it wasn't his.

"The Guarder's."

She was growing irritated with his pithy responses. "And how many were there?"

"At least ten, probably more. At least one escaped. Lost two in a crevice. Irretrievable."

Maybe more details *weren't* better, she considered as she cringed at the thought of the ground swallowing up men.

"They were testing our strength," he added, stabbing at his food.

Eventually the story would all come out. Mahrree might have to get him more breakfast, though. "And how *is* your strength?"

"Not as good as I wished, but enough to impress the general." He pushed around his food with his fork, never once looking at her. "We chased them nearly to Moorland. They have only a dozen soldiers based there, but most were on patrol where we needed them. They helped capture two more prisoners last night." He attacked a fried potato.

"So you captured some?" She was impressed. "That's never happened before."

"That's right," he said dully as he jabbed a pancake.

"Have you learned anything yet?"

"No."

"Are they uncooperative?"

"You could say that." He took a long drink.

Mahrree sighed in annoyance. "So what does the Guarder look like who stained your uniform?"

"Dead."

Mahrree dropped her toast.

Perrin glanced at her plate where it fell. Eventually he looked up at her with blank, cold eyes.

"By whose hand?"

"Unsure," he said impassively. "He was holding a private hostage. Negotiations didn't go well. When he became agitated, Karna and I both rushed him. There's blood on both our swords. Satisfied?" he snapped.

Mahrree was startled by his sharpness. "I didn't mean anything by it, I just . . ." She didn't feel upset enough to cry, but oddly the tears were building rapidly and spilling down her face.

Perrin groaned in disgust and threw down his fork which clattered on his almost empty plate. He rested his head in his hands with his elbows on the table and stared at it.

Mahrree watched him miserably, trying not to sniff out loud. She knew they'd have conflicts, but the tension at the table threatened to break it in half.

Their bliss was gone.

He was quiet for a full minute before he spoke. "It's been a very long . . . my head's so foggy that I don't even know how many days." He rubbed his eyes, his voice weary. "I need rest. I've put the master sergeant in charge for today since Wiles seems to have taken ill. I have to write a report for the High General. I've been surviving on rations and snatches of sleep. I don't think well when I'm tired."

Mahrree nodded that she understood, but didn't dare speak. He was so distant, so unlike the man she fell in love with.

Perrin studied the table again. "Six prisoners, held separately. Brought them together after it was dark last night. We'd had them tied up, but undid them to walk them back to the fort. That was a mistake, because they did the strangest thing . . ." His voice trailed off.

Mahrree nervously chewed on her crust.

"They pulled out these small knives," he continued haltingly. "Didn't know they still had them. Then—they never said a word, just *looked* at each other. Then they . . . *gutted* each other. In front of all of us. Some strange, ritualistic manner. At the same time. As if they *had* to. Forced by . . . something. Before I realized what was happening, it was too late. All dead. Doesn't make sense."

Mahrree held her hand in front of her mouth, trying to calm the wave of nausea that tried to force its way upward. She couldn't think of what to say to the horror her husband had witnessed.

"This isn't . . . this isn't the way Guarders behaved in the past," he stammered as if betrayed by his training.

While she agreed—it was most horrific thing she'd ever heard—she didn't say anything. He didn't seem to be talking to her anyway, but was instead trying to sort out his own thoughts.

"Why . . . why suicide?" he asked the table. "Why . . . what *kind of thinking* has to go on in order to kill each other simultaneously? To be *feeling* the pain, to see the blade plunge . . ."

He made a thrusting and slicing motion in the air, and Mahrree squeezed her eyes shut too late.

"Then *still* continue with it? It was just . . ." He shook his head in dismay, then suddenly pressed his palms against his eyes, as if to force out the images he still saw.

Mahrree swallowed hard and her lower lip quivered in empathy. Of course he was short with her, and distant, and angry. How could he be anything else this morning?

Perrin sat motionless for another long minute, his hands still covering his eyes, while Mahrree tried to think of something—anything—to say. But she had no words that could possibly overcome what he was still reliving.

"This isn't what they do," he murmured. "They've never done this before . . ."

In time he pulled his hands from his eyes, and he appeared to be a different man, as if the disillusioned officer in him was abruptly snuffed out, leaving only her troubled husband.

It was remarkable how he could ignore so much of himself, Mahrree marveled. As if he actually were two different men, just as she thought after the second debate. But she was sure the officer would resurface. Perrin had likely shoved him into a back room of his mind, but he would soon break out.

Still, Perrin's face was noticeably softer as he reached across the table and took her free hand. "This couldn't have been easy for you. I was hoping a day like this wouldn't come for some time. But then again, we made a good enough show of force that this shouldn't happen again for a long while. They'll think twice before coming back," he added with a small, pitiful smile.

She tried to smile too. "I'm just happy you're home. And I know there's no good reason for me to be crying. I think I just need a nap, too."

Half an hour later she collapsed on their bed, and before her husband came upstairs to join her, fell into the deepest sleep she'd had all week.

When she woke up several hours later, she felt more her regular self. It was already afternoon, and Perrin was sitting at the small desk in their bedroom, drafting his report of the raid for Idumea. When she opened her eyes fully he glanced over, smiled thinly, and went back to work.

"How are you?" she asked.

"Fine," he said without looking up.

Mahrree sat up and hugged her knees. "I mean, how *are* you? You know, about . . . the past few days?"

He paused in his writing. "I'm *fine*."

"It's just that we should talk about—"

"We talk all the time, Mahrree," he said to his papers. "I can't think of another couple that talks as much as we do."

"True, but this is different. We should talk about important things."

"We went through the lists, a few moons ago."

"No," she groaned in irritation. Her mother-in-law had warned her about this. "I mean, what you *did*, what you saw, the Guarders, their knives, and how you feel about it, bloodying your sword—"

"I've worked it out. I'm fine. It needed to be done, I did it." He gave her a practiced smile, but she didn't believe it. His eyes, while normally dark brown, were even heavier with gloom. The officer was back. "No need to talk anymore."

"Are you sure?" Mahrree said, because she wasn't.

"Yes."

"Really."

He put down his quill a bit too forcefully, spread out his hands, and took a deep breath. "Yes." He turned in his chair to face her. "Perhaps the more important question is, how are you?"

Mahrree considered for a moment. "Still a little woozy, but I can make dinner." *That's* how you give an answer, she thought to herself. Details, explanations.

"Are you sure?"

"Yes."

"Are you *really* sure?"

Mahrree scrunched up her lips. "I know what you're trying to do."

"*Really?*"

"Perrin—"

"Irritating, isn't it."

She sighed loudly. "I'm only asking because I'm worried about you! That's my duty: to worry about my husband. Don't deny me my duty."

He finally smiled genuinely. "Just don't duty me to death, all right?"

"How can someone just talk you to death?"

"I don't know, but I'm sure *you'll* find a way."

For absolutely no good reason, her eyes filled with tears again.

Perrin winced. "I'm sorry." He walked over to the bed and sat down next to her, the officer shoved again into some recess of his brain. He pushed a lock of hair from her face and evaluated her, seemingly looking for something as he put a hand on top of hers. "Trust me. If something's wrong, I'll let you know. Now, why the tears? You didn't even cry at our wedding."

"I don't know!" she wailed. "Nothing's wrong."

That's when she noticed his side of the bed hadn't been disturbed, and his eyes were still bleary. "You haven't slept?"

He shrugged that away. "Can't sleep when it's light outside. Needed to bring a report to Hogal. I'm sure the whole village has already decided what happened, but he'll deliver the truth to them tonight at the amphitheater."

"Wait, you talked to Hogal?"

"I always talk to Hogal."

"But . . . but you're supposed to talk to me!"

He frowned, confused. "I always talk to you, *and* I talk to Hogal. I have for years. What's the problem?"

"You worked it out *with him!*" she cried. "*I'm* supposed to be who you talk things out with."

Perrin scoffed. "If I talked it over with you, I would have had another vomit mess to clean up. So that's what's bothering you? I didn't *talk* to you?"

"No!" she barked.

But that was a lie. Of course it bothered her, among other things! He'd left her for days with no news, came home angry, and now he told her to stop talking because he already talked?

"So nothing's wrong?" he restated. "Should I trust that answer? Because even though my father doesn't know much about women, he did tell me that when a woman is crying and says nothing's wrong, she's the biggest liar in the world."

At any other moment Mahrree would have smiled, but right now her fury was swirling around her, and she wasn't even sure exactly why she was furious.

"So, nothing's wrong?" he asked again, impatiently.

Mahrree pouted. "Well, I don't want to *talk* when you're like *this!*"

He was mystified. "When I'm like what? Sitting next to you, trying to find out what's bothering you?" his voice grew louder.

"When you're growling at me?!"

"Woman, you have yet to hear me growl!"

"You're growling now!"

"This is not—" He stopped and made a fist with his left hand. His voice was tight when he began again. "This is not *growling*, this is *debating*."

Mahrree shook her head. "This isn't debating, this is—" She started to cry again. She hated crying, and today of all days she couldn't control it. "This is *fighting!*"

She looked at her new husband who was now studying her hand. She'd made a mistake. Why did she marry him? What was she thinking? She could see it now—she'd been blinded, believing everything would be wonderful and ideal, with no major problems.

Most perfect man in the world? Ha!

Perrin continued to study her hand and patted it awkwardly. "How can

I know what to fix if you won't tell me what's wrong?"

"Well, when I figure out everything that's wrong, I'll be sure to tell you!" she declared. "I'll make a new list!"

Perrin's shoulders began to shake.

Mahrree didn't know what to make of it. She bit her lip and wished he would just leave.

When he looked up he was . . . smiling? How dare he smile!

"You're so funny," he chuckled. "You really are."

"What?!" she shrieked. "How can you say that?"

He didn't even flinch at her volume. "You just strike me as funny right now, that's all. What, a new batch of tears? Come on, Mahrree!" He put his arms around her.

She wanted to pull away, but she also didn't want to leave. She'd never felt so, so irrational and girly before, and it was disconcerting. "You're just such a, a . . ." she mumbled into his chest.

"What, such a *man?*"

She snorted at his tone. She didn't know where the snort came from, and she tried to pretend it wasn't from her, but spiders don't snort.

Perrin chuckled again. "Well, I am! And you're such a woman! 'Nothing's wrong,'" he mimicked.

"Perrin, that's not—"

"Look," he interrupted. Pushing her gently away, he held her by her arms and looked into her eyes. "We've both been on our own for many years, and we're bound to have some misunderstandings, right? For ten weeks we've *enjoyed arguing*—" A small but distinct twinkle appeared in his eyes. "But we've never actually fought. We're just due for an actual conflict."

"But if you *really* love me—"

"I'll sit here and try to figure you out!"

Mahrree tried to think of a reply, but couldn't. As much as she hated to admit it, he was right. He didn't *know* her yet, so how would he know what was bothering her? Last year they didn't even know each other existed.

And maybe—maybe—she really didn't know him yet.

"Mahrree?"

"I didn't know where you were," she murmured. "What happened to you."

"So . . . we've jumped to the list?"

Mahrree nodded. "You just left me. Alone."

"You're used to being alone."

"Not anymore!"

He sighed. "That's true. Neither am I, actually. What if I send a messenger the next time I'm detained? So you know why?"

She nodded.

"Next?"

"You were so irritable!"

"Yes. So? Don't you think I deserved to be, just a bit? I haven't had a full night's sleep in . . . I *still* don't know how long, and didn't eat decently for days. I witnessed—"

He stopped, unable to say the words again, and swallowed hard as the memory hit him. She squeezed his hand hoping to convey that she understood. When he continued a moment later, his voice was almost normal. "After all of *that*, you expect Mr. Charm to walk through the door?"

"I've never expected Mr. Charm to walk through that door!" Mahrree finally giggled and wiped her face. "I suppose you have a point. You're allowed to act like a bear . . . *sometimes*."

"Thank you."

"But do you have to take it out on me? I didn't keep you out for four nights."

"No, you didn't. Four nights?" He sighed. "I suppose that's right. But aren't you supposed to be my support? The one who loves and cares for me, no matter what?"

"I've been trying to. It would help if you acted a little more lovable."

"And how lovable were *you* when you got sick all over the stairs?"

She covered her face with her hands. "Please don't remind me."

He carefully pulled down her hands, and to her relief, he was grinning. "I come home, exhausted, expecting to find my beautiful bride waiting eagerly to provide comfort and support, and instead I get another mess to clean up. And you wonder why I was 'irritable'?"

"It's not like I planned to do that, you know!" She looked into his dark eyes, wondering if she would ever get over the effect they had on her. He wasn't perfect, but—well, he was still somewhat wonderful. "I'm sorry. This wasn't a very good week, was it?"

"I'm sure we'll have a few other bad weeks, and a lot more good weeks. This week could still be good," he suggested. "So, is there anything else I should know about? *Anything* at all?"

"No, Captain, I think you can go back to your reports now."

He kissed her, seemed to want to say something else, but then got off the bed and went back to the desk.

Mahrree left the bed and went down to the washroom to check his uniform that had been soaking since morning. She lifted the heavy wool out of the cold water and grimaced. The dirt and blood she could understand—most of it had mercifully dissolved in the large washing basin—but she wondered why so much mud seemed to have been caked onto the gold braid. Bits of filth still remained in the twisted sections.

But it was the small clumps of sticky goo she couldn't understand. She hadn't thought much of it earlier because too many other things occupied her mind. But now, as she saw a few pine needles floating in the water, she began to wonder. She scraped off one of the sticky parts and sniffed it.

Pine sap.

"Oh, Perrin, what did you do?" she whispered to his uniform. She let it drop back into the water to soak, hoping the rest of the sap would dissolve away, along with her suspicions. She walked into the kitchen to begin dinner, and Perrin soon came down and sat on a kitchen chair. He subtly watched her while she worked.

"Everything all right?" she asked as he made notes on his pages. "I think you would be more comfortable in the eating room."

"No, I'm fine here. Just making sure you're all right."

"Your uniform's still soaking. Some unusual stains on it," she said casually.

"Yes, yes," he said, without looking up, "A few tumbles and struggles. I can finish cleaning it. Did so for years. Don't want you getting ill again." He looked up, forced a smile, and went to the washing room to start scrubbing his uniform.

He doesn't want me to know, she thought as she stirred the pot on the stove. Am I supposed to get it out of him, or just wait until he confesses it? That question occupied her mind until dinner, and during it, when she noticed Perrin frequently watching her out of the corner of his eye.

He knows I know something's up, she decided. He's trying to see if I'm going to pry it out of him. She didn't ask anything revealing about his uniform during dinner, nor as they sat on the sofa together afterward. But Mahrree could tell he was paying more attention to her instead of his papers. She rested her legs on his lap and pretended to read a book.

Finally she put it down when she caught him looking at her again.

"All right. I give up. But I'm not a Guarder, if that's what you're wondering," she teased.

"What?" he asked, startled.

"You've been staring at me all afternoon. Something's obviously on your mind, and you're wondering if it's on my mind, too. Aren't you?"

His shoulder twitched. "Maybe. Depends on what you're thinking."

"I think you have something to tell me," she accused. "Something you haven't shared."

She'd never seen such a perplexed look on his face before. "Shouldn't it be *you* telling *me*?"

Now she was baffled. "How would *I* know?"

His jaw dropped. "You're supposed to know first!"

Mahrree blinked. "I'm beginning to think we're not talking about the same thing."

He squinted back. "I think you're right."

"So, what are you thinking?"

He studied her. "How do you feel right *now*?"

She couldn't understand where his question was going, but she shrugged. "Better, but still a bit light-headed. I'm just tired, but I think it's because I haven't slept well."

He didn't seem satisfied by that answer. "Why do you think you were sick?"

"Because you were gone!"

He didn't smile, but something was changing his eyes. "Are you *sure* that's the only reason?"

Mahrree sat up a little. "What other reason could there be?"

"It's just that . . . certain things . . . it could be that . . . you're so *emotional* today . . ." he stumbled with a growing smile. The dark brooding in his eyes began to lighten for the first time since he came home.

It wasn't until he raised his eyebrows in suggestion and nodded at her belly that Mahrree caught his meaning.

Oh.

*Ohhh* . . .

Every morning, her irrationality and queasiness . . .

She looked quickly down at her belly, then back at him.

"Hmm?" he hinted and shrugged with a gentle smile.

"No!" she gasped.

"Are you absolutely *sure*?"

"No, I'm not!" she admitted. His smile was contagious, now growing on her face.

"So how do we know for sure?"

"We wait, I guess. By the end of the Raining Season we should *definitely* know something!" She laughed. Then she started to cry. Already? She had heard it could take seasons and even years, but *already*?!

"I think we'll know a bit sooner than *that*. You're making a good case for it right now!" He dabbed at her tears and chuckled. "My mother told me all kinds of things to watch for, and according to her comprehensive list—"

Mahrree didn't realize until then that *every* Shin was an extensive list maker.

"—you're more than just ill." He sighed—rather contentedly—and his eyes grew shiny. "If you are what I suspect you are, then this will have been a good week after all."

With growing giddiness she covered her mouth with her hands, astonished that the thought never occurred to her. "I just don't dare believe it!"

"So, that's *not* what you've been thinking today?" he reminded her.

"What? Oh, not at all!"

He kissed her. "So my darling wife, who may be getting much larger in size in the next eight moons or so, what was it that you were thinking today?"

"About your uniform!" She kissed him back. "Wondering why it was so muddy with pine sap on it. Why, I completely forgot about it."

"Good," he said shortly. "Now, I suppose once we're sure this is the real thing, we'll need another addition—"

Mahrree held up her hand. "Usually couples wait to see if the baby survives before building an addition. Not that I'm suggesting that . . ." She couldn't bring herself to say the awful alternative, but she knew it was a possibility.

So did her husband, but Perrin wasn't going to accept that. "*Our* baby will live, Mahrree," he said with enough determination to almost ensure it. "Every Shin son for the past four generations came into the world robust and screaming."

"But . . . what if it isn't a son?" Mahrree winced.

Perrin's expression went stiff, as if he'd never considered that. He tried to soften it, but the damage was already done.

Of course he'd think only of a boy, Mahrree thought. That didn't bother her, just *concerned* her.

"You obviously survived," Perrin finally managed. "So too would our daughter."

She was impressed he didn't hesitate on that last word. "We should likely wait anyway," Mahrree decided. "Just to be sure. Now's not the best time to begin an addition anyway, with the—"

She stopped, suddenly remembering the previous conversation he'd so easily steered her away from.

"Wait a minute. We were talking about why you uniform was dirty—"

"Doesn't matter," he waved it off. "I was thinking, if we put the baby's addition against the study, both rooms can share the fireplace—"

She sat up. "Perrin, why *was* your uniform so filthy, with pine sap on it?"

He patted her shoulder. "Now, now. Don't overexcite yourself. Not at a time like this—"

"Oh, don't patronize me!" she snapped. "This is another avoidance tactic, isn't it? Before we married we promised that we'd be honest with each other from now on. I'm asking you a question, and I expect an honest answer. And so does your baby, should he or she be in there!" She patted her belly and tried to maintain her chastising tone, but another wave of joyful anticipation bubbled up and leaked out her tear ducts.

Perrin smiled at her conflicted face. "We can discuss this later."

"We're discussing it now!"

He sighed and sat back, keeping a hand on hers. "I went into the forest," he confessed.

"No!"

"Yes."

"Did you get out safely?"

He raised an eyebrow at her.

She rolled her eyes at her stupidity. "*Of course* you got out safely, what am I saying . . . wait, what are YOU saying? You went in deliberately?"

He nodded.

"Why?"

"That's where the Guarders are, Mahrree," he said simply.

"First rule of the army!" she reminded loudly. "No one in the forests!"

"Yes, yes, yes. I know."

"So how long were you in there?"

"We were there about . . ." He looked up at the ceiling as if estimating, "almost the entire time."

Mahrree's mouth dropped open. "Who else?"

"Karna."

"Willingly?"

Perrin only shrugged.

"What will your father say?!"

"That's why I can't sleep. That's what I've been working on—my excuses, explanations, evidence of success, and a proposal to let me do it again—"

"NO!" Mahrree cried, and protectively held her belly. "You'll die!"

He sat up and took her hands off her belly to hold them. "I don't understand why you're reacting like this. Just last season you proposed that I go in there and stop them."

"Well, now things are different," she insisted, realizing that she *had* completely reversed her position in the last few minutes. True, a few moons ago she wanted her intended to defy the rules, barge into that forest, and scare away all of the bad men.

But that was before she realized just *how bad* the bad men were, and before she realized this was real, not just some vain woman's bravado. Her mind was too frazzled to formulate exactly what had changed but *something* had!

"Back then, you were . . . you were just—" she started.

"Just some man you sort of fancied?" he suggested with a hint of teasing.

"Well, no! I mean, I love you—"

"Oh, *now*, but not *before?*"

"Stop it!" she exclaimed, aggravated by his new attempt to detour her. "I mean, you can't go into the forest because now you might be a father!"

He smiled at that before his face became earnest. "Mahrree, the forest isn't that bad. The trees are the *safest* parts. I can conquer that forest! I scared out several Guarders. They crash around since no one else is there to see them. I'm sure that if I can get an army in there, we can annihilate them, once and for all. Then, Mahrree, *no one* will die." He put his hand tenderly on her belly. "No one."

"You can't be serious about going back," she whispered.

"Ah, Mahrree, believe me—it's just not that bad. Not even the cavern where the two Guarders fell in. It was obvious to see. I stood at the edge and—"

She stared at him, horrified.

He stopped talking and rubbed his forehead. "If your response is anything like my father's—"

"He better be as shocked as me!" she declared. "Perrin, why? Why take such a risk?"

"For you," he said quietly. "For Edge. For everyone in the world being terrorized."

"And not for yourself?"

"Maybe a bit for myself," he confessed, the annoyed officer emerging again. "I wanted answers. Why are they doing this? No one, in all these years, has ever carried on a civil conversation with one of them. It's always been challenges and shouting then blades and then nothing. We have an entire class on them in Command School, and you know what? There's nothing to talk about. If I could just find one willing to explain to me what's going on. Find some truth—*anything*. You understand that, don't you?"

He slumped on the sofa, discouraged.

"It would have been fantastic to find their base or even a settlement, but Mahrree—there was nothing in the forests north of here. Just a few random men chasing each other. And the few men I encountered preferred to die rather than talk. Why? It makes no sense."

"It never has," she whispered. "It's never added up. Perrin, right before we were engaged, I charted when new kings came to power and when Guarders attacked: always a year and fourteen weeks later, as if the Guarders knew. Or as if the kings knew they needed to defeat someone to prove their strength."

"You really did that?" he asked, intrigued. "Where are your notes?"

"I burned them before you arrived that night."

"Good," he nodded. "That's what I did, too. It occurred to me some time ago that Guarder attacks were *convenient*. But when the Administrators came to power, and nothing happened after a year and a season, I realized that now maybe things were different."

"So are they?"

He nodded. "The spy my father interrogated was a hardened, bitter man. He was for real, Mahrree. I remember that conversation we had the night we were engaged, when you questioned their authenticity. To be honest, I have too. Even after the attack on Grasses I still had a fragment of doubt. But now?" His face grew pale, his expression grim. "They're even more mysterious than before. Take that business with the small knives . . ." He closed his eyes and shook his head, trying to dislodge the images. "Anyway, I hate mysteries."

She leaned over to snuggle into him. Everything about him was solid and confident, even when he expressed his doubts, and especially when he demonstrated how much his mind was like hers. As he wrapped a muscled arm around her, she imagined he was the strongest man in the world. Which, she smiled to herself, he likely was. It was precisely his strength she needed— his strength of body, and his strength of thought. It was *almost* as if he was the most perfect man in the world. At least, for her.

"Please don't go back there again," she begged him. "I want answers just as much as you do, but not this way. Should anything happen to you—"

His grip around her tightened and he kissed the top of her head. "I'm asking my father for permission, but I doubt he'll say yes."

"Good. I like him."

He chuckled mirthlessly. "You're terrified of him, and you know it."

"As long as he keeps you safe, so you can be with me and our . . ."

He put his hand on her belly. "Still waiting to know, right? We could ask your mother about it when she returns."

She sat up. "Are you serious? *My* mother? We'll just wait."

The next morning Mahrree awoke to another wave of nausea. She sat up in bed, recognized what the feeling could mean, and cried out, "Oh Perrin! I'm still sick! Isn't that wonderf—" and couldn't say anything more.

But he was ready. He immediately produced a bucket from under the bed, and his timing couldn't have been better.

---

"You're looking much better today, my boy!" Hogal Densal slapped Perrin on the back.

He wasn't the first person to do that today. For his entire walk to the village center, people had been congratulating and thanking him for coming to Edge, and now that he was nearing the markets, the crowds thickened. Speaking to the tanner about his idea for leather armor was going to take a lot longer than he anticipated. Normally this would have been Wiles's duty, but the man was still unwell and spending the day sleeping in his quarters.

When Perrin saw Hogal's proud smile just outside the tanner's, he realized his great uncle had likely presented a most colorful—and perhaps slightly embellished—retelling of the past few days' events. Trying to win him more hearts and minds, perhaps.

"I am better, Hogal. Thank you." But before he could continue, another woman came up to pat his arm. "Yes, all over now. No, you're quite welcome. Army of Idumea's here to serve. Hogal, exactly what—Oh, thank you. Just doing what I was trained to do. Yes, everything's safe again . . . Hogal," Perrin took his great-uncle's arm and steered him between two shops, away from the well-wishers. "Exactly what did you say last night? You didn't tell them about the Guarder suicides, did you?" he ended in a whisper.

Hogal's merry eyes darkened. "Of course not. These people wouldn't be able to handle such details. I'm still struggling with them. No, my boy—" the rector's face brightened again, "I just told them what you told me about the army's ability to keep the Guarders from the village. Everyone here knows too well what happened in Grasses. You prevented another tragedy like that from occurring, and with a smaller army, even. I'm surprised you didn't hear the cheering at your home, especially when I told them about your success in saving a private's life. I wished you'd been here last night."

"Mahrree and I were a bit tired," Perrin explained, "and occupied by . . . other things."

"Ah, newlyweds," Hogal winked.

Perrin opened his mouth to correct him, but realized he wouldn't know what to say without unintentionally revealing that Hogal might be a great, great-uncle in the next year. Hogal could always get Perrin to confess everything. But not this.

Perrin just winked back instead.

# Chapter 19 ~ "He's *finished*, Shin! Out of the army!"

The High General wasn't due to make his report for another hour, but some things will not wait.

That's why Chairman Mal, after reviewing the initial report from the garrison, marched out of his office shouting at his guard to ready his carriage. Within minutes he was whisked to the garrison, with the rest of his schedule destroyed because one man went off on a stupid impulse.

"Will take me days to get it all straightened out again!" Mal growled as he exited the carriage and strode up the stairs to the headquarters of the garrison.

As ornate and elegant as the Administrative Headquarters was, the new garrison was functional and dull. Every building was an inevitable rectangle, made of gray blocks and regularly spaced windows and plain doors that suggested exactness, order, and drudgery.

Army life, depicted in architecture.

But, if army life was as predictable as the garrison, Mal wouldn't have been bursting through the double doors shouting at the top of his lungs. "Where is he? Shin! I want to see you, NOW!"

The officers and soldiers walking down intersecting corridors all stopped to stare at the uncharacteristic outburst from the Chairman of Administrators.

A simple door down one of the hallways opened, and the large figure of the High General slowly stepped out into the hall. "Chairman Mal, what a pleasant surprise," he said sardonically. "A little confused by your schedule? I'm not due to brief you—"

Mal stepped around two large colonels to get to his target. "Why'd he do it, General?" he shouted, not caring who witnessed the argument that was about to ensue with the top wolf of the army. "Lost control over your pup? What's wrong with him?"

General Shin folded his arms. "We can discuss this in my office."

"Why?" Mal bellowed, his face turning as red as his coat. "Don't want the rest of the officers to know your reckless son broke the first rule of the army?"

General Shin's hard glare didn't change, even though more than two dozen officers and soldiers were now looking in his direction, awaiting his response.

"All of them know the risks my son took in order to preserve the safety of Edge and eliminate several Guarder threats," he said evenly. "I have nothing to hide about his success and his fort."

"*His* fort?" Mal barked, a vein bulging on his forehead. "Does that mean *his* rules now, too? And he dragged a lieutenant in with him?"

"Karna is an obedient, faithful officer—" Shin started, but Mal cut him off.

"Unlike your son! He's *finished*, Shin! Out of the army! Bring Perrin back, NOW!"

That finally drew a reaction from the High General. His eyebrows shot upwards and he unfolded his arms to put his hands on his hips, one hand next to his long knife, the other next to his ornate sword hilt.

"Bring him back for what? For keeping the Guarders out of Edge? For confining them to the forests? For preserving the lives of each of his soldiers, while at least nine Guarders died? Take away his commission for being successful, Mal? While he was unconventional—I'll not argue that—he was most certainly *progressive* in his approach to dealing with the Guarder threat!"

Mal took a step closer to the man who stood over a head taller than him, and was close to twice his size in bulk. But Mal had more power. "High General, Captain Shin showed extremely poor judgment by entering that forest and staying there," he seethed. "He was lucky he left that forest alive. It wasn't skill, it wasn't intelligence—it was merely chance. We cannot have commanders of forts setting such dangerous examples for their soldiers or the citizenry they're to protect."

But Mal knew he couldn't end it already. There was still so much to prove. So many years had gone into setting up this experiment, and then to eliminate the primary test subject so soon?

No.

No, revenge was far more satisfying than removal. Indeed, this just may have opened up all kinds of options—

"Still, I realize that Captain Shin is young and new in his position," Mal continued, trying not to sound too conciliatory, "and therefore likely to make mistakes. But—" he held up a finger shaking with fury because, after all, Perrin *had* caused the destruction of nine very capable, very extensively trained men, "—this will be his first and only mistake I will tolerate. You will hereby place Captain Perrin Shin on notice that if he cannot live by every rule established by the Army of Idumea—"

There were rules. Regulations. *Expectations* to how the game was played. Nicko followed the rules, but Perrin had ignored them all and came off looking like the hero.

Mal kept a score sheet in his head. Now as he glared at Relf Shin, and although he didn't want it to, the sheet showed up to mock him.

Perrin—nine; Nicko—zero.

Perrin had cheated.

"—if he can't follow the *rules,* he WILL be relieved of duty and returned to Idumea!"

The High General didn't even seem to breathe.

Mal was nearly screaming now. "And you will also make it clear to the captain that no one—no matter how obedient or willing the stupid soldier is that chooses to follow him—should enter into the forests above Edge or anywhere else in the world! Should anyone else take one step into that forest, he too will be brought immediately to Idumea. Is that understood?!"

It was an impressively long spell that the High General stood there, unresponsive. The tempo of Mal's breathing changed at least three times waiting for Shin to even blink. The top wolf did enjoy his stare downs, especially since there was nothing else he could do. His son broke the rules. Even though Mal knew the general's stalling was to somehow prove he had the upper hand, he obviously didn't. Mal gloated about that victory later, but for now he stared back, feeling his heart pounding in erratic rage.

It was advising General Cush who could no longer stand the tension. The portly man with the thin black beard and mustache—allowed only because he had very little hair on top, and was never going to be anywhere near hand-to-hand combat—finally stepped forward. With his ever-ready smile he put one friendly hand on Shin's shoulder while his other patted Mal's shoulder.

Mal, not one for mollifying gestures, glowered.

Cush pulled his Chairman hand back to safety, but kept the other on the High General. Likely to help hold him back, Nicko decided.

"Already taking care of it, Chairman," Cush said cheerfully. "In the middle of writing to Captain Shin right now. You see, he's actually under *my* jurisdiction, as all new commanders are, and as such I'm crafting the response to his proposals—"

"Aldwyn!" Shin whispered in warning.

"Proposals?" Mal hissed. "What proposals?"

"Suggestions, really!" Cush chuckled in a feeble attempt to lighten the mood. "Perrin had a few suggestions, the Command Board denied them, naturally, but it's nice to see our young officers trying to be progressive, isn't it, Chairman?"

Cush released his grip on Shin's shoulder and daringly put a reassuring arm around Mal. "I've got things under control, and I'll be sure to tell Perrin *exactly* how you feel about everything. You know you can trust me, right Chairman?"

Mal could, he was fairly certain. Some time ago he had his own private talk with the second in command of the army, the subordinate wolf just biding his time to take over the pack. Their discussion was vague enough that Aldwyn Cush never completely understood just what it was all about. But Mal had decided Cush wasn't the man he wanted. While he was experienced and useful, he was simply too social, always trying to bridge the gaps between everyone else.

Mal needed a fellow strategist, not a cloying politician, so he chose another research companion. It was fortunate for the High General that his long-time friend was, while opportunistic, also rather lazy. He'd jump at a bone only if it was laid on his nose.

"I want to see that response before you send it, Cush. In my office."

"Of course, Chairman! I'll bring it by myself."

---

As Chairman Mal stomped his way out to his carriage, High General Shin growled under his breath, staring at the now vacant reception area. The rest of the soldiers quickly dispersed, trying to steal subtle glances at the High General as they fled to offices and exits, but not subtly enough.

"He's right, Relf, I'm sorry to say," Cush said quietly, trying to pull Shin out of his brooding. "Perrin was remarkably bold and completely noncompliant."

"But he *succeeded*, Aldwyn," Shin groused as he turned to go into his office, Cush following him. "Doesn't it make sense to let officers do what works?"

"Relf, your father was the one who wrote the laws of the army, and you pledged to uphold them," Cush reminded as he closed the door behind them. "We can't go turning our backs now on the traditions that have preserved our army for so many years."

Shin sat down at his desk. "Why not? Why don't we be progressive and take a risk?"

Cush wagged a thick finger at him. "I love it how you use Mal's 'progressive' speech every time you want to do something against the law. But it won't work, my friend. There are times to be progressive—as you love to misuse that term—and times to cling to the traditions that keep our civilization stable. The key is knowing which to change, and which to cling to."

Relf sighed again as he picked up his son's detailed proposal. "All of those stuffed red coats are a waste of cloth," he murmured. "Come in here yelling at me about how to do my job . . . Hard to think of a decent one in the lot—"

"Oh, there are a few good ones," Cush said amiably. "There's that Dr. Brisack, for one."

The High General shrugged at that. "Someone in charge of Family Life *better* appear genial. But the others—I swear they sprung out of the same cesspool that spawned Gadiman."

Cush chuckled nervously. "Careful, Relf. Don't want the wrong ears hearing you."

Shin scoffed at that as he perused his son's writing. "Interesting idea with changing uniforms to blend into the surroundings—"

Cush sat down in a chair opposite him. "No, Relf. Not in the least bit! The Command Board already discussed that—"

"They wouldn't kill each other by accident!" Shin burst out. "How absurd."

Cush leaned across the desk, grunting as he did so, and pulled Captain Shin's proposals out of the High General's hands. "I'll let you read the response before I go to Mal. Seeing as how Perrin's your only son, Relf, I'm rather surprised you're not more upset at his willful disregard for his own life."

"Oh, I was!" Relf exclaimed. "Initially. Then I started thinking about what he did and, well . . . fatherly pride replaced my concern."

"Will you still feel that fatherly pride when your daughter-in-law sends you a tear-stained message that her husband has vanished in the forest and no one can find his corpse? After six years of hearing about our grandson Lemuel, Joriana's been telling my wife how excited she is about the prospects of becoming a grandmother," Cush hinted.

High General Shin rubbed his forehead. "Yes, yes, I know. Joriana's already bought a baby blanket. Point made, Aldwyn. Say what you need to, but let me send the response."

---

Tuma Hifadhi heard the knocking on his office door. He looked up from his desk and called, "Come in."

A lean, middle-aged man opened the door.

"Hew Gleace! How wonderful to see you. Come in, come in."

"I hope I'm not interrupting anything—" Gleace said as he came into the room.

"Of course not," the elderly man gestured to a chair next to his desk. "I always have time. You seem to be bursting with something, Hew."

Gleace smiled readily as he sat down. "I am, Tuma. We just received word back from the scouts in the forest."

"The raid is over," the old man began to smile. "So . . ."

"He walked right in, chasing the attackers! And this time, he *stayed*. For three full days and four nights he chased them up and down as if he had been born and raised in the trees. Never once showed fear." Gleace began to chuckle. "His lieutenant, on the other hand . . ."

But Hifadhi ignored that as he sat back and sighed. "Pere Shin's grandson."

"Pere Shin's grandson, yes."

Hifadhi slowly shook his head. "That I lived to see this day . . . *His* grandson, going over the wall . . ." And he closed his eyes.

Gleace waited patiently, having seen him do this before.

Hifadhi's eyes opened a few moments later. "Keep up the surveillance patrols for now. We don't need anyone closer until it's revealed that an intimate presence is required. I'm still not *entirely* sure about this one, but time will tell." He smiled in amazement. "Walked into the forest . . . and stayed there!"

---

Two men sat in the dark office of an unlit building.

Nicko Mal stared at his companion, daring him to speak.

The second man looked back with a slightly amused expression.

Mal drummed his fingers on the armrest.

The second man took a risk. "It's only because you said he always surprises you that I felt safe in speculating that Shin would succeed."

"They didn't even make it into the village because of *him!*" Mal fumed. That had been the true splinter in his foot that sent him into the tirade at the garrison. That, and the fact that Perrin wasn't even injured in the forest beyond a few scratches. He took a deep breath to compose himself. "Shin was, however, a bit slow to respond initially. You must admit that."

"Conceded." His partner smiled.

"Perhaps it had something to do with him being a newlywed and living away from the fort. Unfortunate timing, I suppose," Mal sniggered. "Perhaps this will remind him that duty comes before the wife. But there was that ten minutes. *Ten minutes.* Why didn't they get into the village during that time?!"

"A new tactic," the second man explained. "Eliminate the patrolling soldiers first. In Grasses there were several on patrol that nearly captured some of our men. We didn't want that to happen again."

Mal grunted. "But only two soldiers were injured in Edge. What about the rest?"

The middle-aged man fidgeted. "The patrols weren't on a regular rotation. Up until last week, they were. It seems that only recently Shin varied the rotation times so that the patrols were unpredictable."

Mal formed a fist. "Wiles was in charge of the patrols, was he not?"

"Apparently not even he was aware of the captain's changes. The night of the attack, Shin himself briefed the sergeant on duty as how to stagger the patrols. As if he was concerned something like this could happen."

"Did he somehow know we were coming?" Mal squinted.

The second man shrugged. "I think he was just being a thoughtful commander, anticipating the need. Perhaps he can think like a Guarder. No one knows whose ancestors were among the Guarders, after all. He seems to be one of those you predicted at the beginning would attempt to fight this on his own."

Mal grumbled to himself.

"What I find intriguing," his partner continued, "was his deliberate disobedience to the rules of engagement. Preliminary conclusion to our question: He *wasn't* too comfortable, and marriage *has* made him an aggressive wolf to protect his mate."

That brought Mal out of his sullenness. "Oh indeed," he bristled. "Absolute disregard for anything he'd been trained to do. Pursuing into the woods like that—very brash! Very reckless! We must not lose containment!"

The second man suppressed a smile at Mal's agitation. "I wished I could have seen Relf's reaction to his son's report. I'm assuming General Cush included the admonition that no officers or soldiers return to the forest?"

"He did! Read the response myself. I'm sure the captain will receive the message and he best heed it. We can't have him changing the conventions of warfare and unraveling our work just because he has an impulse!"

Mal sighed, took another deep breath and said steadily, "The fort in Trades is completed, and just in time to put extra soldiers around that gold mine. No one in the far south has had any encounters with Guarders, and the letter skimmers are spending too much time reading complaints from Trades, so we need to lighten their load and alleviate the pain of the complainers. The commander in Trades is a single man with no long-term interests in women. We'll question his readiness for a time."

The second man smirked at Mal's shift in focus. But he had several strategies to turn it back again. First, bring up Perrin Shin.

Privately, the second man was conducting his own study: How quickly can one unhinge Nicko Mal?

"Perhaps if there had been some soldier deaths in Edge, or if the action was closer to Perrin's home—"

"Next time it better be!" Mal snapped.

It is really just *that* easy—the second man made a mental note—to drive Mal to distraction.

Mal drummed his fingers on the armrest again, the raid on Trades already forgotten.

The second man smiled triumphantly to himself. It was fascinating to observe a man that could control the world, yet not himself. Maybe, *maybe*, he didn't control the world as well as he thought either.

"So when activity returns to Edge, you want to create a situation that allows for a variety of observable responses?"

"Yes!" Mal exclaimed as if that was obvious. "You have ideas?"

"A few that I'm working on," the second man assured. "I still have that map, you know. I have to confess," he said thoughtfully, unable to resist pushing Mal just a bit further—for research, after all—"I find myself quite fascinated by the captain. I wonder how long he planned on entering the forest. He deserves a great deal of attention. Perhaps we should consider a closer presence for a time. Someone that can get—"

"I want Wiles OUT OF THERE!" Mal bellowed. "I knew he wouldn't be up to this assignment!"

The second man frowned. "Weren't you the one who said he was 'most fit' for the assignment? Excellent work with the map and all?"

"He's failed the oaths! Failed his duty! Just GET HIM OUT!"

---

Coaches traveling from Edge to Idumea pass many villages along the way, the wide cobblestone road lined with plenty of inns and taverns willing to take in weary travelers. In a hurry, the trip can be done in two straight days and a night, but rarely do people travel in such a grueling manner. One might die of the excessive distance.

Or of boredom. Everyone knew that.

So the rest stations were established at intervals along the main road to provide comfort at an elevated price, with lumpy mattresses that felt like goose down after the jostling of the carriage, and gristly food that slid down mucus-lined throats where it met already nauseated bellies whose owners would attribute their increased illness to the torturous ride rather than the "comfort" they paused for. In such a manner, the journey—for those brave enough or desperate enough to take it—could be extended for weeks, ensuring no one chanced death along the journey. Unless they stopped at a particularly scruffy place outside of Rivers.

But army coaches were different. No one was sure exactly how, but they *never* stopped. Rumor was that they had some kind of privy fashioned into the large black enclosures. But the owners of the comfort stops and taverns grumbled that wasn't true. The soldiers that rode in the coaches simply had stronger willpower than the rest of the world, or did unmentionable things out the window when they passed the less populated areas. To see a dark army coach whisk by, being pulled by four horses which were changed exclusively at the forts or the Administrators' larger messaging stations, was to know that whoever it was carrying was in a hurry.

But Sergeant Major Wiles wasn't aware of any of this as he lay on the coach bench, unsure of his surroundings. Everything had happened so quickly, then slowly, then quickly again as if his mind couldn't regulate the passage of time.

He was ill—that much he knew—then it was light and dark again, and he was put into the coach, and it rumbled for hours and minutes and days and seconds. All was dark inside the coach and out, and for a lucid moment he began to understand what was happening. He hated that moment, because up until then his mind had allowed him to entertain all kinds of possibilities.

But then the coach door swung open while it still continued at a fast pace along the cobblestones, and when Wiles saw the gloved hand reach in toward him, he knew what was coming.

He didn't even have a chance to plead for his life. The oaths wouldn't have allowed it, anyway. The oaths had demanded he do something else days ago, but he hadn't. That's why the massive man dressed in black was there—to fulfill the oaths.

He snatched Wiles easily out of the hurrying coach. The old sergeant major didn't make any sound at all.

The coach continued on, the horses once again speeding up, perhaps sensing their load was now slightly lighter, and galloped their way in the dark toward Idumea.

---

A week after the attacks ended, Captain Shin sat in his office in the command tower and reread the report from General Cush. He looked vainly for loopholes.

> CAPTAIN SHIN,
>
> YOUR RECOMMENDATIONS HAVE BEEN REVIEWED AND DISCUSSED AMONG THE COMMAND BOARD AND CHAIRMAN MAL. WE VALUE YOUR EFFORTS TO IMPROVE THE ARMY OF IDUMEA, BUT FEEL MANY OF YOUR IDEAS ARE PREMATURE OR INAPPROPRIATE.
>
> FIRST, THE UNIFORM OF THE ARMY WILL NOT CHANGE. WHILE IT DOES SEEM LOGICAL TO CREATE A FIELD UNIFORM THAT BLENDS INTO THE SURROUNDINGS, THE DANGER IS THAT SOLDIERS WILL ATTACK THEIR OWN, BELIEVING THEY ARE THE ENEMY. THE UNIFORM IS ALSO ONE OF THE OLDEST AND HIGHEST TRADITIONS THE ARMY HAS, DATING BACK TO THE GREAT WAR, AND ALTERING IT WOULD BE LIKE ALTERING THE ARMY—UNACCEPTABLE.

Captain Shin smirked. That wasn't his father's belief. Relf Shin held up the call for tradition as strongly as his son did. They tried to drop it on its head as often as possible.

"Just create a *field* uniform," Perrin grumbled. "Not something that looks like *them*. That would be as useless as the Guarders dressing up in blue uniforms."

Captain Shin sighed as he continued to read.

> WHILE YOUR SUGGESTION TO REVIVE THE SUITS OF MAIL USED IN THE GREAT WAR SEEMS TO HAVE MERIT, THE CURRENT ATTACK STRATEGIES OF THE GUARDERS MAY NOT REQUIRE SUCH ELABORATE AND EXPENSIVE ARMOR. MAIL AND SHIELDS WERE NECESSARY WHEN THE ENEMY ONE HUNDRED TWENTY YEARS AGO EMPLOYED THE EXTENSIVE USE OF BOWS AND ARROWS, AS WELL AS MACES. BUT GUARDERS SEEM TO BE OUTFITTED ONLY WITH DAGGERS AND ENGAGE ONLY IN CLOSE COMBAT.

IT IS THE OPINION OF THE ARMY LEADERSHIP THAT
EVEN MAIL MAY NOT HAVE PREVENTED THE INJURIES SUS-
TAINED BY YOUR MEN, NOR WOULD MAIL HAVE AFFORDED
ANY PROTECTION TO THE SOLDIER WHICH THE GUARDER
HELD HOSTAGE. NO MAIL WAS EVER MADE TO EXTEND TO
ONE'S THROAT.

"But it could be!" Captain Shin said out loud to the paper. "And what
makes you think they won't start using arrows or maces?" He smacked the
message in frustration. Also not his father's opinion, he was sure. But what
was the point of being High General when all the lesser generals and Administrators controlled the army?

Shin fumed when he read the next line again.

AS FOR BREASTPLATES AND OTHER SHIELDING YOU SUG-
GESTED, WHILE THICK LEATHER WOULD BE EASIER AND LESS
COSTLY THAN MAIL, IT IS THE OPINION OF THE GARRISON
THAT SUCH DEFENSIVE MEASURES MAY ALARM THE CITIZENRY,
WHO ARE OF THE BELIEF THEIR SOLDIERS ARE THE BRAVEST
THE WORLD HAS EVER PRODUCED, AND ARE NOT IN NEED OF
ANY SUCH PROTECTION.

"It would have put three more men to work in the village, making armor! But say what you mean, Cush," he bellowed at the paper, "I'm a coward
for wanting to preserve my soldiers. Oh, but wait. If I really was a coward,
would I have suggested the next thing you've decided is also 'inappropriate'?"

AS FOR BEGINNING TRAINING WITHIN THE FOREST IT-
SELF, THAT TOO IS CONTRARY TO ANYTHING WE HAVE EVER
DONE. THE PURPOSE OF THE ARMY IS TO DEFEND THE CITI-
ZENRY OF THE WORLD. WE ARE NOT AGGRESSORS OR PURSU-
ERS. YOUR BRASH AND RECKLESS BEHAVIOR IN ENTERING THE
FOREST—AND REMAINING THERE—WOULD SUGGEST YOU ARE
TOO AGGRESSIVE TO CAPABLY LEAD YOUR FORT.

That last sentence must have been drafted by Nicko Mal himself. Professor Mal's favorite line to describe Perrin back in Command School was
"aggressively brash and reckless." He scowled as he finished the message.

WE AT THE GARRISON REALIZE THIS WAS YOUR FIRST
ENCOUNTER WITH GUARDERS, AND THE FACT THAT YOUR
SOLDIERS SUSTAINED NO LOSS OF LIFE REDEEMS YOUR OTHER-
WISE DANGEROUS BEHAVIOR. THE COMMAND OF THE FORT OF
EDGE IS STILL YOURS, BUT YOU ARE ADMONISHED TO FOLLOW
ALL ESTABLISHED PROTOCOL IN DEFENDING THE VILLAGE AND
FORT, AND IN TRAINING THE SOLDIERS. YOU MAY, HOWEVER,
CONDUCT TRAINING PROCEDURES ALONG THE EDGE OF THE
FOREST, WITHOUT ACTUALLY ENTERING INTO IT. NO ONE
UNDER ANY CIRCUMSTANCES IS TO BE ALLOWED TO ENTER
THE FORESTS FOR ANY REASONS. THE RISKS ARE TOO GREAT,
THE PAYOFFS TOO SMALL.

IF YOU FIND YOURSELF UNABLE TO FOLLOW ALL OF THE
ESTABLISHED RULES OF THE ARMY, AND INSIST ON PERFORM-
ING IN A RECKLESS MANNER, A NEW CAREER WILL BE DECIDED
FOR YOU.

Captain Shin's left hand formed a fist as he reread those words. That last sentence *may* have come from his father. Or perhaps even his mother, he considered with a dour smile. He sighed and reread the small note that had been attached under General Cush's official signature.

*Take care of that wife of yours and keep her safe from the storms.*
*The sky here is frequently cloudy and dark as of late.*
*By the way, son—excellent work. RS.*

Perrin smiled, peeled the note off the wax attachment and slipped it into his pocket. Then he put the official message on top of the cabinets behind him, planning to "accidentally" nudge it later so that it would fall into the oblivion between the cabinet and the wall.

He pulled out the next message from the packet from Idumea and reread it. He scratched his chin, still puzzled.

Wiles was missing, and High General Shin had sent out yet another message to all forts asking them to inquire with their local law enforcers for additional clues as to what may have happened.

Ever since the captain and the lieutenant emerged from the forest— filthy and scratched, but alive and defiant—and Perrin announced to Wiles and the master sergeant, "We can conquer that forest—I know it!" Wiles had been as pale as a first season private.

Two days after the Guarder attack and the suicides of the prisoners, Wiles didn't even send a messenger to explain his absence yet again in the tower.

Perrin and Karna went looking for him and discovered him in his quarters, clutching his chest. They rushed him to the hospital wing and watched in worry as the surgeon and his assistant tried to help the old sergeant major calm down his rapid breathing.

That's when the message arrived from Idumea, and was delivered to the captain at the hospital.

Chairman Nicko Mal, concerned about the health of his old friend so near the forest, ordered that Wiles be returned to Idumea to retire immediately with full honors. The message was accompanied by release papers signed by the High General.

Perrin thought the offer of retirement was a surprisingly benevolent gesture. But curiously Wiles's breathing became even more labored and his chest pains more severe when he heard that Mal wanted to bring him home.

Even though they laid him in the fort coach that evening to make his ride as comfortable as possible, the weakened Wiles seemed more restless than ever. They even sent a surgeon's aid along to care for him during the long ride to Idumea.

But when the coach arrived outside of Pools for another change of horses late at night, Wiles was no longer in the coach. His crate with his possessions was still in there, but no sergeant major.

The soldiers driving the coach and the surgeon's aid inside were baffled. They hadn't seen or heard anything unusual, and when they changed horses outside of Vines, Wiles was finally sleeping on the carriage bench. The surgeon's aid had nodded off for a well-deserved break, waking only when the carriage stopped for the next horse change.

That was three days ago, and still nothing had been heard about the sergeant major. High General Shin had thoroughly interrogated the soldiers and the surgeon's aid, and was confident all three men were as innocent as they trembled to be. Soldiers from Pools to Vines and even up to Midplain were dispatched to check the roads, thinking that perhaps Wiles had become disoriented and tried to leave the coach while it was moving, but they found no clues.

That struck Perrin as exceptionally odd. The main road to Idumea was well used. And even though the coach traveled at night to get Wiles as quickly as possible to the surgeons at the garrison, it was difficult to imagine that *no one* would have noticed an old man's body lying on the side of the road. At this time of year all the fields, farm after farm all the way to Idumea, were filled with workers bringing in the harvest.

Wiles had simply vanished. Just like people had vanished years ago, when the Guarders were most active.

*Guarder snatched,* as the more paranoid liked to claim.

A string of words he uttered just minutes ago replayed themselves suddenly in Perrin's head. "Guarders dressing up in blue uniforms . . ."

His stunned whisper faded into nothing.

No.

No. That *couldn't* be possible. That wouldn't be *imagined.* Wiles had been around for years. That would mean that *anyone . . . any time . . .* and they could be *anywhere . . .* then they could—

He dropped the message as if it burned his fingers, and stared out at the forest for a very long time.

---

That night he was very quiet as he lay in bed next to his wife.

"You've been lost in thought all evening," Mahrree gently prodded him. "What's wrong?"

It took him another minute to answer her. "Had a thought, earlier. At the fort."

Mahrree tried to keep her sigh quiet. Dawn was only about eight hours away, and at this rate it would take her hours to get him to articulate his thought. "About . . .?"

"Wiles."

Ah, some progress, and faster than she expected. "About him still missing? About—"

Another long pause. "Who he really was."

Now Mahrree went silent, lost in worry. "What do you mean?"

"What if . . . what if he was *one of them?*"

Mahrree huddled closer to her husband, and he put a protective arm around her. "But . . . but that wouldn't make any sense. He's been around for years, right? It's not like he suddenly showed up volunteering to serve in the army."

Perrin's shoulders relaxed. "True, true. He's always been here. I keep reminding myself of that."

"Why would you have to remind yourself?" she asked. "I mean, if you thought he was one of them, that would mean he infiltrated the army years ago. That he's been living among us for decades. Why, why that's *ridiculous!*" Her tone wasn't as light as she hoped it would be.

"Yes. Ridiculous," he answered in a monotone. "But *what if?*"

"Then . . . then . . . it's all over," she whimpered. "We have no hope. They know everything about us, they can destroy us in an instant—"

"But they *haven't*," he reminded her. "If they really have infiltrated the army—the world—then why haven't they taken us over? Why haven't they destroyed us?"

Mahrree sighed in frustration. "It doesn't make any sense."

"It never has, remember? No, the more I think about it, the more I'm sure—Wiles wasn't one of them. None of them are among us. It was just a stray thought that I gave too much attention. Wiles was just a regular old man who met an unfortunate end. That's all. Sorry to bother you with the idea. Good night, my darling wife."

Mahrree lay awake for hours listening to her husband softly snoring. Finally she decided that if he wasn't worried, she shouldn't be either.

It was one of the worst nights she ever endured, and she wasn't even nauseated.

# Chapter 20 ~ "Doorknob, I don't *want* to see everything differently."

"**I** can't stand it anymore," Mahrree announced to Perrin over breakfast.

He sighed and said, as he did each morning for the past four weeks, "Yes, my darling wife, you *can*. And you must."

"But why?"

He put down his fork. "To be sure, remember? Just in case it's not what we think?"

She nibbled on her bread, the only thing she could tolerate in the mornings. "But what else could it be?"

"I really don't know." He smiled. "For now it's just our little secret. Rather fun to keep between just the two of us, isn't it? Besides, you'd be heartbroken if you told everyone and suddenly it wasn't going to happen, right?"

"You're right, you're right."

"*Love it* when you have to admit that." He chuckled as he took a big bite of potatoes.

Mahrree looked away from his plate filled with bacon, potatoes, and scrambled eggs. It was a good thing he was adept at cooking himself a big breakfast each morning.

Strangely, she found herself repulsed by the texture of food. And the smell of food. And the taste of food—

"Four more weeks, Mahrree. That's all. That's what we decided, remember?"

"I remember, I remember."

It was the most sensible thing, but she simply didn't *feel* sensible. She alternated between feeling joyful and jubilant, and woozy and weepy. But, in an effort to feign sensibility, she behaved as if she felt fine even though she was sick each morning and dizzy each afternoon.

But sometimes what she felt was overwhelming. Whenever she saw anything remotely sentimental she began to tear up. Just last week Mahrree and

Perrin went out for an evening stroll to enjoy the Harvest Season air when she noticed a little boy on the side of the road playing with a tiny kitten. Just as Perrin started to pull her away, she broke out of his grip and rushed over to croon at the scene. She knew her behavior was completely irrational, but the little boy and kitten were just *so cute!*

"*Cute?*" Perrin mumbled as he led her away. "Since when do you use the word 'cute'?"

"Should I have said 'adorable'?"

"Neither of those words was on my mother's list."

After that, Perrin began to develop avoidance strategies, or so Mahrree assumed that might be the official term for his behavior. On Holy Day yesterday, a new mother offered to let Mahrree hold her baby girl at the meeting. The infant was in her arms for only a minute when Mahrree began to sniff and grow weepy.

"Ah, must be those allergies, again, huh Mahrree? We better get you home," Perrin said with a tone of hinting. "Before your eyes puff up again. Oh dear, looks like they already are. Let's get going before you bloat and frighten that baby. *Now.*"

Mahrree noticed several of the older women smiling in her direction as they quickly left. They weren't fooling them, and the fact that they suspected what Mahrree and Perrin suspected filled her with even more hope that all their suspicions were correct.

---

Lieutenant Heth heard the quiet knock on the door, but figured it was for a room further down the dormitory. At such a late hour, there was only one kind of visitor that would dare lurk in the halls. And she was obviously lost.

It wasn't until the third time he heard the soft knock that he began to wonder if it was for his room. His roommates were snoring, so obviously none of them were expecting someone. Reluctantly he got out of his bed, lit a candle, and snuck over to the door. When he opened it, he sneered.

"What are *you* doing here?" He looked his visitor up and down with a critical eye.

"Nice to see you too, Sonoforen," Dormin whispered as he ducked into the room.

"Hey, I didn't invite you in."

"Shh. And don't worry, I'm not looking for a place to sleep in Idumea. I just wanted to talk to you. Some place private?"

Heth sighed and gestured to his bed. "My roommates could sleep through a wrestling match. I know that for a fact," he sniggered quietly.

His brother sat on the edge of the bed without commenting.

Heth sat a few feet away from him. "So what do you want?"

"To know what you're doing," Dormin said. "I've been looking for you for weeks."

"And that brought you all the way to Idumea? I thought you were afraid to be seen." In the dim light he eyed his younger brother's dark concealing and ill-fitting clothes, untrimmed blonde hair that was covered by a sloppy hat, and scruffy boots. "You look like a rubbish remover."

"That's because I am. And yes, I *am* worried about being recognized. I move only at night. Twice I've been stopped by soldiers wondering what I was up to."

"Hope you gave them an interesting story to think about during their long night shifts," Heth leered.

Dormin sighed. "You always were so simple-minded. I don't know why I bother."

"I don't either. So leave."

Dormin folded his hands. "I promised someone I would at least try. Sonoforen—"

"It's Heth, now."

His brother rolled his eyes. "Call yourself whatever you want, it doesn't change who you are unless you change yourself."

"And you never made any sense," Heth rolled his eyes back. "Look, I've got early classes—"

"Yes, exactly how are you paying for all of this?"

"How did you even know I was here?"

"There was a message delivered to our aunt's house from Chairman Mal, of all people, asking how I was doing. He said you were in Command School! I don't get it—how are you paying for this?"

"Gold," Heth said easily.

"Whose?"

"Mine. Never told you this, but I had a stash, as the Little King. Great-Grandmother set it aside for me, in case I should ever need it. After mother died, I decided I needed it. Apparently Great-Grandmother didn't leave any gold for you."

Dormin sighed. "Figures. Where was it hiding?"

"I'm not going to tell you."

"So there's more?"

"Wouldn't you like to know."

"Not really. I don't need it. I'm just glad to hear that . . ." Dormin paused to find the right words, "you're doing something useful with your life, finding a way to be productive, to return to the civilization that has given you so much."

His brother scoffed. "Doormat, you sound like an old man, you know that?"

"Maybe it's because I've been spending a lot of time with an old man."

Heth sneered. "Really? Why? Can't get any girls to talk to you."

Dormin took a deep breath and looked up at the ceiling. "*Knew* this was going to be useless—"

"Yep," Heth nodded. "No girls."

Dormin clenched his fists. "Sonof—Heth, why are you here?"

"Why not?"

"I mean, what possessed you to join the army? I thought you hated Mal. And Shin was the one who had our father executed!"

"Nothing better to do," Heth said dismissively. "Exactly why are *you* here?"

Dormin took a deep breath. "Last time we spoke I told you that I was going to read The Writings. Well, I did. I know why Great-Grandmother hated it so much. She was the very embodiment of evil The Writings warn against."

Heth chuckled. "Yeah, she was a piece of work, wasn't she? They discussed her in one of my classes. I really didn't know how tough an old bird she was. Took all my self-control to not puff up in pride."

"She's not something to *admire*, Sonof—Heth." He sighed again. "My point is, there's a better way to live. There's so much in The Writings about how the Creator—"

"Whoa, whoa, whoa—I know what this is. You're trying to get me to read The Writings, aren't you?"

Dormin shrugged. "It's just that I've gained so much—"

"Oh, *please*," Heth snickered. "Don't start, just don't start any of that nonsense. You know what believing in The Writings does? It makes you blind! You don't think for yourself—"

"Stop right there!" Dormin said, almost too loudly. "I think very well for myself. I've been doing all kinds of thinking, and I'm thinking our family has never done anything right. Our father never thought about anyone but himself, he—"

"He was *your father!*" Heth hissed. "How dare you speak against him?"

"No, I'm not speaking against him," Dormin defended. "I'm trying to point out that he simply didn't understand. He never had a chance to be something better, because he didn't know. I loved him, and now I have even more respect for him. He should have been more horrible, considering it was his grandmother who had his mother killed, and then she controlled his every move. But he really *did* try. He could have been good, but he was manipulated by those who never taught him to think. Sonoforen, The Writings have been teaching me to think, to test all things, to ponder, to—"

"Become a bag full of nuts!" his brother finally cut him off. "That's what you are, you know that? You've been talking to a rector, haven't you?"

"I have!" Dormin said eagerly, "and he's the one who—"

"Doo-doo Droppings," Heth said sadly, calling his brother the name he came up with when he was eight. "And you came all this way to—"

"Try to get you to listen. Look, we can fix things. We could do great things for the world, give back for all that we took."

"I am," Heth said coldly. "I'll be giving back all kinds of things. And when I'm done in two more years, I *will* fix everything in the world."

Dormin leaned back. "Why do I get the feeling that while we're saying the same things, we're meaning the opposite?"

"Are you about finished here? Because it's late."

Dormin reached into a pack on his back and pulled out a bound set of parchments. "I want to give this to you, have you read it. Think about—"

His brother snatched it out of his hands and peered at the title in the dim light. "As if I don't have enough reading to do . . . Oh, I am not bothering with *this*, Doorpost."

"I'm not asking for a bed, or for gold, or for anything else. I'm merely asking you to read this. Please. It just may change the way you see everything."

"Doorknob, I don't *want* to see everything differently," Heth said as he shoved the book back into his brother's hands. "I like what I see in my future. And you don't happen to be in it."

"But what if you can see things *better*? Wouldn't that be worth finding out?"

"Look, Doorhead—"

"That one never even made any sense!" Dormin spouted, losing his patience. "What's that supposed to mean: Doorhead?"

Heth sneered. "Just always said it to irritate you. You're seventeen years old now—"

"Twenty-one!"

"—and it *still* works. Look, I realize you came a long way, and what makes it even more pathetic is that it was for nothing. I'm happy. You obviously aren't. Maybe you're the one who needs to see things differently. Now, if you're finally done, get out. They've been doing surprise inspections in the middle of the night and it would be so *tragic* to find that Dormin, King Oren's youngest son, was found breaking into the university dormitories. So many questions would be asked . . ."

Dormin stood up, The Writings clutched in his hands. "I'd hoped this would go better."

Heth shrugged. "Don't know why."

"Because you're my brother. I worry about you. And I . . . love you," he stumbled.

"Ew," Heth cringed. "All right, it's definitely time for you to get out." He stood up and headed straight for the door.

His younger brother nodded. "Well then, that's it. I tried. I failed, but I tried," he mumbled as he got up. "I might never see you again."

"That's fine, Doorgirl," Heth said, pushing him on the back toward the hallway.

"What's *that* supposed to mean: 'Doorgirl'? I never got that either!"

"There are a *lot* of things you don't get, Dormaniac. If ever I see you again, I'll make you a list."

Heth slammed the door.

"And they thought our father was the idiot," he mumbled as he fell back into bed.

---

It took Dormin almost two weeks to get back from where he started, reaching the village by the middle of Harvest Season, just before the Festival. First he finished out the week removing rubbish in Idumea, then told his supervisor he was quitting. He traveled by night along the rivers, avoiding other loners also trying not to be noticed. Eventually he found himself at the small house that sent him. It was before dawn, but he knew he was expected to knock on the back door, no matter the hour.

A few moments later it opened up to reveal a small, middle-aged man blinking sleep out of his narrow black eyes. They popped open when he saw who stood there. "Come in, come in!" he said quickly, pulling Dormin into his small kitchen. "Are you safe? Have you been seen?"

Dormin smiled at the man who seemed genuinely happy to see him. "I'm fine and safe, Rector Yung. No one recognized me."

Rector Yung looked up at the ceiling. "Thank you!" he called as if the

Creator lived in the attic.

"Who is it, dear?" a woman's voice came from behind a partially closed door.

"Our wandering lamb, my love!"

"Dormin's back? Is he all right?" She sounded just as Dormin always thought a mother should: pleasantly worried.

"I am, Mrs. Yung," he called back. "I'm sorry to bother you so early."

"Not at all!" said a cheerful voice. "Let me start breakfast. I'll be right out."

"Come in, son. Tell me everything." Rector Yung led Dormin out of the kitchen and to a small sofa in the gathering room.

Dormin sat down. "I saw him, but Rector, I failed. He wouldn't even take it." He pulled his pack off his back and retrieved the copy of The Writings the rector had given him almost a season before.

"Ah, well. We had to try, didn't we?" The rector took back the book as he sat next to Dormin. He ran his fingers through his black hair speckled with white, as if remembering he hadn't yet combed it that morning. "I suspected it was a long shot, but like feeding an abandoned puppy, sometimes we have to try again and again until it finally accepts the milk that will sustain it."

"Well, the puppy hates me," Dormin exhaled. "Always has. And I didn't do much to win him over, either. He's always been so arrogant, so annoying . . ."

Rector Yung patted him kindly on the back. "Siblings have a way of recognizing our most sensitive points, then stabbing at them, don't they?"

"Yes!" Dormin groused. "I'm sorry. I know I shouldn't have let him control me like that, and for a while I did all right. It's just that . . . I failed. I lost my temper, but I *did* tell him what you said to tell him."

"And how did he respond?"

"By showing me the door," Dormin groaned. "You said it would make me feel better. I must have said the words wrong, because it didn't work."

"The words 'I love you' do indeed have power, but not the kind I think you're expecting. Trust me, Dormin—someday you *will* be glad you said them. At least you'll know that he heard them once from you."

"Whatever you say, Rector," Dormin said wearily. "You've been right about most everything else."

Yung chuckled. "Well, thank you for that display of faith, son."

"Sorry. So now what do I do?"

Rector Yung looked at him in the muted light of the dawn, the sky beginning to lighten and tinting everything a pale orange, matching the dozens of pumpkins growing around the rector's small home. "Now, you will eat some breakfast, then take a very long nap in our guest room—"

"I mean, with my life," Dormin slumped against the sofa. "Rector, I took work as a rubbish collector. Me, the son of King Oren, the descendant of all the kings, removing rubbish!"

"And that was the noblest work anyone in your family line has done in six generations, Dormin," Rector Yung declared.

"Ha!" Dormin scoffed. "Whatever. I have no skills, Rector. The tutors I had as a boy—I realize now they never told me anything true. Merely more rubbish. Maybe that's why I was good at removing it. My supervisor even said I had a *knack*," he shuddered. "Said in maybe five or six years, with 'consistent performance' and 'continued perseverance' I could become a head remover," he said dismally.

Yung swallowed. "Head what?"

"Removing *trash*, Rector. Not *heads*. No, I haven't joined my great grandparents' killing squads, although who knows—maybe that would have been the only other thing I could be successful at."

Rector Yung patted him on the arm. "Dormin, you have remarkable skills. You've been gone for nearly a season getting by on your wits, finding yourself work, keeping yourself from being discovered, and . . . where was it that you finally found your brother?"

"In the dormitory. Command School," Dormin said dully. "Stopped by my aunt's and there was a message for me about him."

Yung's jaw dropped. "Did you get *in* to the dorms?"

Dormin nodded. "Snuck in at night. Watched the guards for a while to time their routes. Talked to Sonoforen—*Heth*, as he now calls himself—then snuck back out again."

"And no one but your brother saw you?"

"I guess not."

Yung breathed out. "Remarkable skills, indeed! Dormin, do you realize how hard it is to get in and out of the Command School dormitory? To be on campus and not be stopped?"

"No one cares about rubbish men," Dormin explained. "I figured that was the best way to slip in and out."

Yung had a smile tugging at both ends of his mouth. "*Very* remarkable, Dormin. Sometimes our skills lie in what we've learned, but other skills are natural. I think we've found your natural ability."

"Great," Dormin rolled his eyes. "I'm good at taking out the rubbish and sneaking in to talk to my brother who cares nothing for me. What's the point, Rector? I know you keep telling me this life is a test, but I'm failing it. I've got no more family—at least, none that cares about me—no friends, and no one that would even notice if didn't exist. In fact, I can think of one or two older men who'd be happy to hear I was no longer alive so I won't pose any threat to their rule. I just take up space, Rector. I'm even a waste of *that* space. I'm rubbish, too."

Rector Yung couldn't help himself. He leaned over and embraced Dormin.

Dormin's chin trembled, but finally he put his arms around the rector and squeezed him back.

"You are a son of the Creator, Dormin," Rector Yung whispered, "and that's far more significant than being descended from some old kings."

"Thanks," Dormin murmured.

Rector Yung released him a moment later. "You've lived such a narrow existence that you simply don't know all there is to know. Well, I know of something you *can* do, something amazing to match your remarkable skills. But I warn you, this may take some time."

"Time is what I've got plenty of, Rector," the young man mumbled. "No gold or silver or home or food or purpose, but plenty of time."

"Time is the most valuable gift the Creator gives us, Dormin. Trust me."

He shrugged. "So what can I do?"

"You will stay with us, Dormin, as our hired hand," Yung decided. "No one here knows you or your heritage. We can say you're our nephew. As scruffy as you appear right now, not even your mother would've recognized you. You can work for us, we'll feed and house you, and during our evenings, I'll teach a few things. Things you've never imagined. But how long this takes depends on your response to one question."

Dormin eyed the rector suspiciously. "All right. I guess I would be foolish to reject your offer."

"If ever you don't want to continue, Dormin, you are free to leave," Yung assured him. "I'm not forcing you, just giving you an option. You'll not be a prisoner in *my* house."

"A *prisoner*," Dormin whispered with growing dread. "How did you know about that?"

"Your family may think they kept quiet the fact that for three generations they enslaved their servants, but Dormin, word has way of trickling out of even the most tightly kept houses," Yung whispered back. "Just know that I know, and I'd never treat you in such a way."

"Of course you wouldn't," Dormin said apologetically. "And I'm grateful for the offer. Actually, I can't think of anywhere I'd rather be than with you and Mrs. Yung. She makes the best biscuits."

"That she does!" Rector Yung said, sniffing the air that was already filling with the scents of breakfast.

"So," Dormin said, clapping his hands on his legs. "What's your question?"

Rector Yung studied him. "Dormin, what color is the sky?"

"Blue," he answered automatically. He didn't even glance out the window at the blazing orange that leaked into the room, tingeing everything around them in a carroty hue. "Everyone knows that."

Rector Yung glanced out the window at the ignored evidence and sighed. "Dormin, you're going to be enjoying my wife's cooking for a *very* long time. But that's all right. That's why we're here."

---

Several weeks after his brother's late night visit, Lieutenant Heth left his last class, marched out onto the greens of the campus, and over a slight rise at the edge of it. The cool Harvest Season air showed his breath as he walked. A few minutes later he strode down the gentle hillside and over to the massive Administrative Headquarters. He kept his cap down low over his eyes, marched up the white stone stairs, and through the grand entrance doors.

The last time he did that, he had a butchering knife in his hands and a flock of guards on his tail. Today no one thought twice about another young man in a uniform entering the Headquarters.

He walked past the old gold and leather throne still on display and proceeded toward a large outer office. He paused at the desk and nodded to the two men in red jackets.

"Lieutenant Heth, sirs."

One checked the ledger. "He's expecting you, Lieutenant. Go right in."

Heth turned toward the large double doors, opened them, walked through, and shut them behind him.

"A much better entry than six moons ago. Sit down, Heth," Chairman Mal nodded to a seat in front of him.

Heth sat obediently in the chair he occupied back in Planting Season and waited.

"Normally I would begin by quizzing you on some of your past exam material," Mal explained, "but you're not a typical officer-in-training, are you?"

"No, sir."

"Dormin came to see you, didn't he?" Mal casually sprung on him. "About a full moon ago?"

Heth's mouth dropped open. "Uh, yes . . . yes he did. How did you know—"

Mal clasped his hands in front of him. "I know all kinds of things, Lieutenant. Why didn't you tell me?" His tone turned sharp.

Heth swallowed. "It wasn't a good visit, sir. He wouldn't have been interested in what you could offer him."

"Are you sure?" Mal asked harshly.

Heth nodded and answered swiftly, "Yes sir! He was trying to give me a copy of The Writings. Wanted me to read them."

Mal pulled a face. "The Writings? Hm. That's too bad," he reluctantly admitted. "He had a good mind. Could have used him."

Heth shifted uncomfortably, having been under the impression that *he* was the one with a "good mind."

"Did he question you about your new position?"

"He did. I told him that my great-grandmother left me the gold to pay for Command School."

"And he believed that?"

"He did, sir."

"Good. Did he ask why you were here?"

"Yes, sir. Told him I had nothing better to do."

Mal squinted. "And his response to that was . . ."

Heth shrugged. "He believed it."

"Coming from you, I suppose it's not unexpected."

Heth wondered if he had just been slighted. "When he left, he said he didn't know if I would ever see him again."

"Where does he live, Heth?"

"I . . . I don't know, sir," he confessed.

Mal leaned forward. "Do you recall that I asked you specifically to find out where he lives if ever you saw him again?"

"You did, sir." He gulped.

"So what is he doing?"

"Moving rubbish, sir."

"Moving rubbish," Mal repeated tonelessly. "Where?"

Heth hesitated. "He didn't reveal that, sir," realizing that he shouldn't add, *Because I forgot to ask.*

Mal analyzed him.

Heth shifted again, perceiving that the Chairman didn't have too high of expectations for him. For some reason that made him feel guilty. It took him a moment to recognize the emotion, because it wasn't one he'd experienced often.

"Did your brother say *anything* useful? Any suggestion of what he might be up to, or who he might be working with?"

Heth eagerly answered, knowing it would make his brother seem more foolish than him. "A rector. He's been working with a rector."

"Hmm," was all that Mal answered.

Heth was disappointed.

"I'm disappointed," Mal said.

Heth began to smile, until Mal finished his sentence.

"—in you. I expected more. If you're going to get what you want, I need to get what I want, too."

"But sir, he's not doing anything," Heth protested. "He's useless!"

"According to your evaluation, which, unfortunately, is all I have to go on," Mal griped. "You're going to have to do better. The next time I require something of you, I expect to be impressed. I'm investing a great deal in you, and when the world gives you something, it wants something *in return.*"

Heth had never heard that before, but he nodded anyway. "Yes, sir."

"I need you to be ready for when the moment is right," Mal said.

"When will the time be right, sir?"

"Well, that's the issue—the time may come up tomorrow, or not for five more years. Whenever I feel it. I need to reach our target while he's still vulnerable, at some moment when he's least expecting it."

"I think I'll be ready, sir."

Mal scoffed. "Think? I'm not training you to *think*, Heth. I'm training you to *react!* And you better be ready to react at a moment's notice."

# Chapter 21 ~ "Something like this shouldn't happen for quite a while considering . . ."

Several moons later, by the middle of Planting Season, 320, Mahrree had had *more* than enough.

Enough of the over-sized tunics and skirts that only emphasized how enormous she was.

Enough of the cringes of sympathy she received as she waddled like a stuffed duck through the market place.

Enough of inane questions such as, "Haven't you had that baby *yet?*" as if it was her fault, and making her feel badly would somehow change the situation.

Even enough of her husband smiling as sweetly as he could and reminding her how beautiful she looked as he gingerly patted her swollen belly.

He was supposed to do that, Mahrree knew. She found it on Joriana Shin's list to her son.

"Number two: remind her how beautiful she looks carrying *your* child."

Mahrree loved the wording of that, almost as much as she loved number seven: "Accept the blame for everything, and don't aggravate her. Remember that this is, after all, *your* fault."

And Mahrree reminded him of that fact, frequently. Maybe if he had been a bit smaller in frame, she wouldn't have been double her size for the past ten weeks. Now, in the middle of Planting Season, while everything else in the world was bursting in new color and life, Mahrree was just bursting.

Oh it had been sweet and exciting a season and a half ago, once she finally got over feeling ill each morning and saw the small bulge beginning in her belly. They had to only tell her mother, and Hycymum squealed so loud the entire village knew within five minutes. Joriana Shin had even come to Edge in the dreary middle of Raining Season to bring baby blankets, clothing, changing cloths, and a new list for her son which he kept secured in his wardrobe for referral.

That was where Mahrree found it one day while rearranging his clothing in a fit of needing to organize things which, interestingly, she saw as number ten on the list: "She will feel the need to reorganize everything. Help her. Remember, all of this is *your* fault."

Mahrree loved her mother-in-law.

All in all the waiting had been fine, and even the forest had been quiet, allowing her to have her husband home every night. But for the past two weeks Mahrree had been "growing irrationally testy"—number one on her mother-in-law's list. Everything was ready. The addition next to the study was completed and outfitted with the cradle she'd used as a baby, and the wardrobe was stocked with blankets, gowns, and stacks of changing cloths which Mahrree was delighted to see Perrin eyeing suspiciously one evening. She was sure she heard him mumble, "Isn't there a better design for these? Maybe something to bury in the ground instead of *washing* afterwards?"

Everything was in place, except the massive creature that rolled slowly like a land tremor in Mahrree's belly. There was nothing else she could do each day, especially since she had quit teaching, but grumble as she straightened up the house, did the laundry, and washed the dishes. Loudly.

"I'm going to break rule number eleven," Perrin said, peeking his head around the door at a safe distance. He came home for his midday meal every day for the past few weeks, just to check on her.

"And what is rule number eleven?" she asked crossly as she leaned across the washing basin, straining to reach a plate. "No matter how tempting, don't use my belly as a shelf?"

He stepped into the kitchen and slid the plate over to her. "No, that's number nine. And I *have* resisted the temptation." He gently took her by the shoulders and turned her, the massive belly bumping into his sheathed sword. "Sorry," he murmured as he tried to hide his amusement. "My mother said I should never tell you that it *will* end, because at this point you simply won't believe me, and may want to hurt me."

"She's right," Mahrree agreed, "because—"

"I know, I know—this is all my fault. But I love you for enduring it."

Mahrree was about to reemphasize his point, but only got as far as opening her mouth.

"What's wrong?" Perrin asked, looking down. "Did your belly actually get nicked?"

She shook her head.

"See a mouse?"

She let out a low moan and gripped his arms.

His eyebrows shot upwards. "Pain?"

She nodded.

"*That* kind of pain?"

"*Yes!*" She gripped his arms tighter.

"It's about time!" He sighed in relief.

"It's not over *yet*, Perrin!" she gasped again.

He stayed loyally by her side that afternoon, the 46th Day of Planting, uselessly rubbing her back and pointlessly promising her that everything would be all right.

Hycymum and the midwives—retrieved by a messenger from the fort wondering where the captain was—tried to encourage Perrin to pace outside once Mahrree felt like someone was whacking her back with a timber.

It wasn't until he saw a midwife strewing a bale of hay across the wooden floor by the hearth in the gathering room—"Makes it easier to clean up the messes," she explained—that he willingly left.

Two hours later an exhausted Mahrree, drenched with sweat and tears, and shocked that so much could change so quickly, stared at the bundle in her arms. Her mother and the midwives were surprised that the baby was so small. Mahrree's seeming enormity must have been a trick of the eye, they decided, magnified by her slight frame. The baby probably came early.

But she didn't know what they were talking about; nothing about the newborn she spent the last hour and a half birthing seemed small.

Downstairs in the kitchen Hycymum was busily stirring up a late dinner, while upstairs one of the midwives helped Mahrree get comfortable in the bed where they had moved her.

"It will be all right," she assured. "Just give him some time. They almost always come around."

Mahrree shrugged. "Thank you again."

The midwife nodded. "I'll be back later tonight to check on—" She stopped when she heard the door slam downstairs.

"Mahrree?!" Perrin's deep voice boomed throughout the house.

The midwife picked up a bag of bloodied cloths, smiled in encouragement, and headed down the stairs. She nodded a greeting to the captain as Perrin bounded up to his bedroom.

"Mahrree!" He stopped at the door and looked at her worriedly. "The other midwife said only that the baby was birthed, and that it's a bit small, and your mother wouldn't tell me anything so is it, is it . . .?"

"It's all right," Mahrree smiled at him. "All the fingers and toes, cried, breathing."

He took another step closer, his broad shoulders tense with concern. "So what's wrong?"

She practiced her brave face. "Perrin, you have a daughter." Then she braced for his response.

He stood motionless. "But?"

Mahrree bit her lower lip. "Well . . ."

His shoulders dropped in relief and a grin spread across his face. "So she's all right? Healthy and everything?" He took another cautious step closer.

"Yes," Mahrree began to smile more genuinely.

"Mahrree," he said slowly, "did you think I would be upset about a baby girl?"

"Umm . . ."

His face softened and he sat carefully on the bed next to her. "I don't care what we have, as long as we get to have a child."

"But are you sure?" she pressed. "Four generations of Shins have produced sons. *Officers!* Perrin Shin's daughter can't even join the army."

He chuckled. "Perrin Shin's son might not want to join the army, either. You know I don't care about tradition. I'm rather *progressive* that way." He winked at her and peered over into the bundle of blankets she held close to her chest.

She held the bundle out to him. "Would you like to hold your daughter?"

To her surprise, his eyes grew wet. "Absolutely," he whispered, and took his newborn.

In his massive hands she really did look small. He could have held her with one hand, which he did. He slid back the blanket covering her head to see her hair. When she first emerged, Mahrree thought her matted hair was black, but after the midwives washed her the newborn's hair was lighter and fuzzy.

Perrin smiled as he ran his hand over it. "Your hair, so far," he said to Mahrree. "What color are her eyes?"

The newborn squinted to see what was making the noise, but she didn't open her eyes more than a crack.

Mahrree felt her own eyes blurring to see how tenderly her husband held their daughter. "Grayish, for now. One of the midwives said newborns she's seen with that eye color tend to go very dark. Your eyes then, later."

Perrin softly kissed her tiny lips, and she squirmed and grunted. "She's beautiful, Mahrree!" he beamed. "Perfect. Welcome to Edge, my little Relfikin."

"Uh . . ."

Perrin looked at her with mock sobriety. "Not Relfikin then?"

"Please no?"

He gazed at his daughter, inspecting her features. "Well then, what if we take two letters from your mother's name, and two letters from my mother's name, and toss in a couple other letters, then mix them all up for something new?"

"Sounds like you've been watching my mother cook."

"So, my tiny daughter," he whispered to her, "how do you feel about . . . Jaytsy?"

Mahrree blinked. "You came up with that rather quickly."

"Jaytsy," he said again, trying out her name. "Jaytsy . . . Well Mahrree, what else should I have been doing for the last two hours while pacing between here and the fort? I wasn't worrying about Guarders."

"You were coming up with baby names?"

"I should be doing something useful, don't you think?" He smiled at his baby.

Mahrree grinned. "I like it—Jaytsy Shin. Just out of curiosity, what boy names did you come up with?"

He looked at her. "I didn't think of any boy names. Only girls'."

That's when Mahrree started to cry.

Perrin smiled at his tiny girl. "Don't be alarmed by your mother's behavior, little Jaytsy. Your Grandmother Shin left me another list for what to expect *after* you were birthed. Crying is on top. It means she's happy you're finally here. And so am I."

Mahrree sobbed.

---

Two men sat in the dark office of an unlit building.

"A *girl?*" the second man said, concerned.

Mal chuckled mirthlessly. "I'm curious to see what happens next. I could tell Relf was trying to make the most of it, but in his eyes I could see his disappointment. Such a manly son, and all he can produce is a female? Ha!"

His partner waved that off. "Oh, I'm sure High General Shin isn't that perturbed by a granddaughter. Without women, there would be no more men, after all. She could still be the mother of another general someday—"

"But Joriana Shin is apparently quite pleased," Mal said, narrowing his eyes. "You sure there isn't some way women can't influence the kind of baby they birth? Some way they sleep, or eat, or carry it—"

The second man laughed. "If there is, every woman would want to know the secret! Granted, men have suspected since the beginning that women communicated things we'll never understand, but knowledge as to how give birth to a girl rather than a boy?"

Mal's shoulder twitched at his companion's continued laughter. "It was a legitimate question."

His companion wiped his eyes. "So what do you think will 'happen next,' as you so ominously put it?"

"He can't be happy with this," said Mal with a developing sneer. "What if having a baby wasn't even his idea? What if it was hers?"

"So what?"

Mal sighed impatiently. "Sometimes you're so slow. Of what use is a girl to a man like him?"

"Many men actually enjoy their daughters," the other man explained. "Find them not as disappointing as their sons."

"Speculation," Mal clasped his hands in front of him. "We will soon see evidence that he is disappointed by having a daughter."

"Such as?"

Mal shrugged. "Some male animals neglect their young. Some leave the mate to raise the offspring herself. Bears have been known to destroy cubs to reduce competition."

The second man studied his companion. "Interesting that you automatically assume some level of neglect or abuse. That's what you're biased to look for, so you'll likely miss what actually happens. Rather sloppy science, Nicko."

"I'm expecting a counter speculation, Doctor!" Mal said coldly.

The second man nodded once. "Counter speculation, then: Shin will surprise us—or rather, *you*—again. We'll soon see evidence that he does enjoy his daughter, and is open-minded enough to see how females are also necessary to the furthering of the world."

Mal's mouth moved into position of a smile, but nothing else on his face did. "Oh, how I enjoy your naiveté. So optimistic. Just fills me with warm thoughts of butterflies and flowers. Will you be traveling to Edge to bring the precious infant a pair of knitted booties, then?"

"What a wonderful idea," the man said. "I've always wanted to check out the fishing in Edge."

Mal glowered as his companion snorted a laugh.

---

On Perrin and Mahrree's first wedding anniversary, the 38th Day of Weeding 292, they didn't celebrate like many other couples did to commemorate their first year together by eating in the marketplace or going to the amphitheater. Instead they sat leaning against each other on their sofa, Perrin cradling their three-moons-old little girl who slept peacefully in his arms, while Mahrree closed her eyes in relief that Jaytsy had been quiet for more than an hour, for once.

"How long until she's sleeping through the night?" Perrin whispered.

"I don't know," Mahrree whispered back, both of them worried they might wake her. "Two mothers last Holy Day told me their babies slept through the night from the very beginning."

"Ah," Perrin nodded, "I noticed you had a murderous look in your eyes. That comment must have been what produced it."

"Then a midwife told me it can take half a year or more before they sleep through the night!"

"You're not going to cry about that again, are you?"

Mahrree chuckled quietly. "Just tears of exhaustion. That was on your mother's list, too. You were there when the other fathers told you about weeping wives, right?"

He smiled. "I have to admit, I never understood the need for parents to sit around talking about their children during the congregational meal. But now? It's nice to know our daughter's normal. And you're *mostly* normal."

"It was a legitimate question!"

"But Mahrree, to describe in detail to other parents, *while they are eating*, the nature and the amount of the fluids Jaytsy produces is not the best dinner conversation."

Mahrree smirked. "None of them flinched. They knew exactly what I was talking about, and you were relieved to know as well that it was normal for her to squirt out so much, and so violently."

He shrugged in reluctant agreement.

"I never appreciated them before until now," Mahrree said, stroking Jaytsy's soft light brown hair. "The villagers, I mean. I've lived here all my life, but I never really understood what it meant to be part of them."

"I rather miss the nightly dinners they brought in," Perrin admitted. "Although some women have strange ideas of what to do with chicken, it was nice that you didn't have to cook for five weeks."

"Mmm, I miss that, too."

"Mahrree, why don't you go upstairs and nap? Jaytsy's got that thumb in her mouth again. She'll be quiet for a while."

"And miss our first anniversary?"

"You're eyes are closed, my darling wife. You're missing it."

"Are you doing anything entertaining?" She forced her eyes open.

"Not until Jaytsy wakes up and I get her to laugh again. That sound has got to be the—" He stopped before he said the "c" word Mahrree had teased him that he would eventually utter.

"I'm not missing anything, then."

Perrin chuckled.

Jaytsy stirred at the low noise, and both of her parents held their breath. She stretched, grunted, and snuggled back into her father's arms.

Her parents exhaled.

"It seemed to be so easy," Mahrree murmured quietly. "Feed them, burp them, change them, put them to sleep."

"We had no idea what we were getting into, did we?" Perrin smiled. "I wonder if we'll ever get the hang of it before she outgrows us. Bath time is entertaining, I'll admit that."

"And you've become quite expert at changing cloths. I think you're the only man in Edge who is."

"Just don't let anyone know about that. Not very dignified for the commander of the fort at Edge to be known as a dirty cloth changer."

"Just remember it's because you have a strong stomach, Captain Shin."

"And don't you forget it!" He ran his finger along Jaytsy's soft cheek. "She's already getting bigger and fatter. That's good, right?"

"Baby fat is very good."

"As surprising as all of this has been, I must admit I'm enjoying it. She really is . . . quite . . ." He faltered to find the right word.

"Say it. I dare you. The 'c' word. As your anniversary gift to me."

"All right—she's *cute*." He sighed in amused resignation. "There. Satisfied?"

Mahrree cuddled into him. "Completely! Happy Anniversary, Mr. Shin."

"It always will be with you, Mrs. Shin."

---

Two moons later Jaytsy was five moons old and learning to sit, snatch food off of her parents' plates, and laugh easily. And Mahrree and Perrin began to feel a bit of confidence in what they were doing.

Until Mahrree awoke one morning in the second week of Harvest to a most unusual feeling. Not that it wasn't familiar, just very *unexpected*. She wished Perrin still had the bucket under the bed, and when the feeling didn't pass she made a quick trip to the washing room. Then she sat, stunned, on the small sofa, wondering if it was something she ate or . . .?

No. It couldn't be that. Absolutely not already.

Now, the law was that each woman could birth only two children, in order to keep the population from overtaxing their resources. And Mahrree had heard that some thought it a good idea that if a couple wanted their full quota of babies, they should have the children close together . . .

But this—*this* close?

By the end of the week Perrin had that same look in his eyes he had over a year before. As Mahrree flopped wearily back into bed from another early run to the washing room, he said, "So I was thinking the next addition should go on the other side of the house, up against the side fence. I have some ideas and I'd like to build this one by myself. I don't know that Jaytsy would like to share a room when she's a teenager."

"I can't believe it," Mahrree muttered. "I mean, it's really quite miraculous. Something like this shouldn't happen for quite a while considering . . ." Then the tears began to fall. "But Perrin, Jaytsy still isn't sleeping through the night!" she wailed. "We'll never sleep again!"

"At least this time we'll know what we're doing. Sort of." Perrin chuckled quietly and gave her a comforting kiss on the cheek. "Last Holy Day I heard someone wonder if the Creator has a sense of humor. I think I now have an answer for him."

---

Two men sat in the dark office of an unlit building.

"The information on the raid in Trades has been most intriguing. I appreciated the chart you made," Mal said.

"Thank you," the second man nodded. "I was cutting up my wife's pie, and had the idea that its shape would lend itself to representing the variety of responses. I never before appreciated her pies. After so many years you would think she could figure out how to make a decent one. This one was still undercooked, but at least I—"

"So," Mal said, cutting off his partner before he went into too much detail about his disappointing dessert, "Edge has been very quiet for a few moons, hasn't it?"

"Well, I suppose you could say that," the second man said. "At least the forest's been quiet. Wait a minute. You haven't heard the news?"

"News? What news?"

"I thought that was the real reason for our meeting tonight, that you were going to twist this into verifying your speculation."

"What are you talking about?" Mal demanded.

His partner chuckled to prolong Mal's irritation. "It seems our Captain Shin has been a very *busy* man. Truly, Relf didn't tell you?"

Mal nearly had smoke coming out of his ears.

"They kept it quiet for a time, the shock of it all, but . . ." The second man leaned closer to him. "The captain's going to be a father again. By the end of next Planting Season, most likely."

"No!" Mal exclaimed.

His companion grinned. "Yes."

"He's taken a mistress?"

"No!" the middle-aged man laughed. "His *wife's* expecting again."

"That will be *two* in just over a year's time," Mal said in disbelief. "Is that . . . is that typical, Doctor?"

The doctor shook his head. "No, but not unheard of. You see, in some cases, the female can still—"

"Ha!" Mal cut him off in sudden realization—and also because the anatomy of women was never anything he was ever interested in. "It *IS* my speculation! He's so dissatisfied with the girl that he's desperately trying for a boy! There!"

The second man shrugged. "Oh, I don't think so. From the bits of evidence we've gathered, Shin seems to enjoy his daughter. You heard the High General—Perrin even carried his daughter up to the fort to visit her grandfather when he was there for a brief inspection. I watched Relf when he recounted that story. Speaking as a doctor, I believe I saw a spark of approval in his eyes."

Mal scoffed at that. "There were women in the room, too. Relf was merely trying to play the proud grandfather role, to show he has a family side to him. That's all."

"That's all you choose to see," his partner said reprovingly. "Nicko, consider that you may be losing your objectivity—"

"Not *that* again. You know how tiresome you sound? 'Nicko, you're not objective!'" Mal whined.

"You know how childish you sound?"

"I'm sixty-seven years old!" Mal snapped.

"Age has nothing to do with childishness." The second man leaned forward in his chair. "Nicko, you're a brilliant man with a fantastic mind. Your ability to analyze is unsurpassed. But for some reason, whenever the discussion comes around to Perrin Shin or Relf, you become completely *irrational.* I see a bead of sweat on your forehead. How's your heart?"

"Fine!" Mal bristled and clenched his fists.

The doctor reached over to him. "Let me feel your pulse."

"NO! It's slightly elevated again, true, but that's only because I'm angry. A natural reaction."

His partner leaned back. "So, you plan to die before you see the conclusion of this extraordinary study of yours? Because that's what your fury is going to do to you: stop that heart before your mind is ready to quit."

Mal took a few deep breaths. "See? Better already."

"Oh, yes," the doctor nodded cynically. "I see the tranquility in your eyes. Nicko, you're not fooling me. Tell me, why do you let him get to you? How can you be so analytically objective in everything else, but not when it comes to the Shins?"

"I don't know!" Mal hissed. "Do I need a reason? You think running the world is easy? You oversee only one twenty-second of it. I oversee it all! Every soldier and citizen is under my watch, and I'm doing an exceptional job. If I choose to vent my irritations and rage on one family, who isn't even around to feel it, how is that such a problem? Objective? *No one* is objective, my friend! Irrational? Every person in the world has their moments of irrationality. Look on that shelf; I've documented thousands of displays of irrationality. If I had enough time, I could find a moment of illogical thought and reasoning in every last person in the world. You're the one who keeps telling me to take a walk every now and then. Do my heart some good to get the heart rate up. Well, it's up now! How is *this* not as healthy as taking a walk, Doctor?!"

His partner only blinked. "Are you about finished with your little tirade?"

"We need a new plan for Shin."

"Wait a minute—I barely compiled the report on the raid in Trades. It will take seasons to go through all of the information. What do you mean, a new plan for Shin?"

"I want him tested, now. Again."

His companion exhaled. "Still on your tirade."

"I'm about to prove to you that I'm a compassionate man, Doctor," Mal said calmly. "I want Perrin Shin to have a son."

"Uh-*huh*," his partner said. "And how are you going to ensure that?"

"Eliminate his wife and daughter."

The doctor choked and coughed before regaining his voice. "What?!"

"Consider, what if the second baby is another girl? He's already had one, chances are overwhelming he'll have a second. Then Shin's chances at a son are over. What a waste. Even officers are allowed only two children. But," Mal continued as easily as if he was musing over dinner choices, "as the law states, should his wife and children *die*, he can remarry and have up to two more children. Another two chances at a son. Now, what's not compassionate about that?"

It took the doctor several long, heavy moments to respond. "That's . . . that's . . . An expecting woman? That's a little *much*, don't you think? And a baby?"

Mal eyed him. "Shin's a test subject, remember? Consider the wealth of information we can gather from such a scenario. How would someone as strong as Shin respond to the loss of his wife and daughter? What we learn could better the entire world in terms of recommendations coming out of the Office of Family on ways to handle grieving. Then again, if he doesn't have any strong feelings for them, we will have done him a tremendous favor. In one way, we stand to gain a great deal, another way *he* gains a great deal. That's what we call a gain-gain situation."

Had there been any more light in the room, Mal might have discerned the growing horror in his companion's eyes. But perhaps that was why they always met in the dark.

"Nicko, you can't be serious. You can't do this . . . not to them."

"Not to *them?*" Mal repeated. "Are you sure you're not bonding to him, just a bit? I made that mistake once with a horse. When it died I actually felt some sorrow, and couldn't fully appreciate the information its death provided me. It was almost not worth killing the beast for. Don't fall into that trap now."

The doctor held up his hands. "I'm not, I'm not. It's just that . . . well, that wealth of information you mentioned—perhaps there's more to this than we realize, a full range of possibilities we haven't considered. Do you know how rare it is for a man, especially an officer, to have *two* children? And so close together? Nicko, we shouldn't eliminate a potentially captivating research project."

Mal was unconvinced. "You realize I had others to choose from, but I thought you were the most intelligent and open-minded. There are others willing to take your place, you know."

His partner scoffed. "Who, Gadiman? The most paranoid creature to have ever skulked in the world? When we began this you said you wanted *balance*. Gadiman is as unbalanced and shifty as the land around Mt. Deceit. You replace me with him, you'll both be discovered and overthrown in less than a year. There's tragedy, and then there's outrage. Keep this research to creating *tragedy*, and you can continue it for decades. But if it produces *outrage*, someone will start digging, and at the bottom of the pit they'll find you!"

Mal met his stony glare. "The return of the Guarders is tragic, my good doctor," he said slowly. "If Shin wants to avoid tragedy, and wants his woman to birth another baby, he's going to have to make sure of her safety himself. Shin's a test subject. If you can't handle that, I'm sure Gadiman can. What's it going to be, Doctor Brisack?"

Brisack swallowed hard. "Speculation—fatherhood has made Shin so fierce a bear that not even a dozen Guarders could bring him down."

"A dozen you say? Fine," Mal smiled thinly. "A dozen for Captain Shin it is, then."

---

It wasn't unusual to see the Administrator of Family Life out in the city of Idumea, not even this early as the sun was rising. Of all the Administrators he was the least intimidating and most gregarious. He smiled at people as he passed and was known as The Good Doctor, be it for his effectiveness or his manner, no one was quite sure. But his eyes had that sparkle one hoped to see when they're being told that it *was* indeed a raging infection, but he just might have something new to treat it that didn't involve cutting, sucking, or bleeding, so don't worry, sit tight, and be sure not to touch anything on your way out.

Ten years ago he joined the university working with other surgeons to experiment with sulfurs, resins, herbs, and anything else Nature provided that might be medically beneficial. The university work was occasionally more time-consuming but certainly more predictable than panicked knocks on his door at all hours.

Still, he was frequently stopped along the road to "take a quick look" at something. It never failed to amuse him how modesty vanished in public places when the most famous doctor in the world could be persuaded to examine a body part usually kept under wraps, even in one's darkened bedroom.

But The Good Doctor marched with single-mindedness this morning through the mansion district and on to the official messenger service several blocks away. Something like this shouldn't go through the regular messenger service, because that mode of delivery would serve only to confuse, not enlighten.

The fifty-five-year-old man, his gray-brown hair balding on top—and no, he wasn't working on a cure for something as vain as that; besides, balding men are more virile, everyone knew that—didn't notice the waves to get his attention, or the elderly man who held up a wrapped foot barely outside his peripheral vision. The Good Doctor stared only ahead of him, dodging citizens, carts, horses, and anything else that suddenly appeared in his shortened view.

He only hoped he worded it correctly. It had to be subtle yet obvious, while vague yet telling. But writing complex details, cataloguing findings, choosing words for their specificity, not their ambiguity, was all he'd ever done before.

Yet he couldn't allow this. This was beyond research, running into senseless revenge. Revenge for a purpose, yes; he could see the reasoning for balancing the scales once they'd been brutally upset.

But this? To call it research insulted science, and he wouldn't stand for that. It was now a cruel game, and the main participant didn't even know he was playing. He deserved a fighting chance.

The Good Doctor was going to give him one.

After all, it was the doctor who gave Wiles' map of Edge to Mal, marked with the future Mrs. Shin's home. He was merely evening the odds.

---

Chairman Mal took a deep breath and sighed. "Yes, I actually do want to see him again," he said to the page that stood at the door.

"Told you!" said a voice full of heartless glee, and the lanky man barged through.

The page backed up quickly, shutting the door behind him.

"Well, Gadiman?" Mal asked calmly.

"I had him followed all the way. Found the message, too!" His small eyes brightened as he licked his lips.

"Where's the message *now*, Gadiman?"

"On its way. That's what you wanted, right?"

Mal nodded. "Yes. Were you careful?"

"I'm always careful!" Gadiman bristled. "No one will be able to tell the seal was broken or the message read."

"So what did it say?" Mal clasped his hands together.

"He wrote, 'Captain Shin, a dozen will be awaiting in the shadows to assist in the care of your wife and daughter.'"

Mal pondered that while Gadiman puffed and bounced from one foot to another.

"Don't you get it? He told Shin! About the twelve men you're going to send!"

Mal nodded slowly. "I could tell that he couldn't let this happen. He knows he can't stop it, but thinks he can send a warning."

"So can I bring him in for questioning?"

"No! Of course not! What has he done wrong, as an Administrator? Nothing. I can handle him—*if* there's anything to handle. Shin may understand the warning, but he won't know when, or how, or what. In fact, it will make him all the more edgy." His smile sucked all the warmth out of the room. "Indeed, Brisack just made this more intriguing. How will a paranoid man behave if he knows that an attack is imminent, but doesn't know when? Oh, how I wished I had eyes in Edge right now! Hmm. That's not a bad idea, is it now?" he muttered to himself. "My own set of eyes in Edge . . ."

Gadiman scowled at the Chairman, following only half of what he was saying. "Sir?"

Mal looked up.

"What should be done? Shin will know!"

Mal's smile frosted the windows. "He's been warned there are twelve. That's why I already sent word that *fourteen* will be on this mission."

# Chapter 22 ~ "Do I *look* like I'm about to do something stupid?"

"**A**nd so that resolves the concerns about soldiers patrolling along the canal system, but we're still having some complaints from farmers in the east. It seems that—" Captain Shin's face began to contort.

Karna started to smile and glanced over to the new staff sergeant and master sergeant who were sitting with him in the forward command office. The master sergeant glanced over at the sand clock on Shin's bookshelf, nodded in admiration, and winked at the lieutenant.

Shin's face continued to twist until he could no longer fight it.

He yawned.

The rotund staff sergeant smiled. "Well done, sir! Nearly time for dinner, and that's your first yawn."

The three men chuckled as Shin glared good-naturedly at them. "You said you weren't doing that anymore."

"There's so little to entertain us now, Captain," Karna sighed in feigned sadness. "Quiet forest for over a year, and now that it's the Raining Season again—well, Guarders hate the snow. Nothing will be happening for at least another moon until Planting begins. We keep ourselves sharp by guessing how much sleep you lose each night."

"And it's only going to get worse when that second baby comes, sir," the gnarled master sergeant drawled. "Why, we can take bets for at least another three seasons."

Shin smiled reluctantly as the men laughed. "Grandpy Neeks, knowing you there's a chart somewhere in your quarters. You know how I feel about gambling."

"No slips of silver—only bragging rights. And being right is better than being rich around here. We all accept that, sir," he said with a smile in his eyes. "So far, I'm the rightest one around."

"You always are, Neeks." Shin couldn't help but chuckle.

For as long as Perrin knew Neeks, the man had been called Grandpy. His red hair went prematurely gray when he was twenty, and he had a naturally weather-beaten look as if he were a decades-old stockade fence. He also had a monotonous way of slow-talking that said, "Don't interrupt me boy, or I'll take you out to the woodshed after I finally finish this story and make you chop four cords of wood then make you build another shed to hold it all, so help me, now sit down, shut up, and show some respect because I'm not gonna take no mouth from no one."

He was perfect for whipping the new recruits into shape.

Perrin had requested him specifically as Wiles's replacement, and was stunned to realize that, when he opened Grandpy's file from the High General, Master Sergeant Neeks was only forty years old. Perrin wondered if he would seem as ancient and gnarled in ten more short years of serving in the army. Maybe the weathering effect only occurred to the enlisted men.

The other new addition to the fort, Staff Sergeant Gizzada, replaced the master sergeant who retired right after the forest raid, and was almost a complete opposite. While Neeks was as pale and gray as the strongest mortar, Gizzada was as dark and brown as the richest soils. And even though he was six years older than Perrin, he looked more like an overgrown boy with a round face that matched the rest of his body, dark cheeks that were hued a deep red, and a tongue that was always licking his lips as if knowing dinner was on the way.

The former head cook of midday meal at the garrison was a good fit as supply master. "Sir, *I'm* not for lack of things to do around here," Gizzada said jovially. "I keep myself well entertained."

"So that's the problem, Karna? Not enough entertainment for you?" Shin asked. "I didn't realize you were so eager to get *back into the forest*. I can arrange for that, if you insist."

His lieutenant paled as the sergeants sniggered. "No, sir, I don't want you violating your father's orders again. Why, he might promote me ahead of you."

Shin's eyebrows went up as the sergeants chuckled.

There was a knock on the office door and Neeks opened it. "You're a little late today, messenger," Grandpy said severely to the young man holding the bag from Idumea. Neeks never passed up an opportunity to dress down a young soldier.

"Yes, sir. Sorry, sirs," he nodded toward Captain Shin. "The messenger I met in Vines said there were some last minute administrative additions to the pack in Idumea. And as you know, we're not allowed to leave until all of them are satisfied." He took the pack off his back and handed it over to Grandpy, who kept the eyebrow up.

"Then I suppose it's remarkable you get to leave at all," Karna mumbled daringly.

Shin nodded back to the messenger. "I won't have anything to return for at least an hour while I sort through this. Might as well take your meal here rather than in Mountseen."

"Be first in line at the mess hall," Gizzada recommended. "Roast venison in a button mushroom sauce with buttered spuds. Mmm!" He kissed his fingers.

"Thank you, sirs," the messenger said happily, before having his grin wiped away by Neeks' still-menacing eyebrow.

As he bolted down the stairs, Neeks dropped the pack on Shin's large oak desk. "Feels a little heavier today, Captain. Need some help going through it?"

"Probably," Perrin said, pulling out some of the contents. "More notices. We're going to have to build larger notice boards around Edge to hold them all."

"Or ask the Administrators to be more concise," Karna nodded as he picked up a large document detailing something mundane.

Shin sat down at the desk and sorted through the pile. "Ah, this one looks promising. Nice and small."

He grinned as he looked at the plain beeswax seal. Something in his belly tightened, but maybe it was because he was now thinking about venison, and he could hear Gizzada's round abdomen rumbling. As the other soldiers sorted through the message pack, Perrin opened the small folded document, frowned at the unfamiliar writing, then swallowed as he read the sentence.

For a minute none of the other men noticed that he hadn't moved, until Neeks glanced up and saw the dead look in his eyes. "Sir? Something wrong?"

Shin didn't answer.

"Captain?" Karna tried.

Shin only swallowed again and refolded the message. "Men, take care of the rest of this for me, please. Anything important, leave on the desk. I'll be back in forty-five minutes." He stood up and put on his cap.

"Sir?" Karna said, stunned that the captain would leave while messages needed addressing.

"And when I come back, you may find something far more interesting to do than timing my yawns."

---

Rector Densal released a heavy sigh and looked at the note in his hands.

"Perrin, I think your father might have more insight than me."

"I don't think I have that kind of time," Perrin said gravely as he sat across from Hogal at his eating table.

Tabbit stood behind Hogal, reading over his shoulder. "Are you going to tell Mahrree?"

Perrin shrugged. "According to number three on my mother's list, I shouldn't give Mahrree anything unnecessary to worry about. One never knows when the mother bear instinct may arise."

Tabbit nodded. "Joriana was always very smart in these things."

"I don't know," Hogal mused. "Mahrree might need to know that a dozen Guarders have her and little Jaytsy marked."

"Oh, that's not *really* what it means," Tabbit blanched. "Is it?!"

"What else would it mean, Auntie?" Perrin said, trying to keep his growing rage and worry out of his great aunt and uncle's house, unsuccessfully. "It's written in a hand I'm not familiar with, and by the tightness of it, it looks like they even took pains to disguise it just to be sure. Somehow it got smuggled into the message bag. Only Administrators and the army can submit messages to that service. The messenger said the pack was delayed in leaving Idumea early this morning, and that's why!" he gestured furiously at the note. "Someone took great risks to get me that warning, and they wouldn't bother unless it was a real threat!"

Hogal patted Perrin's hand. "It will be all right, my boy—"

Perrin stood up abruptly, knocking his chair backward. "*HOW* will it be all right, Hogal? They want my wife and babies! They've been successful before, in eight different villages. How do I know those people weren't warned like this, and failed to stop them?"

Tabbit covered her mouth in terror and slipped into a chair next to her husband.

"They're cowards!" Perrin bellowed at the message. "Going after the most vulnerable and innocent? What could be easier targets than an expecting woman and her nine-moons-old daughter? NO!"

"Perrin, sit down," Hogal said firmly. "Now."

Perrin's broad chest heaved up and down as he met Hogal's determined gaze. For a tiny old man, he was profoundly persuasive.

Perrin eventually sighed, picked up his chair, and sat down again. With his head in his hands he murmured, "How do I fight this, Hogal?"

"With one hundred soldiers, Perrin!" Hogal reminded him. "Keep her under guard, at all times."

"Or make up an excuse and move her and Jaytsy to the guest rooms at the fort," Tabbit suggested. "Say there are bugs infesting the house, and it needs to be cleaned out with herbs that might affect your next baby."

Hogal nodded. "Not a bad idea."

"There are no bugs in the middle of Raining Season," Perrin mumbled in irritation. "Not under a foot of snow. And Mahrree would never agree to living at the fort. Sorry, Auntie," he said more quietly. "I didn't mean to get angry."

She patted his hand. "You have every right, Perrin."

"Perrin, just tell her. She's an intelligent, thoughtful woman. She can handle this," Hogal promised.

Perrin looked at him glumly. "When she's *not* expecting, yes, she's a very intelligent, thoughtful woman. But when she's expecting? She's a little *emotional*. Even though she's only halfway through this expecting, she's still—well, take last week, for example. She said that since the fort had been so quiet, maybe my father would consider shutting it down and letting me take on less dangerous work, like being a rancher."

Hogal and Tabbit laughed sadly.

"Obviously she doesn't know that cattle run away from you," Hogal said.

Perrin smiled halfheartedly. "She didn't believe me. But then she went on to list all kinds of other work I could do. Something safer that will ensure that our children always have a father."

"Perrin," Tabbit said gently, "she knew what she was getting into when she married an officer. I talked to her about it, and so did your mother."

"But this is precisely the kind of thing she's fretting about," Perrin explained. "I know once she's birthed this next baby, she'll be a little more rational, but for the next three moons or so? She's terrified something will happen to me. So how am I supposed to tell her that it's not *me* she should be worried about? There's something more," he said, his shoulders sagging. "We haven't been getting much sleep lately again—"

Tabbit frowned. "I thought Jaytsy was sleeping through the night."

"She is," Perrin sighed, "but recently Mahrree's been . . . There's a problem. For the past week she's already been feeling strong pains. We were up most the night last night counting them. It's far too early, and the midwife says Mahrree needs to relax and not feel any stress so that she doesn't risk birthing too soon. Hycymum knows, and has been coming over every day to clean up and cook, and drive Mahrree a bit crazy with too much attention, but can you imagine what this kind of news would do to Mahrree? She could lose the baby," his voice cracked and he stared at the table again.

"I had no idea," Tabbit whispered. "I'll go over tomorrow to help Hycymum. Maybe I can entertain Jaytsy."

"Thank you, Auntie," he smiled at her, but his eyes were wet. "We didn't want to worry either of you, but now I see that we need all the help we can get."

"That's why we're here, my boy." Hogal examined the message again. "No time frame given."

"I know," Perrin said. "Something could happen tonight, or in five weeks from now."

"They always attack at night, correct?" Hogal said.

"So far. Which means I need to beef up patrols every night until something happens, but we can't *look* like we're expecting something. They'll strike when we appear the most susceptible. They likely won't want to be out in the freezing temperatures for long. Their black attire stands out rather well against the whiteness . . ." His voice trailed off. "Black *against* white . . ."

Hogal and Tabbit exchanged glances. Tabbit immediately recognized the rector's look of, *We need to be alone, dearest.*

She nodded at her husband, got out of her chair, and went over to kiss her niece's son on the cheek. "You'll find a way to succeed, Perrin. I have complete faith in you. Mahrree, Jaytsy, and the new baby will all be fine."

"Thank you, Auntie." He gave her a practiced smile.

After Tabbit left, Hogal said, "Perrin, why did you come to see me? You're surrounded by far more experienced men than me in matters of battle and Guarders."

Perrin stared at the table. "About eleven years ago I sat with you talking about things," he said vaguely.

"I remember," Hogal smiled. "That was a wonderful time."

Perrin scoffed. "I was an insufferable eighteen-year-old beast! You're too kind. Always were." He hesitated before saying, "One evening you were teaching me about . . . the Refuser."

Hogal nodded slowly. "I remember that quite well, too. What did I say to you then?"

Perrin continued to examine the table, yet without fully seeing it. "That he was a son of the Creator who refused to take this test we're all in, and that many of the Creator's children followed him into exile. Their spirits are here, in this world. While the Creator gave us this world, the Refuser stole it for himself and has sought to control and destroy those of us willing to take the test. He's here, with those who followed him, making this existence as miserable as possible."

"Very good," Hogal said. "You could teach it for me this Holy Day."

Perrin didn't smile.

"But that wasn't *all* I told you, was it, my boy?"

Perrin shook his head. "No," he whispered. "You said something else that I've chosen to forget over the years, but keeps coming back at the most unexpected moments. It came back again today, when I opened this message."

"What did I tell you eleven years ago, Perrin?"

Eventually Perrin said, "That the Refuser knows me intimately, and that while he hates all of us, he feels that hatred even more keenly for me. There are a few he most ardently seeks to destroy, and I am near the top of that list. The world really *is* out to get me."

Hogal sighed. "Perrin, you have no idea how hard it was for me to say that to an eighteen-year-old boy. But you had to know it. I didn't know if I would ever get another chance, and I also knew I would never get a decent night's sleep until I did. For weeks I was plagued with the same dream and the same message that I had to deliver to you."

"Why *me*, Hogal?" Perrin whispered. His chin began to tremble and he pressed his lips together tightly for a moment to regain control. "Why my wife? My children? They're so innocent."

"I really don't know, Perrin." Hogal's voice grew husky. "You must have a great future ahead of you. Enormous power, influence, abilities. The Refuser targets those who can do the most damage to him and his plans. You could take it as a great compliment that he hates you so much."

Perrin rolled his eyes. "I've done nothing special, Hogal. Not as if I'll do anything important, either."

"What did you tell me you were going to become, the first day of that visit eleven years ago, Perrin? Remember?"

Perrin closed his eyes. "I don't want to be a general anymore, Hogal," he said. "I look at what my father does, and who he does it with—I want nothing of that life. But I could never tell him that. I don't ever want to leave Edge. I *can't* be the general."

Hogal put a hand on his shoulder. "Don't think about that right now, Perrin. Much can happen in the next twenty years. Think instead about the next twenty days. Or twenty minutes. You're not alone in this. When the Refuser targets someone, who steps in to help?"

"The Creator," Perrin said, his voice breaking.

Hogal slid the note over to him. "Here's the first bit of assistance. Someone with knowledge, *on their side*, went to extraordinary measures to get this to you."

"And I wonder why." Perrin picked it up. "If they're so evil—"

"Not necessarily, Perrin. Each one of us has tendencies toward good and evil. The test of this existence is to see how often we listen to one side or the other. Whoever sent this to you has spent much of his life in darkness, but occasionally a spark of light catches his eyes, triggers his conscience, and reminds him of who he truly is—a child of the Creator, not a slave of the Refuser. For one moment the author of that note followed that memory and was seared by a conscience he's neglected for who knows how long. I'll pray tonight that he clings to it."

"Then so will I, as well as pray for many *other* things," Perrin murmured.

"For what it's worth, Perrin, I think you would make a fantastic general. The world needs to be led by men like you."

"Right now, I think I'd do better leading a herd of cattle."

Hogal smiled faintly. "You need to go, Perrin. I feel that nothing will happen tonight, but very soon. You need to start preparing immediately."

"I feel it too. We'll be up all night working on plans. I refuse to give in to the Refuser. Hogal, pray for me?"

"I always am, my boy."

---

Mahrree's mouth moved up and down before she could make any words come out. "But . . . you barely got in! And you have to go out again? All night?"

"I'm sorry, again," he said, kissing her on the lips. "But you just said you haven't felt any pains since midday meal, right? Maybe the danger has passed."

She didn't kiss him back. "But . . . I was really counting on you being here tonight."

His eyes sparked mischievously. "Mm, so was I! A few things to *argue* about . . ."

Mahrree exhaled in exasperation. "You know what I mean! Besides that," she giggled in spite of her frustration. "I need an extra set of hands to help me with her," she gestured to Jaytsy who was crawling fast to her father.

"I ran into Tabbit this afternoon, and she said she can come over to help tomorrow. She can give Jaytsy a bath in the morning, and I'll get her tired before I leave." He picked up his daughter, grunting loudly as he pretended to strain at the effort, and Jaytsy squealed. "You're so big!" he rubbed noses with her. "Look at my big girl, and those tiny teeth, sharp as knives. I should start feeding you steak."

Mahrree couldn't stay mad at him, not when he played with his daughter who adored him.

Jaytsy grabbed at his face and squealed again as he tried to bite her fingers. They always played more aggressively than Mahrree did. She sat and read books to her daughter, which was about all she could handle right now. But Jaytsy didn't mind; she saved up all her energy for her father. He growled at her, she screamed at him—they were a great combination.

Mahrree plopped on the sofa and grumbled.

Perrin put Jaytsy on the floor and started crawling and growling after her. Jaytsy growled too, screamed in delighted terror, then turned to bat at her father.

"You're turning her into a wild animal. You know that, don't you?" Mahrree accused.

"I'm toughening her up!" Perrin said in a loud growl which Jaytsy matched.

"When do you have to leave?"

"In about ten minutes!" he roared. Jaytsy screamed and laughed.

"And when will you be back?"

"I'm not sure!" he howled in a wolf impersonation. Jaytsy started to chase him back, gnashing her small teeth.

"And your father didn't tell you about this until now?"

"The message came in the late afternoon." Perrin scrambled to hide behind a stuffed chair. Jaytsy kept up her pursuit, giggling all the way.

"So for how many nights?"

"Unsure!" he cried in a mock squeal of horror as Jaytsy touched his leg and roared at him.

"Days? Weeks?"

"Maybe!"

"Can you come home during the day? To sleep? For us to see you?"

"I'll try!" he squealed in a high pitch as he scramble-crawled away from Jaytsy. "Have to get a clean uniform!" Jaytsy was laughing so hard she could barely crawl.

"Yes, Jaytsy's looking exhausted now. I thank you for that," Mahrree said, dejected. "It's so cold outside, too. Full fort night patrols? Really, what kind of Guarders will be out now?"

"We're drilling in case they change their tactics!" he said in the frantic tone of one being pursued by an infant with sharp teeth and a desire to taste her first meat. He came around the sofa where Mahrree sat, got up on his knees and kissed her belly. Panting, he looked up into her worried face. "I'll dress warmly, and I'll be just fine. You stay here and . . . don't worry." He kissed her again and this time she returned it.

"I don't like the sound of this, Perrin. For some reason I'm feeling very uneasy."

He waved that off. "That's just your condition," he assured her, putting his hand on her belly. Whoever was in there rolled and kicked at his hand. Perrin chuckled as Mahrree grimaced. "Jaytsy never kicked that hard, did she?"

"Not that I remember," Mahrree said. "But the motion is very much like you at night. I'm guessing Little Perrin is in there this time."

"That's why I need to toughen up Jaytsy," he winked at her, "to handle a little brother. I heard those can be rough—OW!" He'd forgotten about Jaytsy in pursuit.

Mahrree and Perrin looked down at their daughter, her teeth sunk deep into her father's calf. She released him, his trouser's leg clearly showing eight small indentations in a circle. She looked up at them with dark brown eyes, enormous with worry.

"Oh, she's tough all right." Mahrree giggled. "Jaytsy, don't cry, sweety. Your father didn't mean to startle you."

Perrin twisted to pick her up, gave her kiss, and placed her on the sofa next to Mahrree. "Did I at least taste good?"

Jaytsy giggled.

Perrin sat down on the floor and pulled up his trouser's leg to inspect the damage. "Look at that. She nearly punctured my flesh. No, she can handle a little brother, all right." He chuckled and looked up into Mahrree's face.

Her eyes were filled with tears. "Why am I so worried, Perrin?"

He placed a hand on her belly. "No pains, right?"

"No pains, but—"

"Your condition, my darling wife. Merely your emotions running away with you again. I'll be fine, all will be secured, and you and Jaytsy will be fine, too."

"Dress warmly?" she sniffed.

"I've got my overcoat and gloves, so don't worry."

"Telling me to not worry is like telling Jaytsy to not bite you. Useless."

"I love you," he said before giving her one last kiss.

"So much that you leave me?" she moped.

He stood up and put his cap back on. "So much that I *have* to. See you in the morning."

---

Tuma Hifadhi didn't feel even a twinge of guilt for knocking loudly on the door so early in the morning. He kept pounding to make sure the message was received. It was.

Hew Gleace yanked opened his door, still blinking the sleep out of his eyes. "Tuma? Tuma! What's wrong? Why are you here so early?"

Without waiting for an invitation, the stooped man with faded gray hair and skin stepped quickly into the room so Hew could shut the door to the outside cold.

"We have very little time, Hew. We need to move men out, immediately."

Hew massaged his bleary eyes. "What? Why?"

"It was made known to me very early this morning. We need them readied and on their way within the hour."

Hew both nodded and shook his head to shake out the sleep and to make sense of Tuma's words. "Are you sure?"

Tuma didn't move a muscle.

"I'm sorry," Hew said. "Of course you're sure. Who am I to question . . . So, how many do you need?"

"How many do we have?"

---

Staff Sergeant Gizzada stood outside the shop trying not to look conspicuous as he waited for it to open. He shifted nervously not because he was cold—his army-issued woolen overcoat kept him quite toasty—but because he never visited this part of the market. He was usually several shops away at one of the bakeries awaiting the fresh goods to come out of the ovens. They even knew his name down there, but no one here was familiar with him.

That was probably why the older woman coming up to her door regarded him suspiciously. "Is there something wrong, soldier?" she asked, looking him up and down as she pulled out her key for the latch on the door.

"No, no!" he beamed, his dark rosy cheeks nearly purple with the cold and his nervousness. "I just need a . . . coat."

She unlatched the door. "That overcoat is as fine as anything I have in here."

"It's not for me," he said quickly. "It's for my brother. His birthday. Want to get him something nice."

The woman shrugged and opened the door to let him in. "I hope you can find something you like. Anything in particular?"

"Yes, actually," he said with an awkward chuckle. "Do you have anything in . . . white?"

"A *white* coat?" she pulled a face. "White in Raining Season?"

He nodded eagerly. "My brother has always liked white. Why? Is that wrong?"

"Nothing wrong with white," she answered quickly. "It's just not very common."

Gizzada nodded and looked at the clothing hanging on rods along the walls of the shop. His eyes were drawn immediately to one in particular. "Ah, this one, perhaps?" He walked over to a long white coat with a hood, edged in fur. "This is white!"

The woman winced. "Yes it is, but—"

"This is fur, isn't it?" Gizzada stroked the fluffy white edges along the front and bottom. "Feels like a bunny I had once as a child."

"It *is* rabbit," the woman said gently trying to take it out of his hands. "The latest Idumean fashion. Perhaps such a coat would be inappropriate since it reminds you of a beloved pet—"

"Not *that* beloved. We turned it into an excellent stew. Carrots, turnips, onions—"

"Well, you see," she said, clenching her teeth as he put it on and strained to wrap it around the front around his ample body, "it being the latest Idumean fashion means it's also very *expensive*—"

The staff sergeant, stroking the white fur on the front, paused. "How expensive?"

"Twenty *full* slips of silver!" She looked appropriately shocked.

The sergeant went back to petting the memory of the stew. "That's within my range, actually. At the very end of it, but—"

"It's a *woman's* coat!" the shop owner blurted. "You can't buy it for your brother!"

Gizzada only slowed in his petting. "Doesn't look like a woman's coat to me."

"But it will to everyone else. Look at the design of the rabbit fur—it's stitched in butterflies!"

"Do you have any other white coats?"

"No," she admitted, looking around frantically in case a coat decided to pale overnight in order to fit the sergeant's odd need. "And it doesn't close completely on your front. If your brother is the same size—"

The sergeant shook his head. "Need it only to close around the chest area. My brother is the same size there, but not down here," he chuckled as he patted his round belly. "I'll take it! It's perfect."

The woman rubbed her cheeks with one last protest. "But . . . people will laugh at your brother if he wears that in public."

"He's not expecting to be seen much in public with it, ma'am. And certainly not in Edge."

"Not in Edge? Oh, well then. That's different. Shall I wrap it for you?"

---

Karna walked tensely to the feed barn outside the compound as the sun was setting. Although the entire reason for what was about to take place had been explained to him, he still felt very ill at ease. His only consolation was that he wasn't the only one unhappy about it.

He glanced around before stepping into the barn, but it was unnecessary. Nearly every soldier was out on patrol on the new all night training regime devised by the Command Board in Idumea.

Or so they were told.

Edge was the first to try the "experiment," and while the soldiers weren't too thrilled about altering their sleep schedules so that every last one of them was on the night shift, they were obedient. Besides, it had been dull for the past year, so this was definitely something new and even a bit exciting.

The lieutenant slipped into the barn and saw the lamp light coming from the middle of it. He quickly made his way there, weaving around large bales of hay, and when he saw the scene, kept his *pfft!* in his head.

"I still can't believe you're doing this, sir."

"Not 'sir'," Perrin said as he finished unbuttoning his uniform jacket. He took it off and handed it to Grandpy Neeks, who also groaned in displeasure. "Without my uniform, I am no longer the captain. Just call me . . . Perrin," he winked. "Told you that before, Brillen." He stood in the frigid air in only his thin white undershirt, goose bumps developing on his large shoulders.

Gizzada winced and looked at the other two soldiers.

"When Idumea finds out . . ." Karna shook his head. "You remember what General Cush said after that first raid?"

"Yes, Brillen, I remember," Perrin intoned. "*If* Idumea finds out, I'm out of the army. Well you know what? I don't care what Cush, Mal, or even my father has to say about this. I'm not about to sit waiting for Guarders to come after my family! It's not as if I'm violating the Creator's law. It's a rule made by a man who didn't anticipate such a scenario. I have no doubt Pere Shin would approve of my breaking his rule to save his granddaughter-in-law and great grandchildren."

Karna, Neeks and Gizzada exchanged dubious looks as Perrin began to unbutton his trousers.

"But you could lose your commission—"

"Brillen," Perrin stopped unbuttoning midway, "I'd rather be an impoverished sausage-on-a-stick vendor in Moorland with a family, than be the next High General of Idumea knowing that I let my wife and children die. Mahrree would prefer to live as well, I'm sure. So I'll do what's right and let the Creator decide my fate."

Grandpy Neeks sighed loudly and shook his head, while Gizzada bit his lip.

Karna cleared his throat. "So she believed your 'night training' story?"

"Of course she believed my story," he said tersely, removing his trousers. "She trusts me completely, as she should. She knows I have to go out a second night, and perhaps for many more, to do my duty. But since none of you is married, I can see why you don't understand."

Neeks rubbed his mouth. "Can't believe I'm watching this happen," he murmured as Captain Shin—*Perrin*—handed him his trousers.

"You have no choice, Grandpy," Perrin said, almost as coldly as he felt. "So quit complaining, all right?" He glanced down at himself in only his thin undershirt and shorts. "At least these are white, too." He shivered, picked up a thick knitted wool tunic—white—that lay on a bale of hay and pulled it over his head. Next he took a pair of brown woolen trousers and pulled those on.

"Sorry if they're a little loose," Gizzada apologized as Perrin fastened them in the front. "I had to guess at the size."

"Not a problem," Perrin said. "Better than being too tight." Over the trousers he put on the only kind of white leg coverings Gizzada could find in the middle of Raining Season—thin linen dress trousers.

"Fit for a picnic, those are!" the staff sergeant smiled. "That's what the shop keep told me. He wasn't even sure why he still had them in stock, but fortunate for us, right sir? I mean, Perrin?"

Karna and Neeks glowered at Gizzada.

He looked back at them confused, unsure of the cause of their irritation.

"And now, for the final touch," Perrin said as he lifted the long white coat off another bale of hay.

Gizzada sighed. "It's simply lovely, isn't it?"

Perrin stopped in mid-motion and stared at the staff sergeant.

"Could let your wife wear it when you're finished. They do alterations at that shop," Gizzada assured him.

"Do they also remove blood stains, Gizzada?" Perrin said heavily. "Because when I'm done with it, I anticipate this rabbit fur looking worse than the day it was slaughtered."

Gizzada swallowed. "Perhaps Mrs. Shin would prefer another coat, then."

"Perhaps Mrs. Shin will never *hear* about this coat, or any other coat from you, Staff Sergeant! That's the entire reason I sent you, so no one would see me purchasing these things and telling my wife she might be getting a surprise. This is one surprise I never intend for her to find out about, right?" He thrust a fist through the sleeve.

Gizzada shrank in his own overcoat and nodded quickly. "Of course, sir. Of course."

"We all understand, Captain," Karna said walking up to him. From his overcoat pocket he pulled out thick white gloves and a white knitted hat.

Perrin pulled the hat over his head, concealing his black hair underneath.

"Not that we approve, *Perrin*," Karna added.

The nearly all-white man acted as if he didn't hear Karna finally calling him by his first name. It was likely because Brillen's tone was as foul as a sulfur pit.

Shin slipped on the gloves and said to his lieutenant, "Where are they?"

Karna pulled out the two long knives from another pocket, dulled so as to not catch any light that might reflect down from the two moons, nearly full that night.

"Excellent," Shin said with a half smile. "Good work." He slipped the two dulled knives into his waistband and put on his boots—the only things still black. He took two more shiny knives from a bale of hay and put them into the sides of his boots.

"Four knives," Neeks said, slowly shaking his head.

"Yep," Perrin said easily. "Not that I'm planning to lose all of them, but one can never be too sure." He took up the full quiver of arrows waiting on another bale of hay and slung it over his shoulder. "Are the other two quivers placed where I wanted them?"

Karna nodded. "Did it about half an hour ago. You have enough arrows to kill an army now."

Perrin picked up the large bow and checked the string. "Nice choice, Brillen."

"Your strength is in the sword," Neeks reminded him.

"A sword is loud and obvious," Perrin reminded back.

"Just like you," Karna bravely whispered.

"Karna, I can't help but notice my 'second mind' gets more vocal and braver the closer I get to the forest. And Grandpy, I'm sufficient with the bow," Perrin assured him. "Not as skilled as Brillen, mind you, but I can take something out from a distance this way, unseen and mostly unheard."

"This is madness," Neeks hissed. "Goes against every single rule in the book. If the High General knew—"

Perrin rounded on the older man. "He will know *nothing*, Neeks! Not unless something goes terribly wrong. And then it will be too late for him to demote me. But if everything goes *right*, then what I'm about to do won't matter at all. Is that understood, Master Sergeant?"

Neeks simply folded his arms. He'd been in the army too long to be intimidated by mere officers. "You said you're no longer the captain, remember? And since I have more experience than Karna, in a battle situation *I'm* in command. And if I don't like what I see happening, I'll use that position and pull rank. Is *that* understood, Perrin?"

Perrin took a deep breath, accentuating his broad chest. Implausibly, even the white bunny fur stitched into butterflies appeared threatening. "You do something stupid, Neeks, *you'll* have to explain why to my wife and my daughter. Tell them why they are now vulnerable. Is *that* understood?"

Neeks didn't flinch. "Don't do anything stupid then, Captain."

Shin pulled the fur-trimmed hood over his knitted cap. "Do I *look* like I'm about to do something stupid?"

Karna couldn't hold in the *pfft!* "Are you expecting an honest answer for that, sir?"

"Not really," Shin said, almost smiling. "Now remember, tell the men I'm still point commander, but I'm at a hidden location in order to observe without interfering. Any questions from the soldiers will be funneled directly to you two," he pointed to Karna and Neeks, "with the understanding that I will receive the message only from either one of you. The moment I see or hear anything, I'll sound the signal, and you call for defensive positions. Gizzada, you're in charge here at the fort."

"We know, we know," Lieutenant Karna said impatiently. "Let's get this over with."

"That's the problem," Neeks mumbled. "We may be doing this nonsense for weeks."

"I don't know why you're still complaining, Grandpy," Shin glared at Neeks. "*I'm* the one wearing a woman's fur coat to go on a midnight picnic in the middle of the forest during Raining Season."

---

Mahrree didn't even hear him come into the bedroom. When she opened her eyes, there he stood hovering over her. All she could do was whimper.

"I'm not very happy with you," Perrin growled. "You didn't even lock the doors! What's the point of reinforcing the windows and doors with iron bars if you don't use any of it?"

Mahrree pushed herself up in a sitting position. Jaytsy stayed snoozing next to her. "I wanted to make sure you could get in this morning. You realize you're such a bear when you've been up all night?"

He'd taken off his uniform jacket and was setting it properly on the chair again. "I thought I explained to you, *very clearly last night*, that we're practicing for attack scenarios. That, Mrs. Shin, includes YOU!"

Mahrree's eyes grew large.

"You will BAR those windows and LOCK those doors as you have been instructed, as soon as I leave the house tonight. Understand?"

"Yes." She blinked back tears. "You have to go out again tonight?"

"Yes!"

Jaytsy sat up, her light brown hair in wild disarray, and beamed at her father. Then she screamed at him.

"Not now, Jayts." He sat down on the side of the bed and Jaytsy crawled over to him. He smiled and kissed her cheek. "Want to rest with me for a while?"

She roared in response. He lay down on the bed and she immediately thumped his chest with her fist.

"So how did it go last night?" Mahrree asked timidly.

"Fine. Boring." He closed eyes. "Which is good. Sort of."

She dared to kiss him. "I missed you."

He only grunted.

Mahrree pulled Jaytsy away, quietly got off the bed, and shut the bedroom door behind them.

---

That night in the barn Perrin put on two extra pairs of socks. "My feet started to go numb last night. Until I found that one spot."

Neeks, holding his weapons, squinted. "What spot?"

"A place where the snow was all melted and steam rose from the ground. Even some scrawny deer were there, eating the last of the grasses. Fascinating, really. You see—"

"I don't want to hear it," Neeks shook his weather-beaten head. "I can't claim innocence about your doings if I know too many details."

"Ah, Grandpy," Perrin chided as he put on the white knitted sweater again. "I told you—I left the letter with the surgeon. Should anything go wrong, that letter exonerates you, Karna, Gizzada and everyone else at the fort. My father will know that I acted alone and that no one else at the fort participated with me, or had any power to prevent my activities."

He slipped on the two pairs of trousers.

"The surgeon even signed it, verifying that I was of sound mind. What he was signing, he still doesn't know, nor will he know unless . . ." He left the rest up to Neeks's imagination as he put on the white coat. "This really did the trick last night. Kept out the chill quite nicely. Indeed, a lovely coat."

Grandpy grunted that he was not amused and handed Perrin his long knives, then his quiver and bow. "Just bring that lovely coat back again tomorrow morning, still white."

---

Deep in the forest the man in white and gray mottled clothing peered up at the boulder field faintly illuminated by the light of the moons. It was another cloudless night, which meant it would be exceptionally cold again. But that wasn't a concern as long as he sat by the warm steam vent.

His mouth dropped open as he saw them come, pouring out from a thick stand of trees, as if the entire neighborhood was dropping by his eating room for a snack.

"What are . . . what's going on?" he whispered to the first man to reach him. "Why so many?"

"Something different," the man told him as he was joined by many others eager to warm their hands and feet by the vent.

"But, but," stammered the man whose cozy surroundings had been invaded, "it's cold! Nothing ever happens in the snow—"

"I told you—something different, and we have little time to find our positions."

---

Mahrree was watching the back door as she stirred the cracked wheat for breakfast. She smiled when he marched up the back stairs and yanked on the door. She would have heard his yelp of surprise all the way up in her bedroom.

"All right, all right, you locked the door. Very good. Now let me in!"

Mahrree chuckled and went to the back door, unlatched the locks and slid away the three long iron rods that secured it.

He pulled it open. "Now, how did you know it was me? What if I was a Guarder?"

"I knew it was you, Perrin. I watched you jump over the fence."

"But what if I wasn't alone? What if a Guarder was holding a knife to my throat, making me say those things?"

Mahrree sighed. "You'd never submit to that. I'd sooner find a dead husband at my door."

To her surprise, he smiled. "Yes, you would. Very good."

"Another boring night?" she asked as he kissed her on the cheek.

"Yes."

"How many more?"

He shrugged. "Not sure."

"Breakfast, then bed?"

He nodded. "Where's Jaytsy?"

"Actually asleep in the cradle in her room."

They heard a high-pitched scream.

"But now she's awake and wants you." Mahrree sighed.

He smiled. "I can give her, and you, ten minutes."

---

It was Karna's turn that night to help prepare the captain. "No more finding warm spots in the forest, all right?"

"Grandpy told you about that?" Perrin adjusted his gloves.

"I have to admit, I'm curious as to what else you find out there. In the dark. Everything covered with snow—"

Perrin shook his head. "Not everything is covered with snow. The ground is warm, even hot, in many areas we were in before. Then there's—"

"Stop! Stop—I don't want to hear it." Karna covered his ears like a toddler. "Grandpy said you'd start talking again, and we really shouldn't know."

"Your name is on that letter too, Brillen. You won't be in any kind of trouble."

"But I already feel I am! Perrin—" Karna dared say his first name because sometimes 'second minds' really needed to get through to the first ones, "—maybe, maybe it *is* nothing," he said earnestly. "Maybe it's an elaborate hoax. Was there anyone mean-spirited that you went to Command School with?"

"Brillen," Perrin said as he put on the quiver, "only about half of my class. But this is no trick. I feel it, deep in my bones."

"Sure that's not just the cold you're feeling? It's another clear night."

"It's real, Lieutenant."

Brillen took a deep breath. "And you're sure you're the *only* one who can break this rule, go over this wall, barge into this forest?"

"You know it as well as I do. I can see it in your eyes. Besides, your skin's not pale enough."

Brillen exhaled in unwilling agreement.

~~~

Mahrree was putting the iron bars back into her windows again, grunting as she did so. "Why did your Grandmother Peto insist on taking these down today, Jaytsy? So what if they look 'uninviting'? That's kind of the point! She knew I'd have to put them back up again."

Jaytsy pulled out some wooden blocks from the bottom shelf.

"Good idea, Jayts. Trip up any intruders on your scattered toys. We could—"

The sudden knock on her front door filled her with immediate fear. No one would be coming by this late at night, unless . . .

She hesitated until she heard the knock again.

"Mahrree? It's cold out here!"

"Hogal!" She rushed to the front door, unlatched the bolts and opened it as quickly as she could. "What are you doing here? Is Tabbit well?"

Hogal stepped quickly inside and shut the door behind him. "Tabbit's just fine, my dear," he said as he undid the long scarf wrapped around his face and unfastened his thick coat. "We're actually worried about you, with these all night training sessions. Tonight I had a feeling that maybe you might appreciate a little company. I'd be happy to sleep on the sofa there, keep the fire going, and get Jaytsy for you when she wakes in the night," he offered, a little bashfully.

"Oh, Hogal," Mahrree felt herself growing weepy. "I'd hate for you to sleep on the sofa, or to spend the night away from Tabbit." But that wasn't what she meant at all.

And Hogal could tell. "It was Tabbit's idea, and I was more than happy to agree with her. If you send me home, she'll only be angry with me."

Mahrree swallowed and nodded, sniffing her gratitude.

"Any recent pains?"

"Some this morning," Mahrree admitted, "but after I rested this afternoon they stopped again."

"Well, let's make sure it stays that way. Now," Hogal said, clapping his hands, "I see some bars that need replacing. I think I'm up to that! Why don't you get little Jaytsy ready for bed and let me finish down here?"

"Thank you, Hogal." She kissed him on the cheek.

About fifteen minutes later Mahrree left her bedroom after lulling Jaytsy to sleep. Mahrree really didn't want Jaytsy disturbing her great-great-uncle tonight, so she would stay in her parents' bed. From the storage trunk on the landing, Mahrree pulled out a thick blanket and two pillows, and started to make her way downstairs. She paused when she saw that Hogal, who had finished securing the iron rods in the windows and doors, was now standing near the eating room table.

Not realizing he was being watched, he slowly slid open the secret drawer and retrieved the long knife. He peered suspiciously at the blade as if it might suddenly come to life. Hogal touched it gingerly, winced and then did something extraordinary—he slipped the long knife into his waistband, making sure the handle was concealed under his knitted tunic.

Mahrree was stunned motionless. What in the world did an eighty-two-year-old rector think he could accomplish with a long knife? She stepped noiselessly back up the stairs to her bedroom and sat down on the massive bed to think.

Why was Hogal here, and so worried about securing the house? Why—

Mahrree realized she was the dumbest woman in the world. How could she have been so self-absorbed to not see it? Last year Perrin spent Raining Season teaching his soldiers hand-to-hand combat in the indoor training arena. He said he wouldn't force the men into the bitter cold unless there was a legitimate—

"Oh, dear Creator!" Mahrree whispered and held her belly. "There really *is* something happening, isn't there? Why wouldn't he tell me?"

A tightening of muscles in her lower back that spread around to her front told her why. She took a deep breath to calm herself, although that never worked.

"He didn't want me to worry. So, naturally, I'm worrying even more. And the only reason Hogal is here is because—"

She closed her eyes to try to stop the tears, the stupid tears that so easily trickled out whenever she was expecting a baby.

"Because tonight, the world is out to get my husband."

# Chapter 23 ~ "And if it is Your will, let me walk out of here again."

Perrin was beginning to know the forest rather well. And it wasn't nearly as fearsome as he remembered it a year and a half ago. He thought of himself as a manifestation of snow as he moved quietly, looking for anything that would signal twelve Guarders had finally arrived. He'd plotted his course for this night, moving in erratic patterns that wouldn't suggest any kind of deliberate behavior to whoever might see him. He also stooped to avoid being recognized for his size, but he saw no one, again.

He knew he was effective, though. Several times during the past two nights he'd come within a stone's throw of his own soldiers, crouching at the edge of the forest like a snow-covered rock while his soldiers rode and walked right past him.

The forest had become familiar. Instead of feeling cold terror, he felt as if he'd come home. There was something about the trees that called to him like a foggy memory he'd forgotten. And *that* was what was so unnerving about the woods. He considered once asking his parents if there was any dormant Guarder blood in his veins. He suspected that's why all the family lines were lost after the Great War—to hide who was related to Guarders. But he could imagine the look of shock on his father's face should he ask such a question.

Instead, Perrin focused on the trees. Or rather, the areas behind, in front, and between the trees where no one normally looked. That's where he moved as well, so close to shrubs and pines to become part of the numerous boulders caked in frozen white. He was grateful he remembered to bring along a white scarf tonight, lifted from Mahrree's wardrobe, to wrap around his mouth and nose in order to trap his breath so he left no telling steam clouds behind. The only thing he couldn't control was the crunching of the snow underneath him. He practiced walking on his toes to minimize his impact, but he was a large man, and sticks even under a foot of snow still insisted on snapping with disturbing regularity.

As he crept and scanned the area, he felt the same unexpected sense of tranquility that surprisingly enveloped him the first night. He could stay there all Raining Season if necessary. He wouldn't mind at all.

---

One of the men in mottled white and gray clothing held out his arm to stop his companion. The group had dispersed from the steam vent high in the forest and now moved, two by two, throughout the trees just as they had the night before. This pair was close to the forest's edge and had watched the usual patrols of the soldiers. They also saw the *other* patrols, close to the tall timber walls of the fort, noticeable only to those who knew how to recognize the unnoticeable.

But this—*this* was completely unanticipated.

"What is that?" the man's companion breathed.

"Must be a soldier," the other one whispered in awe. "He has a bow and quiver."

"Is he one—"

"No, he's not! He's dressed in white."

The men froze in position as the large being continued to creep along, almost noiselessly, and turned down into a small ravine.

"Remarkable!" the first man exhaled.

"But if it's not . . . Wait a minute." The second man peered carefully. "Might that be—"

"Yes, it's him!"

"But why? How?"

"He must know," the first man sighed.

"What do we do?"

"Tell everyone!"

---

Perrin saw it out of the corner of his eye, but he needed to discern if the movement also saw him. He stopped, held his breath, and hoped that he looked like one of the boulders around him. Only his dark eyes were still exposed, and they shifted to look to his right.

Definitely movement—and human. The dark shadow was loping along an elevated ridge about sixty paces to the right of Perrin. His sloppy gait indicated he didn't know he was being watched.

"This is it." Perrin sighed, almost disappointed that this would be his last night in the forest. He slipped between two of the boulders, noiselessly took his bow off his arm, nocked an arrow, and took aim.

The figure in black stopped to look around.

"Always two together," Perrin whispered. "Waiting for your companion? I've got time." He shifted his aim to where the figure had come from.

A moment later another shadow burst out of the trees. He never heard the twang of the bowstring, but his companion saw him drop to the ground.

"One," Perrin whispered as he rapidly nocked the next arrow.

The first figure in black ran back to his fallen companion and dropped to his knees. Panicked at seeing the arrow protruding from the still body's chest, he scrambled back to his feet and looked anxiously around.

"Two," Perrin whispered as he released the arrow. It struck true with a muffled thud, felling the man on top of his companion.

The urge to run up to the ridge to see if they were dead or merely injured overwhelmed Perrin, but he knew he had to stay where he was, in case they moved in fours now, instead of twos.

He'd wondered how he'd respond to taking a life from a distance. Stabbing that Guarder with his sword a year and a half ago had felt as if he was stabbed himself. But this time, he wasn't even sure where he hit the men.

Mostly likely their chests, which was what he was aiming for. Neeks was right—the bow wasn't his strength, but he was a fair shot.

He'd expected to feel the crushing burden of taking a life to overwhelm him as it had when he and Karna killed the Guarder. But instead it hovered in the air as if it were a black cloud, knowing more was to come, so it was waiting until it could engulf him.

It was better that way, he reasoned. He wasn't finished for another ten men.

The forest remained silent and he looked around to orient himself. He was probably two miles west of Edge, and the men had been running from the west. Maybe several more pairs were on their way, or had already passed him below or above his point near the boulders.

A surge of heated dread rushed through Perrin. Targets might be slipping past him, or he might be surrounded and not even know it. It would take only two men to make it into Edge, to find his house—

He darted out of the cover of the boulders, not entirely sure where he was headed. He readied another arrow as he made his way through a thicket of trees, trying not to bump into any of them.

He stopped, closed his eyes, and whispered, "Think Perrin, think . . . don't panic, just think. How can you find them?"

Tracks.

He rolled his eyes. Yes, no problem tracking at night.

He peered into the dark forest and whispered, "Dear Creator, please guide me. Please save my family. And if it is Your will, let me walk out of here again."

It was in the corner of his eye that he noticed the movement. Without even thinking, he raised the bow with the arrow already in position and let it fly. It hit its target, barely fifty paces away. The man holding the jagged dagger fell to the ground with a soft thump.

Perrin already had the next arrow readied, waiting for his companion. A cascade of snow falling from a tree to his left spun him to look to see what caused it.

The black shadow burst out so fast that initially Perrin thought the tree was falling, until he saw a glint of steel right in his face. He fell backward as the weight of the Guarder pushed him down. The bow was no longer in his hands as he wrestled with the man, much smaller and weaker than him.

Perrin flipped the Guarder off of him, throwing him into the snow. As the Guarder rushed to stand up, Perrin lunged, pushing the man on to his stomach. Perrin kneeled down on his back, shoving his face into the hard snow. With his free hand, Perrin pulled out one of his long knives as the Guarder wriggled to free himself from suffocating. Perrin lay on top of the man, crushing him with his full weight.

With the blade of his long knife up against the Guarder's throat, he whispered in his ear, "Where are the others?" He yanked up his head to allow the man to answer.

"You'll never get out alive!"

"That's not what I asked. Where are the others?"

The man merely laughed.

Until Perrin cut his throat. "Four. And all of that was just to divert me from seeing your companions, wasn't it?"

He stood up quickly and faced the forest. He barely registered that another man was rushing him until he felt the smack in his face. Instinctively, Perrin went on all fours and rolled down the ravine to a cluster of shrubs. There he stopped to look around to find his attacker.

He came trotting down the ravine, his jagged blade out and ready. Perrin charged up the slope, his own long knife still brandished.

The Guarder never had a chance. He was obviously not used to running in the snow, because his feet slipped out from underneath him, sending him sliding right into Perrin's blade.

"Five," he whispered as he dropped the body on to the ground. "Where's number six?" It took only a moment to discover him. Perrin beckoned him with his knife that was dripping red drops into the snow.

The man thirty paces away instead turned and ran to the south, toward Edge.

"Oh, no you don't!" Perrin took off in his own slip-sliding race toward the man who was narrower, swifter and unfortunately, more elusive. Perrin looked ahead through the trees to try to determine where he might be.

"Yes!" he whispered as he continued his pursuit. Karna should be about eighty paces away from where the Guarder would break from the forest in his race toward Edge.

Perrin stopped to catch his breath, and a second later the silence of the woods was broken by his ear-piercing whistle. He practiced it frequently as he strode along the forest's edge. He knew it carried far, because on several occasions when he puckered to the trees, a flock of birds would fly out in alarm, at least five hundred paces deep. He followed the long, high-pitched noise with three shorter whistles. Then he held his breath and waited for the response.

One quick whistle. Karna would be waiting.

Perrin bent over to slow his breathing and waited to hear if Karna was successful. About half a minute later Perrin heard shouts, the clang of metal, and a cheer that was immediately muffled, most likely by a sergeant's hand covering an over-eager private's mouth.

"What did I say about keeping it quiet?" he groaned silently at the premature victory. "Six more. Keep your eyes open!"

Six more.

---

"To the west! The west!" the man whispered hurriedly as he came upon three other companions. "He's taken down five, chased one to the soldiers."

Two of the men in white and gray mottled clothing looked at each other in surprise.

"Impressive," one of them said, "but he'll never get everyone."

"Agreed," said another. "It's time. The rest should already be on the move."

The three other men nodded, stood up, and ran toward the west.

---

Perrin had been walking for ten minutes now, but saw no one else. He kept fighting down the fear that they'd slipped past him and were on his way to his house. But there were soldiers there, too, walking in quiet patrols through the neighborhoods. Another four would be dispatched to watch over his home specifically. Karna would have understood the three short whistles telling him the Guarders were in the forest, and this was not, repeat—*not* an exercise.

He nocked another arrow and held up the bow, stepping past boulders and staring into dark shadows.

---

They were in the clear, and they knew it. While the large man in white was wrestling one of their own in a ravine, their group of four in black moved above them, heading east before they turned south.

They still couldn't understand where the man like snow had come from, but that didn't matter. There was a mission to accomplish.

That's why they each stopped short, staring in astonishment at what blocked their path.

"What . . . what . . ." one of them stammered, but the other three had already turned and were running, chased by what appeared to be a mysterious hoard of men, dressed in gray and white.

They all ran west.

---

Perrin continued to step cautiously, looking down the shaft of his arrow. He twisted and strained to hear any sound. He'd already pushed back his furry hood and slipped the knitted cap up off his ears. Some time ago he lost Mahrree's white scarf, but she never wore it and wouldn't miss it. He was filled with a raging heat so strong he was surprised the snow didn't melt around him.

Six more.

They could be anywhere, within miles of his position. The longer he walked the more helpless he felt. They were gone, maybe even snuck past Neeks and Karna and the ninety soldiers patrolling between here and his home. All it would take was one determined, fierce man.

Mahrree better have put those iron bars back up in the windows. He'd have some angry words with Hycymum in the morning if—

Sure.

If a Guarder made it through, and the window and door reinforcements weren't in place, and his family were dead, yelling at his mother-in-law would be the first thing he'd do.

He shook that off, along with the thought that he should have run home and checked the windows and doors himself. All he could do now was watch, listen, pray, and hope that—

He blinked, and blinked again.

Two more men in black, running parallel to his position, were about to skirt the trees below him. He didn't wait for the moment, but released the arrow. A shout of agony told him he hit his target, but only wounded him.

"Go, go!" shouted the downed man, and Perrin quickly grabbed another arrow.

He let that one fly blindly, and it sailed without striking anything. Scanning the area for the unseen companion, he snagged another arrow out of his quiver.

A sound behind him spun him around. It was the other man in black running erratically, as if unsure whether to pursue his partner's attacker or head toward the village. Perrin ended his wondering with an arrow to his belly. A second arrow quickly followed to put him out of his misery.

"Eight!" Perrin whispered in momentary triumph, then looked back up to the man he had injured. Seeing no more movement, he jogged over to the site and noticed the man was obviously dead. Perrin stepped closer and saw where the arrow penetrated his body. Oddly, it was protruding out of his thigh—not a life-threatening hit.

Baffled, Perrin pushed over the man with his boot. When he saw his chest, he jumped back.

The man in black was lying in a fresh pool of blood, stemming from a chest wound.

He'd been stabbed.

---

Grandpy Neeks was right on top of the black shadow as he bolted from the forest. Quite *literally* on top of him. His horse had been acting skittish, and when the two figures in black broke in a dead run from the trees, Grandpy's mare reared and threw the master sergeant right on to the Guarder, sending them both sprawling into the snowy field.

Neeks acted as quickly as the startled Guarder. He had his long knife out from his boot slightly faster than the Guarder pulled his jagged dagger. Although Grandpy earned a nicked cheek and a gash in his arm, half a minute later the man in black was bleeding from an incurable throat injury.

Tracking down his partner took a bit longer.

Not that the soldiers were unprepared—six of them converged on his position, riding horses that had grown stiff with the cold. But the Guarder was shifty and elusive, darting and dodging then diving under a horse and through the line of six in a remarkable escape attempt.

That's why there was another line of eight soldiers waiting in the shadows of the fort wall. The foot chase would have been comical in any other circumstance, Neeks considered later, but as he held his bleeding arm shouting instructions at the soldiers that slipped left and right trying to catch the infiltrator, there was nothing amusing about their attempts.

But in the end they succeeded, three soldiers piling on top of the Guarder when he slid on a patch of ice, and each one of the corporals plunging their long knives into him.

It wasn't until Neeks got the word that the Guarder was dead that he finally sat down in the snow and allowed a surgeon's assistant to wrap his arm with a bandage.

"We've got three so far tonight, Captain," he cringed as the dressing was wrapped tightly to staunch the bleeding. "How many do you have?"

---

How did he get stabbed? Perrin wondered as he jogged toward the east again. That's where they came from, which means they must have gone *past* him, but were now coming back. But why? Why not just head to the village?

Perrin wished he'd looked around the ground for an explanation for the chest wound. Perhaps the Guarder had his dagger drawn and fell on it. Maybe there was a sharp tree branch that he was impaled upon. Maybe—

But Perrin hadn't seen any evidence, in the short shocked moments he stared in disbelief, of a weapon or bloodied branch. The snow underneath the man was wide and unbroken by anything except the pool of blood.

Someone had stabbed the Guarder.

Was it his companion, knowing he wouldn't be able to escape? Perrin couldn't remember seeing anything near the dead man, but perhaps his companion was sneaky.

Or maybe it was something—or *someone*—else.

---

"He doesn't know how many are left," one of the men in mottled white and gray whispered to his three companions as they jogged a safe distance behind the large man in white.

"He's not quitting, not yet."

"But someone *has* to get to—"

"Don't worry, they are."

"I just hope we brought enough," another man whispered.

"Don't worry," one of the men repeated. "We know how to count to fourteen. That's all that matters."

---

Four more, Perrin thought to himself. Four more. Maybe a pair or two had made it out beyond the forest, or all of them were already accounted for, and he was wasting his time.

That's why he was making his way to the edge, hoping to find good news . . . and the other quiver full of arrows he had Karna hide for him in a cavity of rock right inside the trees. He reached it in about five minutes, traded his empty quiver—most of the arrows had fallen out when he was wrestling the Guarder—and reminded himself that he still had four long knives. More than enough for four men.

At the border of the forest he whistled again, a short-four pattern. A moment later a sergeant came riding up to him, his eyes wide in surprise.

"You didn't see me like this," Captain Shin told him.

The sergeant nodded that he understood, then shook his head.

"Report!"

"We have three Guarders, sir. One that Karna brought down, another that wrestled with Neeks until he killed him—"

"Who killed who?" Perrin demanded.

"Neeks killed the Guarder," the sergeant clarified, still staring at the captain in white with red splatters on his rabbit fur that for some odd reason reminded the sergeant of butterflies. "Grandpy was injured, but will be fine. Caught the third man just outside the fort. He's dead, sir."

Perrin sighed. Two more, still out there. "Report to Karna. Tell him there are still two more, but I don't know where. Two more!"

"Sir, how do you know there are two—"

But the captain had already vanished back into the trees.

---

"Are you sure he said two more?" Karna asked the sergeant.

"Positive, sir. Captain Shin was very specific."

"Remember, sergeant: you didn't see him."

"But sir, I did! I saw—"

Lieutenant Karna's groan told the sergeant that he couldn't believe his eyes on a night like this.

"Ah. Sorry, sir. I already told the captain—that I *didn't* see—that I did not see him."

"That's right," Karna nodded. He looked up at the forest and rubbed his gloved hands together. "Two more. They could be anywhere. But at least we know where they're headed."

"There are ten around the house, sir. Do we need more?"

Karna shook his head. "We don't need Mrs. Shin waking up and seeing her home surrounded. Ten will be noisy enough. The more men we keep here, the fewer the chances they'll get near the village. *Two* more . . ."

---

In his heart Perrin was praying for guidance, but it felt wrong.

First, he wasn't on his knees with his head bowed—he was walking with his bow strung and his arrow searching for a new target.

Second, he struggled with the wording. Initially he prayed to find the last two men to *kill*, but those seemed to be entirely the wrong words to utter in a prayer.

Then he tried asking for guidance to *stop* the men, but the Creator certainly knew what Perrin meant by "stop."

He felt as if he traveled with a cloud following him, the horrible realization that so far ten men had died that night, seven by his hand. At some point the cloud would descend upon him, and he feared with what paralyzing power it might overtake him. He had to be successful before then. If there was any other way he could find and flush out the last two men without having to kill them, then maybe he could go home with a less heavy heart.

She could never know about tonight. He'd have to go home with a smile on his face and tell her cheerfully that the night training was over and she had back her husband. But he suspected he wasn't that good an actor.

As he crept through the forest he felt a presence as if another cloud, larger and lighter, was coming to absorb the one that hung heavily over him. It was as if this cloud could cleanse his horror, allowing him to do what no one else in the village—or even the world—would dare to do.

In some way he felt his actions that night were good, even sanctioned, because he was preserving the innocent. It wasn't his choice to be out there taking lives; he was forced into it by others who were out to destroy his family. He was expected—required—to do this. And while the deaths tonight would remain in his memory forever, their heaviness would be nothing compared to the oppressive weight that the death of his wife, daughter, and unborn child would have caused.

He didn't choose his steps but let his boots go in whatever direction they led him, in a northeasterly direction, past the fort to the south, and toward some end.

---

Hogal couldn't sleep because of the cold steel next to his hip, he decided about three hours after he had lay down on the small sofa made up into a bed for him by Mahrree. Exactly *how* did Perrin walk around all day with something this cold, sharp, and threatening against his hip?

Hogal shifted the long knife frequently, trying to find a more comfortable position.

For a time he tried lying on his back with the long knife in his fist resting on his chest, but he couldn't decide which way the tip should be pointing.

Up toward his face seemed most ominous, especially if he should fall asleep, awake with a sneeze, and forget what was clenched his hands.

Pointing it downwards also seemed quite dangerous, for reasons his mind chose not to entertain for long.

Facing it toward the sofa felt rude—what if he accidentally cut the cloth?

And lying with the tip toward the door, and ready for anyone who may somehow barge through it, was simply too violent for the rector to consider.

Eventually he sat up, turning the knife over and over in his hands, wondering if this one had ever been used.

It was happening tonight, the 56th Day of Raining Season. That impression had come to him forcefully that evening, and just one look told his wife what he'd be doing that night and why. She answered nothing but retrieved his coat and gave him her scarf, along with a kiss.

Exactly what was he doing at the Shin home? What could he accomplish that one hundred soldiers and his brawny nephew couldn't? He put the bars up on the windows and secured the doors. Maybe that was enough. Maybe he wasn't there so much for Mahrree as he was for himself, to know that she and the next generation would survive the night.

Hogal eventually got up from the sofa and walked quietly to one of the front windows. He peered out the thick wavy glass hoping to see something, and hoping *not* to as well. After a few moments of his breath fogging up the glass, he noticed a dark smudge moving stealthily across the road.

He wiped the wavy glass and firmed his grip on the long knife.

The smudge paused in front of the house, looked toward it, and continued on again. Hogal noticed a glint of dim moons' light coming from the smudge's side. A sword. It was a soldier, patrolling the road. Another joined him, coming from a different direction.

Hogal exhaled so heavily that the entire window was nearly encased in his breath. The house was being watched, by men younger than him and with much larger pieces of sharpened metal.

He made his way back to the sofa and wrapped himself in the thick blanket. The fire was dying away on the hearth, but he didn't need it. No matter how warm the room was, he was filled with an inner chill that wouldn't subside until he saw his nephew come walking through the door. Hogal went back to what he was doing for the past three hours, the real reason he likely was there.

"Dear Creator, protect him, guide him, help him. He has no idea what he's up against, nor the great things that await him. Please watch over him, strengthen him, and send him help. Dear Creator, protect him . . ."

Upstairs, Jaytsy slept peacefully sprawled on Perrin's side of the bed. And, despite herself and her worry, Mahrree slept more soundly than she had since before she was expecting her firstborn.

She dreamed of children, gardens, and a large wooden house with window boxes filled with herb plants.

---

He was perspiring heavily now, the tension of the moment lasting excruciatingly minute after minute. He was getting closer to something, but to what he didn't know. Perrin only knew to let his boots guide him.

His hands began to feel cold, the nervous sweat of his palms seeping through the gloves and freezing. He frequently flexed his fingers on the bow to make sure they would still move properly for when he finally saw his last targets.

He wasn't normally the kind of man to fall prey to his anxiety, but he couldn't deny his increasing jitteriness. Passing a loud spout that shot hot water into the air more than irritated him. And the loud belching of the earth infuriatingly drowned out all kinds of sounds he needed to hear. Beyond him a few dozen paces was another gap in the ground that coughed constantly, again too loudly for him to notice anyone's footsteps.

But then again, the noise also masked his noise. Sweat trickled down his face, and he would have removed his knit cap except that he feared his black hair would stand out too much against the whiteness of the laden pine trees.

Then it came to him distinctly—the urge to turn to his right and look deep into the woods.

There they were running, two of them, as if being chased. They glanced behind them nervously, their pursuer as yet unseen by Perrin. He tensed again, in case a mountain lion or wolf appeared behind them. He could take out the attacking animal first—to make sure he didn't become its prey—then the Guarders.

He had such an unobstructed view of them, still about two hundred paces out and illuminated dimly by the light of the moons, that he smiled faintly at the singularity of the site. There couldn't be any other section of the entire forest so clear and devoid of trees.

He sighted in the men, running nearly in a panic as they approached him. Behind them he saw nothing threatening that needed his first arrow. Whatever had been pursuing had apparently broken off the chase. He took a deep breath, let out half of it, then released the arrow. It flew true, striking the first Guarder in the chest.

"Eleven!" Perrin whispered as he pulled out another arrow to nock.

But the same moons' light that illuminated the Guarder also shone down on Perrin. The Guarder cut hard to his left, ducking behind a cluster of boulders, and Perrin's arrow bounced harmlessly off of them.

He threw down his bow and pulled out one of his long knives. He dove behind a stand of scrubby shrubs and looked at either side of the boulders, waiting to see which way the Guarder would sneak out.

He waited for fifteen seconds. Thirty. Forty-five.

Nothing.

Either the Guarder was waiting for Perrin to reveal himself, or he had already slipped out of his hiding place and was coming around to meet the man in white.

Perrin spun around, his heart pounding near his throat, checking every shadow for someone to lunge out at him. "Guide me, guide me, guide me," he whispered, impatient to find the last threat to his wife and children.

Then he saw the movement that, under any other circumstance, he was sure he would have missed. But there it was, a black shadow in the distance taking off in a quiet jog down toward the south and the village.

The twelfth Guarder.

"I see you!" Perrin grinned furiously and took off in pursuit. He had so much pent up anxiety that it propelled him faster than any other being in the world.

The Guarder glanced behind him to see the man in white gaining on him, and took off in a zig-zagging pattern.

Perrin wasn't deterred. He kept on in a straight shot toward the man who was getting closer to the edge of the woods.

"Go on, *run* to my soldiers! In either case, number twelve, I win tonight!"

The man tried to cut around a large boulder, but he slipped, twisting his leg and going down in a loud grunt of pain.

Perrin was by his side just moments later, his blade brandished. He plunged it, almost too eagerly, into the Guarder's neck.

The man went limp.

Perrin leaped to his feet. "TWELVE!" he bellowed to the forest, his arms held up in triumph. Not only did he conquer the forest, he took out its greatest threat. Twelve fewer Guarders in the world to terrorize and threaten his family.

An odd noise traveled up to him from the forest, and he turned hear it. Every muscle tensed in preparation, but a moment later he relaxed.

It was cheering. The army had heard his shout of "Twelve" and was celebrating with him.

Perrin finally smiled and dropped to his knees a few paces away from the dead man. He looked up at the black sky speckled with stars, grinned, and bowed his head.

"Dear Creator, thank you!" he said quietly. "Thank you for preserving me, for allowing me to be successful, for—"

A twig snapped behind him, muffled under snow.

Never expose your back. *Never* expose your back!

He scrambled for one of his long knives, but the thick arm around his neck was faster. Perrin's fingers fumbled and dropped the blade. Instantly he felt his throat constrict as the arm tightened around him, and his training kicked in. Don't bother grabbing the arm choking him—pulling at it would only be in vain. Instead, find another way to divert the attacker.

Perrin groped around his waist to retrieve another long knife, but as soon as he gripped it he felt the familiar sensation of beginning to lose consciousness. Everything in the world of black shadows and white snow turned gray. The body behind him was exceptionally large and heavy, probably specifically matched for him.

Normally Perrin would have thrust the long knife up into the man's arm, causing him to release his grip. But Perrin could smell the thick black leather covering his attacker's arm like a shield.

Or like *body armor*, he thought in irritation. Exactly the kind he wanted to fit his soldiers with, but was forbidden to. The leather even appeared to be around the man's legs—Perrin's other possible place to stab. But he knew of one spot still likely exposed on the Guarder.

With his last bits of consciousness, Perrin lunged backward, trying to throw off his attacker's balance, and wished he wasn't still stuck on his knees. He was successful for only a moment, but it was enough to loosen the man's grip and allow Perrin a shortened gasp of air.

He knew he had only moments left. Perrin shifted his grip on the long knife and thrust it blindly behind him over his shoulder where he hoped his attacker wasn't expecting it.

Right into the Guarder's face.

He heard a low cry of pain in his ear, followed by a wheeze. The muscular arm around his neck suddenly released, and Perrin scrambled to his feet, coughing to refill his lungs.

He turned to face his attacker, a beast of man in black clothing who was bleeding heavily from a deep slash in his cheek and—surprisingly—was flat on his back in the snow.

Perrin's air-deprived head swirled, but he grabbed a tree branch with his free hand to steady himself. The man in the snow was lying far too still from having received just a knife in the cheek. Perrin kicked at his leg, but it didn't move. He glanced around and then took hesitant step toward the body.

The thirteenth Guarder was dead, because of a second gash near the base of his throat.

Perrin fought to regain control of his breathing. He had hit the man only once with his long knife—he *knew* that.

Yet there were *two* wounds on him.

Perrin looked wildly around. "What's this all about?" he shouted raspily, no longer worried about who else might be lurking in the forest. "Are you after my wife and children? Whose side are you on anyway? Show yourself!"

"Gladly," said a cold voice from behind another cluster of trees.

Guarder number fourteen.

He charged Perrin, his toothed blade out and ready. Perrin bent down, snatched another long knife from his boot, and readied his stance. Two blades in two fists.

With a screech, the man ran straight for Perrin, hacking wildly. Perrin sidestepped him, delivering a slash across the man's knife arm that barely penetrated his leather armor. Perrin firmed his stance once more as the enraged

Guarder turned and ran toward him again, any discipline he may have had gone as he attacked with pure hatred and no strategy.

Perrin preferred it that way. Enraged men were easy to conquer; it was the ones who channeled that rage into calculated fury that made him nervous.

He stepped forward to meet the Guarder, but his foot hit a slick patch of hardened snow and he abruptly went down just as the Guarder came on him. Perrin struggled to right himself, but not before the Guarder slashed Perrin's back, cutting so deeply that immediately Perrin knew the white fur coat was damaged beyond repair. His back seared with hot pain that quickly numbed, his flesh gashed open and bleeding.

With a roar, he pushed himself upright again, both knives still in his hands, and lumbered after the Guarder who was turning for another run on the snowy man now bleeding red.

Perrin lunged toward him—faster than the Guarder expected—and thrust one blade into his neck, and the other into his chest. Perrin held his breath as he watched the Guarder take his last one.

This time Perrin didn't gloat as the body slumped at his feet. Instead he waited, listening for the trees or bushes to tell him there was still another one in hiding.

Thirty seconds passed. A minute. Two minutes.

The forest remained quiet, as did the soldiers at the edge of it. They must have heard his shouting and the Guarder's yells. And now they waited, wondering what had become of their captain.

The familiar tranquility of the forest returned to him, enveloping him with comfort and giving him the assurance that yes, the last threat had been eliminated.

"Thank you," he whispered to the black sky speckled with white stars. Then he called out hoarsely, "FOURTEEN!"

Again the cheer rose from the barren strip of land that bordered the forests.

Perrin flopped weakly against a tree with white bark. It was then that he remembered he was injured, the trunk of the tree pressing the fact vividly into his mind. Slowly he began to pull himself to his feet, feeling a sudden depth of exhaustion that he'd never before experienced. He took one last look around the forest that, barely two hours ago, had felt comforting.

Oddly, it still did.

He looked closely again at the body of the thirteenth Guarder and felt unnerved by the second wound that killed him. In the dim light it was evident the wound was left by a blade with a straight edge, not a jagged dagger like Guarder number fourteen had brandished.

Perrin felt a chill course through him, with an accompanying thought that he needed to get back to his soldiers, quickly, so they could tend to his injury. The mystery of the second slash on the thirteenth Guarder—along with the Guarder with the unexplained chest wound—would have to remain a mystery. A most confounding, overwhelming, fantastic one.

Perrin glanced around one last time, his head beginning to sway with the sensation of losing too much blood too quickly.

"Thank you," he said again to the forest, wondering if anyone was there to hear it. He stumbled south toward the sounds of cheering soldiers.

---

Back behind a clump of pines, a man in white and gray mottled clothing nodded. "You're welcome, sir. My pleasure and honor." He raised his hand, gashed and bleeding, to his forehead in salute.

So did the men behind him.

# Chapter 24 ~ "Remarkable the kind of damage a mere tree branch can do, isn't it?"

"**W**ell, it *was* a lovely coat." Gizzada sighed as he evaluated the jagged slash drenched in blood.

"It likely saved his life," the surgeon said, continuing to work. He wore a perpetual scowl of concern on his pasty face. "The thickness seemed to keep the dagger from going in too deep. Had he been wearing only his overcoat, he would be in much worse shape right now."

Captain Shin didn't say anything as he lay on his bare stomach on the surgeon's table, since an obliging long block of wood knocked him to the ground ten minutes ago. The surgeon worked quickly while the captain was unconscious, finishing the last of twenty rough stitches just as Perrin began to groan.

"He came out of that a bit faster than I expected, but at least the worst part is over." He nodded as an assistant handed him thick layers of cotton.

"Karna," Perrin mumbled.

The lieutenant, who had been watching with a grimace as the surgeon worked, squatted next to the captain. "Right here, sir."

"How bad?"

"Bad enough to keep you from doing somersaults for a time," the surgeon said, setting the cotton in place and unrolling long bandages to wrap it. "But you'll live, as long as you can come up with a convincing story to tell *Mrs.* Shin."

Perrin groaned loudly, and not because of the stitches in his back. The snow they had packed over his wound earlier to slow the bleeding and numb the area still had lingering effects.

Gizzada looked sadly at the bloodied coat. "Can't even give her this as a peace offering. But maybe if it were altered into a tunic?"

Karna cleared his throat and shook his head at the staff sergeant.

"And Neeks?" Perrin whispered.

"He required seven stitches in his forearm," Karna told him, "but he's already back on duty, making sure the men know the official story before they go to bed."

"And what's the story?"

"Only a handful of soldiers saw you come out of the forest looking like a bloody man of snow. They've pledged silence to protect your wife. Kind of hard to argue against that. The rest of the men have been told you violated the first rule again, but only to the extent of about twenty paces."

"Thank you," Perrin said slowly. "Good work, Brillen."

"Not nearly as good as you, Captain. Fourteen? Where did the other two come from?"

"Brillen, there were *more* than fourteen," Perrin murmured as the surgeon and assistant helped him into a sitting position so they could secure his wrappings.

"More than fourteen!" Karna exclaimed. "How?"

Perrin tried to shake his head but seemed to forget how to do so halfway there. "I have no idea . . ."

Karna stepped up to help support him as he began to drift forward. The surgeon and his assistant quickly wrapped the bandages around his chest and back before he toppled over.

"Lieutenant," the surgeon said in a low voice as they worked, "I wouldn't put too much credence in anything he says right now. He's had an extraordinary night and lost a fair amount of blood. And whenever we plank a man, his mind isn't right for several hours."

Karna nodded as he strained to support the deadweight of the captain, who was now drooling on his lieutenant's shoulder.

Gizzada rushed over to help. "What do we tell Mrs. Shin?" he whispered to Karna as he propped up one side of the captain. "He won't be in any condition to go home in the morning. Dawn's just a few hours away."

The surgeon scoffed as he negotiated his way around the helpers to wrap the bandage around the swooning captain one more time. "And he wonders why none of us is married."

He secured the end of the bandage and helped the soldiers lay the captain down again. "Where's that rector uncle of his? Send for him. He should be able to come up with something believable."

---

Hogal hadn't slept all night, which was why he was eagerly watching for the dawn. He was hoping Perrin would show up and tell him everything was fine, so he could put down the long knife. It was still dark outside when he saw several dark smudges he assumed were soldiers converging together in front of the house.

Hogal's stomach knotted in his throat. Whatever it was, he needed to hear it before Mahrree. He fumbled with the iron bars at the front door, unlatched all three of them, and slipped quietly outside. He trotted down the front stairs, forgetting that he was still wrapped in the thick blanket, and made his way over to the soldiers.

They looked at him in surprise.

"Well?" Hogal breathed in the frigid air. "What news from the forest?"

"No news, sir. Forest is quiet, as always," a young sergeant said convincingly.

"Nonsense!" Hogal snapped. "Perrin Shin is my nephew! I know there was trouble, and no one's going to tell his wife about it but me. Understood?"

Later he felt a guilty streak of pride that Relf would have been amazed as each young man jumped automatically to attention.

"You're Rector Densal, sir? I was sent to retrieve you. I'm pleased to report Captain Shin was most successful, sir," the sergeant said in formal tone tinged appropriately with awe. "Fourteen Guarders were killed this night."

Hogal twitched. "Fourteen?"

"Yes, sir. But the captain was also injured."

Hogal's shoulders sagged. "Ah, *no*. He's not coming home soon then, is he?"

The sergeant shook his head.

Hogal looked back at the house, decided it seemed quiet, then said to the soldiers, "Can one of you bring me to him?"

---

Rector Densal walked quietly into the surgery recovery room and winced when he saw his nephew. His torso was bare except for white wrappings around his midsection, and he rested belly down on a cot.

"Ah, my boy. By the number of bandages, I'm guessing it was pretty severe."

Perrin squinted open his eyes and tried to smile. "Merely an overly enthusiastic surgeon, Hogal."

"That and twenty stitches," the surgeon said, folding his arms. "It *was* severe, Rector. And he's in great pain. He just controls it well. We're getting another batch of snow to pack on his wound again."

Perrin's smile faded. "Mahrree! Does she know?"

Hogal sat down on a nearby cot. "No, no she doesn't. I stayed the night at your house, worried about . . . well, everything. I secured all those windows and doors again. She was still sleeping when I left."

"But you haven't slept at all, have you Hogal? I've never seen such bags under your eyes."

"Well, you don't look so grand yourself, Perrin. But I've been up all night before. Part of the calling as a rector. But I've never been up all night with one of *these*," he said, pulling out the long knife from under the blanket he still wore as a cloak. "Can't seem to put it down."

Perrin cringed. "Oh, Hogal. You should never have touched that."

Hogal nodded feebly.

"Sir, may I help you with that?" said a quiet voice. Lieutenant Karna crouched in front of Hogal and gently pried the long knife from his fist.

"Thank you!" Hogal and Perrin breathed at the same time.

Karna chuckled. "I'll see that this gets back to your home, Captain," and he slipped it into his waistband.

"How exactly do you *do* that?" Hogal said, more lighthearted now the knife was a safe distance away. "Don't you ever cut yourself? Or sneeze?"

"We simply don't talk about it if we do, sir," said Karna soberly.

Hogal chuckled, then put a hand on Perrin's bare shoulder. "What happened, my boy?"

"Guarder," Perrin whispered. "I slipped on the snow, he came over the top of me, right through the coat and tunic. But I got him. Hogal, there were *fourteen*."

"I heard that, from the soldier that accompanied me here. I've been thinking about it, and I think I know what might have happened."

"What, Rector?" Karna sat down on another bunk, and the surgeon stepped closer to hear.

"Your informant was found out, Perrin," Hogal said gravely. "It was discovered that he sent the warning, and those above him sent two more to finish the job in case you ensured the other twelve failed. Just when you'd be confident that you had them all, the last two would arrive."

Perrin closed his eyes. "That's exactly what happened. Can't count on hearing from our friend ever again, can I?"

"If he was discovered, he's most likely dead," Karna suggested.

"That would be the Guarder way," the surgeon said with disgust.

"But she slept through it all, didn't she?" Perrin said with his eyes still closed.

Hogal smiled. "That she did, my boy. Without a pain, I imagine."

"Which poses a new problem," Perrin said, "and I hope you can help me with it."

"What to tell her about that?" Hogal gestured to his torso.

All the soldiers nodded.

Hogal clucked his tongue and shook his head. "Remarkable the kind of damage a mere tree branch can do, isn't it? When a horse goes down in the snow, and throws one at just the precise angle? Really, that branch should have broken sooner, but if it had held longer, Perrin would have been impaled on it, instead of severely slashed. Good thing Relf sent the message that the night training experiment is over. Just in time for his son to have a nice three or four days off to sleep at home and annoy his wife by being around *too* much."

The surgeon nodded at him. "That's why the forests are so dangerous, Rector, and why we never allow any soldiers *into* them. Perhaps now they should even stay away from the edges!"

He shot a severe look at the captain. Shortly after they'd packed Shin's back in snow, the surgeon opened and read the captain's letter he'd signed a few days before. Then he threw it angrily into the fire and went to work on the noncompliant officer.

"I'll write instructions for Mrs. Shin on how to care for her husband. I'm sure he'll be more comfortable at home. We can move him after midday meal, when he's a little stronger."

Karna nodded at the rector. "I'll be sure the soldiers know the dangers of *branches*. Most should still be getting breakfast," and he left the surgery.

Hogal patted Perrin gently on the shoulder when they were alone. "Excellent work, my boy. I couldn't be prouder. I suspect you were sent some help?"

Perrin's eyes became damp. "Hogal, you have no idea, and I think only you would understand."

"I look forward to hearing the story. But first, I'll go get Mahrree."

---

It was a little over an hour later, as dawn was breaking and ending that very long night, that Perrin heard the whimper.

"I don't believe it! Look at you! Oh, Perrin!"

He attempted a smile. "Hello, my darling wife. How did you sleep?"

"Wonderfully, I'm ashamed to say." She kneeled down by his cot and gingerly touched his back. "You must be in so much pain."

"I'm fine—they froze the area with snow again," he whispered. "Where's Jaytsy?"

"Tabbit came over so she and Hogal are both there for when she wakes up."

"And our little kicker?"

Mahrree held her belly. "Still kicking, but no pains right now."

He closed his eyes. "Thank the Creator."

She wiped away a tear and attempted to stroke his bare back, unsure of where to touch him. "This is so awful! A tree branch? Thank goodness your father stopped these ridiculous night drills. When I get home I'm going to write to tell him exactly what his little experiment did to his son!"

"No, no, no," Perrin whispered earnestly. "You'll do no such thing. Let me handle it. How about I dictate a message and you write it down?"

"And make my own additions as I see fit?"

He would have chuckled if he could. "We'll see."

She kissed his bare shoulder and stroked his dark hair. "I'm so sorry, Perrin. I'm so sorry this happened to you."

"It's all right, Mahrree. I'm just sorry I got injured when you've been having pains."

She kissed him on the lips. "How about we both laze around for a few days together?"

"Sounds perfect," he whispered back.

From several paces away the surgeon, Karna, and Neeks watched the two of them talking quietly. The men looked away when they kissed again.

"Guess there are one or two reasons to get married," Grandpy said, gruffly clearing his throat and holding his bandaged arm.

Mahrree turned and noticed the audience behind her. She blushed and pushed herself to stand up. All three men rushed over, but she was on her feet before they got there.

"You all right, Mrs. Shin?" the surgeon asked with unusual gentleness.

"Yes, I'm doing well this morning, thank you. When did you say we can bring him home?"

"After midday meal. He needs to rest and get a little stronger so he can help us help him. I've given him some tea so he'll sleep for a few hours."

Mahrree nodded. "I'll go home and get things ready. Probably shouldn't be going upstairs to bed, should he?"

The surgeon shook his head. "Give him a night or two on your main level, then we'll see how he's feeling."

Staff Sergeant Gizzada came in to the surgery and gave a meaningful look to the three other men. All of the white-now-stained-red clothing was being burned, destroying the evidence. He put his finger to his lips when he saw the exhausted captain drifting off to sleep. "Just checking on him," he whispered.

"He'll be fine in a few days," the surgeon said. "I'll get the notes, Mrs. Shin. I'll also be by this evening to evaluate him."

"Thank you," Mahrree smiled as the surgeon started for his desk. "Well, I suppose I should take his uniform jacket and overcoat with me. Doesn't look like he'll be wearing them home today."

"I'll walk you home when you're ready, Mrs. Shin," Karna told her.

"And I'll get the uniform, ma'am," Gizzada nodded. He walked to where the folded blue overcoat and jacket sat on a chair, and carried them over to Mahrree and Karna. The lieutenant took the bundle from him as Neeks tipped his cap good-bye and started for the door of the surgery.

"I should see if the damage is repairable or not," Mahrree murmured, lifting the overcoat from off the top. "After it's soaked for a few hours."

All four men stopped suddenly.

Karna turned abruptly to Mahrree. "Repairable?"

Neeks stopped at the door and slowly pivoted.

The surgeon at his desk looked up sharply.

Gizzada's eyes doubled in size.

"Yes, his overcoat and jacket," she said, letting the overcoat unfold from her hands. "Not that I'm much of a seamstress, but my mother . . ."

The four men looked desperately at one another, but it was already too late.

Mahrree had turned the overcoat to look at the red-soaked gash she anticipated seeing there. She held it up in front of her face while the surgeon, Neeks, Karna, and Gizzada held their breaths, waiting for her response to the overcoat in pristine condition.

Slowly she lowered the coat and looked at the four men, her face ashen. "He wasn't wearing his uniform, *was he?*"

The men looked at each other, unsure of what to say.

Captain Shin snored softly.

"There was no tree branch either, *was there?*"

Karna shifted his feet, Neeks swallowed hard, the surgeon cleared his throat, and Gizzada licked his lips.

"And he doesn't want me to know why, either. *Does he?*"

That, the men could answer. They all shook their heads ever so slightly.

Mahrree closed her eyes and clutched the overcoat to her chest. "Thank you for taking care of him. And me."

"Happy to do it, ma'am," Karna whispered.

---

"But Perrin, are you absolutely sure you only stabbed him in the cheek?" Hogal whispered, not worried that Mahrree would hear him—she was in the kitchen with Hycymum and Tabbit cooking a big dinner—but because Jaytsy was snuggled up against her father, napping soundly. She and Perrin lay on the large down and straw mattress, placed in front of the hearth in the gathering room by the soldiers that helped bring Perrin home. The sofa and stuffed chairs were pushed to the sides to make room for the bed. Hogal sat on a pillow next to Perrin who spent the day—and would spend many more nights—shirtless and on his belly with his back exposed.

Hogal removed the last of the cotton and winced at the stitched bloody gash. In a few minutes they would be packing snow over his wound again.

"I've run it over and over in my mind." Perrin rested his chin on his hand and gazed into the fire. "That earlier incident, with the Guarder I hit only in the leg with my arrow, I could imagine a few scenarios for why he suffered a wound in the chest. Fell on his own dagger, or his companion stabbed him, or he fell on a broken stump . . . But that thirteenth Guarder, there's simply no explanation. I was losing consciousness as he was choking me. It took all my remaining strength to thrust the knife behind me, and I didn't have a lot force going over my shoulder. There's no way I slipped and stabbed him in the neck. The wound was too deep, at the wrong angle, and delivered by someone with great strength. Even after he released me, I wouldn't have been in any condition to take him out until I could breathe easily again. Hogal, someone *else* was in that forest!"

Hogal nodded slowly. "I can't think of any other explanation, either."

"My question is," Perrin whispered, "who? How? Why?"

"That's actually three questions, my boy, but who's counting. Perhaps a sympathetic Guarder? Maybe even your informant?"

"Maybe," Perrin whispered, patting Jaytsy's back with his free hand as she slept next to him. "Maybe he heard that more were being sent, and he came to help." He shook that off. "No, that's not right. I don't know why, but I just feel it's not right."

"Agreed," Hogal said. "What happened out there to you—*for you*—is remarkable. I prayed all night for you to receive help, and you most definitely did."

"I was on my knees after that twelfth Guarder, Hogal. I was thanking the Creator when I heard the thirteenth come up behind me."

"He sent you help you didn't even know you needed."

"Hogal," Perrin's whisper was barely audible, and his great uncle leaned down to hear him better, "only you could understand this but, somehow I felt as if *He* was in the forest."

Hogal squinted. "The Creator?"

Perrin shrugged then winced as he regretted the movement that shifted his back. "That's not quite right either. I'm not saying the Creator was killing that last Guarder, but somehow it felt as if His *presence* was there. For a place so cold and dark, it was actually comforting. I can't explain it."

"I don't think you have to, Perrin," Hogal said. "There's so much in the world that's beyond our explanation. Sometimes we think we know everything, but when we finally see all that this world really involves, we'll discover we knew nothing at all. All our ideas were just as pitifully inaccurate as four year-olds arguing over what kind of baby snake a worm is. No, for now our understanding is so limited, our minds so small, the world so large—the Creator's power is simply beyond our comprehension. Don't try to explain anything, but be grateful for the experience and, after Mahrree has birthed this next baby and she's steady again, tell her about it too. She needs to know."

"Agreed," Perrin whispered. "I feel awful not telling her the truth."

"Not only because of that," Hogal said as he removed the last bit of cotton, "but because . . ." He hesitated.

"What is it, Hogal?"

The old rector was quiet for another moment before he continued. "I wished I didn't have to say this, but it's very clear to me now: Perrin, the Refuser isn't only after you. He's after you're entire family."

"No!" Perrin whimpered, putting his large hand back on his daughter's small body. "Because of me—"

"No, my boy!" Hogal gripped his nephew's arm. "Not because of you, but because of who *they* are. Who they will become."

Perrin craned his neck to see his great uncle better. "What are you talking about?"

"I wished I could understand more, but I don't have the sight of a guide. I'm merely a lowly rector who receives impressions." Hogal sighed. "Perrin, it's no coincidence you married Mahrree. She poses just as great a threat to the Refuser's plans as you do. She may prove to be a most dangerous woman some day. In fact," he hesitated again, "I'm sure of it."

"Mahrree? My small Mahrree?" Perrin scowled. "Dangerous?"

"That's why she was targeted," Hogal nodded. "Remember the saying, 'The smallest annoyances—"

"—grow into the biggest pains.'" Perrin sighed and finished the familiar phrase. "'It's not the boulders in your way that slow you down, but the pebble in your boot.'"

"Exactly. And your children? I believe the Creator doesn't randomly send souls to families. He has a plan. For you, your wife, your daughter, and your *son*."

Perrin's eyebrows shot upwards.

"They'll all someday do things to anger the Refuser. The four of you are in the same family for a reason: you must all fight this war together."

Perrin closed his eyes, not only because of the increased twingeing in his back, but now also because of the twingeing in his mind. "War," he whispered.

"I'm afraid so," Hogal whispered back. "I wished I *was* a guide—they could bestow blessings of protection. I can only pray. But remember, you've won two battles in the war so far. I also don't think the Refuser's going to give up easily. Whoever he's influencing isn't about to quit. The third battle—who knows?"

"And how many more after that?" Perrin murmured, his eyes still shut.

"I wouldn't even dare guess," Hogal said softly. "This isn't a war that will end anytime soon. Maybe not even until the Last Day."

"You couldn't even give me one full day to enjoy my victory, could you?" Perrin opened his eyes to glare, only half in jest.

"Oh, they're cheering you, Perrin Shin!" Hogal declared with smile. "In the Paradise of our ancestors, there's great rejoicing!"

Perrin scoffed. "If you say so, Hogal Densal. I'm not hearing much."

"We rarely do, but trust me: they're there."

His nephew smiled faintly, and then it faded. "How can I tell Mahrree any of this?"

"Don't tell her my impressions about your family, my boy. Simply tell her about what happened in the forest." Hogal put the soiled bandages in a bag to be washed later. "She already suspects something else happened. Your lieutenant told me—of all your planning and care, there was one detail that was overlooked."

"What detail?"

"Your uniform. Completely undamaged and unbloodied?"

Perrin groaned. "My uniform! How could I have forgotten that? What did she say?"

"Not much, but thanked your officers for taking care of you and her. Uh, Perrin," Hogal paused. "Exactly what *were* you wearing, if not your uniform?"

"White furry butterflies," his nephew grumbled.

Hogal pondered that. "I see. And exactly *how hard* do they hit you to knock you unconscious? They're *sure* planking doesn't cause any memory problems?"

A voice prevented Perrin's response. "I believe you're expecting this?" Tabbit said brightly as she came in with a bucket half filled with snow, the weight of it slowing her down to a shuffle. Her smile vanished when she saw the ragged wound that was nearly the width of her nephew's back. "Oh. My. If Joriana saw that she'd—"

Hogal held up his hand for the bucket. "Thank you, my dearest. Why don't you go back and help with dinner?"

"Hycymum's got it," she said, her voice breaking and her eyes transfixed by the oozing around the stitches.

"Then ask Mahrree for some thick cloths to put around the snow on his back, so as it melts it won't make the bed wet."

"We have enough of that with Jaytsy in our bed so often," Perrin chuckled quietly, trying to lighten his great aunt's—and his—mood.

Tabbit's shocked expression softened to hear her nephew joking. "Yes, of course," she said, backing up. "Thick cloths, on the way!"

Mahrree's voice came from the washing room. "I've got them already, Tabbit. Why don't you go help my mother? I still can't follow her kitchen talk."

Tabbit nodded and willingly headed back to the kitchen as Mahrree came and kneeled down next to her husband.

Perrin glanced at her furtively, trying to see that small woman with delicate hands, growing belly, and soft yet piercing eyes of green—

No, wait.

Gray, or . . .

Moldy mud?

Well, while he still couldn't figure out the *exact* color of her eyes—her eyes that were trying hard to be brave, but were unsuccessfully masking her horror—there was something he did know: she wasn't nearly as brave as she pretended to be. Oh sure, she talked a supposedly dangerous talk on the platform, but no one ever took Edgers seriously. Idumea knew all intelligence was centered in the middle of the world, and it became diluted the further one traveled away. By Edge of the World, people were considered geniuses if they could put a hat on the correct body part.

And Mahrree knew that, too. She never would have been so brave on the platform in Pools, or even Mountseen. And it's not as if she'd ever be bold enough to enter the forests. How can one be dangerous without courage? No, underneath it all she was timid and wary and that was exactly the way Perrin wanted her—

*Most dangerous woman.*

Maybe it was because Hogal was still in the room that the improbable words insisted on mashing themselves into his brain. He tried to shake them loose as he looked at her perfect lips pursed in worry. How could she possibly ever be dangerous? What in the world could that mean?

No. No, Hogal must have got it wrong.

Although Hogal never got things wrong.

Perrin decided not to think about it anymore. Besides, something more immediately worrying was about to happen.

Mahrree took a deep breath and said analytically, "So, I suppose it could be worse." But her tone suggested she'd never seen anything so terrible in her life as the roughly stitched gash. She placed some of the thick cloths around his wound. "Then, um, we're to pile the snow on it, a few inches deep," she said in an almost passable imitation of the surgeon, if her voice hadn't been quavering. "The cold numbs the area while also controlling bleeding and swelling. We'll do it again before you go to sleep tonight—"

She accidentally brushed one of the thick black-threaded stitches, and he flinched.

"I'm so sorry!" she whispered, the last of her detached pretense vanishing.

"Mahrree, shall I—" Hogal started, but Mahrree shook her head.

"No. No, I can do this. Thank you, Hogal. My husband, my responsibility. So," she said trying to calm her voice, "do we put the snow on in layers, or just as one clump?"

"I'm not sure," Perrin said, his eyes squeezed shut in anticipation. "Perhaps just plop it all on at once, so you don't have to look at it anymore. It will probably all feel the same to me."

Hogal gently scooted Jaytsy to the far side of the bed, making sure her thumb stayed in her mouth so she'd remain asleep.

Mahrree nodded a thanks and plunged her hands into the bucket to pull out a mass of cold icy snow. "At least you got injured during the Raining Season, when we have all this snow." She winced as she dropped it on the jagged injury.

Perrin writhed and arched his back.

"I'm so sorry!" Mahrree gasped.

"No, just cold!" Perrin gasped back. "Really, it's good, it's good."

"If you say so," she whimpered, putting another handful on his back and smoothing it to cover evenly.

He squirmed and shut his eyes tight, a strangling noise coming from his throat.

"What is it?" Mahrree whispered frantically.

"Leaking. Down my side. *Tickles*," he breathed. "Wipe it up!"

Mahrree broke into a relieved grin and took an unused cloth to wipe the melted snow that the dam of cloths failed to retain.

"Thank you, my darling wife," he whispered.

"Anything for you!"

Hogal patted Mahrree on the arm. "I think you've got things here. I'll see if Hycymum needs a taster," and he shuffled off to the kitchen.

Perrin's shoulders relaxed as he grew used to the freezing sensation numbing his back. With Hogal gone, it was easier to push aside what his great uncle suspected about his family. For a moment he could even ignore the idea that it was the "most dangerous woman in the world" he trusted with his injury.

"How are you feeling?" he asked Mahrree.

"I'm all right," she assured him, wiping up more melting snow that trickled down his ribs. "How are *you*?"

"It's not as bad as it seems. I should be able to get up and walk around tomorrow. Help you a bit."

"Don't need to," she said. "My mother and Tabbit cooked enough for us for days and Mother also did the washing, so we can rest here and enjoy watching Jaytsy destroy the house."

He chuckled quietly. "You know, I was thinking that under different circumstances, this would be rather romantic. Our bed on the floor in front of the fireplace . . ." He turned slightly and raised his eyebrows suggestively at her.

She giggled. "Your back incapacitating you, our daughter here, my mother and your great aunt and uncle in the kitchen—"

"So, you *do* want to argue?" he said in the low rumbling voice that he knew always drove her to distraction.

But sometimes, a woman simply won't be distracted.

"How can you be thinking like *that* at a time like this?" She chuckled as she continued wiping.

"What else should I be thinking about?" he asked, trying to avoid the many thoughts clogging his mind.

"Your story."

"What story?"

"The one you should be coming up with, to explain why you're wounded, but your uniform is unscathed?" She raised her eyebrows at him, but she wasn't suggesting the same thing he was a minute ago.

Perrin exhaled as he stared into the fire. "I was wondering when you might ask. Thought I might have more time, but . . . Mahrree, I *really* didn't want to tell you this. I wanted to spare you the knowledge that, well, that your husband's an idiot."

Mahrree nodded soberly as she readjusted a cloth. "It's all right. From our first debate I had my suspicions."

He smiled. "Well, here it is. You realize that men are merely overgrown boys, right?"

"Unfortunately, yes."

"And that sometimes men will dare each other to do stupid things, like boys dare each other?"

"Well, this is far more interesting than I anticipated. Go on."

"And the later at night, the more outlandish those dares become?"

"I'm not going to lie, Perrin—I'm praying we have another girl."

"Well, Mahrree—" he decided not to tell her Hogal already knew it was a boy, "—it's like this: in Command School there was this dare. The older classes would dare the younger classes to run across the campus in the middle of the night during the coldest part of Raining Season in only their . . . underpants. And sometimes even less than that."

"Uh-huh," Mahrree said thoughtfully. "I see why women are not allowed in Command School. Here I always thought it was because they were considered less intelligent."

"Well, Karna and I were getting bored last night, so we started reminiscing about life in Command School, and well . . . he went first since he's younger. He stripped and ran to the feed barns and back. I told him that wasn't impressive, so I went next. Stripped down to my underpants, mounted my horse, and rode to the forest."

"Any mead involved?"

"Mahrree, you know I never drink mead."

"So you were completely sober when you did this." She shook her head. "Somehow that just makes it all worse."

"My horse grew skittish and bucked, and the next thing I know I'm flying backward in the air, right toward a dead tree. So if it seemed to you as if my officers were trying to cover up something, it's because we're *all* idiots. Neeks was going to go next—something about proving enlisted men's worth—until he saw what happened. I understand his trousers were off."

"Hmm. Indeed, you all are idiots," she decided. "Tell me, does this dare involve anything else, like perhaps a white scarf?"

Perrin swallowed, having forgotten about that as his story had unraveled in his mind.

"Because, you see," she continued casually as she put another pile of snow on his wound, "I was looking for mine earlier. I never wear it because I think white is impractical, but I thought it might be comfortable to wrap around your bandages. Yet I can't find it anywhere. Almost," she said slowly, "as if it were *Guarder snatched*."

Perrin hesitated for only a moment before ignoring her last comment. "Yes, yes the dare does involve a bit more. I took the scarf last night expecting this might happen. The actual dare is, 'Run across the campus wearing only a piece of your girlfriend's clothing.'"

"Rather wordy."

"Rather drafty. At least I won last night, since I'm the only one with a 'girlfriend.' Lost the scarf, though. Sorry." He didn't add, *Because it likely was Guarder snatched.*

"I guess I should be proud of you. And that's the story you're sticking with?"

He blinked in innocence.

She smiled sweetly.

"I just confessed to being an idiot! You really think there's something more?"

She kissed his cheek. "Have I told you today that you are the most perfect man in the world, and that I love and adore you more than words can say?"

He smiled. "I love you, too."

"I think that's obvious. Now, not that I wasn't thoroughly entertained by your story—although I *really* didn't need that image of Grandpy Neeks and his lack of trousers because now I can't seem to shake it," she shuddered dramatically as Perrin chuckled, "—I'm merely wondering, how long until you tell me the truth?"

He sighed. "As long as I can get away with it."

"You have to report this injury to Idumea, you know. Too many soldiers know about it."

"I know," he whispered. "I'll find a way to take care of that."

"Perrin, just tell me—what happened?" she whispered back. "While it's jagged, this slice is too clean to be caused by a tree branch. I can tell that much. It looks more like a knife wound. Or . . . a dagger."

He twisted his arm to pat her belly. "At least another three moons until you can birth this one safely, right?"

"So the midwives are guessing."

"I'll tell you in thirteen weeks, then."

---

Two men sat in the dark office of an unlit building.

They stared at each other in the growing shadows, silently daring the other to claim the upper hand.

Brisack broke first. "Any news from the observers in the forest above Edge?"

It was a good opening line. Didn't claim victory or admit defeat, just asked for information.

"No news," Mal said plainly.

Another good line. No concessions or challenges. Just ending his opponent's questioning.

"Wonder why that is," Brisack pressed, putting the burden of response on the other party.

"Cold weather," Mal said shortly.

Accurate. But also irrelevant.

"Too cold to move messages, then," Brisack nodded once. "But not too cold for the fort at Edge."

The staring match heated.

Both men knew what news came from Edge. High General Shin had been quite vocal about what he called a deliberate attack on his son. Within minutes of the news reaching the High General, messages flew out to every fort to watch for snowy attacks, since Edge had been singled out by at least fourteen Guarders. That's how many the soldiers encountered, Captain Shin killing eleven of them himself. And the High General made sure every last person knew *that*, too.

What didn't come from the general, interestingly, were any details. Unlike the previous time, when Captain Shin violated the first rule of the army, there was no information about the attack. Not from either of the Shins, nor from any observers in the forest.

Everything and everyone in the north was unusually silent.

"Forts have more resources through which to send information," Mal explained.

"Not that our observers might also be dead?" Brisack suggested.

"There's no evidence either way to form any kind of conclusions. May never be any."

Silently they glared at each other again, the temperature in the room increasing in relation to their tempers.

"You said twelve," Brisack finally seethed.

"And you told him twelve!" Mal boiled back.

Brisack swallowed hard, but recovered. "You have the map!"

"He's a test subject!"

"And he succeeded!" Brisack bellowed. "Even against fourteen! Just as I predicted!"

There.

Brisack claimed victory, which meant Mal had only one option as he gripped the armrests of his chair. "You invalidated the study by influencing the test subject with your interference."

"You created an unnatural situation," Brisack countered.

"*All* of this is unnatural, Doctor!" Mal gestured to the shelves of his library packed with notes and writings. "But I never cheat to see a result I want."

"You have Wiles's map! You told them exactly how to reach the house!"

"We did the same thing in Grasses, with the captain's sister and parents. Why is this any different than Grasses?" Mal leaned back with a smug expression. "I see it now, Doctor Brisack. *You've* lost your objectivity. Couldn't stand to see him lose the mate and litter, so you gave him a little hint. You know Gadiman found your message."

"That's obvious," Brisack said steadily. "I've told you, he's as subtle as a twister in Weeding Season and just as damaging, throwing around his glares thinking no one notices. I don't regret warning Shin. And considering how successful he was, I rather suspect he didn't even need my warning."

"There will be no evidence gathered or analyzed concerning this raid," Mal decided. "The test was compromised, so no information will be worth our effort."

Mal wouldn't even evaluate his failure, and Brisack gloated about that later.

"Anyway," Mal's shoulder twitched, "Perrin's out of the army, so—"

"Wait a minute," Brisack interrupted, "What do you mean, *out of the army?*"

"Neeks's report stated that the captain stepped into the forest—" Mal began calmly.

"Only a few paces!"

"Nevertheless, Captain Shin knew what would happen if he violated the first rule again," Mal clasped his hands in front of him. "He would be relieved of duty, and—"

"You haven't done that, have you?"

"Tomorrow morning I'm going to visit his father," Mal said.

"No you won't. You couldn't bear to do it."

"What do you mean?"

"You already would've done it if you were serious," the doctor pointed at him, "but so much of what we do is because of him. And to lose him, already? Oh, no. If you let him go now, he'd be a regular citizen and all your connections, ability to watch and test him would be reduced to almost nothing. In a way, he'd win."

Mal's shoulder twitched again.

Brisack began to smile. "That's it! He wins no matter what. Yesterday you didn't push Relf about what happened, because you suspected Perrin went back in the forest, and that would kick him out of the army and your experiments. So he wins by doing what he wanted *and* by staying in the army. You've lost twice, and the captain doesn't even realize the size of his victory!"

Mal glared his best, but Brisack was in far too good a mood.

"We have other matters needing attention," Mal said abruptly. "We haven't fully evaluated the information from the past raids, especially in Trades. Who died there, and what were the effects?"

"Just that easily, eh?" Brisack shook his head. "Just replace one citizen with another? One didn't die here, but oh good—a few died there. Let's get to analyzing!"

Mal rolled his eyes at the doctor's attempt at sarcasm. "Citizens die every day. More are born to replace them. We can study one just as easily as another—"

"They're not horses, Nicko. They're humans! People are not interchangeable!"

"That's where you're wrong!" Mal's patience finally wore out. "That's the whole purpose of this study—the animalistic nature of humans. I'll agree that there are subtle differences in personalities, responses, whatever. But when you get right down to it, you can use any mule to pull a cart, any woman to birth a baby, and any man to wield a sword. Just teach, manipulate if you must, bridle, threaten, and control, and it will perform."

"And one will not out perform another, through sheer will or determination or desire?" Brisack pressed.

"No!"

"And that's why you're invalidating the study on Perrin Shin," Brisack snatched the upper hand, "because he proved everything you just claimed to be completely false. He's defied your every attempt to control him, and he keeps succeeding!"

Mal opened his mouth, but no words came to it. As Brisack smirked, Mal finally came up with something to say. "New procedure. I want the forts to have a set of eyes *in* them."

Brisack frowned. "*In* them? None of our men in Command School—"

"Not officers," Mal said. "What I have in mind are enlisted men. Shy boys requiring the frequent attention of their fort commanders to 'bring them up' a bit, take them under their wings, so to speak."

Brisack let out a low whistle. "That's never been done before."

"Neither has been using the Administrators' messaging service to send a warning from a Guarder," Mal intoned.

"I'm not one of *them*," Brisack declared. "Only an observer."

"You swim in the same pond, Doctor."

"There's a great difference between the swans and the leeches, Nicko. And just what are you hoping to accomplish with this?"

"Keep an eye on the commanders. Nudge them back into place from time to time."

Brisack shook his head. "You're talking about putting in mere boys, Nicko. They aren't nearly understated or experienced enough to pull off something so complex. They'll be found out within days, especially if they're trying to send messages."

"I wouldn't require constant messages," Mal waved that off. "Only communication in times of extreme situations or unexpected opportunities. They could be successful once or twice a year."

"Hmm," Brisack considered, in spite of himself. Research was research, after all. Who was to say what was acceptable and what wasn't?

Well *they* were, of course. They made the rules.

"You know," the doctor mused slowly, "if just the right men are placed, they could deliver a wealth of information. How many forts will you begin with?"

Mal's mouth formed a suggestion of a smile. "For now, just one. Training for this new position begins as soon as the right man is located."

"But I haven't sent any messages—"

"No," Mal cut him off. "Only I do that now."

Brisack bristled. "May I at least know which fort is receiving this new procedure?" he asked coldly. "Might it be Edge?"

Calmly Mal said, "Yes, to understand what makes him Perrin Shin. My good doctor, I will prove to you that he's just another horse," he continued with the determination of a man who would never be proven wrong again. "He may be more stubborn and willful than average horses, but I have yet to meet an animal I couldn't break. It just takes the right amount of force. And the right man!"

---

"Are you comfortable?" Mahrree asked Perrin as she tried to find a way to cover his still-oozing wound with the blanket. Realizing the weight could irritate his stitches, she instead tossed a few more logs on the nearby fire.

"I'm comfortable—and warm—enough," Perrin assured her. "You need to sleep too, my darling wife."

Mahrree nodded grudgingly and crawled into bed between her husband and daughter, who whimpered briefly in her sleep. Mahrree smiled at her and thought, I've been wanting to whimper all day, Jaytsy.

"It's sadly funny," Perrin said as she tried to get comfortable, "you'd give anything to sleep on your stomach, and I'd do anything to sleep on my back."

"We'll never be satisfied, will we?" she sighed dramatically. "By the way, I saw the plans you drew for the new baby's bedroom."

"I think I should be able to start working on it in a few weeks when my stitches are fully healed."

"You could get help," she suggested. "Your plans are so detailed anyone could follow them. Three layers of cross-hatched planking, with a space between two of the layers? Should regulate the heat much better."

"I'll add the extra layer to Jaytsy's room first. It just gets too cold in there for a baby, especially on nights like this."

"And if it works well, perhaps you could . . ." She paused. She knew he wasn't going to like her idea, but she was feeling desperate that night.

Actually, that entire day.

Ever since she saw that horrible gash on his back—

"I could what?" he prompted.

"You'd be an excellent builder, Perrin. You're strong, meticulous, creative—"

"What are you getting at, Mahrree?"

"Why don't you be a builder instead of a . . ." She hesitated again.

"What, a *destroyer*?" he snapped.

No, he wasn't coming over easily to her idea at all. She sighed. "I was deciding between saying 'captain,' 'officer,' or 'commander.'"

"Which probably all mean destroyer to you," he exclaimed quietly so as to not disturb his daughter. "We've been through this. No one else can keep Edge safe, and have you considered—"

"Have *you* considered," Mahrree interrupted evenly, "that there are other commanders in the world? Idumea churns out a new crop of officers every year."

"None that I trust to keep us safe!"

"If you weren't the commander, you wouldn't be a target, Perrin," she pointed out. "I'm not stupid, you know. Your injury is a result of your job. And if you had a different job—"

"I'd still be a target, Mahrree. And so would you and our children."

"How?" she demanded, beginning to lose patience with his stubbornness. "Why? We could drop out of sight, live a quiet little life, and no one would care about us. We're nothing special, Perrin. It's not like . . ."

She had to say it, just to see how he'd react. Her own little test of him.

"It's not like . . . . the world's out to get us."

"And how can you be so sure?" he challenged.

Mahrree swallowed hard. "Because . . . because . . ." she faltered.

Someone just failed the test. She suspected it was her.

Then she felt her husband's large hand tenderly caress her cheek.

Oh, and he was passing it so well, too.

"Don't you ever get the feeling the world *is* out to get us, Mahrree?" he said gently. "And I thought you said you could handle being married to an officer. It's what I was before I met you, what I planned to be ever since I was a child."

"When I was a child, I planned to find Terryp's land," her voice quavered. "Sometimes we have to change our plans."

He groaned quietly. "It's just not that easy, Mahrree. This is what I *have* to do."

She propped herself up to see him better. "Are you sure? Just explain to me why."

"I can't," he whispered, his eyes pained. "I just know that we aren't safe, nor might we ever be, no matter what I do."

Mahrree rolled her eyes. "What a comforting thought to consider right before I go to sleep."

He chuckled. "You're so funny sometimes."

"I wasn't being funny."

She wanted to say something else, but didn't dare. She'd been feeling *him* near her all day, reassuring her that her husband would eventually recover, and trying to keep her calm so her belly wouldn't tighten.

He also wasn't pleased that she tried to push away his last mortal advice to her. He was waiting patiently—on the sofa it seemed—for her to come clean with the truth he told her long ago, and what he still told her frequently.

"Perrin, I suppose I should tell you. The night of our first debate, I heard my father whisper in my ear and . . ."

She sighed again, unsure of how he would respond to such an odd revelation.

"He said the world *is* out to get me. Actually, I thought he was alluding to *you* at first," she gabbled on hurriedly, until Perrin's loud exhale interrupted her.

"Will you believe *him*? And me?"

Mahrree didn't expect that. She actually thought he'd begin inquiring about the state of her mental health. That he so easily accepted that his father-in-law still communicated with her—

Well, maybe he was willing to take any ally he could get tonight, even one that resided in Paradise.

She got the impression that the someone on the sofa was grinning in appreciation before he faded away.

"I'd really rather not believe either of you," she admitted. "I now realize why it's easier to just imagine the sky is always blue, no matter what you actually see."

"But Mahrree," his tone became tender, almost pleading, "how will believing a lie save you from the truth?"

"It can't," she sighed in reluctant agreement. "And I don't even need to look outside to see the color of the sky. It truly is black, and getting darker."

"Yes, Mahrree. It is."

"We could use a little blue," she decided.

---

Lieutenant Heth had just returned to his quarters late that night, ending a disappointing evening because he was returning alone. What was the point of one's roommates being out all night if one can't take advantage of it? He was just unbuttoning his jacket when his door flew open.

"Where is he?!" Chairman Mal barked.

Heth stared at the unusual sight of the Chairman, his white hair disheveled and his red jacket untidy, yelling at him in the middle of the night. Heth glanced around. "Who, sir?"

Mal slammed the door. "You know who—Dormin!"

"I've told you sir, I don't know. He said—"

"I've investigated every rubbish remover from here to the edges of the world!" Mal seethed. "No one matches his description, and now I need him more than ever."

"Why? He's useless."

"Not as useless as YOU!" Mal spat, turned, and left the room, shutting the door with a resounding thud.

"And *he's* the greatest leader the world has ever seen?" Heth scoffed.

"The world doesn't expect much of its leadership, does it. See?" he said with a smile of planning, "I could still be king."

He withdrew his long knife from his waistband and gingerly caressed the thin, sharp blade.

"Because I'm fairly certain the same methods to eliminate a Shin will also work on a Mal."

---

Early in the morning of the 64th Day of Raining Season, 320, Tuma Hifadhi leaned on his cane to watch the young men as they filed before him. Behind the elderly man stood several middle-aged men, their arms folded, watching critically. Last week's failed raid in the forests above Edge brought everyone out in the snow sooner than they expected.

Things were different now, and the time had come.

Hifadhi evaluated the young men as they lined up in the field covered with new snow, the light of dawn just reaching them. Some of them were as large and strong as draft horses. Others were as quick and sneaky as coyotes. Still others were as quiet and subtle as deer. And each one of them was sharp, clever, and focused.

These ten had been selected out of several dozen, and now each waited patiently for the next stage. The weeding process had been most thorough. Even one of Hifadhi's grandsons had been rejected, but it wasn't because of his size or ability; it was because he was married and a father. Whomever Tuma chose would lead a life very different than he had known, and he couldn't have any ties that might influence him to neglect his duty.

Hifadhi smiled at the confident faces that tried to conceal their apprehension. Some were more successful than others. He looked up and down the line, his gaze pausing just a moment on one young man a little taller and a little broader than the others.

Draft horse.

Hifadhi tried not to say anything with his eyes, but he suspected the young man could read them anyway.

*He* would be the one.

While he had the largest and strongest body of the men, his face was as smooth as a twelve-year-old boy. Even though he was as powerful as a team of oxen, he looked as sweet as a lamb. Everything about his body was contrary to who he was.

He was perfect, Tuma knew already. He was the sharpest and cleverest, with eyes that sparkled an innocent—and deceptive—sky blue.

In a few weeks, he'd be the newest man in the fort at Edge.

# Acknowledgements . . .

First, thank *you* for reading this, and for being charitable with the niggling errors that I fear still remain, hiding like crabgrass despite my continuous weeding. (Mahrree and I both have gardening issues.)

My thanks next to my daughters: Tess (who's read the entire series—several versions of it—and realized we needed someone named Sonoforen), Alex, and Madison Pearce, who each gave me responses that ranged from, "I loved this part!" to "I hated this part!" (Can't beat children for honesty; it's against the law.)

Thanks also to my friends and neighbors who willingly read drafts—sometimes more than once—and weren't afraid to tell me what they really thought (and they're still counted as friends, mostly): Marci Bingham, Stephanie Carver, David Jensen, Robbie Marquez, Cheryl Passey, Kim Pearce, Liz Reid, Liz Riding, Paula Snyder, Alison Wuthrich, and my sister Barbara Goff, whose constant nagging to "get this finished already!" has been motivating as only an older sister can motivate.

Also thanks to Dr. Daniel Ames, who taught me track changes and that revising the same passage fifty times is perfectly acceptable, and to our neighborhood cop, Cory Thomas, for reviewing some of the fighting sequences to make sure they sounded plausible.

I also appreciate the rest of my children for coping with my neglect (but I almost always remembered to make dinner). And thanks to my husband David who—after a cursory reading of the first book realized I wasn't spending hours each day writing something vampy, and that Perrin Shin bore a remarkable resemblance to him in both face and spirit—just shrugged when the house looked like nine tornados touched down, because he knew writing this made me oh so happy.

# About the author . . .

Trish Strebel Mercer has been teaching writing, or editing graduate papers, or revising web content, or changing diapers since the early 1990's. She earned a BA in English from Brigham Young University and an MA in Composition Theory and Rhetoric from Utah State University. She and her husband David have nine children and have raised them in Utah, Idaho, Maryland, Virginia, and South Carolina. Currently they live in the rural west and dream of the day they will be old enough to be campground managers in Yellowstone National Park.

(This page left intentionally blank.)

(Oh, crud. Now it's no longer blank.)

(This page doesn't have anything vital to the story written on it.)

28960629R00204

Made in the USA
Middletown, DE
06 February 2016